SHE'LL NEVER TELL

Books by Hunter Morgan

THE OTHER TWIN

SHE'LL NEVER TELL

SHE'LL NEVER TELL

Hunter Morgan

ZEBRA BOOKS
KENSINGTON PUBLISHING CORP.

ZEBRA BOOKS are published by

Kensington Publishing Corp.
850 Third Avenue
New York, NY 10022

ISBN 0–7394–4388–7

Printed in the United States of America

Prologue

Marcy glanced at the digital clock on the dashboard glaring accusingly in green and groaned; she was going to be late picking her daughter up from band practice. Katie would be in a pissy mood by the time Marcy got there. The rain would have turned her hair to frizz *and* her taxi service was late again.

Of course, these days, it didn't take much to put Katie in a pissy mood. Marcy just couldn't do anything right for the thirteen-year-old. Jake said Marcy was making too much of the teen's mood swings. It was better just to ignore her. But Katie didn't put it to him the way she put it to Marcy. Katie wasn't ashamed of Jake. She didn't ask him to pick her up at the corner so no one from school would see her get into the car with a fat woman.

Not that Marcy could blame Katie. She might have felt the same way if her mother had been this overweight. Elizabeth Seibel had never had an ounce of fat on her, nor had Marcy's absentee father. And Phoebe. The skinny, beautiful bitch. Last week she'd actually said something to Marcy about drinking protein shakes to put on a couple of pounds.

Marcy tucked a damp lock of her blond hair irritably behind her ear and switched the windshield wipers to high. It was raining so hard that she could barely see the gray pavement against the gray December sky, surrounded by the lifeless trees of the woods line. She gripped the steering wheel of the new minivan a little tighter with one hand while she reached for her biggie Coke with the other.

A pile of burger wrappers and a jumbo-sized fries carton lay discarded beside her on the seat. Dropping the drink into the cup holder, she began to stuff the greasy, wrinkled papers into the plastic trash bag that hung from the cigarette lighter. She'd have to hide the evidence before she got home; two double cheeseburgers, a large fries, an apple pie and a super-sized soda were not on her diet.

Not that it was any of Jake's business, but she wasn't up for the healthy eating/healthy living diatribe tonight. She'd had a lousy day at work; payroll was due tomorrow and she was way behind on the end of fiscal her boss at G & A Construction was waiting on. She'd have to work all weekend to get them in by Monday morning.

A yellow diamond-shaped sign, warning of the turn in the road and the single-lane bridge ahead, rattled in the wind on the side of the road. Marcy squinted, gazing out through the foggy windshield. She turned up the defrost fan. The rain was coming down harder, pummeling the van roof. The sound was earsplitting. Criminy, not hail, she thought. It would ruin the finish on the new car.

Marcy touched her brakes gingerly, knowing she had to be careful on pavement this slick. To her disbelief, the minivan didn't respond. She tapped the brake pedal again, this time making sure her sensible shoe met the rubber squarely.

Still the minivan didn't slow.

A sense of panic fluttered in Marcy's chest. The moment seemed surreal. The driving rain. The old wooden bridge looming ahead. The hum of the defrost fan.

She was going too fast to make the turn.

She hit the brakes hard. Gripped the wheel with hands that had suddenly turned sweaty.

She felt the wooden slats of the bridge, irregular beneath her tires. Heard the thunderous crash as the railing gave way. She gripped the steering wheel as the door flew open, blasting her with cold wind and rain.

It was funny the thoughts that ran through a person's mind in the last moments of life.

Marcy wished she had buckled her seat belt.

She wished she'd thought to stop and toss the remnants of the fast food in a trash can somewhere. When they found her dead, she'd be floating in a sewer of greasy burger wrappers.

The windshield exploded. Horrific pain enveloped Marcy as she felt herself hurl forward, out of her seat. Then no pain, only blessed darkness.

Who said there wasn't a God in heaven?

Chapter One

Six months later
Albany Beach, Delaware

"Hey, there." Patti walked up to the car as he rolled down the window.

"Hi." He grinned.

He had a nice smile. And he was sweet, really. He never came on to her the way a lot of guys did. Like he thought she was trash or something.

"You walking home alone this time of night?" he asked. "It's really not safe, a pretty girl like you."

She took one last draw on her cigarette and dropped it, grinding it out with the ball of her foot. "Car's been in the shop for a month. Two-fifty to fix it."

He winced. Nodded. "Everything's so expensive these days."

Patti glanced up the dark road and down it. There weren't any other cars in sight, though it wasn't that late. Just after eleven. Her feet hurt from the cheap high-heeled sandals she'd bought at the shoe mart, and she was coming down off the beer buzz. She'd missed work again, and she knew she was in danger of being fired and then what?

All she wanted now was to crawl into bed.

She turned back to the driver, resting her hand on the sleeve of his shirt as she gave him her best smile. "So, you going to offer a girl a ride home, or are we going to just stand here and shoot the shit all night?"

He laughed and hit the switch on the power locks, unlocking the front passenger door. "Sure. Jump in. I'll have you home in no time."

Patti walked around the front of the car and blinked against the bright headlights. She opened the door and slid in, closing it behind her. A strange smell immediately caught her attention. "What's that—" Patti turned her head toward him. Saw his hand from the corner of her eye as he raised it to her face. A whiff of the strong-smelling stuff.

Then nothing.

Patti was groggy, half asleep, half awake. She felt sick to her stomach, like she was going to puke. She hadn't had that much to drink. Her eyelids fluttered as she tried to figure out where she was . . . who she'd gone home with this time. Only her eyes wouldn't focus. She was sitting up in a chair . . . in a car maybe? It was dark except for a single bright light that hurt her eyes, even shut.

Had someone slipped her some of that date rape shit going around? She almost laughed. Like a guy had to drug her to get some. All he had to do was be nice to her, buy her a drink, maybe a burger. She wasn't a girl who was hard to—

Patti opened her eyes and she stared at a dark puddle on the floor. *What the f—*

She lifted her sagging head to stare into her lap,

where a clear plastic tablecloth or something lay neatly folded. She was tied to a chair . . . no, it felt like tape. Duct tape?

What kind of kinky thing had she gotten herself into?

The nausea rose in her throat again and she closed her eyes. Swallowed. She couldn't remember how she'd gotten here or who she'd come with. Her head was spinning . . . throbbing. She was so damned tired that she felt like just going back to sleep. Waiting for the beer and whatever other shit she'd taken to wear off. Waiting for the buzz to clear.

But she smelled something . . . maybe just sensed it. Something warm . . . A trickle of fear slid down her spine. What was going on here?

Then she remembered the puddle beneath her. Had she pissed her pants? Her panties didn't feel wet, but right now she felt so weird . . . who knew?

Patti was only able to open her eyes part of the way to stare at the dark puddle. It was a dirt floor beneath her feet. No, sawdust. The puddle was widening. She began to shake, suddenly afraid.

A drop fell, hit the puddle creating little ripples, like on a pond. A drop of what?

God, she wished she hadn't had that last beer . . . But how many had she had? Four, maybe five? It took a lot more than that to tank her. Someone *had* to have slipped her something. . . .

Her head hanging, she watched as another drip hit the puddle at her feet. It was like she was there, but not really.

Blood?

Shit. *Shit.* She jerked back in the chair, her eyes flying open despite the piercing pain of the bright light. It was blood! That was red, thick blood on the floor. She could go with a little kink on occasion, but this . . . this was . . .

Where was the blood coming from?

Patti still wasn't thinking clearly, but she knew that if this was blood, it had to be coming from somewhere. From someone.

Licking her dry lips, she turned her head that felt like it weighed a ton. Just ever so slightly.

Her arm was taped to the wooden arm of the chair. A wave of dizziness washed over her as she stared at the silver band of tape wrapped around her forearm, still not quite comprehending.

Her gaze shifted, lower along her arm. More blood.

A choking sob of terror rose in her throat as she stared at the cuts across the inside of her wrist. She hadn't tried to kill herself! She would never—

Not wanting to, unable to stop herself, she turned her head, let it droop and focused on the other arm, taped to the chair.

More blood.

Patti lifted her head and let out a scream, peeing her panties for real this time.

She screamed again, and her voice echoed overhead in a black abyss.

"Please don't do that," came a male voice out of the silky darkness.

It was a calm voice. Pleasant . . . even sexy.

Then Patti remembered who had picked her up on the road and she was even more frightened. More shocked.

He moved out of the darkness, something shiny in his hand. Light from the blinding lamp reflected off it.

"No," Patti murmured, tears running down her cheeks. She tried to pull back, to get away, but she couldn't. She couldn't move.

"I don't understand," she sobbed as he took a step closer, raising the sharp object to cut her again. "I don't understand."

"I know," he soothed. "I know . . ."

* * *

Leaning on the shovel, the Bloodsucker stood over the puddle of gore and stared at it with great interest. He hadn't known blood could be so dark . . . so rich. The pool looked black to him, not red.

He wasn't stupid. He knew the iron in hemoglobin was what made blood red. But here, spilled in the sawdust on the floor, it was black . . . and exquisite in a way he knew few would be able to understand. He glanced at the dead woman in the chair, her shoulder-length blond hair covering her face. Her shame.

Patti's blood was black. He wondered if she had known.

She must have. She had not been a good person. Not by society's standards, at least. He had heard people talk about her behind her back, even the ones who had been nice to her to her face. Dated her. Slept with her.

They said she had been too free with her body. Too free with the substances she had consumed, smoked, drank. She had not appreciated her body the way she should have. They had said she was wasting her life, that she was too smart, too pretty to be working in a diner, picking up men she didn't know in bars on Saturday nights.

Watching her, he had wondered if she was just lonely.

The thought made him a little sad.

The Bloodsucker knew about loneliness. He knew what a big black hole it could be. It could just suck you up, or it could nibble at you, bite by bite, until it consumed you. Loneliness started with an empty aching, but it could turn mean. Hurt you. Kill you again and again, but not let you die.

He rubbed his inner arm absently. Studied the blood.

Granny said blood held evil humors, but she said a lot of crazy things. Maybe, in this instance, though, he wasn't giving credit where credit was due. Patti's blood did look evil lying there at his feet. Was it because of the men she had slept with? Because of the lying? The drinking? The drugs?

The Bloodsucker wondered if his own blood would be black if he dripped that much onto the floor.

Granny said he was evil. Said he was bad. A bad boy. It was hard to understand, sometimes.

The Bloodsucker didn't have promiscuous sex. He tried not to masturbate. He knew that was bad. Weak and disgusting . . . maybe proof that he was unworthy. But he didn't smoke tobacco or do drugs either. And he had made something of himself. He had a good job. People in the community respected him. Depended on him. Looked up to him.

He glanced at Patti again. The way her head hung. He was sad for her, but he felt good inside. Right now he felt strong. Powerful.

It was funny. Ironic really. He doubted that Patti had ever felt this good.

With a smile, he lifted a shovel full of fresh sawdust and threw it over the blood. It would sop it up, making it easier to clean. He'd already burned the plastic sheeting that protected against accidental spatter. In an hour's time, there would be no evidence left that Patti had ever been here. Had chatted with him.

It had been hard at first. Trying to get her to understand, but she had come around quite nicely. She had told him some interesting things. She had listened to him. Had realized what he was.

Patti had been a good listener.

He stared at the black blood again. He guessed being a good listener hadn't been enough to save her, though. Sometimes there just wasn't enough to save you. Enough of anything.

As the Bloodsucker threw another shovel of sawdust onto the floor, he glanced up at her still sitting. Waiting patiently. She was so beautiful that a heartbreaking ache came over him.

He shouldn't have done this. It wasn't intentional . . . not really. But still . . . he shouldn't have—

Then the Bloodsucker's gaze fell to the black blood once again. Black blood that was proof that she was evil. Proof that she was bad. There was no need for him to feel guilty. There really wasn't.

And it was silly to spoil his good mood with these foolish misgivings. He should treasure the moment. Take pleasure in this elation he had never known before, never realized how to tap into.

And he needed to get to work. He didn't have all night. He'd have to dispose of her. She couldn't stay here.

But that wouldn't be hard, not for a bad girl like Patti. He set his jaw. He knew just where she belonged.

Marcy sensed she was awake before she was actually physically aware of it. It was as if someone had thrown on a switch in her head. One moment the light had been off, the next it was on. She heard the muffled sounds of soft-spoken voices. The squeak of a rubber-soled shoe on clean tile. She smelled floor wax. Her mind swirled, a jumble of confused thoughts.

Where was she, the kitchen? She didn't remember waxing the floor, and heaven knew no one in her house would have ever picked up a mop.

But she wasn't in her kitchen; she was lying down. Her bed? No, the sheets felt slightly scratchy. She always bought two-hundred thread count or better. The sheets didn't smell right, either. She'd used a different detergent, a different fabric softener. Downy fresh.

Confused, Marcy felt her heart flutter with fear. Then she recalled feeling the same way just a moment ago.

She had been afraid.

All of a sudden she remembered the sound of the

rain pounding on the van roof. The smell of the fast food she'd eaten that still lingered, mingling with the new car scent. She'd wrecked the new minivan. She remembered driving off the edge of the road, onto the bridge, through the railing. She must have totaled the van. Jake had to be beside himself. There was certainly no financial advantage to owning a brand-new vehicle five days before running it off the road into a river and totaling it. They hadn't even made the first payment yet.

Marcy felt her heavy lids flutter, but she was hesitant to open her eyes. Her head was swimming, her stomach gurgling, and she felt as if she'd been beaten with a tire iron. She wasn't in the mood to argue with Jake tonight. Not about wrecking the van or eating the forbidden burgers.

Slowly she opened her eyes. Startled by her surroundings, her gaze shifted from one thing to the next. She was in a single bed, tucked in neatly with white sheets and a white thermal blanket. The room was small, with subtle flowered wallpaper in yellows and greens. Sound caught her attention, and she glanced upward to see a TV mounted in brackets in the corner of the room. An afternoon soap opera flickered on the screen, but the volume was too low for her to hear it.

Marcy half sat up in the bed, then fell back weakly. She was in a hospital bed, so not only did she wreck the car, but she was running up a hospital bill, too? She squeezed her eyes shut against the tears that stung them. Jake was going to be so angry with her.

"Well, looky who's decided to join the land of the living."

Marcy opened her eyes to see a black gentleman peering down at her. He held an armful of newspapers.

"I'm sorry, do I know you?" she asked. Her throat was dry, her voice so raspy, she barely recognized it as her own.

He grinned, showing perfect white teeth. The man had to be eighty if he was a day. "Don't reckon you do. Name's Parker and I deliver papers 'round here. But I know you, missy." He shuffled away. "Let me go get that lazy nurse of yours for you." He shook his head. "I told that girl you were wakin' up. Told her two days ago."

Marcy watched the old man disappear through the doorway. A moment later, a perky brunette in a bright purple smock hurried into the room. "Marcy, you're awake!" She rushed to the bedside and grabbed Marcy's hand.

Marcy wondered if . . . *Nancy* . . . she read it on her name badge . . . was going to shake her hand, but instead she checked her pulse.

"I can't tell you how happy I am to see you, Marcy."

Marcy was beginning to feel a little weird. She was light-headed, but it wasn't just that. She didn't know how she had gotten there or who these people were, though they all seemed to know her. Was this how Alice had felt when she tumbled down the rabbit hole? "Do I know you?" she asked the nurse.

"We got to know each other pretty well these last few months." Big smile. "So I suppose you could say we're acquainted."

Marcy rested her head back on the pillow, feeling slightly nauseated. "I was in a car accident," she said softly.

"You remember?" Nancy the Nurse was now hovering, making Marcy nervous.

"Is Jake here?" She picked her head up off the pillow. "My husband, Jake Edmond?"

"You remember your husband's name? Excellent. And how about yours, sweetie?"

Nancy the Nurse was talking to her as if she was a child or maybe just at nitwit. "Of course I know who I am. I'm Marcy Edmond. I live at 223 Seahorse Drive in

Albany Beach, and I want to speak with my husband this minute." Her voice trembled with her last words.

"It's all right, Marcy." Nancy patted her shoulder. "Don't get upset. I'll call your husband at work, and Dr. Larson should be here any minute. I had him paged the minute I heard you were awake."

Marcy closed her eyes. She had been in a car accident, and Jake was still at work? Why did that not surprise her? Ever since he'd made partner in the CPA firm, he'd lived, eaten, and breathed the place. She just hoped someone had picked Katie up at school.

After school? Her eyes flew open. The soap opera on TV came on at three. She hadn't even left the office until four. She hoped to God she hadn't been here all night. She needed to get those reports in.

"Marcy?"

She opened her eyes to see her family doctor standing over her, and she pushed up on her elbows, her heart fluttering in her chest again. "Dr. Larson, what's going on? How long have I been here?"

That was when she looked down at herself in the bed and realized it was her, but not her. Her body, but not her body. She must have been sixty pounds lighter. . . .

"Six months," Marcy murmured, still in disbelief.

Dr. Larson had broken the news to her of the accident and subsequent coma hours ago, but it was still sinking in. He hadn't given a lot of details because he'd said she didn't need all the information at once. All she knew now was that it was the first of June, and she had been in a coma since December twelfth. She'd lost all the weight because she'd had to be hooked up to a feeding tube.

She kept patting the sheets, feeling her new body beneath them. No one had brought her a mirror yet, so she hadn't seen what her face looked like, but she knew she had to have lost some of that pudge. She was so excited, she could barely think straight. All those years of cabbage soup and grapefruit diets, and one silly accident and coma had been the answer to her prayers. Why hadn't she thought of it sooner?

"I know it must be hard for you to believe," Jake said. "Pretty scary, I would think."

Her whole family was there. Jake, the kids, Katie and Ben, even her twin sister, Phoebe, who was downstairs getting coffee and having a smoke right now. After the initial round of hugs, Katie had settled down out in the hallway to do her homework, her ever-present headphones covering her ears. Ben was seated on the floor in the corner of the hospital room with a video game clasped tightly between his hands.

Six whole months of her life gone in a blink of her eye. The kids had grown so much . . .

Her gaze settled on Jake. He was being incredibly nice to her. Attentive. He'd brought her a sandwich from her favorite deli off the boardwalk. She'd only been able to nibble a corner of the bread. After all these months of a liquid diet, her stomach had rejected the very suggestion of solid food, but it had been thoughtful of him all the same. Now he was just sitting beside her on the edge of the bed, clasping her hand so tightly that he was cutting off her circulation . . . and staring down at her. His eyes kept clouding with tears.

She guessed he was relieved he wouldn't have to empty the dishwasher anymore, something he always hated to do. All that housecleaning and running the kids here and there all these months alone must have been tough on him.

Phoebe waltzed into the room, smelling of menthol cigarettes and peppermint. She was as beautiful as she had ever been in her size-eight designer jeans, with her blond hair halfway down her back, and those cheekbones women paid thousands of dollars to have plastic surgeons create. Marcy had always been jealous of her twin sister. Their mother had used to say that Phoebe got all the looks, while Marcy got the brains. Marcy couldn't count how many times in her life she would have been willing to give up a few brain cells just to have those sensuous lips or that pert nose.

"So'd you tell her?" Phoebe spoke to Jake as if Marcy wasn't even in the room.

"Tell me what?" Marcy looked to Jake, her breath catching in her throat. All she could think of was that someone else had been involved in the accident. She didn't remember another vehicle, but she hoped to God no one else had been hurt. She didn't know if she could live with herself, knowing she had injured or killed another human being.

Jake didn't answer either of the sisters.

Marcy looked to Phoebe. Phoebe could be brutally honest—when she wanted to be. "Tell me what, Phebes? Whatever it is, I want you to give it to me straight. I don't want either of you protecting me."

Jake's and Phoebe's gazes met. There was a flicker of something between them. Something Marcy couldn't identify. Then it was gone.

"I'm going to start shouting here in a second," Marcy warned them.

Phoebe reached into the fashionable sack purse that hung on her slender shoulder.

Jake nodded, then turned back. He spoke softly, which scared Marcy even more. "Dr. Larson thought it wise not to tell you everything at once. The accident was bad, hon."

What was he trying to tell her? She knew she wasn't paralyzed. She could still feel her feet and wiggle her toes. Everything was still intact. She'd just been gazing at her skinny calves in wondrous awe a minute ago.

Phoebe drew a small compact from her purse and offered it to Jake.

Marcy trembled, looking from her husband to her sister. Her stomach twisted in knots.

Her face.

That hadn't occurred to her. She'd been thrown from the car, into the trees. Jake had already told her that much. But she hadn't thought that her face might have been damaged. She might be scarred for life.

She recalled the young woman she had known her freshman year in college who had been gruesomely burned in an automobile accident. The girl had committed suicide the following year, leaving a note behind saying she could stand the pain, but not the ugliness. Not the pity of others.

Marcy gripped the sheets and stared into Jake's eyes. Good old Jake and his trusty brown eyes. "Tell me," she whispered. "It's bad, isn't it?" She wanted to reach up and touch her face, feel the hideous scars, but she was afraid. She had never been beautiful like Phoebe. Plain was the word her mother had used to describe her, but at least her face had never been scary—like the teenager with the burn scars.

"It's not what you think." Jake held her gaze, and for a moment it seemed as if there was no one in the room but the two of them. He took the gold compact from Phoebe without taking his attention off Marcy.

He opened it, and the click of the tiny gold clasp seemed thunderous.

Marcy reached for the mirror. How bad could it be? Katie and Ben had kissed her cheek and never reacted. But then, they had had months to get used to seeing her, hadn't they? All these months she'd lain there, maybe the whole family had practiced what they would say if she ever woke up. They had rehearsed how they would not look away, no matter how frightening her face might be.

Marcy's fingers curled around the cold metal of the compact, and she closed her eyes as she drew it in front of her face. She tried to breathe through her mouth the way she'd been taught years ago in childbirth classes.

Jake rested his hand on her thigh. It was trembling.

Marcy counted silently to three and then opened her eyes.

For a moment she thought she had fallen down that rabbit hole again. Or maybe this wasn't real at all. Maybe it was all just a dream.

Staring back at her in the tiny compact mirror was Phoebe. It was her sister's beautiful face she saw, not her own.

Yet when she blinked, the Phoebe in the mirror blinked back. When she pressed her lips together, Phoebe pressed hers together. Marcy could feel her own facial muscles responding to the signals she sent from her brain to her body.

Holding the compact with one hand, she raised her other hand to the face still looking back at her. "Jake, I don't understand," she breathed. Her fingertips found the soft skin of her cheek, the tip of her delicate nose. Only it wasn't her rough, blotchy skin, it wasn't her too-long, too-chubby nose.

"When you were thrown from the car," Jake said carefully. "There . . . there was—"

"Oh, Jesus Christ on a mountaintop, Jake, tell her." Phoebe walked up to the bed, hand planted on her slender hip. She was obviously irritated, but then, any conversation that did not relate directly to her irritated her.

"You weren't wearing your stupid seatbelt," Phoebe said. "You went through the windshield, Marcy. Your face was all screwed up. Nose gone. Lip over your eyebrow. No one thought you were going to live, but Jake wouldn't hear it. You were flown by helicopter to Shock Trauma in Baltimore, not to save your life, but because Jake insisted plastic surgeons repair your face. He said his Marcy deserved the best there was."

Marcy had been staring at her sister, but she looked

in the mirror again, still trying to comprehend. "But . . . but this isn't my face, it's yours."

Phoebe pressed her pink lips together. Though it was only June, she already had a nice tan. "They had to have something to go by." She didn't meet Marcy's gaze this time. "Jake gave them a picture of me instead of you because apparently he couldn't find any pictures of you."

Because she never allowed anyone to take her photograph. Because, ashamed of her weight, she had destroyed the few photographs there were.

Marcy couldn't take her hand off the smooth skin of her face. She was beautiful. Not just pretty, but beautiful. Gorgeous. Six months ago, she had driven off that bridge fat and ugly, and this afternoon she had opened her eyes to find that she was thin and gorgeous.

If this was a rabbit hole, she was staying down here. If it was a dream, she prayed she didn't wake up.

Jake rubbed her thigh. She could feel the warmth of his skin even through the sheet. "You're beautiful, Marcy," he murmured. "Just beautiful."

Phoebe walked away.

Marcy dragged her gaze from the mirror to Jake's face. It wasn't until she saw the tears in his eyes that she began to cry.

"There you go. All done." A nice-looking man in his early thirties, wearing a white lab coat, placed a Band-Aid in the crook of her elbow. "Good luck, Marcy."

His name tag said Alan. She watched as he tucked her vial of blood into his tray and headed out of her room and down the hall for his next patient. She was amazed how many people in the hospital knew her. And they were all being so nice. But as Nurse Nancy had pointed out, she had been here six months. "Thanks, Alan," she called after him.

Dr. Larson passed the phlebotomist on his way into Marcy's room. "So I understand you're ready to go home," the gray-haired man said, smiling pleasantly. She slid off the edge of the hospital bed and sat on a chair to tie her sneakers. She was amazed at how far she could lean over without the spare tire she once had around her middle. "I can't wait to get out of here."

He flipped open her thick medical chart. "I'm not thrilled about letting you go so quickly. It's only been two days since you woke." He hesitated. "But—"

"But I promise to take it easy, and I'll back weekly for the blood tests and the CT scans you've ordered." She patted the overnight bag Jake had brought her this morning. "I've already got the paperwork right here."

Finishing his notes, he tucked his pen into his lab coat pocket and held her records to his chest to look down at her. "You really do look amazing, Marcy." He shook his head. "I have to confess, I always thought your sister was a knockout, but I swear, I think you're prettier. It's astonishing what these plastic surgeons can do these days."

She felt the heat of her embarrassment in her cheeks, but it was a pleasant embarrassment. It still all seemed too good to be true. "It is amazing. I still don't recognize myself in the mirror." She gave a laugh as she stood. Her legs were a little wobbly. Dr. Larson said it would be months before she regained all her muscle strength, but she felt good. She couldn't wait to get out and go shopping, a task she had once dreaded. But for now, she was content to wear Phoebe's sweat pants and T-shirt. She'd even had to borrow a bra and panties. Right now, the only thing she was wearing of her own was a pair of socks and sneakers.

Marcy pushed a lock of blond hair behind her ear, hair that had grown inches in the six months she'd been unconscious. "Don't worry about me. I'm fine and I'm ready to go home."

"So home you go." He offered his hand, and she shook it. "Good luck, Marcy, and remember—"

"Call you if I have any problems." She laughed. "I promise I'll call."

Nancy the Nurse rolled a wheelchair into the room, passing Dr. Larson on his way out. "Your chariot awaits, madame."

Marcy grabbed her overnight bag and sat in the wheelchair, allowing Nancy to put the foot rest down for her. "I know it's a waste of time to tell you this," she told the nurse, "but I really can walk."

"Come on, you've seen the movies," Nancy teased.

"Hospital policy," they finished in unison.

Marcy shifted her bag on her lap and they rolled down the hall. Suddenly she felt a little self-conscious. The hallway was busy, not just with medical personnel who already knew her, but patients, too. People were smiling at her. People who hadn't known her before. "Jake went to get the car," she said hesitantly, "so we can just meet him at the entrance."

"You got it."

A familiar face in Marcy's hometown came striding up the hallway toward them, her long legs pumping, blond ponytail swinging. Police Chief Claire Drummond was lost in thought, her pretty mouth taut. But as Nancy wheeled Marcy by, Claire spotted her and halted.

"Marcy, it's so great to see you. Welcome home."

Marcy smiled hesitantly, looking up at Claire in her smart green-and-tan police officer's uniform. She had known Claire Drummond her whole life. They were both Albany Beach natives and had attended the same high school. But Marcy had always found Claire intimidating; maybe it was her nearly six-foot stature or her beautiful face, or maybe it was that unwavering confidence she seemed to exude.

Claire hadn't returned to Albany Beach after college, but five years ago, after what everyone said was a

nasty divorce, she had moved back to her own hometown. A little more than a year ago, her father had retired after more than thirty years as the town's police
chief. She'd been hired to replace him, and she was not
only Albany Beach's first female police chief, but the
county's. Marcy bumped into her once in a while, at the
diner, the post office, but they had never exchanged
more than a few words in years.

"It . . . it's good to be back," Marcy managed. "Though,
honestly, I don't feel as if more than a few days have
passed since I ran the van off the bridge." She grimaced.
"I am really sorry about the bridge. I hope the city sent
my insurance company a bill."

Claire patted Marcy on the shoulder. "Don't be silly.
We're just all glad you survived. It was a heck of an inci-
dent." She glanced up to see one of her officers waiting
for her in a doorway. McCormick. Marcy had always
thought he was cute; he just looked like a cop. "Listen, I
better run." Claire pressed her lips together. "I guess
you heard that we found the missing Lorne girl."

Marcy nodded. In this small town, word of anything
traveled fast. She already knew Patti Lorne had been
missing; she'd read it in the local paper the day before.
Jake had heard about the waitress's death this morning
when he stopped to grab a cup of coffee at the local
diner before coming to the hospital to pick Marcy up. It
was a shame. Patti had seemed like a nice girl. A little
mixed up. Maybe drank a little too much, went out with
the wrong kinds of guys, but none of that was a crime.
Certainly not one punishable by death.

"They say it's our first murder in the town in sixty-
some years," Marcy mused.

Claire offered a quick smile. "Well, Patti's death has
not yet been ruled a homicide, but if it is, she'll be the
first in a long time, not since old man Potter killed his
brother for sleeping with his carnie wife."

Nancy and Marcy both smiled. Everyone in the town

knew the story. Two bachelor brothers had lived together in one of the many farms that dotted the coun-
tryside west of Albany Beach. Noah Potter had gone to
a county fair and brought home a bride, one who was
said to have had a tattoo—pretty scandalous for the for-
ties. Less than a month later, poor Noah caught his wife
in bed with his brother. He shot Jessup. Noah went to
jail, and Sylvia ran off with the carnival, never to be
seen again.

"Take care, Marcy." Claire gave her a final pat and
strode past her, down the hall toward the officer waiting
for her.

Not yet been declared a homicide? Who was Claire kidding? Slit wrists or not, there was no way Patti had killed
herself, and the police chief knew it. There was no blood
where Patti had been found next to a trash barrel in the
state park, and she sure as hell hadn't walked there on
her own. Not with more than fifty percent of the blood
in her body gone.

Claire walked past Patrolman First Class Ryan Mc-
Cormick, who waited for her. She pushed through the
swinging door that read "Employees Only". Down the
steps, she would find the morgue where Patti Lorne's
body waited for transport to the ME's office in Wilming-
ton for an autopsy. They'd be here any time for her, so
Claire wanted to get another look without the interfer-
ence of others. Get a couple more pictures.

Her stomach twisted in protest at the thought of seeing Patti again. This was not only Albany Beach's first
homicide in sixty years, but it was her first here on the
job. Sure, in college she'd seen a couple of dead bodies
in a forensics class, and then she'd worked a couple of
fatal auto accidents as a state policeman, but this wasn't
the same thing. Those dead people had never served her
coffee, never laughed and told her not to worry about
her daughter, that all teens went through crazy phases.

Claire's footsteps echoed in the stairwell that seemed

to smell of formaldehyde. Death. She knew it was just her imagination. No one mopped the stairs with formaldehyde, or even used it here for that matter, but that assurance didn't settle her stomach any.

In the narrow, tiled hallway in the basement of the hospital, Claire found the morgue door, white with plain block letters. It seemed innocuous enough, despite its implication.

"You coming in?" she asked McCormick, taking the camera bag from his shoulder. Thirty years old, he was nice-looking in a soldier of fortune kind of way. Clean-cut, clean-shaven, buffed with a full membership at the only gym in town. A little too gung-ho for Claire's taste, but she heard he never wanted for dance partners in the bars in town on a Saturday night.

"I thought I'd stay here, if you don't need me."

"I'll holler if I do." She opened the door and stepped in, closing it quietly behind her.

Claire didn't mind coming into the morgue alone, and she didn't blame her officer for not wanting to join her. He had known Patti pretty well apparently, not just from the free coffee she served him daily at the diner. Supposedly, he'd dated her a couple of times. Of course, rumor had it that every single male in Albany Beach between the ages of twenty-five and thirty-five had, too. And a few who weren't single, as well.

Claire set her camera bag on a small, stainless-steel table, opened it, and took her time attaching the lens she would use for the close-up shots. She pulled her pen and notepad from her breast pocket and placed them neatly beside the camera bag. Then she took a deep breath and turned around to open the stainless-steel drawer where she knew Patti's body would be.

The drawer glided out effortlessly, soundlessly, as if Patti's passing meant nothing. Just a dead waitress who had maybe drunk a little too much, given her love a little too freely.

Biting down on her lower lip, Claire pulled back the sheet and blanched. Breathing through her mouth, she swallowed hard against the sour bile that rose in her throat. She hadn't realized this was what a body looked like if you drained a good deal of its blood. Patti hadn't just bled to death. Someone had tried to make sure that as much blood flowed out of her body before her heart stopped as possible. Her wrists, slit numerous times, were pretty clean, as if someone had wiped the blood from them, keeping the cuts from clotting.

Claire picked up the cool, lifeless hand that appeared blue. Translucent. She straightened it out as best she could, and reached behind her for her camera.

"I'll find out who did this," Claire said softly, blinking back the tears in the corners of her eyes. "I swear I will, Patti."

There was no response in the cool, dimly lit morgue except for the whirl of the camera shutter.

Chapter Two

Marcy walked in the front door of the Cape Cod she and Jake had bought when Katie was two. After being unconscious for six months, she had expected that coming home would feel strange. It didn't; it was as if she had just left the house that morning, rushing out the door, coffee in hand, hollering to Jake that he would have to pick up the dry cleaning if he needed his gray suit. The biggest difference she noted was that the day of the accident had been cold and rainy; today was warm, and the sky was clear. She'd missed Christmas, the snow of winter, the daffodils and crocuses of spring. It was the first week of June. School would soon be out, and vacationers would be flooding the town that blossomed from a population of twelve hundred to four thousand at the peak of the summer season in August.

The house didn't feel strange at all, but this new body of hers certainly did. No thighs rubbing together, no pouch for a belly. As Marcy passed through the front hall, she caught a glimpse of herself in the antique mirror her grandmother had given her. Her entire adult life she had avoided mirrors, but since she woke from the coma, she couldn't stop staring at herself. The fact that she now looked like Phoebe's identical twin still spooked her a little, but the psychiatrist who had stopped by her hospital room the day before had said that was to be expected. He had given her his business card—*"in case you want to talk"*—but she didn't think she needed a shrink. Just some time to adjust.

"House smells good," Marcy said. "You make dinner?"

Jake closed the front door behind them. "You know better than that," he teased and inhaled deeply. "Smells like Phoebe's lasagna to me."

She glanced at him as he set her overnight bag at the foot of the staircase to be carried up later. "Phoebe's here?"

Jake lifted his shoulder in a half shrug. He had lost weight too in the time she had been ill. Lost the slight paunch above his belt. And even though his sandy blond hair seemed to be thinning a little, he was still an attractive man. He had nice eyes, dark brown with lashes a woman would kill for. She didn't know to this day why he had married her. He could have done so much better.

"She thought you might be hungry." His face grew lined with concern. He acted as if he was afraid she was going to fall into a coma again at any moment. "Or would you rather just go up and lie down?"

She hesitated. Actually, she *was* hungry. The lasagna wasn't the problem, Phoebe was. The day Marcy had driven off the bridge, she and her sister probably hadn't spoken in a month, though they lived in the same town. They had never been the best of friends to begin with, even as children; their personalities were too different. But there had definitely been more than the usual amount of friction in their relationship back in December. Phoebe had been in the middle of a divorce, declaring bankruptcy, and had hinted she needed a place to stay. . . .

Marcy glanced over her shoulder at Jake and lowered her voice to a harsh whisper. "Is she living here?"

He nodded hesitantly.

"Jake." She turned to face him head-on. "Didn't we talk about this? Didn't we agree that if we bailed her out again, she'd just assume we'd help her fix her next screw-up, too? You know the nine months she lived here last time nearly drove me to drink."

"I know, you're right."

"So what's she doing here?" She gestured toward the kitchen. She could hear Phoebe and Katie talking, though she couldn't make out the conversation. Katie was laughing about something her aunt had said, and it galled Marcy; Katie never laughed at anything Marcy said.

Jake avoided eye contact with his wife. "We did agree she wouldn't move in, but then you had the accident. Marcy, I couldn't drive back and forth to see you in Baltimore, work, *and* get the kids to school and to their lessons. I'm sorry, but I just couldn't do it all." He hesitated. "You don't know how scared I was that you were going to die."

She listened, but didn't say anything. Talk of the accident, her three months in the hospital in Baltimore, then three months here in Albany Beach; none of it seemed real to her. It was just a story others were telling her. She still wasn't absolutely positive this wasn't a dream.

"So when she offered to pitch in, I was thankful," Jake continued.

The phone rang, a dull background noise.

"And you should be, too. I don't care what happened in the past." He pointed in the direction of the kitchen, his voice low but surprisingly forceful. Ordinarily, he was the kind of man who took the low road, the path of least resistance. "Your sister was here for you when you needed her. When *I* needed her."

Marcy glanced in the direction of the kitchen. Jake was right, of course; he always was. She sighed, brushing her now below-her-shoulder hair out of her eyes. It was amazing that a body could be clinging to life and grow such nice, healthy hair. "So let's eat."

She walked into the kitchen and put one arm around Ben, who sat at the counter doing his math homework. She kissed the top of his head. The nine-year-old, going on fifty, didn't usually appreciate her displays of motherly affection, but he wiggled with nervous energy and grinned. He was glad to have her back.

She glanced at her sister through the space between the kitchen counter where Ben was working and the cabinets above. "Hey, Phebes, smells good."

Phoebe pulled a tray of lasagna out of the oven. She was wearing faded denim shorts and a baby tee. The yellow apron hung considerably lower than the hem of her short-shorts showing off her long, slender legs that were tanned an even sun-kissed brown. Marcy wondered absently if her own legs, right now as white as a fish belly, would tan like that.

"You always liked my lasagna." Phoebe plucked the flowered hot mitts off her hands. "Ben, tell your sister to get off the phone and come to dinner."

"Dinner, Katie!" Ben shouted at the top of his lungs. "Get off the stupid phone, talking to your stupid boyfriend!"

"I could have done that," Phoebe chastised. "Now go get her."

Ben rolled his eyes, but obediently slid off the stool.

As Marcy watched Ben go through the kitchen to the family room, she fought a wave of resentment. Jake was right. She should be thankful Phoebe had been there for him and the kids while she was in the hospital. But did she have to sound so much like she was Katie and Ben's mother?

"I'll set the table," Marcy offered, feeling guilty for her thoughts. What was wrong with her that she didn't feel more appreciative to Phoebe and Jake?

"Already done."

Marcy glanced at the kitchen table that was bare except for the napkin holder filled with napkins.

"Oh, in the dining room." Phoebe smiled. She had pink lipstick on. No matter how much she ate, drank or talked, she always sported pink lipstick. Marcy would have thought her lips were tattooed pink if she hadn't seen her sister remove the tube of lipstick and apply it a million times since they were sixteen.

"Phoebe thought we didn't use the dining room often enough," Jake explained, unaware or uncaring of Marcy's annoyance. "We eat in there all the time, now."

Marcy's first impulse was to tell Phoebe that she was impressed that her sister could work all day, keep a house that was cleaner than it had been in the last ten years, *and* make gourmet meals on a work night, but she bit her tongue. She was tired and probably overreacting.

"Hanging up the phone," Katie announced, strolling into the kitchen, gesturing grandly for everyone to see. "Watch closely as I hang up the phone to join my family for a nightly communal meal."

Marcy glanced at Jake, wondering what that was all about. Even after her Sleeping Beauty act, she could still read his face. *Don't ask*, he said silently. *Not if you want to eat dinner while it's still hot.*

A couple of hours later, Marcy entered the bedroom she and Jake shared. She had tucked Ben in and stuck her head in Katie's bedroom door to say good night. Suddenly she was so tired, she could barely set one foot in front of the other. She wondered how a person could ever be tired again after sleeping for six months.

"Ben in bed?" Jake asked, walking into the room behind her and closing the door.

"Out for the count." Marcy plopped on the edge of the bed, noting how little the mattress sank beneath her now. "I swear, I think he's grown six inches in six months."

He sat beside her and slipped off his loafers. She could smell the faint scent of his cologne. He'd been wearing the same stuff since they were in college, but she had always liked it so she didn't mind.

"He really missed you, hon," Jake said, rubbing her shoulder. "I mean, Katie missed you as much as any teenager can miss their parent considering they don't want to claim us." He chuckled. "But Ben was lost without you."

She smiled at the thought. It was nice to be appreciated by someone.

"Of course, I was lost without you, too. The most lost of any of us." He slid his hand down and around her waist and she stiffened.

He kissed her arm just below the hem of her short sleeve.

"Jake—"

"I still can't believe it's you. Awake, walking, talking. The doctors had no idea how good recovery would be, if you ever recovered."

Marcy sat on the edge of the bed, staring straight ahead. She could see herself in the mirror above her dresser. See Jake kissing that beautiful woman. But she felt nothing sexual. Just annoyance. The same annoyance she had felt the morning of the accident when he had used the rest of the milk in his coffee so that she had to drink hers black. He knew she hated black coffee.

He kissed her bare arm again. Her shoulder. When he tried to kiss her neck, she pulled her head away. "Jake—"

"I'm sorry," he said quickly, letting go of her. "I know. It's too soon. I just missed you so damned much, Marcy. I—"

"Jake—" She stood up, glancing away from the mirror, not so much because she didn't want to see her own face, she didn't want to see his. Who was he kidding? He hadn't been this amorous in years. It wasn't her, his wife, he was kissing, it was this beautiful woman in the mirror. A woman Marcy didn't know yet. "Let's not play games here."

"I know, I need to give you some time," he went on quickly. "I know you have to be overwhelmed."

"Look, Jake, we're kidding ourselves if we're going to pretend things were good between us before the accident," she said flatly. She walked to the dresser and opened her pajama drawer. It still held her winter PJs. All flannel, baggy. Ugly. She closed the drawer. She wouldn't wear them. Not ever again. That part of her life was over. "As I recall, last December you were sleeping most nights downstairs on the couch."

"Because you weren't sleeping well, and I know I snore." He sat on the edge of the bed looking more like a forlorn boy than a forty-year-old CPA. "It just seemed easier—"

"Wait one minute," she interrupted him. "You're not putting the blame on me. You weren't sleeping in our bed because you didn't want to sleep with me." She pulled open another drawer and removed a T-shirt she'd bought in Disney World two Easter vacations ago . . . no, three. She had missed Easter this year. She had once worn the shirt with shorts, but now it would hang long enough for a sleep shirt. "You were sleeping on the couch so you wouldn't have to talk to me. God forbid, bump into me in bed."

She clutched the T-shirt to her chest, all her insecurities about her looks, about what she had looked like before, coming back, filling her with a gamut of feelings from self-loathing to anger at the world. "So don't come on to me, now that I'm a size eight with this face, and say that it's the old Marcy you're coming on to, because I don't buy it."

He rose from the bed. "Marcy, you're wrong," he said quietly.

She turned away, not wanting to see his face. "Am I?"

There was silence for a moment, silence that stretched out until every second became more painful than the previous one.

"Marcy, you're tired," he finally said. "You have to be overwhelmed. We don't need to be talking about this right now." Jake grabbed his pillow off his side of the bed. "Why don't I just sleep downstairs tonight? Give you some privacy. You get some sleep. I know things will look different in the morning."

She turned to face him, but her gaze fell to the bed. There was a new bedspread on it, but she hadn't even noticed it until now. Peach and tangerine flowers. She knew instantly who had put it there. Jake wasn't into flowers, and even if he was, he'd never have ventured into a department store to buy a bedspread. Not if it was the last spread, the last store, on earth.

The spread was Phoebe's, like the new wallpaper in the powder room downstairs, and the new water glasses with the funky geometric print in lime and yellow. Had Phoebe just waltzed into Marcy's house and taken over completely?

Guess you couldn't beat free rent, free food, and laundry service.

Lost in her thoughts, Marcy didn't see Jake move until she realized he was on his way out the door. She didn't say anything to him. Didn't know what *to* say.

Once he was gone, the door closed quietly behind him, she went into the bathroom. She brushed her teeth with the toothbrush she hadn't used in six months, taking care not to look in the mirror. In the bedroom, she shut out the light before she undressed and pulled the sleep shirt over her head. She didn't want to see the new face, the new body anymore tonight. Didn't want to think about it. She'd had enough.

Marcy jerked the bedspread off the bed, throwing it on the floor, and then climbed under the sheets, hoping they weren't pink. She realized she was reacting childishly, but she couldn't help herself.

She fluffed her pillow, thinking that maybe Jake was right. Maybe she was just overwhelmed. Maybe everything would make a little more sense, seem a little easier, in the morning.

The following morning, Marcy watched the passing scenery as Phoebe's yellow convertible zipped along the country road headed toward town. Phoebe had asked Marcy if she wanted to drive, but Marcy wasn't sure she was ready. Truthfully, she wasn't sure she could ever get behind the wheel of a car again.

But it felt good to be outside, to feel the sunshine on her face and the wind in her hair that she had left down after her shower this morning. She'd always had nice hair, silky, blond, but she'd worn it short for years. Close-cropped was sensible on a woman who had a demanding job, a husband and two kids. So what if it was dowdy? She had never been the kind of woman anyone would see as sexy anyway.

Now Marcy liked the feel of her hair brushing her shoulders. She liked the way it swished when she walked, tickling her face and her neck. She'd get a trim because she needed it desperately, but there would be no "helmet hair" for her again.

"Here we are," Phoebe announced as they passed the Albany Beach city limits sign. Down the street, she turned into a parking lot and zipped into a parking space in the front of the town's only diner.

"Loretta's" looked like it was right out of the fifties and had been there that long. A structure built with a series of flat tarred roofs and small additions, painted silver to look like it had once been a railroad car, it was the gathering place of the locals year-round. The coffee was great and the homemade pancakes and pies were to die for.

Marcy got out of the car and followed Phoebe up to the front door, feeling a bit conspicuous in the shorts and tank top she had borrowed from her sister. The size-eight shorts were actually big on her and hung too low on her hips. The tank top barely touched the shorts' waistband, so if she lifted her arm, her bare belly showed. Even her bra felt strange—also borrowed from Phoebe. It was just one of those cotton stretchy athletic kind, instead of the armor she had always worn. And tucked inside were someone else's breasts. Had to be. These were barely B cups, and amazingly pert considering their age and the months of breast feeding they had endured. Marcy felt like an alien inhabiting another body . . . her sister's body at that.

"God Almighty, look at you!"

The moment Marcy walked through the diner door, she was bombarded with the heavenly scent of coffee and the pudgy arms of Loretta Pugh, proprietor of the diner. Loretta was a big woman in height and girth, covered in a huge flowered apron that looked like a tablecloth. As far as anyone knew, Loretta never left the place. She was here day and night. The diner had probably been built around her and she would, most likely, live as long as the walls stood.

"I can't believe it's you, Marcy, sugar pie!" Loretta swore, her entire body jiggling with delight.

Marcy gave her a pat around the shoulders, not so much because she felt like hugging the woman, who was somewhere between fifty and a hundred and fifty years old. It was just the only way she knew she'd be released from the embrace of the tablecloth and Loretta's arms.

"How'd you know it was me and not Phoebe?" Marcy asked curiously. Phoebe's hair was a couple of inches longer, a little blonder from the sun, but beyond that, they truly were identical. "We look just alike now."

"Pshaw!" Loretta released Marcy so that she could breathe again and gave a wave of the beige menus, forever preserved in laminate and smelling of maple syrup. "You don't look a bit alike."

Marcy raised a pale eyebrow.

"Phoebe's got that trashy look," Loretta explained matter-of-factly. "Something you can't copy. You either have it or you don't, sister."

Phoebe slid into a Naugahyde-covered booth seat and turned a coffee mug, already set out, right side up. "I love you, too, Loretta," she said, not in the least bit offended. "Coffee for both of us, and a number four for me." She glanced at Marcy.

Marcy nodded. She usually ordered the wheat toast, dry, and grapefruit with artificial sweetener, then watched her sister consume a stack of pancakes, two scrambled eggs, and three slices of scrapple. She knew full well she couldn't eat this way every day or she'd be tipping the scales over two hundred again, but this morning she was having the number four and she was going to enjoy every bite.

"Okay, which one are you?" Ralph, who bused tables and washed dishes in the back, approached the table, carrying a coffee pot.

"Which one is who?" Phoebe asked, teasingly. She was a flirt with any man, young, old, attractive, unattractive, it made no difference.

Ralph chuckled. He'd been at the diner for years, too. In his late fifties, early sixties, he sort of looked like someone's grandfather. He was tall, thin and bald except for a ring of white hair around his head. Despite his harmless, grandfatherly looks, he had always made Marcy feel a little uncomfortable. He was very mysterious about his past, and sometimes the strong odor of cough syrup permeated his clothes.

"Which one's Phoebe and which one's Marcy?" he said.

Before Phoebe could tease Ralph any further, thus extending his visit to the table, Marcy raised the cup he had poured full of coffee. "I'm Marcy."

He peered down at her with cataract-cloudy eyes.

"Damn, I'll be. It's true. Patrolman McCormick was just in here this morning telling us how spooky it was. I guess he'd seen you at the hospital." He glanced at Phoebe and then back at Marcy again. "You look just like her now." He shuddered. "Weird, if you ask me, how doctors can do that. I saw this show that explained how JFK was really killed in the war. They took somebody else and gave him that new face. So JFK wasn't really president. Have you seen that one?"

"Nope. Missed it. Must have been asleep." Marcy gave Ralph a quick smile and reached for the cream and sweetener. When she looked back to Phoebe, Ralph had moved to the next booth with the coffee pot. "I see some things never change," she said under her breath. "Ralph's as loony as he ever was."

Phoebe blew on her coffee and took a sip. She drank it black, the stronger and thicker, the better. "You should have seen him yesterday. It was pretty pathetic. Crying about Patti, slobbering all over everyone. Saying how he loved her and how he wanted to marry her." She rolled her eyes, pursed her pink lips, and took another drink of coffee.

Marcy watched Ralph duck under the counter and disappear into the back. "I ran into Claire Drummond on my way out of the hospital yesterday. I guess Patti's body had been transported to the hospital before going upstate." She shook her head, sipping her coffee. "I just can't believe someone killed Patti. She was a nice girl—"

Phoebe gave a snort. "If you think that, you didn't know her very well. She was the town whore."

Marcy cut her eyes at her sister. "She's dead, for heaven's sake. Murdered. Don't you have any sense of couth?"

"Two number fours," Loretta announced, sliding the oval plates across the authentic Formica table. "Anything else I can get you lovely ladies?"

"That's it, thanks, Loretta." Marcy smiled up at her as

she reached for her silverware wrapped in the paper
napkin. Her first bite of pancake was a sensuous experience.

"So did you hear how she died?" Phoebe scooped up
egg on her fork.

"I've been asleep for six months. I haven't caught up
on all the gossip."

Chuckling, Phoebe took a mouthful of egg. "She
bled to death. Slashed wrists."

"She killed herself at the state park? I thought everyone was saying someone killed her. A lover's quarrel or
something. That's what the nurses were saying."

Phoebe shook her head, a silly grin on her face. She
loved gossip, and she especially loved gossip no one else
had heard yet. "It wasn't suicide. The body was dumped."

Marcy took another bite of pancake. It was only her
third mouthful, and she was already beginning to feel
full. She could see she was going to have to take this eating thing slowly. "How do you know?"

"Ryan McCormick."

"The cop?" Marcy took a nibble of scrapple. "Are you
dating him again?"

Phoebe lifted a thin, suntanned shoulder beneath
her bright pink spaghetti strap. "I saw him at Calloway's
last night. He bought me a drink."

Calloway's was a local bar built out on a dock over
the bay. It was open year-round, unlike most of the bars
in Albany Beach, so it was a locals' hangout.

"You've gone out with him before, Phoebe. You said
he wasn't good for you. Wasn't he the one who you said
liked it rough?" She glanced around to be sure no one
was eavesdropping. "Handcuffs and stuff?"

"We're just talking about a drink and a little juicy information, Marcy. For God's sake, I didn't fuck the guy."
Her tone became conspiratorial again. "But apparently
Patti did. *Regularly.* " Phoebe lifted her coffee cup. "Loretta, more java?"

Marcy stared at her plate, still heaped with all the treasures of the number four breakfast platter. She set down her fork, her stomach protesting. She couldn't eat another bite. "McCormick say who they think might have done it?"

"They're going to look into that guy, Billy, she lived with for a while. Apparently she still hung out with him sometimes. Doper. Of course, if it was someone she was dating who killed her, could have been any number of guys."

Phoebe had always used the word "dating" in a different way than Marcy. When Phoebe said *dating,* she meant *having sex with.*

Phoebe lowered her voice, giving her sister the eye. "Including Patrolman First Class Ryan McCormick."

"Phoebe, that's ridiculous. You shouldn't be making such accusations." She looked around at the patrons in the diner. Many she knew, but already tourists were moving in for the summer, bringing their minivans, bicycles, and beach umbrellas . . . and millions of dollars of revenue. "Someone might hear you."

"I'm not making any accusations," Phoebe scoffed. Then she grinned slyly. "But you have to admit, it is food for thought. A dead girl, a dozen guys she's slept with this winter. An on-again, off-again relationship with a pothead. Who did it? Was it a drug deal gone bad? A jealous lover? Someone who didn't like the way she served the coffee in this dive?" She laughed at her own joke.

Marcy wrapped her hands around her coffee mug. "So's your divorce final?" she asked, changing the subject.

Phoebe spread butter and then strawberry jam on a piece of white toast. "Almost."

"That like being *almost* not pregnant?"

"I'm definitely not pregnant." Phoebe laughed. "No, all the paper work is in; we're just waiting for a court

date. The restaurant makes things more complicated."
She was studying her plate intently now, not meeting
Marcy's gaze.

"Jake said that after the accident, you offered to stay
with the kids. That was nice of you."

"You'd have done the same for me." Phoebe sawed
off a bite of scrapple, giving it great attention.

"Of course I would have." What Marcy didn't say was
that she was shocked as all get-out that Phoebe would
have voluntarily done anything for anyone else, her of
all people. She hadn't known her sister had it in her.

Marcy used her fork to push around some uneaten
egg on her plate. "So, you working?"

Phoebe glanced up, instantly hostile. "What's with
the twenty questions?"

"I haven't seen you in six months. I know a lot's happened in your life . . . was happening when I had the accident. I just—"

"You mean my life was a disaster again, six months
ago."

"No, I didn't mean it that way," Marcy defended herself. And she didn't. She just wanted to know what was
going on . . . with everyone. Six months was a long nap.

"I've got some applications in." Phoebe leaned back
to let Loretta pour her a second cup of coffee. "You
know how hard it is to get a job around here in the winter."

Meaning Phoebe hadn't worked the entire time Marcy
had been in the coma. Meaning, she had been living off
her and Jake all this time, because she certainly hadn't
left her marriage with anything.

Phoebe and husband number three, Matt, a small-
time gambler from New Jersey, had been up to their eye-
balls in debt when they parted company. Their credit
cards had been maxed out, and food and liquor bills for
their restaurant were past due all over the state. After
the bankruptcy hearing when her five-bedroom beach

house was seized, as well as the restaurant, Phoebe had probably been left with nothing but the convertible she paid cash for seven years ago with her inheritance from their parents, and the clothes on her back.

As Loretta turned to go, Marcy brushed her hand against the older woman's arm. "I'm really sorry about Patti, Loretta," she said quietly. "I know you cared a great deal for her."

Loretta's pale eyes filled instantly with tears. "I appreciate that, Marcy. That kid was like a daughter to me. Always come in here with some cockamamy scheme to get rich on. Always thinking the new man in her life was going to take her away from this." She gestured to the diner with the coffee pot. "Guess one of them did," she finished sadly.

Marcy let Loretta go, taking a minute before she glanced at her sister across the table. "I'm sorry you had to put your life on hold for me," she said carefully. "I want you to know that I appreciate it. All you've done." And she meant it, at least on some level. "But I'm okay now. The doctor said he sees no reason why there will be any residual brain damage. I'm going to be fine, so please don't feel like you have to hang around and baby-sit me."

Phoebe dropped her fork and it clattered on her plate. "Jesus, didn't you hear me? I said I was looking for a job, Marcy. I'll be out of your hair and your house just as soon as I get a job."

Marcy knew better than to argue. Phoebe always had to have the last word and it always had to be about her. Today, Marcy let her have it. She drained her coffee cup and reached into her shorts pocket for the twenty Jake had left on the counter for her this morning. "I'm going to get some change for the tip." She slid out of the booth, sweeping the bill up with her hand.

When Marcy returned to the table, Phoebe had already gone. Outside catching a smoke, probably. No smoking in public places in Delaware anymore.

Marcy left too large a tip on the table and then walked out to the gravel parking lot. The sun was incredibly bright, and she shaded her eyes with her hand. Phoebe was standing in the gravel parking lot, leaning against her car, inhaling deeply on a menthol light.

"I've got some stuff to do," Phoebe said. "Want me to run you home first?"

"Mind dropping me off at the beach instead?" Marcy slid into the passenger seat and reached into the glove compartment for the spare pair of sunglasses she knew her sister kept there. "Maybe I'll walk home."

Phoebe took one last deep drag and dropped the cigarette in the gravel, grinding it out with her sandal. "You sure you ought to be doing that?"

"Why not? It's not much more than a mile if you let me out near Dauber Street. I've walked that a million times, even as a fat girl. You don't think I can walk a mile sixty-five pounds lighter?"

Phoebe slammed the door. "I meant, do you think your doctor would approve. Jake'll freak out if he finds out I left you on the beach."

"So you *are* supposed to be baby-sitting me?"

Phoebe pulled her sunglasses down off her head, over her blue eyes that were identical to Marcy's, and started the engine. "Suit yourself."

At the dunes that separated the street from the beach, Marcy slipped out of her sandals and picked them up. Behind her, she heard Phoebe tear down the street in her convertible. She hadn't intended to anger her sister this morning, or seem ungrateful, but she knew Phoebe too well. She had to be told in no uncertain terms that she couldn't stay with them forever. She had to get a

job, support herself, and find her own place. With the
luck Phoebe had, she'd have a new husband within the
year to support her anyway. At least until that relationship fell apart, too.

Marcy followed the footpath over the dunes onto the
beach that was already dotted with early-season sun-
bathers. A mother walked a toddler in a bright orange
bathing suit along the water's edge. An elderly man and
woman sat under a large rainbow beach umbrella in
sweatshirts and long pants, reading a newspaper. She
smiled to herself. She had always loved the beach. The
briny smell of the ocean, the warm sand under her bare
feet, the blue sky that seemed endless overhead. As if on
cue, a seagull soared overhead, calling.

Reaching the water's edge, Marcy turned north.
She'd only walk a couple of blocks and then turn back.
Despite her bravado with Phoebe, she knew she had to
be careful not to overdo it physically in the next few
days and weeks. The physical therapist she had spoken
with at the hospital the day before had explained that it
would take a while to regain muscle tone. Even with the
exercises physical therapists did each day with their unconscious patients, muscles still atrophied. It was one of
the reasons Dr. Larson didn't want her going back to
work. Not that she was anxious to go. With this new
body, this new face, she was thinking that maybe she
needed a new job, too.

Marcy sidestepped an incoming wave, giving a squeal
of surprise as the cold water washed over her feet. Not
looking where she was going, she bumped into a jogger,
running with his dog in the opposite direction. She
glanced up, embarrassed. "I'm sorry," she sputtered.

The guy had grabbed her arm to keep them from both
tumbling into the wet sand, and released her. "No problem."

She looked up to realize it was Ty Addison, a recent
college graduate who had baby-sat the kids for her on

occasion when he'd been in high school. He was shirt-less and wearing orange swim trunks like the ones life-guards were issued. He was handsome, with the blond surfer look that was so popular these days. He had a nice face . . . and an even nicer chest.

"You okay?" he asked. His dog barked and sat down in the wet sand.

"Yeah, yeah, I'm fine." She laughed, flustered. Through the dark lenses of Phoebe's spare sunglasses, she could see Ty checking her out.

"It's Marcy Edmond," she said. "You used to watch my son Ben and my daughter Katie for me."

"Mrs. Edmond." He snapped his fingers and grinned. "I'll be damned. I've heard the gossip, but I wouldn't have believed it if I hadn't seen it for myself. You look—"

"I know, just like my sister."

"Actually, I was going to say great." He grinned.

"Thanks." She smiled back, feeling a little awkward. "Well, sorry to slow you down." She gave a lame wave and headed north again. When she glanced over her shoul-der, he was still standing there, watching her, and ap-parently admiring her caboose in the size-eight shorts that hung too low on her hips.

She turned around, feeling her cheeks grow warm. Horny college boys. She was embarrassed, but pleasantly so. She'd spent what seemed like her whole life watch-ing men watch Phoebe that way. Now it was her the cute guy was looking at, and it made her feel shamelessly good inside. Hopeful.

Marcy continued to walk along the wet, hard sand, glancing up occasionally to be sure she didn't run into anyone else. As she walked, she let her mind roam. Things still seemed a little fuzzy in certain areas of her memory, but her mind was still her own. The plastic sur-geons had only altered her face, not her brain.

She recalled that before the accident, she had been very unhappy. Depressed. She hated her job, she hated

Jake, she hated herself. She had felt trapped and unable to do anything about it. She'd known that if she left Jake, she'd spend the rest of her life alone and that wasn't what she had wanted. What she had wanted was to be thin and beautiful.

And suddenly that wish had come true. The accident that had given her this new body and face was a fairy tale come true. Her mind raced. She could start her life all over again. Leave Jake, take the kids with her, find a job that was rewarding, that made her want to get up in the morning. Maybe she'd even meet a new man.

She smiled at the thought. She'd been a virgin when she'd slept with Jake her senior year in college, just two weeks before they graduated, three weeks before they married. She'd never even "dated" anyone else, not by her definition or Phoebe's. In college, she had been in love with Jake, thrilled that a man as good-looking as he was would have paid any attention to her. She had married him because he had asked. Somewhere between getting real jobs, applying for a mortgage, and having two children, that love had faded. She could barely remember now what it had felt like.

Marcy passed a couple in their late twenties, walking hand in hand, obviously in love by the way they were looking at each other, talking in hushed, intimate tones. Maybe newlyweds. She wanted to walk hand-in-hand with a man who looked at her that way.

So now she had the chance. The question was, did she have the guts to take it?

Chapter Three

"I don't understand why I have to go to school." Ashley slumped in the front seat of the dark green police cruiser, arms crossed over her chest. "There's only four days left."

Claire glanced at her fifteen-year-old, forcing herself not to cringe. Her beautiful blond-haired daughter had dyed her hair jet black, outlined her blue eyes in thick black eyeliner, and added a nice gray lipstick to complete the makeover. To finish off the look of the dead, Ashley had crafted an ensemble of black: intentionally torn jeans, black T-shirt sporting a screaming skull with snakes shooting from the eye cavities, and a hardware store-quality chain around her waist for a belt.

Police Chief Claire Drummond's daughter had gone Goth. It was the talk of the town. Or at least it had been before Patti's murder.

"Because there *are* four days left. That's why you have to go," Claire said, signaling to make the turn into the school's circular driveway. She didn't dare leave Ashley out front on the street where her daughter preferred to be dropped off. That almost guaranteed a call from the attendance officer checking up to see how Ashley was feeling, since she had missed another day of school.

Ashley groaned and slid down farther on the bench seat, shielding her face with her right hand so the students walking up the sidewalk wouldn't see her in the police car.

Claire took notice of the silver rings on her daughter's slender fingers. The count was up to one bat, three skulls, and a python. The black fingernail polish was a nice touch.

"Stop looking at me," Ashley huffed. "Why are you always looking at me?"

"Just trying to figure out how I spawned you from my loins," Claire said lightly.

When Ashley had taken this bizarre turn on her dazed and confused teenage journey, Claire had vowed to try not to be judgmental. She'd promised herself that she would try to tolerate the phase, reminding herself again and again to choose her fights carefully. Life wasn't about what clothes or shade of lipstick a person wore. It was about who they were inside.

Ashley's grades were still decent, she only missed curfew on occasion, and she never missed a day at work at the local garden center. Claire was still fascinated that a girl wearing black lipstick and a chain around her waist could take such pleasure in working in a greenhouse. She had actually caught her daughter a few weeks ago talking baby-talk to a tray of geranium seedlings while watering them.

"Please," Ashley groaned. "I try not to think about the fact that you and Dad had to have sex to bring me into the world. *Gross.*"

Claire laughed as she pulled up to the curb. Comments like that actually pleased her. It meant, chances were, Ashley wasn't considering have sex with anyone anytime soon. "Go straight to work after school, then to Grandmom and Grandpop's."

"I know."

"Do not stop at the Dairy Cream."

"I know."

"Do not pass go, do not collect two hundred dollars."

"*Mom,* I know." The moment the cruiser rolled to a stop, Ashley had the door open and was reaching for her backpack on the seat behind her. Black, of course.

"I might be late tonight. I've got several interviews to conduct." Claire's mind began to shift as she transformed from mother to police chief. Switching hats was difficult sometimes. Even harder when she was concerned about Ashley the way she was right now, and she had something big going on at the station. Patti's murder definitely qualified as something big.

"I can get Pop to take me home after dinner."

"No."

Ashley cut her kohl-lined eyes at her mother. "Why not? I stay home alone by myself all the time."

"Not when there's a man out there who just killed a woman."

"Her boyfriend did it," she said, her voice taking on that "you're an idiot" tone that teen girls did so well. "It doesn't take a genius to figure that out."

Claire arched an eyebrow. "And you have evidence to support this theory of yours?" She gripped the wheel. "The truth is, between the two of us, I don't think Billy Trotter did it. I can't see him working up enough energy to kill someone. And if he didn't do it, that means someone else out there did."

Ashley frowned. "Whoever it is, he better not come after me. I'll kick his ass."

Claire shifted her gaze to look out the windshield. "Language, young lady."

Ashley yanked her backpack onto her shoulder and climbed out of the cruiser, black army boots untied with the laces dragging behind her.

"Bye," Claire called after her. "I—"

The door slammed.

"Love you," Claire finished quietly. Then, with a sigh, she shifted the Olds into drive and pulled slowly around the school, making sure Ashley was inside the front door, being greeted by the principal, before she turned onto the street.

Using her car radio, Claire checked into the station-house with Jewel, the gum-popping dispatcher, saying she'd be right in after a coffee stop. Jewel had already called in their order.

"Morning, Claire," Loretta greeted her at the diner's cash register.

"Good morning, Loretta. How are you?" Claire took a stool at the luncheon counter and gave a wave to Ralph, who was serving up someone's plate of fried eggs, sunny-side up, and a double of link sausage.

"I'm doin' all right, considering." Loretta closed the old-fashioned cash register with a *ching* and handed the departing customer his change.

Claire nodded. "You get any sleep last night?"

Loretta leaned over, parking her huge, flower-covered breasts on the counter. "Hard to sleep thinking of my sweet Patti dead, lying next to that trash barrel."

Claire smiled grimly and patted Loretta's swollen hand. "We're going to find out who did this to Patti. I swear we will."

"I got every faith in you." Loretta stood up and slapped the gold-speckled Formica countertop. "Now, what can I get you for?"

"Jewel called in the order for two blacks to go, two jelly donuts—"

"And a bran muffin," Loretta finished for her, already grabbing two Styrofoam cups.

"So I'm predictable." Claire lifted one shoulder in a half shrug. Today the badge affixed to her neatly pressed uniform seemed heavier than usual. "Boring."

"Not boring, just *regular*," Loretta teased.

Claire smiled, glancing around the diner, taking in who she saw, what she saw. In this line of work, she had learned to be observant wherever she went, on duty or off. When Loretta returned with the coffees and a white paper bag, the police chief met her gaze. "You have time to talk for a sec?" she asked quietly.

Loretta's gaze flickered to her customers, then back to Claire. "We got 'em all fed. They can sit tight for a second without a top-off on their coffee."

Claire pulled a small pad of paper from her breast pocket. "I need any information you can give me on Patti that might help us figure out what happened."

"Well, like I told Patrolman McCormick, she didn't come into work that day like she was supposed to. But then, Patti didn't always get around to giving me a call when she was out sick or whatever."

Claire didn't have to ask what she meant by *whatever*. She knew Patti. The young woman had drunk too much and dabbled in drugs on occasion, though nothing too bad, to her knowledge. Mostly a little weed she scored from Billy Trotter.

"Do you remember seeing anyone around that week who stood out? Any strangers?"

Loretta stroked her chin that sported several hairs. "It's June, Claire. We've already got some early birds staking out their section of the beach. Seth Watkins said he had half his company's condos rented last Saturday night. Been a lot of strangers sittin' at these tables in the last week."

Claire made a note to check with the Realtor on his weekend renters. Maybe he noticed someone who didn't fit the usual early summer vacationer profile. "But anyone who stood out? Anyone who didn't strike you quite right?"

Loretta leaned on the counter again. "I tell you who you need to be lookin' at, and that's that no-good trailer trash, Billy Trotter. You know his father went to jail for beatin' the hell out of Kat right before she left him a few years back. Happened in Ocean City. I guess they got tanked and things got out of hand. They say that kind of thing can run in a family."

"I'm aware Billy has an alcohol problem, and I am going to talk to him. But I still need you, and Ralph, too, to think through the last week. Any arguments Patti might have had with a customer? Any new man in her life she might have mentioned?"

Loretta grinned wryly. "Well, you know how Patti was. Seemed like there was always a new man in her life."

Claire tucked the pad and pen back into her pocket and reached for the coffees and paper bag. "You think on it. Give me a call. Now what do I owe you?"

"Not a thing, and you know it."

Claire started for the door. "Loretta, how can you make money if you never charge me or my boys for breakfast?"

"A couple of donuts a week, a couple pots of coffee, is pretty cheap security, considering the times, sweetie. Knowing you and the boys are out there keepin' our streets safe makes us all breathe a little easier."

Apparently we couldn't keep Patti safe, Claire thought, but she kept it to herself. "Thanks, Loretta. You have a good day."

"You, too."

Going out the door, Claire ran into Morris Tugman.

Damn, she thought. *To think, a minute sooner and I could have gotten out of here without this aggravation this morning.*

"Claire."

"Morning, Mayor." She nodded, but kept going, hoping she'd get lucky and he'd go about his business.

He blocked the door. "So how's the investigation going?"

She halted. The luck just wasn't with her this morning. "Very early stages, Morris. I really can't say. Patti's been dead less than forty-eight hours."

"But you've picked up that Billy kid? The one who works in that head shop on the boardwalk, lives on his grandparents' farm in that eyesore trailer?"

The head shop was a constant source of aggravation

to Claire. Owned by a man from Pennsylvania who had a string of them, the locals hated it. But it apparently made good money, and the business did employ half a dozen local kids Memorial Day to Labor Day. They didn't sell anything illegal, just T-shirts most parents would find inappropriate, incense, band stickers for cars, that kind of crap. It was currently Ashley's favorite store because they had an entire section of studs to place in various pierced regions of the body, necklaces and bracelets that resembled dog collars, and racks of black clothing. So far, studs only adorned Ashley's ears and nowhere else . . . that Claire was aware of.

"Actually, Billy's been working at Calloway's all winter." She was tempted to tell him how surprised she was he hadn't remembered seeing him behind the bar. Apparently Morris liked to park himself on a bar stool at Calloway's, with a shot of Jack Daniels, on occasion. "There's certain protocol we follow when questioning suspects, you know that, Morris." She tried to focus on the mayor's bushy eyebrows and not the ridiculous toupee he wore. Ashley and half the people in town called him *Mayor Rug Man*, her father, the retired police chief included. "I intend to speak with Billy myself today. I was just doing some preliminary interviews first."

"You look into Ralph?" The mayor leaned against the glass door, propping it open, but still preventing Claire from escaping. He pointed in the direction of the diner's kitchen. "He's a crazy bastard, always talking about aliens and shit. And he admitted himself here in front of half a dozen people that he had been in love with her."

It was difficult to take a man who was wearing a green and yellow shirt with multicolored parrots on it seriously. Especially when it had to be a size triple-X shirt to accommodate Morris's ever-increasing spare tire, and the parrots were life-size. "The coroner promised to fax me her initial report by four. I'll draw up a full list of people I need to interview, once I have that information."

"Well, sounds like you have everything under control." He shook a finger, obviously unconvinced. "But the minute you think you're over your head, Claire, you call in the state police. You hear me?"

"Yes, sir." She ducked under his arm. "I'll keep you posted."

"You better. Unsolved murders make it hard on employment contracts up for renewal, you know."

Morris's words that sounded close to a threat were still ringing in Claire's head when she reached the station, used her pass card to get in the back door, and delivered the coffee and donuts to Jewel.

"What's up this morning?" Claire asked, grabbing a pack of sweetener from the counter behind Jewel's desk. The dispatcher, a cute brunette, also served as a receptionist and worked in a glass room that was accessible only from the rear offices, with a reception window in the public waiting room. Everyone at the station called it "the fish bowl."

"Let's see." She took a sip of her coffee and gave a crack on her gum. "Mrs. Peterson's locked herself out of her house again. McCormick just sent Savage out to climb through the bathroom window . . . *again.* Mr. and Mrs. Arquette think someone has broken into their house and stolen the remote control to their new plasma screen TV—"

Claire glanced up, stirring her coffee with a red plastic stirrer. "This thief didn't steal the TV, just the remote?"

Jewel glanced down at her purple legal pad. "Nope, just the remote. I took notes just the way you showed me. Mrs. Arquette called at seven thirty-four, said someone had broken into the house between the end of the news last night and when Mr. Arquette got up at six-thirty and tried to turn on the Weather Channel."

Claire sucked the coffee off the end of the stirrer. "No one else in town even has a plasma TV. What the hell are they going to use the remote for?"

Jewel giggled. Popped her gum.

Claire gestured with her finger, twirling it in a circular motion. "Skip forward to something I need to know."

"Captain Gallagher, headquarters, state police, wants you to return his call." Jewel handed her a pink "While You Were Out" slip and then slid into her office chair. "Thanks for the donuts." She pulled Claire's muffin from the bag, placed it on a paper plate, and took a bite from her own donut.

Claire grabbed the muffin and walked out of the fishbowl, closing the door that automatically locked behind her. Jewel had been working for her for eighteen months, and she still couldn't get used to watching the dispatcher eat with gum still in her mouth. "I'll be in my office."

"All righty."

Claire closed her office door behind her before sliding into the chair behind her desk. Setting down the coffee and muffin, she stared at the pink slip of paper with Kurt's work number on it. Before accepting the position as Chief of Police of Albany Beach, Claire had been a lieutenant with the state police and had worked with Kurt on a couple of cases. He had thought her taking this job had been a step down for her, instead of up. He didn't understand her desire to follow her father's legacy in the town she had grown up in. He also hadn't understood why she had broken up with him after they had dated for two years.

It had been that tired, age-old, male versus female commitment issue. He said he loved her and he saw no reason to spoil what they had by getting married. She thought that if they had no intention of making the relationship more permanent than a quickie on the nights she could get a baby-sitter, there was no sense in continuing the relationship, period. Though by choice, the breakup had hurt Claire deeply. Deeply enough that she hadn't even attempted to date since then, but she was still certain it had been the right decision.

She punched Kurt's number and extension into the phone and reached for her bran muffin. He picked up on the first ring before she had a chance to chicken out.

"Captain Gallagher," he said, his tone clipped. She could see him now, hunched over his paper-scattered desk, sensual mouth pulled in a frown as he thought through some detail of a case that didn't sit right with him.

"Kurt—Claire."

"What the hell's going on down there in Sussex County, Claire? First week of June, families heading for our beaches, and you've got a dead woman in a dumpster?"

She pulled off a piece of the bran muffin, thinking that from the sour tone of Kurt's voice, he needed the *regularity* more than she did. "The victim wasn't in the dumpster, she was next to a trash barrel."

"Wrists slashed, but not a suicide?"

Claire breathed a little easier. She could talk to Kurt just as long as it was about work. As long as they didn't cross the personal threshold, she was just fine. "Not unless she's one of the walking dead. My ER doc says that she'd bled out more than half the total blood volume of her body."

"Dumped, then."

"No blood at the scene. Had to be."

"Any obvious evidence?"

She took another bite of muffin. "Like the killer's name printed in blood across the barrel? No."

"So . . . you need a hand?" Kurt's tone had changed slightly. He was edging toward personal.

She sat up in her chair, annoyed. "Did Mayor Rug Man call you?"

"I'm just offering my assistance." He ignored her question. "You know we're available to aid local municipal forces."

"You're at headquarters now. A big-shot captain, headed higher up the ladder soon, I hear. You don't work murder cases."

"Claire—"

"No, I don't need your help—not yet, at least. I don't even have the autopsy report back."

"Well, you know I'm here."

Didn't she. "Thanks, Kurt. I appreciate that."

There was a tap at her door, and McCormick stuck his head in. She held up her finger.

"You just want to bounce some ideas off someone," Kurt continued, "call me."

"Will do. Listen, Kurt, I have to run. We've got a remote control thief on the loose."

"I'm not even going to ask." His tone was husky now, teasing.

She groaned silently. No matter how she tried to deny it, she still had feelings for him after all this time. "Bye." She hung up the phone before he had time to answer, waving Ryan in.

"I checked out Billy's place like you asked," Ryan reported. "Nothing unusual. Dog's still tied to that old car in the back yard. His pickup is in its usual parking place out by the mailbox, but so's his grandmother's Honda. No sign of life yet, but it's early for Billy."

He stood in front of her desk almost at attention, his chin squared, his uniform, as always, immaculate. He would have made an excellent officer in the military. Claire always felt as if he were wasting his life here in Albany Beach being a town cop. Not that she didn't appreciate him, she just thought that his aspirations could have been higher. Of course, Kurt had said the same thing about her.

Claire nodded, thinking about Billy. The dead girl. Something chilling, deep inside, told her that her life in Albany Beach was never going to be the same. Maybe it had something to do with lost innocence. She didn't know. Maybe something more sinister.

"You want me to go pick him up?" McCormick asked.

"No. Not until the autopsy report comes in."

* * *

It was after five when Claire eased her cruiser into a parking spot along the dock. Glancing at the manila envelope on the seat beside her that contained Patti's autopsy report, she climbed out of the car. There were only a few cars in Calloway's parking lot; it was early in the day for the barflies and too early in the season for the restaurant crowd.

She nodded to several familiar faces inside, finding her way to the bar. She slipped onto a stool, dropping the envelope on the mahogany bar that had recently been wiped down and smelled of glass cleaner. Billy was stacking glasses under a mirror that ran the length of the bar, his back to her. Someone had written the beer specials for the night in lipstick on the mirror. Rolling Rocks were "buy one, get one free" from seven to nine tonight. Claire hated Rolling Rock. She hated beer.

Billy turned around, empty glass tray in one arm. He caught a glimpse of her reflection before he actually saw her. "Wondered how long it would take you to show up," he mumbled, letting the dishwasher tray ease to the floor. He was about six feet tall, willowy with brown shoulder-length hair pulled back in a ponytail, a tuft of brown whiskers jutting from his chin. He was wearing baggy khaki shorts, and an orange Calloway's T-shirt sporting a flying marlin.

"I'm sorry for your loss."

He shrugged a thin shoulder, pulled a white towel out of his back pocket, and gave the bar top in front of her a swipe. "I was done with her."

"How far done?"

He glanced up. "Look, Pats pissed me off, but I wouldn't want to see her dead or anything."

She watched him carefully. His eyes were red, a little bloodshot. Probably came into work high. If she searched him or his pickup, she might come up with an eighth, but she didn't want to be a hard ass. Not yet, at least. "You want to tell me what she pissed you off about?"

To Claire's surprise, Billy walked away, disappearing into the back. She was just lifting her weight from the stool to see what he thought he was doing walking out on a police interview when he appeared again. He tossed a yellow card onto the bar.

She reached for it. A time card. The evening of Patti's murder, he worked from four-thirty to twelve-fifty in the morning. Patti disappeared between eleven and midnight.

Claire gave the time card a push and it glided across the glassy bar top. "That doesn't mean anything, Billy, and you know it." She lowered her voice. "I've seen you driving around town at night making your *drops* when I know you're clocked in here."

It was a bluff. She'd never seen him driving around when he was supposed to be at work. If Billy did deal in marijuana, it was small time. Most likely he was just supplying a few friends. From the look of the trailer he lived in, the truck he drove, he obviously wasn't making much money at it. Maybe smoking his profit margin?

"I didn't kill Pats. I would never kill anyone." He lifted his peace hand, making a peace sign. "Make love, man, not war."

Billy met her gaze directly when he spoke and didn't look away when she narrowed her eyes in challenge. People with something to hide didn't do that, not unless they were sociopaths. Claire's gut feeling, from the beginning, when she had stood there at the dumpster studying Patti's body, had been that it wasn't Billy who killed her. Even now, with the time card on the bar top, it wasn't his alibi so much as her gut feeling that told her Patti's killer wasn't here.

Claire slid off the bar stool, reaching for her envelope of photos. She didn't want to share them with anyone she didn't have to. "I have any questions for you, you'll be around, right? No plans for a vacation?"

Billy lifted his hands. "That's it? You don't want to know when the last time I saw her? You don't want to know where I went after work that night?"

"I'll let you know if I have any more questions."

He reached under the bar and pulled a bottle of beer from a sink full of ice. "On the house." He pulled his church key from his pocket and popped off the top.

She glanced at the green beer bottle. "Still on duty."

He shrugged and lifted the bottle to his lips, his gaze still locked with hers.

Claire walked out of Calloway's knowing she'd hit a dead end with Billy. The question now was, which way did she go from here?

"It was nice of your sister to keep an eye on the kids tonight," Jake said stiffly, downing the last of his beer. He sat across from Marcy at the small table out on the restaurant's deck, dressed in khakis and a plum polo shirt. He looked nice. He'd even put on cologne for their "date." Still hoping to get lucky, probably, which would be hard to do considering the fact that he'd been sleeping on the couch since she came home from the hospital a week ago.

Marcy reached for her iced tea. She had considered ordering a glass of wine, but she wasn't sure she was comfortable enough with herself in this body, with this face, yet, to lower any inhibitions. She didn't answer Jake, just sipped her drink. They'd already had their meal, and she wished the waiter would come back with the check. Sitting here with Jake like this was making her very uncomfortable. She didn't feel like she knew him anymore. She certainly didn't know herself.

Over dinner, they had talked mostly about the kids— how well Ben had done in math with the help of his tutor and whether they were going to let Katie baby-sit this summer for a neighbor. They had both purposely avoided the subject of Phoebe.

"Marcy, you look beautiful tonight," Jake said, leaning forward on the white linen-covered table for two. He slid his hand over hers. "Sexy in that dress."

She gazed down over the red, low-cut halter dress she'd borrowed from her sister. In her "Miracle Bra," her newly acquired normal-sized breasts did look pretty good. Aside from being a little loose at the waist, the dress fit perfectly. She'd even found an old pair of very high heels in the back of her closet to go with it.

She lifted her gaze to meet Jake's, not sure why his compliment struck her the wrong way. Maybe because everything he said struck her the wrong way—or at least it had last fall before she'd hurled herself over the bridge. "It's not my dress."

"I know. It's Phoebe's." He gave her a half grin. "She looked damn fine in it too, but I have to say, you—"

Marcy snatched her hand from his. "My sister looked good in this dress, did she? You get a lot of chances to see her in this dress while I was in that coma, Jake?" She didn't know what made her say that. It hadn't even occurred to her until this moment that this was why she had been upset all week. She didn't like Phoebe in her house because she knew how men felt about Phoebe. They didn't just like the way she looked; they liked the way she talked, the way she flirted, playing innocent and coquettish one minute, then slutty the next. Phoebe had been at the house six months. What if in that time—

Marcy stood up abruptly, tossing her white linen napkin on the table. "I'll wait for you outside." She didn't give Jake the time to answer, hurrying across the deck and down the steps into the darkness.

Jake found her in the parking lot leaning against the SUV he had bought to replace the minivan she had totaled. It was the SUV she had wanted in the first place; now she was too scared to drive it.

He walked up to her slowly, his hands in his pockets. Under the circle of lamplight, he looked sad, but he didn't look like a man who had been cheating on his wife and gotten caught. She felt bad that she had been mean to him in the restaurant. He was trying so hard.

"You want to go home?" he asked, then went on tentatively, "or would you maybe like to take a walk?"

She pressed her lips together, tasting her new lipstick. She'd chosen a coral shade she'd never been bold enough to wear before. "A walk might be nice." She ran her hand over her flat stomach that still didn't seem like her own. "I ate too much. I feel stuffed."

"Me, too." He took her hand in his and she let him. "There's a blanket in the back. I can grab it and we can sit in the sand. We could watch the waves wash up the way we used to."

She nodded.

At the edge of the dunes, they took off their shoes and walked down the path that led through the grass that had been carefully planted to preserve the coastline. When he reached for her hand, she let him take it. At the water's edge, they walked north, passing an older gentleman sitting in a lawn chair surf fishing, and a young couple walking hand in hand in the opposite direction. The woman was laughing as they strolled past, that sexual laugh that couldn't be mistaken. Probably more June newlyweds, Marcy thought.

"Want to sit down?" Jake asked when they'd walked a while. The beach was empty here, lights from a couple of cottages and condos twinkling in the distance beyond the dunes.

"How about up there?" She pointed, and they walked up toward the summer houses, the ocean at their backs.

Jake shook out the blanket they used to sit on at the kids' soccer games, and Marcy watched it float and settle on the smooth beach. The sand-cleaning machines had already come by, picking up lost shovels and pieces of trash, leaving perfect squiggles as tracks in their wake. She sat on the edge of the blanket dotted with soccer balls, digging her bare feet into the sand that was still warm, though the sun had long set.

Jake sat beside her, his hip pressing against hers, his arms wrapped around his knees. She glanced behind them, forward again, getting the strange feeling that someone was watching her. There was no one there, of course. She felt like everyone was watching her because they were. Ever since she'd left the hospital, people had been staring, and it made her uncomfortable.

Jake slid his arm around her waist and for once, his touch felt comforting. "You get those blood tests today?"

She stared at the white rush of water churning onto the shore. "Yup. Results will be back next week, but I'm sure they're fine. I'm fine. I feel great."

"Do you?"

His soft, husky voice made her warm inside, a feeling she could barely recollect from their dating days. "Well, I'm still a little tired, but Dr. Larson said that's to be expected."

He lifted his hand from her waist to her shoulder and brushed his lips against her bare arm.

"I was considering trying jogging," she told him, thinking the sensation wasn't all bad. "I walked around the neighborhood twice yesterday and again today, but that's a little boring." She glanced at him. "You think I could do it?" she asked hesitantly.

"Sure. Just take it easy. Quit when you get tired."

A smile touched her lips. She liked the idea that Jake thought she could run for exercise. She liked it so much that when he brushed his fingertips across her cheek, guiding her mouth to his, she let him.

Jake tasted familiar . . . and yet not. She tasted the beer he had drunk at the restaurant. The years they had shared, good and bad.

She parted her lips, feeling the heat of arousal warm

in the pit of her stomach. Her heart rate kicked up a beat. When she pulled away, breathless, she was panting. She'd never been a frigid woman; she'd enjoyed the occasional orgasm the way any other overweight married woman with kids and a mortgage did, but usually it took more to heat her up than this.

Jake eased her back on the blanket, and she moaned as he brought up his hand to cup one breast. Her nerve endings seemed more alive than they had been in a very long time. When he rubbed his thumb against her hard nipple, the sensation seemed to lead a path directly between her thighs. They kissed again, her tongue touching his, and she pressed her hips against his, feeling his arousal for her.

Jake slid his hand over her bare thigh and the next thing she knew, he was tugging on her panties with his finger.

Marcy couldn't believe she was doing this. On a public beach?

But she realized she needed Jake; she needed him in this elemental, non-thought-provoking way. She didn't want to talk. She didn't want to explore her feelings about her new body or face or about how she felt about her husband. She just wanted to have hot, feral sex in the sand on the beach.

Jake pushed up her dress, pulled down her panties. She kicked them free as she slid her hand over the front of his bulging khakis and grabbed his belt. "Come here," she whispered.

He groaned, bringing his mouth down over hers hungrily as she unhooked the buckle, unfastened the clasp and slid his zipper down.

"I like that sound," he murmured in her ear.

Jake caught the lobe of her ear between his teeth as she slid her hand into his BVDs. He was just never a boxer kind of guy.

"Like the feel of that even better."

Nuzzling his neck, Marcy smiled to herself as she caressed him, cupped his balls in her hand, squeezed them gently. It had always fascinated her that a man could become so pliable with just the brush of a woman's fingertips. For men, it was all about mechanics. She admired that, wanted it. Especially tonight.

Still stroking him, she lifted her chin to meet his kiss. She thrust her tongue into his mouth, tasting the beer he'd drunk with dinner, enjoying the thrill of penetration, as it was, on her part. She had always enjoyed French kissing with Jake; he was good at it. As he pushed his tongue into her mouth, she wondered why they had stopped kissing this way. Why their lovemaking, before the accident, had become so . . . *clean* and impersonal.

"Marcy," Jake mumbled, tearing his mouth from hers. He brought his hand up under her breast and, even through the fabric, she could feel the heat of his hand. He opened his mouth, covering the tip of her breast, wetting the dress with his tongue.

She laughed, throwing her head back, slipping her hand out of his khakis to run her fingers through his hair. She held his mouth to her breast as little trills of erotic sensation ran through her, all seeming to find their way to that warm, damp place between her thighs.

"I hate to be a party pooper," he whispered in her ear. "But . . ."

She laughed, her voice sounding odd, breathy in her own ears. For once she wasn't upset that he wanted to push to the big event. For once, it seemed to be just what she needed. What she ached for.

Marcy slipped her arms around Jake's neck and lowered herself back onto the blanket, pulling him down on top of her. He fumbled to slide his pants to his knees and she ground her hips against his, pleasuring herself. The old Marcy would never have dared . . . or at least not been so obvious about it.

Jake at last freed himself of the tangle of his pants,

and she felt him hard and warm against her thigh. She parted her legs, pulling him down, lifting her hips upward, her desire incomprehensible to her now.

He slipped inside her, harder than usual, and she groaned.

"I'm sorry," he panted. "You all right?"

She tipped her head back, laughing at him . . . at herself. "I won't break."

"I know." He moved slowly inside her. "It's just that—"

She bit down on his lower lip to silence him. At the same time, she raised her hips, forcing him deeper inside her. She moaned. Did it again.

"Christ, Marcy . . ." Jake pressed both his hands into the blanket on each side of her head, thrusting faster. Harder. She rose to meet him each time, refusing to close her eyes, wanting to saver every moment of the pleasure as the stars overhead swirled around them.

Too soon, she felt that shudder just before she came. She tried to hold back, not ready for it to be over.

She was too late. With a brazen cry, not caring who on the beach heard her, she met his thrust one last time and her insides exploded with the heat and the pent-up desire. Desire that had maybe been smoldering beneath the fat and ugliness for years.

Jake was right behind her. He grunted and fell against her, breathing hard.

Marcy laid back on the blanket in the sand, throwing her arm over her face. She was still breathing hard, the last tingling sensations of her orgasm giving her that strange sensation of floating. "I can't believe I just did that," she muttered.

Jake laughed, kissed her flushed cheek, and dropped onto the blanket beside her to pull on his pants. "Why? You said yourself, sex was one thing that's always been good between us."

"I know. It's just that—" She sat up, getting that creepy feeling of being watched again. She looked over her shoulder, toward the lights of the cottages. She heard a man's voice, a dog bark, but they were on the other side of the dune. She turned around to look at Jake again. "Where are my panties?" She felt around in the dark on the blanket.

Jake shifted his weight as he zipped and buttoned his pants and came up with her panties that had been under him.

She snatched them from his hand and scrambled to get up. "I think we better go home."

"You don't want to stay for another go-round?" Jake teased.

Marcy pushed down the skirt of the red dress, debating whether or not to try and stand on one foot and pull on the silk panties that had somehow gotten sandy. With her luck, she'd get sand in the crotch and then wouldn't that be a comfy ride home?

Jake pulled the blanket up and folded it in his arms as they walked south, angling toward the water where it was easier to walk. The moon was beginning to rise now, making it easier to see than it had been earlier. As they passed a large garbage can, Marcy tossed the panties into it.

Jake laughed. "I always knew you were my kind of woman, Marcy."

This time, when he reached for her hand, she darted away and they walked in silence back to the car.

The Bloodsucker held his breath as they passed. They were arguing now. He could tell by the way she wouldn't let him take her hand. She had certainly been eager for him to touch her earlier, though, hadn't she, his lovely swan?

The Bloodsucker walked farther up the beach, unnoticed by the swan and her husband. Past the old man sitting in the lawn chair, drinking coffee laced with brandy, holding a surf rod. It was like he was invisible. They saw him, yet they didn't. And even if they did make eye contact, he would just smile. Wave. No one knew who he was because everyone knew who he was. That was the best part about it all. The swan knew him, just as Patti had.

The Bloodsucker stopped at the trash can. Scuffed his pale white bare feet in the sand that was beginning to feel cool now. He looked up the beach. Down. No one was paying any attention to him. Marcy and Jake had crossed the dune and disappeared into the parking lot.

He reached into the trash can and was rewarded with the smoothness of a piece of silk fabric. He smiled in delight and lifted it carefully, looking again to be sure no one was watching. They were red panties; he could see that now in the white light of the rising moon. He drew the red silk across his shaven cheek and let his eyes drift shut for just a moment.

The Bloodsucker wanted to keep the panties, but he knew he couldn't. He couldn't because he wasn't a stupid idiot. He knew that if he took the panties, it would be considered a trophy by law enforcement. Trophies were a no-no. If he allowed himself this one, the next thing he knew, he'd be taking them from the women he took back to the barn with him. Some people wanted to get caught. Wanted to be seen. He wasn't one of them.

He drew the red silk panties against his cheek one more time and then let them fall into the darkness of the trash can. He walked back to the parking lot along the dune, and as he crossed the path, back toward his car, his shoes in his hand, he watched Marcy and Jake pull away.

Who would have thought she would ever be so beautiful?

The Bloodsucker wanted her now. He was sure of it. He would just have to be patient.

Chapter Four

"Apathy, for fourteen, on a double-word score for twenty-eight points," Marcy announced, setting her letter tiles on the Scrabble board.

"Aw, Mom." Katie noted her mother's score on the pad of paper.

"That's not fair, I don't even know what apathy means," Ben griped, resting his chin on his hand.

Marcy sat on the screened-in back porch of the house, playing the game at the table with her kids. She'd been trying to do things like this, play games, straighten out their closets with them, give them a chance to reconnect. So far, so good. Ben was clingy and a little whiney, and Katie was sometimes aloof, but she knew that was to be expected. After all, she'd been "gone" for six months and come back looking like a different person. She wasn't the only one who needed time to adjust.

"It means *disinterest,* like if you're kind of bored with something," Marcy explained, reaching for new tiles.

"Like this stupid game." Ben got up from his chair, dumping his tiles into the lid.

"Quitter," Katie accused.

"Mom! She's calling me names again."

Marcy glanced at her teenaged daughter. She'd been hesitant to reprimand them since she got home from the hospital, but she had realized that Phoebe would continue to act like their mother as long as Marcy didn't. "For heaven sake, you're four years older than he is. No name calling." She grabbed the sleeve of Ben's T-shirt as he went by. "And *you,* no whining. You know I can't abide whining."

She let go of him, and he walked into the house. "I'm going to bed to read my new book on saving the rainforest."

"Night, Ralph," Katie called after her brother. It was a nickname meant to be funny, but somehow it didn't come out that way when she used it. Ben was so preoccupied with safety and environmental concerns that Jake had started calling him Ralph Nader a few months ago . . . a year ago now.

Ben stuck his tongue out at his sister and disappeared into the brighter light of the family room.

"Guess we're done. You win." Katie picked up the game board.

"Hey, you and I could have kept playing." Marcy reached for the board, but it was too late. Katie spilled the tiles into the lid of the box.

"It's okay." Katie made a face. "Aunt Phoebe's waiting for me anyway. She's going to paint my toenails for me." Her face immediately brightened. "We do it all the time. She's got a whole pedicure kit with this buffing stone and mint lotion that smells really good and makes your skin tingle."

Inwardly, Marcy winced. How could she compete with her daughter against Phoebe with her pedicures, chick-flick movie nights, and apparently endless credit card limit to buy Katie anything she wanted? Ben didn't seem to be nearly as taken with his aunt as his sister, but it still bothered Marcy that she seemed to have been displaced from her family while she was in the hospital. It seemed so unfair. In her mind, it was still as if she had just been driving in the rain down that winding road a little more than a week ago.

Marcy closed up the game box. "Put it back in the closet."

"I will," Katie sang, scooping it up and leaving her mother alone on the back porch.

Marcy flipped off the light that hung over the table to deter a mosquito she heard buzzing near her ear. Thankful for a quiet moment alone, she sat back in her padded wrought-iron chair and stared out into the darkness. She could see the outline of Ben's "fort" that Jake had built him a couple of years ago from salt-treated timber. She could make out the shed, too, where they kept the lawn mower and bikes, just a faint outline at the edge of the property.

Marcy felt the hair rise suddenly on her bare arms. There it was again, like on the beach the other night, that feeling that she was being watched. There was no one there, of course. The neighbor's German shepherd hadn't barked. The outside light that was triggered by a motion detector hadn't come on.

She closed her eyes for a second, willing her heart to slow to a normal pace again. If she told anyone she thought someone was watching her, she would end up on that psychiatrist's couch, or worse, back in the hospital again for more tests.

Taking a deep breath, Marcy opened her eyes. Dr. Larson had warned her that she might feel strange at times, that there might be moments in her day that didn't quite make sense. It was all part of the brain's recovery he had patiently explained in that monotone voice doctors liked to use. So, a little touch of paranoia didn't seem all that strange, considering the circumstances, did it?

"Marcy?"

Jake laid his hand on her shoulder from behind, and she leaped out of the chair.

"Jake! Don't do that." She pulled away and sat down again. "You scared me half to death."

"I'm sorry."

He grabbed a chair beside her, and she looked away. This wasn't working. Him tiptoeing around her, constantly apologizing. Being so stinking nice to her. Marcy had been thinking about it since the other night on the beach. The sex had been great, she'd give Jake that. But that didn't mean she wanted to remain married to him. She just hadn't had the guts to bring it up yet.

"I just wanted to tell you that I'll be late tomorrow night. I've got a meeting with Dick Magee—"

"Jake, I want you to move out," Marcy interrupted. She turned to face him, thinking she owed him at least that.

"What?"

Even in the darkness, she could see the distressed look on his face. She was glad it was dark so he couldn't see hers clearly and be reminded of how beautiful she was now. She didn't want the facts to be distorted by her face or nice boobs.

"I think you need to move out." she repeated, more sure of herself now.

"Marcy—"

"Jake, you know we were on the verge of this before the accident. I can't pretend we weren't, even if you can."

"Honey—"

He reached out for her, and she drew back. His touch did still excite her, and she didn't want that distorting the facts either. "Please, Jake?" She swallowed against her fear and the tears that threatened to well up in her eyes. "You know how it was with us. Barely talking. Always arguing over stupid stuff when we did speak. Stuff like who ate the last of the cereal, who left the toothpaste in the sink?"

"Marcy, those are just the things that married couples fight about. Everyone bickers. That doesn't mean we don't love each other."

She shook her head, pressing her lips together. "I don't want to be *everyone,* Jake! And I don't know that I do love you anymore." She hadn't meant to shout those last words. They just came out that way.

Jake stood up, his arms loose at his sides. "I don't know what to say."

She looked away, into the dark yard again. "Don't say anything. Just find some place to go. A hotel would probably be expensive, but maybe you can find a rental for a couple of weeks."

"You want me to go tonight?"

She kept her eyes focused on the big lilac bush beside the shed. Now that her eyes had adjusted to the dark of the porch, she could see the yard better. There was no one there. "That would be better."

"But just until we sort this out, right?" he asked hopefully.

He sounded so sad that Marcy didn't answer, afraid she'd have second thoughts and tell him not to go. After several long moments of painful silence, he walked back into the house.

Phoebe must have been waiting inside the door because she passed Jake on her way onto the porch.

Marcy drew up her legs on the chair and wrapped her arms around her knees, still amazed she could do it. She wiped at her eyes and sniffed. "You heard that."

Phoebe sat down, opened her cigarettes that she had left on the table, and flicked her lighter. Marcy didn't allow smoking in the house; it bothered Ben's asthma. The flame glowed for a moment, illuminating her sister's face. "I heard."

Was there nothing in her life that could be hers alone? Marcy looked down at her hands. No wedding or engagement rings anymore. Someone had taken them off after the accident and given them to Jake for safekeeping. Marcy had found them in her velvet-lined jewelry box. They were too big now and would have to be sized. If she ever wore them again . . . ."You think I'm nuts?"

Phoebe shrugged. She was wearing two pink tank tops, one pale, the other darker, layered over each other the way teen girls wore them. No bra. "You know me— I'm not one to give advice on relationships, but you weren't getting along very well last year. At Thanksgiving you told me you were thinking of separating."

Marcy ran her hand through her hair, pushing it back over the crown of her head. She had gotten a trim, adding some layers, and she loved the way it felt now. Loved the way it brushed her cheeks when she turned her head. Phoebe had liked the way she got it cut so much that she had gone and had hers done the same way.

Marcy studied Phoebe in the darkness that served as a buffer between them. Somehow it was easier talking this way, not having to see this reflection of herself too clearly. Marcy didn't remember saying anything to her sister about wanting a separation from Jake, but it was probably just one of those holes in her memory that Dr. Larson said might occasionally occur. "I'm not saying it's permanent."

Phoebe inhaled, and the end of her cigarette glowed brighter for a moment. "No, of course not."

"I just need some time to think."

Phoebe nodded. "This way you can have some space. And I'll be out of your hair in no time." She lifted her hand and let it fall. "I've got applications out all over the place. I got called in for an interview over at O'Hara's already. Assistant Manager. Salaried with benefits."

Marcy glanced out into the dark yard again. She could hear the frogs along the woods line peeping. Insects chirping. No one could be out there, she told herself, fighting that feeling again. She glanced sideways at her sister, then through the screen into the dark yard again. "Have . . . have you noticed anything strange around here the last few nights?" she asked softly.

A cloud of smoke drifted over Phoebe's head. "What do you mean?"

Marcy hesitated. The mosquito buzzed in her ear again, and she swatted it absently. She didn't want her sister saying anything to Jake. She didn't want anyone talking to Dr. Larson, either. This town was so small; everyone knew everyone's business, and she was tired of everyone talking about her accident. About her. "I don't know. I just keep getting this weird feeling that . . . that someone's watching . . ." She let her words trail off, not knowing how to verbalize what she was sensing.

Phoebe glanced into the yard. "Ryan says Billy Trotter's no longer a suspect in Patti's murder. Got an alibi. They're looking into some transient guy who was seen hanging around the diner the week she was killed. *Maybe he's out there*," she teased, altering her voice to sound spooky. "You know, like the night stalker."

Marcy cut her eyes at her sister. "Very funny." She got up. "I'm going to bed."

"Where's Jake sleeping tonight?"

Marcy walked into the light of the family room, feeling more secure there. "Don't know, don't care," she called over her shoulder. "So long as it's not here."

The Bloodsucker stood in the shadow of the shed and watched Marcy walk off the porch, through the open French doors and into the family room. As she went, he imagined following her. Walking right in with her, like the house was his. Like Marcy was his. If it had been him there on the porch tonight and not Jake, he wouldn't have agreed to move out. If it had been him, Marcy wouldn't have asked him to move out. She would have wanted to take him by the hand and lead him upstairs where she could tuck him warm and safe into their bed. She would have kissed his cheek and told him how much she loved him. She would have said how glad she was that she hadn't died because now she could be there with him.

Watching Marcy's interactions with her family tonight had been like watching a Sunday night movie . . . no, better. It had all the drama, the angst of any award-winning drama ABC, NBC, or CBS had to offer. But the best part was that Marcy had been the star. She made such a wonderful heroine, so brave, strong, courageous. Unlike her sister, Phoebe.

The Bloodsucker didn't like Phoebe. And now that she had gotten her hair cut like Marcy's, it was sometimes hard to tell them apart. At least until Phoebe opened her mouth. Then all the trash spilled out. The filth. He wondered if Phoebe's blood would be as black as Patti's had been.

He shifted his weight from one foot to another, suddenly uncomfortable inside his undershorts. He didn't like that feeling. It was bad.

He swallowed, trying not to think about it. Thinking about it only made things worse . . . .

The Bloodsucker wondered about Phoebe's blood, but it wasn't Phoebe he was interested in. It was Marcy. Marcy who had been fat and ugly and then been transformed in a miracle. Her life could have been a miniseries. He could make it one. They could do it together.

The Bloodsucker told himself that Patti had been a mistake. He swore to himself that he would not do that again. It was too dangerous. So many ways to get caught. But as the days passed . . . as the elation waned until it was nothing but a dull throb . . . he wondered why he couldn't do it again. Better this time. It would be better. The joy would last longer if he had a woman like Marcy. A woman who could truly understand him. Understand his needs. It would make him strong.

Marcy disappeared from his view inside the house, and his disappointment was so pungent that he could almost taste it in his mouth. He liked the taste of things in his mouth. Taste had always been good. Something Granny was never able to take away from him.

His gaze wandered to Phoebe, who remained on the porch. She leaned back in the chair and propped her feet on the table. He watched the end of her cigarette glow as she inhaled.

Smoking was bad. Unhealthy. And he didn't like the smell of it. Patti had smelled like smoke. But Marcy . . . he knew she wouldn't ever smoke cigarettes because she understood how important it was to take care of her good health.

She was even jogging now. First, she had just been taking walks, but now, she jogged through town. That made the Bloodsucker happy because he could see her more often. Watch her.

Coming here tonight had been an impulse. He had known he shouldn't have and yet . . . His hand found its way to his pants.

No. Bad.

He tucked his hand behind his back. Then the other hand. He had to have the strength to resist.

Patti had given him strength. Somehow he knew in his heart that Marcy could give him strength. That her strength could become his. And she was such a good person. Surely she'd be willing to share.

A dog barked next door, startling the Bloodsucker. Suddenly, his heart was racing.

"Shhh, shhh, don't bark, dog. Nice dog." He backed up behind the shed, then turned and ran through the woods.

Coming here had been so bad. Granny would have said it was very bad.

It had felt so good.

* * *

Marcy sat in the driver's seat of the green SUV, her fingers gripped tightly around the wheel. The garage door was still shut. No one knew she was here. No witness to her moment of temporary psychosis. Phoebe had dropped Ben off at the pool for his swimming lesson, and Katie was down the street baby-sitting for their neighbor's twin toddlers.

She had been sitting here like this for almost an hour, trying to get up the nerve to start it. She knew her fear was illogical. It wasn't raining, and there was no ice on the road. It was a sunny eighty-three degrees already, according to the radio. No chance of skidding off the road and crashing through the railing of a bridge. She wouldn't even have to cross the bridge to get to town. She had only been involved in one automobile accident in her entire life. What were the chances she'd get into another today? Her brain dwelled on the logical while her body still seemed to be clinging to this irrational fear.

But Marcy wasn't going to let it overwhelm her. Jake had moved out of the house two nights ago. Tonight he was coming to the house for some of his things and then moving into a friend's condo. When Phoebe got a job and moved out, Marcy would be here alone with the kids. She had to be able to drive to function as a mother. As a person. If she wanted independence, she had to be able to drive. Albany Beach wasn't a town big enough for public transportation.

Marcy grasped the brown leather of the steering wheel, then released it, flexing her sweaty fingers. She could feel her heart beating in her chest beneath her white T-shirt. Taking a deep breath, she willed herself to reach down, grab the key, and turn over the engine. It started right up, and she grinned. As she reached up to punch the garage door opener, she caught a glimpse of herself in the rearview mirror.

Coral lipstick. Hair pulled back in a ponytail. She was

actually getting some sun now, out on her walks that were turning into jogs. She looked younger with a little color. She adjusted the mirror, still finding it hard to believe that that was her looking back at herself. That beautiful woman whose possibilities seemed endless.

If she could just back the car out of the driveway . . .

Biting down on her lower lip, Marcy shifted into reverse and eased the SUV out of the garage. So far, so good. Of course she'd been moving forward at the time of the accident.

Her little joke made her smile and gave her the courage to shift into drive when she reached the pavement in front of her house. She inched down the street, out onto the main road, and slowly pressed the gas pedal. Her heart was still pounding, but by the time she reached the edge of town, she was breathing normally again. She had done it. She had driven the car. And now she was going shopping.

By noon, Marcy had three shopping bags of clothes, mostly T-shirts and shorts, but a pair of running shorts and a nice jog bra, too. New socks, panties, bras, and a hooded sweatshirt for cool evenings. She was just tossing the last bag into the back of the SUV, feeling more than a little proud of herself, when she heard someone come up behind her and she whipped around. Why was she so jumpy?

"Marcy?" It was Claire Drummond in full police uniform. From the tone of her voice, she wasn't positive she had the right sister.

Marcy made a conscious effort not to look like she'd had the bejesus scared out of her. "Claire. Yup, it's me."

The police chief, who had apparently cut across the parking lot, stopped at the edge of the SUV. "Sorry, I wasn't sure."

"I know." Marcy closed the back of the car. "We look just alike now."

Claire chuckled. "Must be strange."

"Very."

"So how you doing?" The police chief reached out, touching Marcy's arm. "Feeling okay? You must be; I saw you jogging last night. I was on my way home."

"That's right. You live out my way." Marcy nodded, feeling a little uncomfortable.

She and Claire had attended the same schools. Though Claire was a few years older, they'd known each other since they were kids in Sunday school together, but they'd never been friends. Claire had always been beautiful. Smart, well liked. She'd been a cheerleader in high school and the president of the senior class, too. While Claire had always been a part of the "in" crowd, Marcy had tended to hang with the other fat girls and with the guys who were just a little too odd to fit in anywhere else. She'd always gotten good grades, too, but it hadn't been enough to bridge the gap between her and a girl like Claire.

"I see you've been shopping." Claire picked up the conversation that Marcy felt she was letting drag.

"Yeah." Marcy laughed. "Nothing I have fits. I can't wear my sister's clothes forever. Then I'd really look like her."

Claire laughed with her and then hooked a thumb in the direction of the row of stores at the edge of the parking lot. "I was just going into The Greenery for some lunch. You have time to join me?"

Marcy's first impulse was to say no thanks and make a quick escape. What was she going to say to Claire Drummond over an entire lunch? But a part of her wanted to have lunch with Claire . . . wanted a friend. "Um . . . yeah. Sure. That would be nice. I'm still not eating a lot, but I am hungry." She clicked the remote key lock and the car beeped.

"Great."

Seated inside the funky little lunch shop, Claire and Marcy both ordered salads, Claire a Caesar and Marcy a

Greek. They both added sweetener to their iced tea and stirred loudly to fill the silence.

"So . . . I've been following the paper," Marcy said finally, licking her spoon and setting it down beside her glass. She was still ill at ease sitting here with Claire like they were lunch buddies, but not as nervous as she had been. After all, why should she be? Claire was the one who had asked her, so she must have thought Marcy had something of interest to say. Some worth, even if it was just the novelty of being a woman who had crashed her car off a bridge and had plastic surgery that made her beautiful.

"No idea what happened to Patti Lorne yet?"

Claire sipped her iced tea, shaking her head. She was a beautiful woman with that white-blond hair Marcy had always admired, cut just above the shoulder in what looked like one of those shaggy Meg Ryan do's. Her own blond hair was more golden, with subtle streaks of red that become more pronounced in the summer. And Claire had the most profound blue eyes. She didn't look like a police chief, or even a cop. She could have been a model.

"Of course I can't tell you exactly where we are in the investigation," Claire confided. "I can tell you no one's been arrested."

"I heard you were looking for some homeless guy." Marcy didn't give her source. She didn't want to get Patrolman McCormick into trouble. Claire probably wouldn't appreciate one of her officers giving out information to women on barstools.

"Work gets around quick, doesn't it?" Claire flashed a smile. "One of the joys of living in a small town. Yes, we're looking into a guy who was seen hanging around town."

Marcy studied Claire across the table from her, noting the lines of concern at the corners of her mouth. "But you're not too hopeful?"

Claire stared into her glass of tea. "Let's just say it's not looking too promising."

"Do you think Patti knew her killer or was he a stranger?" Marcy thought of the creepy feelings she kept getting and Phoebe's ridiculous comment about a "night stalker."

"I'm not even sure if the killer was male or female yet, Marcy."

"Women kill other women like that?"

"Not often, but it's done. Usually out of jealousy, according to what I've been reading." She gave a humorless laugh. "Needless to say, I've been up late nights brushing up on my *traits of a killer.*"

Marcy lowered her gaze, lifting her glass to her mouth. She could see how what Claire said could be true. She would never kill anyone, of course, but she understood jealousy. She'd been jealous of Phoebe her whole life, and it was an emotion that could possess you, eat at you like a cancerous tumor. For some, maybe it turned to rage.

"A Caesar and a Greek," the waitress announced, sliding huge wooden salad bowls in front of them. "Anything else I can get you ladies besides free refills on the teas?"

Marcy glanced up and smiled, shaking her head.

"Nope, we're good. Thanks, Trina."

Marcy and Claire attacked their salads and moved on to less morbid topics. They commiserated on having teen daughters, and Marcy found herself thanking God that while Katie could sometimes be difficult, at least she hadn't dyed her hair black. Not yet, anyway.

As they talked, Marcy marveled at how easy she found Claire to talk to once she relaxed a little and stopped feeling so self-conscious. She'd never been good at conversation before. Not had any real girlfriends for years. They just seemed too hard to make, too hard to maintain. Talking to the police chief this way, she realized how much she missed female companionship with someone other than her sister, whom she always felt she was in competition with.

"So how are things going at home?' Claire asked, pushing her salad bowl aside and wiping her mouth with her napkin.

"Okay." Marcy set her bowl aside, too, though she had only eaten half the salad. She didn't know if it was because she was afraid of getting fat again or not, but she just didn't have the appetite she had once had. Six months ago, she'd have devoured the salad and a double-decker BLT, too. "It's going to take Ben and Katie a while to adjust, of course." She didn't meet Claire's gaze. "But Dr. Larson said that's to be expected."

"It's got to be a big change for you, too. Waking up to look like a different person," Claire offered gently. "Jake, too."

Marcy lifted her gaze to meet Claire's gaze. "You've heard." she said softly.

Claire nodded, and Marcy grimaced. "Talk about a small town. Jake's only been gone two nights. I suppose he's been crying all over town that I kicked him out."

"Actually, he's been pretty quiet. I ran into him at the diner last night. He seemed mostly concerned about how you were making out alone with the kids."

"Well, my sister's still staying with us for now."

Claire didn't say anything.

"But you know Phoebe."

"She can be a handful," Claire offered with an understanding chuckle.

"You're not kidding." Marcy pressed her lips together, pausing for a moment. "I know you're divorced. It had to be hard. Everyone says it's worse with kids."

"My ex and I should never have gotten married, Marcy. I knew it the day I stood at the altar. I should have listened to my instincts and my dad." She was smiling. "But you and Jake . . . you always seemed different. You made a good couple from day one."

Marcy fiddled with her napkin. "Maybe. But things haven't been great in a while." She glanced up hesitantly. "And now after this accident, everything that's happened, I think I need to take a good, hard look at my life. I was even thinking of checking out some other line of work. You know, I've always hated accounting."

"You're a smart woman, Marcy. You could do anything you set out to accomplish. What are you considering?"

"I know this is going to sound silly." She looked up, unable to believe she was actually telling Claire this. She hadn't told anyone yet. "I've always wanted to own a restaurant. Like a little French Bistro or something. You know, with good bread and homemade soups. Fancy desserts." She hesitated. "Crazy?"

"Not at all. And this is certainly a good area for restaurants."

Claire didn't mention Phoebe and her husband's failed restaurant, but Marcy knew that was what she was thinking about. What Marcy was thinking about.

The bell on the door jingled as someone entered The Greenery. "Hey, Chief."

Marcy looked up to see Ryan McCormick approaching their table. He was dressed in a uniform similar to Claire's in green and tan, and looking mighty fine with his broad shoulders and GQ-meets-GI good looks.

"McCormick." Claire acknowledged. "You looking for me?" Her hand went to the radio on her shoulder. "No one called in."

"Nah. Jewel said you were on your lunch break. I just stopped in to grab something to go." As he removed his dark sunglasses, he turned to Marcy, a hint of a sexy smile beneath the cop poker face. "Good to see you, Mrs. Edmond. I hear you're making a heck of a recovery."

She blushed, unused to the attention he was giving her. But she couldn't miss the look of interest on his face. It wasn't that Marcy had never been able to see that sexual attraction in men before, it had just never been directed toward her. "I'm feeling, good. Thank you for asking." She closed her hands around the cool, wet glass in front of her.

"I have to tell you, I'm pretty amazed, considering what the scene looked like. I don't know that I've ever seen anyone else survive a wreck like that, certainly not come out as beautiful as you did."

"Patrolman First Class McCormick and his partner, Patrolman Savage, were the first on the scene of your accident," Claire said. "He pulled you out of the water."

Marcy looked at him again, forcing herself to meet his gaze despite her discomfort. She was tired of her habit of always looking away, always feeling undeserving of anyone's attention, especially with a man as attractive as the officer. If he deemed Phoebe worthy of his attention—which he obviously did—why not her, too? "Then I have to thank you." She offered her hand. "I guess you saved my life."

He closed his hand over hers, warm and firm. His touch sent little tingles of pleasure up her arm. She pulled back. He was still looking at her. Definitely smiling now.

Claire glanced at her officer and rolled her eyes. "McCormick, pull your tongue back in your mouth. You're drooling on the table." She wiped it with her hand. "You are still on the clock, aren't you?"

He seemed to snap out of it and took a step back from the table. "On my way, Chief." He nodded toward Marcy. "I hear you're alone now, Mrs. Edmond. I'm sorry to hear that, but you need anything, you just call me . . . I mean, give us a call."

Marcy couldn't help smiling back. "Thanks, Patrolman McCormick. Have a good day."

"You bet."

Marcy watched him swagger off before looking at Claire across the table. "Nice guy," she remarked. "I

think my sister has gone out with him a couple times."
She tried not to think about what Phoebe had said about
the rough sex and handcuffs. He seemed too nice for
that sort of thing . . . and her sister did tend to sensa-
tionalize things.

"Yeah, I hear he's quite a ladies' man." Claire slid out
of the booth, taking the check the waitress had left on
the table.

"Oh, I'm sorry, let me—" Marcy opened her purse.

"Nah, let me get this. I'm the one who asked you to
lunch. Next time you can get it."

Marcy nodded, sliding out of her seat. She liked the
idea that they might do this again. She liked Claire. Liked
how sensible she was. Strong minded. "I'd like that."

Out on the street, Claire surveyed the parking lot.
"I'm parked over there." She pointed to the tan cruiser.

"Well, thanks for lunch."

Claire hesitated, meeting Marcy's gaze. "I don't mean
to stick my nose where it doesn't belong, Marcy, but you
should give this thing with you and Jake some time. Not
do anything permanent right away."

Marcy was touched by her kindness. "Thanks. And
thanks again for lunch."

"You bet."

This time when Marcy climbed into the SUV, she
started it up and backed it out of the parking space
without a moment's hesitation. She felt good today.
Better than she could remember feeling in years.

The Bloodsucker watched Marcy from the sidewalk
in front of the strip mall. He'd been lucky today. Lunch
break. Right place at the right time.

Through the dark lenses of his sunglasses, he observed
her walk to her new car. Long shapely legs. Blond hair
fluttering in the warm breeze. It was a big green SUV,
and somehow it fitted her new look.

He watched her back out of her parking space and pull out of the lot, heading home probably, from the direction she was going. Of course, he already knew where she lived.

He'd already been there. That had been very bad of him, to go there. To watch her. It was wrong. It was dangerous. The police were looking for him.

Of course they didn't know it was him because he was so clever. So smart. Granny had never known just how smart he was.

And he wanted Marcy. That was why he had gone to see her. Because he wanted her. Needed her.

She made him feel good. Something he never recalled feeling before, really. Not like this.

Of course, Patti had made him feel good.

The blood. Her blood.

He swallowed hard, squirmed a little. He glanced up quickly, making sure no one was watching him. He didn't want to draw any attention to himself. He couldn't.

Not if he wanted to avoid suspicion. Not if he wanted to bring Marcy home with him.

Two days later, Marcy walked into the kitchen to find Phoebe folding the clothes she had tossed in the washing machine that morning.

"You take Ben swimming?" Phoebe asked.

Marcy dropped her keys on the counter. She wanted to go for her jog before it was too warm out, but she didn't feel like she should be out running when her sister was standing here folding her underwear. "Swim lessons first, then he's going to Pete's house. Liz said she'd pick them up." She went to the kitchen table and pulled one of her new T-shirts from the laundry basket.

"Oh, I can do these. You rest."

Marcy eyed Phoebe. "I don't need to rest. I slept

eight hours last night, and you don't need to keep doing things like this." She added the tee to a growing pile and reached for another piece of static-crackling clothing.

"I'm sorry. I was just trying to help."

From anyone else the statement would have sounded properly contrite, but somehow Phoebe didn't quite pull it off. Maybe Marcy was being overly sensitive, but somehow her words didn't quite ring true, and she couldn't put her thumb on why. Maybe because she knew her sister too well?

"Jake's coming after work to get the kids," Marcy said, changing the subject, "so don't start anything for dinner."

"I was going to pick up some mahi mahi at the seafood place."

"Well, don't." Marcy glanced at her sister and saw the hurt look on her face. "Phebes, you're stuffing me like a pet pig. I'll be back in my old jeans in no time if you keep feeding me this way."

"I'm just trying to help you get your strength back." Phoebe added a folded pair of shorts to the pile.

"I swear, I don't know how you eat that way and still stay so skinny." Marcy shook her head, looking at her sister in knit shorts and a baby tee. "And you never exercise. I figure I need to run three miles a day just to maintain."

"Just my metabolism, I guess." Phoebe dropped a yellow sock on the table and dug for another piece of clothing. "I can run the kids over to Jake's after work if you want me to. Just so you don't have to—you know, deal with him."

Phoebe had been good about helping out since Jake left, not just with the kids but with handling Jake, too. She glanced at Phoebe as she dug into the basket in search of a mate to the sock she held in her hand. "No. It's fine. He probably wants to get some more of his stuff anyway. So how was the interview?"

Phoebe glanced up blankly.

"The one at O'Hara's? The assistant manager's position you told me about the other night?"

"Oh, that." Phoebe gave a wave and began to stack the piles of clean clothes in the basket. "It wasn't worth taking."

"I thought you said it was salaried, with benefits."

Phoebe busied herself with the clothes. "You know how it is. People advertise something they're really not offering. I'm not worried. Everyone will be hiring soon. Mid-June, schools are getting out everywhere. People will be flocking to the beach. Restaurants will be desperate for people with my kind of experience."

Marcy wanted to tell her sister that she didn't think she was in a position to be turning down any job offers, not considering the fact that she had no others. Then she reminded herself that she should be grateful Phoebe had been unemployed and able to be here all these months, looking after Jake and the kids. "I'm sure something better will come along." She added the last of the clean clothes to the basket. "Was that Matt on the answering machine for you this morning? He must have called late."

"I don't know why he calls here. He had my cell number." Phoebe grabbed the basket.

"The divorce close to being settled?"

"Of course not. He's trying to say we weren't equal partners in the restaurant, even though *he* was the one who took out those extra loans. Prick." She headed out of the kitchen with the clothes. "If no one's going to be home for dinner tonight, I'll probably go out." She halted in the doorway. "You'll be okay here alone while the kids are with Jake?"

"Of course." The truth was, Marcy was looking forward to a few hours of peace and quiet. Mostly from Phoebe. She fussed over her like a mother hen. It was so unlike her that it made Marcy uncomfortable. Though

Phoebe was older by twenty minutes, she had never had
that big-sister quality about her. Growing up, it had always been every girl for herself.

"You going out to jog now?"

"Yup."

"See you later," Phoebe called as she disappeared down
the hall.

After changing into her new running clothes, Marcy
stretched, grabbed a bottle of water out of the fridge,
and headed out of the house. Her plan was to walk a
quarter of a mile, jog a quarter of a mile, and then do it
again. Her goal was to make it into town and back without collapsing on the road and having to take another
ride in an ambulance.

Marcy made it all the way into town, but as she turned
to head back, she realized she should have started with a
bigger bottle of water. The one she was carrying was
empty. She had no money with her to run into the mini
mart, and she was dying of thirst. Walking along the sidewalk next to the diner, she cut across the parking lot.
Trying to catch her breath, she darted inside. The place
was empty except for a couple of teenagers, all dressed in
black with dyed black hair, seated in the rear. She spotted
Claire's daughter, at least who she thought was Ashley,
seated next to a guy with spiked black hair, and a nose
stud. He rested his arm possessively around Ashley's
shoulder. When he made eye contact with Marcy, he studied her for a moment, lifted his chin in a quick acknowl-
edgment and returned his attention to his milkshake.

"Well, well, well, little lady. Marcy, right?"

Marcy glanced up to see Ralph leaning over the lunch
counter toward her. Instinctively, she moved back. She
could have sworn he was staring at her breasts. "Right.
Marcy." She offered a half smile.

"So what can I do for you?"

Marcy wished now that she'd come into town in something more than her running shorts and new matching

blue and green jog bra. When she left the house it had seemed perfectly decent enough; she was wearing a sight more than most women wore on the beach. But the way Ralph looked at her made her wish she'd worn the beach towel, too.

"Um." She dropped her water bottle on the counter. "I was out jogging and I ran out of water, and I was wondering if Loretta could just fill it up from the tap." She made an effort of looking for the diner's proprietress.

"Loretta's gone to the Save-A-Lot. Left me in charge." He stroked his chin. "But I'll be happy to fill 'er up for you. As pretty a thing as you are now."

"Thanks." She looked away as Ralph scooped up her bottle and lumbered into the back.

Marcy again caught the eye of the teen with the spiked black hair. He had been watching her. Self-consciously, she wrapped her arms around herself, covering at least part of her bare midriff. She didn't remember seeing the boy before. He looked older than Ashley, but still in high school. Of course, if he had undergone the same transformation the police chief's daughter had, she might know him from town and just not able to recognize him any longer.

"Here you go, little lady." Ralph leaned over the counter, offering the bottle of water as he leered. "Filled it from cold in the fridge."

She offered another quick smile, realizing she was going to have to take the bottle from Ralph's hand and risk touching him. "Thanks." She grabbed it quickly and darted for the door. "Tell Loretta I said hi."

"Be careful out there," Ralph warned. "It's hot for a little thing like you to be runnin'."

Outside, Marcy gave a shudder of disgust and jogged slowly across the parking lot, sipping the icy water. Instead of following the path she had taken coming into town, she took a parallel street. She crossed the Coastal Highway and headed inland. As she slowed to a walk, she glanced at the marquee in front of the Waterfront Realty building. *Business space,* it read. *Restaurant Possibilities. Excellent location.* It gave a property number.

As she headed down the country road that led to her development, Marcy thought about the marquee. She'd checked in with G & A Construction, reiterating what Dr. Larson had said about her not going back to work yet, but she had encouraged her old boss to go ahead and find a replacement for her. She'd been thinking more and more about her restaurant idea. She had money of her own, money her parents had left her when they died. Phoebe had blown through hers in less than a year and had nothing to show for it but her convertible. Marcy had been the conservative one. She hadn't spent a cent, but had invested sensibly instead. She could use the money as collateral to start a restaurant if she wanted to.

So far, though, she'd done nothing but daydream and tell Claire about the prospect. By the time she walked into her house, hot, sweaty, but feeling good, she had decided she would make the call to the real estate company. It was time for Marcy to take action.

The Bloodsucker lowered the flame on the stovetop and put a lid on his spaghetti sauce. Granny had never made spaghetti sauce. That was why he made it so often now. Why he liked it so much. He just bought the stuff in the jar, but he always added spices to it to brighten the bland taste; a little garlic, Italian seasoning . . . some other things. His mouth watered at the thought of it.

Something bumped into the Bloodsucker's leg and he glanced down. "Max." He smiled as he stooped down to pet his dog. Max had just been a stray he'd found eating fish guts out of a trash can behind a restaurant one night. He was a good dog, who never bit and never pissed on the floor. Best of all, he never complained. Never called a person ugly names.

The Bloodsucker scratched behind Max's ears and made little soothing sounds the way he had seen people on TV do. "That's right, Buddy. What a good boy. What a smart boy."

He said things to Max that a person might say to a boy. Things Granny had never said to him.

Enjoying the attention, Max rubbed up against the Bloodsucker's black pant leg, leaving little brown hairs all over him. He laughed and brushed them off, then walked to the cupboard to get a dog treat. Getting a little animal hair on their clothes might have upset some people. It might have made them so angry that they would hit someone . . . or worse. But the hairs didn't make the Bloodsucker angry. They didn't because he had control. He was strong.

He made Max sit for the treat and gave him a pat as the dog bounded over. Then he went down the hall to the bathroom and used a lint remover to roll away the dog hair from his pant leg.

Back in the kitchen, he went to the stove to stir his sauce. It was cooking down nicely now, looking dark. It reminded him of Patti's blood, in a way, though it wasn't so black.

The thought of Patti sent a pleasantly surprising trill through him. He liked the way she had made him feel. Strong. Capable.

But the feeling wouldn't last forever, the Bloodsucker knew that. It was already fading. He had to keep scooping it up, pulling it back toward him. Making it his own again.

He would have to kill again. He knew that. He had known it the first time he had seen Marcy with her slender new body, her lovely pale face.

"Patience," he whispered. "Patience." And then he lifted the wooden spoon dripping with red sauce to his mouth and let his eyes drift shut as the pleasure of the taste washed over him.

Chapter Five

"It's so nice of you to do this on such short notice." Marcy dared a look across the diner table at Seth Watkins. Both of them were armed with a cup of Loretta's coffee.

Marcy was glad she'd taken the time to dress nicely, not just so the Realtor would take her seriously, but because he was kind of cute.

Seth Watkins was a little "cleaner," a little "smoother," than she usually found attractive, but a woman had to be open about these things, didn't she? Granted, his fingernails were professionally manicured and every hair on his head was glued precisely into place with some serious hair gel, but he was very friendly. And the fact that she got the idea he thought she was attractive didn't hurt.

"Not at all, Mrs. Edmond."

"Please." She added sweetener to her coffee and stirred it. "Call me Marcy."

He glanced at her left hand. "Divorced?" he asked, his voice low. He was wearing khakis and a form-fitting polo. She could tell he worked out and either spent a lot of time on the beach or had a membership at a tanning booth.

"Separated."

"I've never been married myself."

"Well, due to my *situation*, I'm very interested in buying property suitable for a restaurant. If I find what I'm looking for, I may want to move quickly." She lowered her voice, adding to the intimate feeling between them that he had already established. Though it was early for the lunch crowd, she knew several people in the diner, like her, stopping for a cup of coffee. "I haven't told my—Jake about this yet, so I would appreciate you keeping it to yourself."

"Of course, of course," he assured her, reaching out to pat her hand. "You sure you wouldn't like a donut? A piece of pie?"

She laughed and shook her head thinking to herself, *If he only knew how easily she once would have been tempted.* "No, thanks."

"Loretta makes a mean lemon meringue pie," he cajoled, smoothing his already smooth hair at his temple. "I eat here more often than I eat at home."

"I think everyone else in town does, too," she said, laughing.

He leaned forward on the table. "Listen, before we get started, I have to confess something."

She lifted a freshly plucked brow. She'd treated herself to a facial yesterday at the salon in town, in anticipation of this meeting today. She had hoped it would give her the extra boost of confidence she needed. So far, it seemed to be working.

"I pretended not to know who you were when I returned your message," Seth said. "But it wasn't true. Even though I haven't been in town long, I knew who you were the minute I heard your name on my voice mail. I've seen you around town, jogging, in the grocery store . . ." He had a handsome, boyish grin to go with his blond hair and all-American good looks. "Okay, so maybe I've been watching you around town."

She hid her smile by lifting the cup of coffee to her

mouth. "I have to pick up my son at two; he's having lunch with his father. I'd really like to see what you have to show me in your folder there, and maybe look at a couple of places?" She glanced up. His attention made her feel bold. "If that can be arranged, *Seth?*"

"Of course that can be arranged. Now, let me give you a copy of the listings and one of my pens." He slid the folder across the table to her, along with a cheap plastic lime-green pen with his name printed on it in bold letters. "You can see my phone numbers are on there. Call me any time, day or night."

She flipped open the folder, trying not to think about how much she hated cheap ink pens. She couldn't hold that against the guy, could she?

Half an hour later, they were at the site of one of the available properties. Even though Seth said he liked to drive his clients around town, she had taken her own car. There'd be gossip enough when it got around that she had met with a Realtor; she didn't want to fuel the fires with any other juicy tidbits considering the fact that everyone knew Jake had moved out.

The property was at the end of an upscale strip mall on the south edge of town and presently unoccupied. A Mexican restaurant had been there before. As Marcy walked past Seth into the dimly lit main dining room and gazed up at the sombreros still hanging from the ceiling, she heard him lock the outside door behind her. She turned around, her gaze shifting to the door, then to him. The idea of being locked inside with a man she didn't really know made her a little uneasy.

"It's a safety precaution," Seth explained, adding a grin for good measure. "You never know what kind of people might be hanging around."

She nodded, thinking that did make sense. And there were people walking by outside on the sidewalk. The entire front wall was glass; anyone who went by could see inside. She supposed she was safe enough. After all, a Realtor wouldn't make much of a living if he attacked his female clients, would he?

She turned back to the main dining room, listening as Seth began telling her about the property, practically touting it as one of the Seven Wonders of the World, falling somewhere between the hanging gardens of Babylon and the three great pyramids of Giza. She could tell that Seth was a brilliant salesman, but she also recognized quickly that she would have to take each thing he said with a grain of salt.

After the tour of the elaborately decorated dining room and the full kitchen, Marcy and Seth stood near the front door and talked. Somehow they got on the subject of France and he was telling her about his trip there the previous year. Marcy had only been there once, the summer after she graduated from high school. A gift to both her and Phoebe from their aging parents. Their mother had given birth to them late in life and had carried over certain ideas from her own youth, one being that young ladies should tour Europe. It was on that summer trip that the first seed had been planted in Marcy's head to own a bistro. But then, at the end of the summer, she had returned to the States and reality. She'd chosen a major in college that would put food on her own table and ultimately snag a husband, although the way things were looking now, maybe that wasn't such a plus.

Marcy glanced at her watch. "Oh, no!" She pressed the heel of her hand to her forehead. "I'm late. Listen, I have to run." She gestured for Seth to unlock the door. "But I'm very interested in this property and also the one just off the boardwalk on Seagrass Drive. Could you get those particulars together for me?"

"Sure." He turned his key and made a show of graciously holding the door open for her. "I'll call you. Tonight okay, if I get the info together?"

"Sure. Call me. You have my home number and my cell."

"And you have my numbers if you have any questions," he called after her. "The pen, right?"

She turned back to him, waving the pen as she climbed into her SUV. "Thanks, Seth."

"You bet. See you soon." He lifted his hand, cocking his thumb as if shooting her.

Corny, but he made her smile. It wasn't until she walked into Jake's office and saw her sulking son, seated in a chair in front of his father's desk, that her euphoria over the meeting subsided. She threw up her hands. "I'm know, I'm late. I'm sorry, sweetie."

Jake looked up from his computer screen filled by an Excel spread sheet. "It's okay. You're not that late."

"But look at this puss." She reached out to stroke Ben's chin.

"You said we would go to the Big-Mart." Ben pouted. "I want to look at carbon dioxide detectors. You promised."

"I said I'm sorry." Marcy shifted her new khaki-colored Sak purse on her shoulder. She'd never owned anything so trendy, but it had looked so nice with the khaki pants and crisp white shirt that she had let the sales clerk talk her into it. "I told you I had an appointment."

"I knew you got your hair cut," Jake said, admiring her. "It looks nice."

Marcy hadn't told Jake what her appointment was for when she'd asked him if he'd like to take their son for lunch today, but if he wanted to think it had been for a haircut, she'd let it go. Obviously, if she went through with this whole crazy restaurant scheme, she would have to tell him eventually, but that wasn't necessary yet.

Jake rose from his chair. He'd removed his suit jacket and was wearing a pale green shirt with a coral tie. He looked nice. She'd always liked that shirt and tie on him, and it looked even better now that he had lost a few pounds.

Marcy self-consciously brushed her hair off her shoulder, suddenly feeling guilty for not being entirely truthful. Despite the problems in her and Jake's marriage, dishonesty had never been one of them. She felt even worse because she'd been late, not because her appointment had taken longer than expected, but because she'd been busy flirting with Seth Watkins. Well, maybe she'd not been actively flirting, but she had certainly let him do his share.

"We should leave Daddy to his work, Ben." Marcy gave her son a nudge toward the door. "We'll stop at the Big-Mart on the way home."

"Thanks for coming." Jake put his arm around his son and kissed the top of his head, then tousled his sandy brown hair. "You mind waiting outside for your mom for a sec, buddy?"

"Sure." Ben put out his hand to his mother. "Keys."

She laughed, giving him one of those *over my dead body* looks. "Wait in the lobby, Ralph."

Jake watched him walk out the door, and then turned back to Marcy. She felt funny being alone with him like this. They hadn't been alone together since the night on the porch when she'd told him he had to move out.

Jake slipped his hands into his pants pockets. "So, how are you?"

"Good. Fine." She nodded, studying her sandals.

"Ben says swim lessons are going well. He's saving his allowance to buy the rainforest?"

She smiled, not looking up at him, knowing he was looking at her. "A square inch, is all. It's some kind of preservation thing. I thought it would be fine. He'll get a certificate for his wall."

It was Jake's turn to nod. "And Katie tells me she's rich now?"

"She got her first paycheck. She and Phebes have already made plans to spend it a hundred times over. I'm not sure my sister is the person to be giving our daughter advice on finances."

He chuckled. "Phoebe always was good at spending other people's money, wasn't she?"

"Speaking of which, that reminds me." She hadn't intended to bring this up with Jake today and start an argument with him, but now that he had opened the door, she thought she might as well waltz through it. "You didn't tell me she had our bank debit card."

He lifted one broad shoulder, hands still in his pockets. "Didn't get a chance, I guess." He halted, and then went on. "Look, I had to do something when you were in the hospital. Leaving money on the counter didn't always work. She was always stopping for groceries, picking up my dry cleaning. I couldn't very well expect her to use her own money, could I?"

Marcy bristled. For some reason, the idea of Phoebe picking up Jake's dry cleaning irked her. It wasn't that she was particularly fond of the chore; she just didn't like the idea of her sister doing it. *Talk about irrational thoughts. Maybe she did need to see that psychiatrist.*

"Well, just so you know, I made her give it back to me and she's pretty pissed. Not with you, of course. Me. Is there something you needed?" Marcy's tone turned short, mostly to cover her own inner conflicts. She was angry with Jake for making her be the bad guy and have to ask for the bank card, but at the same time, she didn't want to argue with him. She really missed him. "If not, Ben's waiting."

"I just wanted to know how you were."

"I'm fine. I—"

He reached out and brushed his fingertips against her cheek. She lifted her lashes to gaze into his brown eyes and felt a lump rise in her throat. Out of nowhere, she found herself so filled with emotion that she had to look away from him.

She was so confused. She had wanted Jake out of her life for months, years, hadn't she? Now that he was gone, what was this sense of regret that kept popping up whenever she saw him?

"You'll be by Friday night to pick up the kids, right?" She stepped away from him, toward the door.

"Yeah, right. Right after work." He hesitated. "I was wondering, could they stay the night? I mean, now that I have a place. An extra bedroom. Ben can sleep with me and Katie can have the other room." He stopped, then started again. "If you think they'd like to." He faltered again. "Marcy, I really miss them."

She gripped the door frame, refusing to turn back. She made herself concentrate on the property she had seen today and the infinite possibilities it held rather than the emotion in his voice. "You need to call them and ask them yourself, but I'm sure they'd both like it. Overnight is fine."

"Good. Okay. Well . . . see you later." He followed her as she passed through the doorway into the hall.

She didn't look back as she hurried down the hall because she didn't want him to see the tears in her eyes.

Claire's phone on her desk buzzed; a red light lit up. She punched the speaker phone with annoyance. "Jewel, I said hold my calls." She ran a hand over the glossy black-and-white photos of Patti Lorne's body spread on her desk.

"Sorry." Gum pop. "It's your daughter. She's called twice in the last hour. I thought you might want to talk to her."

Claire sighed, pushed back in her chair, and ran her hand over her face. "Sure. Yeah."

"Put her through?" Pop.

"Yes, Jewel, put Ashley through."

The light on the phone blinked again. Claire picked up the receiver. "Hey. What's up?"

"I've been trying to call you," her daughter said tersely.

No hi, Mom, how are you? How's your day going? Claire noted.

"You tell me you want me to let you know what I'm doing," Ashley continued, "and then I can't get through to you."

Claire's gaze strayed to the photo in front of her of Patti's pale body sprawled on the grass next to the galvanized drum in the state park. Completely clothed; denim miniskirt, bare midriff tee, high-heeled sandals, purse on her shoulder. She was practically dressed like a hooker, but there had been no sexual assault. Strange.

Claire sighed, looking away to a blank spot on the wall of her office. "You're right. I'm sorry."

"An apology. That's a first," her daughter quipped.

Claire forced herself to take a deep breath, to not reply with one of the many retorts that played on the end of her tongue. "What do you need, hon?"

"I'm getting off work in a few minutes, and I wanted to make sure it was okay if I went to the boardwalk with a friend."

"This friend have a name?"

No answer on the other end.

"Ashley?"

There was a big sigh on the other end of the phone. "Chain."

"What?" Claire reached for her Diet Coke and took a sip.

"You asked me what my friend's name was. It's Chain," Ashley repeated.

Claire swallowed the soda. Flat. "Your friend was baptized *Chain?*"

"I don't know," Ashley snapped. "No, of course not. Look, Mom, is it okay or not if I go to the boardwalk? April and Shawna are going, too. And some others. I think I'm pretty safe from the waitress killer, in a group. You can pick me up on your way home from work or . . . just let Chain bring me home."

"Or not." Claire dropped the soda can into her garbage can under her desk. "Okay, you can go, but you be on the designated corner at eight-thirty, or I'm coming with handcuffs and leg irons, looking for Chain."

"I'll be there."

Ashley hung up without a proper good-bye, and Claire dropped the receiver onto its cradle. "God save me from teenagers," she muttered aloud.

There was a knock at her door.

"What happened to not disturbing me?" Claire called out.

The door opened a crack. Jewel didn't stick her head inside. Probably afraid Claire would throw something at her. "I told him you were busy," she whispered loudly. "He wouldn't take no for an answer."

"Who?" Claire asked the door.

"Claire," a male voice bellowed.

The door swung open.

Claire forced her grimace into an adequate smile. "Mayor."

Jewel stuck her head around the corner of the door. *Mayor Rug Man,* she mouthed silently. *Sorry.*

"Thank you, Jewel. That will be all. Get back in your doghouse." Claire rose, offering her hand to Morris. "Good to see you."

He clasped her hand. His was warm and damp with perspiration.

"Sit down." She gestured to the chair in front of her desk and then discreetly wiped her hand on her pant leg. Still standing, she began to collect the crime scene photos spread in front of her.

The mayor peered down at her desk. "Those pictures of the waitress?"

"Yes, but you know, of course, that I can't share them." She glanced up. Smiled. Returned to what she was doing. "I'm just going over some details."

"I heard you found the bum. You lock him up?"

Claire eased back into her leather executive chair, stuffing the eight-by-tens into a manila envelope. "Now, Morris, you know very well I can't walk up to some guy and just arrest him because he doesn't live in a half-million dollar house like some of us."

Either he didn't catch the reference to his nineteenth-century Victorian house, or he didn't care. "He was seen at the diner," Morris said. "Seen talking to her."

"So were you."

He looked away quickly. "That isn't even funny, Claire!"

Her father was always telling her she had to be more political in this job. This was probably the kind of thing he was talking about. She took a second to collect her thoughts and her sarcasm. "Morris, my point is that Patti had contact with a lot of people. Without any obvious evidence, this isn't going to be as easy as you might think. As for the transient who'd been seen at the diner talking to Patti, we found him in Rehoboth. A Joseph Caterman. But he didn't kill Patti."

"How do you know that?"

"Because a local church had put him up the night she disappeared and the following two nights after that. He was having dinner with the pastor the evening her body was dumped and then he got a ride to the hotel. He couldn't have walked all the seven miles here with Patti thrown over his shoulder, disposed of her body, and then walked back." She picked up a sheet of paper she'd been doodling on. "What I did find out interesting is that, according to preliminary reports from the ME's office, Patti died only a short time before she was dumped. Close to twenty-four hours after we think she disappeared."

Morris's plump face grew flushed. "You . . . you mean

he picked her up one night, killed her the next? You can tell that from the body?"

Claire nodded, then lifted a finger in warning. "But don't you tell anyone that detail. Not even your wife."

"I don't tell her anything," he snorted.

"First it goes around the beauty parlor," Claire warned, "the next thing we know, it's in the newspapers."

"Well, she's in Florida visiting her sister." Morris pulled a white handkerchief from the pocket of his shorts and wiped his mouth. "You're sure this Joe fellow couldn't have gotten to her?"

"I'm telling you, his alibi is airtight."

Morris thought for a moment. "And you checked that boyfriend of hers again?"

"They weren't living together anymore. He said it was over, but yes, I checked into him. He was at work both nights. I saw the timecard."

"So two weeks after the murder and we're still no closer to figuring out who the hell dumped that girl in our park?" the mayor demanded.

Claire stared at him from across her desk. "No, sir, we're not."

"So what happens?" He rose from the chair. He was sweating profusely despite the cool air pumped in from the air-conditioning unit. "We just close the case?"

"It goes unsolved for the present, but we don't *close* it. Sometimes evidence pops up in the weeks to come, months, sometimes even years. Killers usually talk, Morris. It's the way most of them get caught. They get drunk, brag to a buddy. Happens all the time."

"So now you're the expert?" He wiped his sunburned forehead with the already sweat-soaked handkerchief. "One unsolved murder case and you're an expert?"

She bit back another imprudent reply. "Morris, let me do my job. I'll find out who killed Patti Lorne."

"So do it," he barked. "We're already up to twenty-five percent summer occupation. We don't need a murder keeping tourists away." He started for the door, then turned back. "So if it's not solved now, maybe it ought to be tabled . . . 'til fall."

Claire couldn't believe what she was hearing. One minute the mayor was shouting at her to find the killer, and the next minute he was suggesting she "table" the investigation. She paused before she replied, keeping her father's advice in mind. "I'm still piecing together the evidence. I'm going back to Patti's place again, just in case we missed something. The landlord wants to clean it up, get her stuff out of there so he can rent it again."

She didn't tell Morris that she didn't think that was where the killer had taken Patti from, but she kept it to herself. The mayor didn't care how the murder had taken place, anyway. And he didn't care about Patti either. Just the town revenue.

"I'll keep you updated." Claire opened her office door.

"You better."

After he was gone, she sat a full five minutes in her chair staring at the wall. She'd stared at that spot so long in the last two weeks that it was a wonder she'd not burned a hole in it. After a quick argument with herself, she picked up the phone and dialed the number on the pink slip of paper she'd tucked in her ink blotter. She got Kurt's voice mail.

"Cutting out early again?" she quipped into the phone. "It's Claire. Call me, will you?"

She hung up the phone, gathered the envelope of photos of Patti and all her notes, and stuffed them into a briefcase. If Kurt could do it, she could do it. She had two and a half hours before she had to pick up Ashley, and she was already well over the hours the city would pay her for the week. Maybe she'd go home and get a shower. Sit out on the deck and stare at something besides the wall in her office for a while. Maybe something would come to her on this investigation, something she missed. Maybe Patti's photos would talk to her.

*   *   *

Marcy saw the headlights and moved over to the side of the road, trying to pick up her pace. It was later than she realized, and she knew the country road her development was located on wasn't the safest to be running on this time of evening. Dusk was a difficult time of day for drivers, especially ones who had worked all day and were tired. Their vision wasn't as sharp, and neither was their reaction time.

She realized now that she shouldn't have started out so late. But she'd been busy all day. She'd met with Seth again to look at two more properties. He'd asked her out to dinner, but she'd declined. She wasn't sure she was ready for dating, and if she was, if Seth was someone she'd be interested in. So far, the professional services he had provided had been stellar, but she couldn't shake the feeling that his delivery was something akin to a used car saleman's.

After meeting with Seth, Marcy had gone to the bank for an appointment with a loan officer. She'd also spent several hours on the Internet investigating the distributors she would want to do business with if she opened the bistro.

In between all that, she'd picked Katie up from her babysitting job, dropped her off at a friend's to work on a dance routine for her church youth group, and taken Ben to the library so he could do some more research on carbon dioxide detectors for home use. After taking him to the Big-Mart after lunch with his father the other day, her son had decided to hold off buying until he was sure which model he wanted. When she had time, she thought she might spend some of it worrying about his fixation with safety, but it would have to wait. She was too tired tonight.

The car headlights behind her grew brighter, and Marcy scooted over into the grass a little farther. Phoebe was taking the kids out for pizza and a movie, so the house would be quiet when she got home. All she wanted right now was a shower, a pair of comfy knit shorts, and a glass of wine. Microwave popcorn was on the menu for dinner tonight. Definitely not bistro fare.

The car was still behind her and Marcy glanced over her shoulder nervously. It had slowed down. The same thing had happened to her a couple of nights ago. A car had slowed down behind her, seeming to follow her through the one lonely stretch of the road, through a woods, but then it had sped up, whizzing by her, heading west. She had tried to make out the car, but had been unable to.

Was it her imagination, or had someone been following her that night? Was someone following her again?

She jogged faster.

She heard the car draw closer. She heard loose pebbles off the pavement shoot out from under the tires, and she glanced off to her left. The woods were dense, tangled with briars and ground cover. Even if she wanted to dart in, hide until the car had passed, she didn't think she could get through the trees.

A trickle of sweat ran down her back beneath her athletic tank, along her spine. She realized that she was afraid.

She threw another quick look over her shoulder. The car was definitely slowing down; it wasn't her imagination.

A sense of panic rose in her chest. What if it stopped? What would she do? She wished now that she'd gotten a can of pepper spray. Ben recommended she carry some in her little fanny pack, along with spare change for a phone call and an extra water bottle and a properly filled-out identification card that included her medical history.

Sweat ran in her eyes, stinging them, and she wiped her face with her hand. She was breathing hard now, pumping her arms, lifting her legs. *Heel toe, heel toe,* echoed in her head. Push.

Like she could outrun a car . . .

The vehicle was almost on her now. Drifting across the road toward her. On the wrong side, into oncoming traffic.

She thought of Phoebe's night stalker again. Of the dead waitress. Maybe she'd get lucky and a car coming from the other way would appear and save her.

She heard the hum of an automatic car window go down.

"Hey, it's dark out. Want a ride?"

For a moment, the identity of the male voice didn't register. Then she snapped around, slamming her hand on the car door. "Damn it, Jake, you scared me half to death!"

"Sorry. It's awfully late to be out on this road jogging. I can hardly see you. Didn't Ben tell you you ought to wear one of those reflective vests if you're going to do this?"

She walked around the front of the car, ignoring him, and bent over, panting hard. She climbed into the passenger's side and slammed the door. "Would you please get over?" She motioned to the correct side of the road. "Before someone hits you head-on?"

"You all right, Marcy?" Jake eased the car back into his lane and sped up. "I really did scare you, didn't I? I'm sorry."

"It's all right," she panted, chugging down the last of her water from her fanny pack. It was lukewarm, but she didn't care. It was wet. "I scared myself." She reached over and gave him a push on the arm. He smelled good, and she knew she smelled awful. "What are you doing following me?"

"I wasn't *following* you."

"Yes, you were. Wasn't that you behind me on Main Street?"

He glanced at her, then back at the road. They were almost to the development now. "Okay, I *was* following you. But I saw you jogging down the road and it was late. I wanted to make sure you got home safely. I'm sorry, damn it, for caring about whether or not you get hit by a car!"

Strangely, his raised voice didn't upset her. She actually kind of liked the idea that he could express a strong opinion. She screwed the lid back on the water bottle, her heart finally slowing to an acceptable pace. "So I suppose it was you the other night, too?"

He frowned. "What other night?"

"Tuesday. I was out about this time again. You followed me all the way to the entrance to the neighborhood, then kept going."

No." He signaled and turned onto their street.

"No?" she demanded.

"I worked late Tuesday."

She glared at him.

"Marcy. I'm not a stalker. I'm your husband. I'm telling you, I didn't follow you home Tuesday night." He pulled into the driveway, and the front light over the garage popped on, illuminating the driveway and the interior of the car. She could see the concern plain on his face. "You really think someone was following you the other night?"

She hesitated. "No," she said quickly. "Of course not." She got out of the car, fumbling for her key in her fanny pack.

"Because you know they haven't found Patti Lorne's killer yet." He was a step behind her on the sidewalk that led up to the house.

"Jake, a killer was not following me." She opened the front door and stepped into the hallway.

He remained on the white-trimmed porch, hands stuffed in the pockets of his tropical-weight gray trousers.

Marcy glanced into the house, then back at Jake. Unsure of herself. She knew what he wanted; she just wasn't sure what she wanted. After a second, she said, "You want to come in?"

"I'd like to," he responded quietly. "If you want me to."

"Jake." Now she was exasperated with him and herself. "I'm inviting you in. Take it or leave it. I'm going up for a shower. The kids went out with Phoebe, so there's no dinner, but there's probably better leftovers in my fridge than yours."

"How do you know? Maybe I have leftover shrimp scampi and chilled butternut squash soup in my refrigerator." He followed her in, closing the door behind him.

He knew both were her favorites.

She stopped halfway up the staircase. "I know because Ben and Katie told on you. A jar of mustard, a bottle of ketchup, some half-and-half for your coffee, and a banana." She ticked the items off on her fingers, surprised she had turned so playful with him. It was probably just her relief at not being followed by some mysterious would-be killer.

"How about scrambled eggs?" Jake said, laughing as he disappeared down the hall.

"Anything you make would be fine," she hollered back, already peeling off her sticky, perspiration-soaked clothes as she went down the upstairs hall. The nice thing was, she meant it.

By the time Marcy came downstairs half an hour later, Jake had scrambled up some eggs with green pepper and cheddar cheese just the way she liked it. He was just sliding the eggs onto a plate when she walked into the kitchen, barefoot, in gym shorts she'd borrowed from Katie, with a towel tied around her head.

"I thought we'd sit out on the back porch. It's nice out there tonight." He cut through the kitchen.

Marcy hesitated. Ever since that night on the porch when she had felt that someone was watching her, she'd been uncomfortable out there. She hadn't sat out there since.

"You coming?" Jake called.

She pulled the towel off her head, giving her wet hair a shake. She knew her fear was irrational. This paranoia had to have something to do with her brain injury that had caused the coma. She'd been dragging her heels, but maybe she did need to see Dr. Larson or the psychiatrist, or both. "I'm coming," she called.

Marcy was pleasantly surprised to discover that Jake had found a candle and lit it, setting it on the middle of the table. He'd also dug out a bottle of Australian chardonnay that she liked and poured them each a glass.

"Wine and scrambled eggs?" she asked, slipping into her chair.

"Sure. Why not?"

He grinned, and for a moment Marcy caught a glimpse of the man she had fallen in love with in college. All those years ago there had been something about him that made her smile. The very same thing that was making her smile now.

The phone rang and Claire picked it up. She was sitting on her back deck, enjoying the early evening sounds of the woods that surrounded her. Her father had thought the cabin she bought after her divorce was too isolated. Even though she was only five miles from town, it was two miles to the nearest neighbor. This was precisely why she had fallen in love with the place.

"Hello."

"Claire?"

"Kurt." She settled back in her redwood lounge chair that she'd stained herself.

"Got your message. And no, for your information, I hadn't taken off early. I was out on a case."

"Anything big?" She was stalling. Now that she had Kurt on the phone, she wasn't sure she wanted to talk to him about the Patti Lorne case. Albany Beach was her town. This was *her* murder.

The minute that thought passed through her mind, she realized how ridiculous it was.

"Nah. Car theft. What do you need?"

She checked her watch. She'd needed to leave to pick up Ashley. "The mayor's really on my back with this murder."

"You couldn't expect any less of the Rug Man, could you?"

She smiled. Kurt had always been able to make her smile, she'd give him that. "When I admitted I had no real leads right now, he actually suggested I *table* the whole thing until after the summer season."

"You think he had something to do with the girl's murder?"

"Nah." She ran her hand over her Virginia Tech T-shirt, brushing off a sandwich crumb. "He's too fat to have been able to carry Patti's dead body; he gets out of breath mounting the diner steps."

"Evidence of a struggle?"

"Not really, which is strange. There were ligature marks at her ankles and wrists, tape adhesive residue around her mouth, but that's understandable. He had her tied to something. A bed. A chair. Used a ninety-nine cent roll of duct tape to keep her quiet."

"No evidence on her body?"

"Nothing recoverable. No skin under the fake nails. No foreign fibers. Everything we found was from the dump site."

"Sounding premeditated to you?" Kurt asked.

"Yup."

"Someone she knew."

"My guess is that she climbed into a car with the wrong person."

"Anything else stand out? Anything at all?"

"Not really, except that apparently this sick SOB didn't kill her straight off. ME sets time of death two to four hours before her body was found. She was last seen leaving the bar more than twenty-four hours before we found her."

"Did you locate her car?"

"It was in the shop. She didn't take it to Calloway's that night; she got a ride with a girlfriend there. Friends say she had a history of hitchhiking home from bars late at night."

"Nice friends. Couldn't be bothered to give her a ride themselves and keep her from getting murdered?"

"She was last seen leaving Calloway's." Claire grabbed the book she'd been reading and headed into the house. She took the time to lock the double glass doors and then drop down the wooden bar that would prevent anyone from sliding it open. "She'd been drinking, but she wasn't *too wasted,* according to said friends."

"And no one saw her after that?"

"Nope. Not until she was lying beside that trash can." She dropped her book on the counter and padded down the hall to her bedroom to get her sneakers.

Kurt made a sound of empathy. "Sounds like it's going to be a tough case to crack."

"Tell me about it." She dropped onto her bed to pull on her shoes.

"I hate to say this, but your best bet is going to be that someone talks."

She frowned. "Exactly my thinking."

There was a pause between them.

"Well . . ." Claire cradled the phone between her ear and her shoulder as she tied her sneakers. She hated these silences between them. It made her think about how much she missed him. "I've got to get into town to pick up Ashley. I just wanted to run this all by you, make sure I was thinking clearly."

"Sounds good to me. I mean, I'll look over your evidence if you want, Claire, but so far, this sounds like good police work. I don't know what TV shows you're watching, but in real life, we don't always get the bad guys the first time out of the gate."

And sometimes we never get them, Claire thought.

* * *

"Dad. What are you doing here?"

Katie burst into the family room, and Marcy got up off the couch where she'd been sitting with Jake. They had the TV on, but they hadn't been watching it. They'd been talking. She glanced at the clock over the mantel. Apparently longer than she realized. She felt guilty for not getting rid of Jake before the kids arrived home. She didn't want to make separation any harder on them than it had to be.

"Your dad just gave me a ride home. That's all." She swept up the two wineglasses, headed for the kitchen. "Give him a kiss. He's got to go. Work tomorrow."

Phoebe followed Marcy into the kitchen. "What's he doing here?" She eyed the wineglasses as Marcy rinsed them and put them in the dishwasher.

"Who are you? My mother?"

"You two talking about getting back together?" Phoebe sounded agitated.

Marcy busied herself cleaning up the kitchen. She put the frying pan in the sink to soak. Returned the carton of eggs to the refrigerator. "We were just talking, that's all. He's the father of my children, Phoebe."

"I understand that," she whispered. "I just think you need to be careful what kind of signals you send Ben and Katie. This was a big step for you. Realizing you were unhappy and asking Jake to move out. You don't want to undermine your decision." She glanced in the direction of the family room. They could hear Jake and the kids talking. Laughing. "You don't want to let Jake undermine your decision," she whispered. "You know how manipulative men can be."

Marcy rinsed off the utensils and dropped them into the basket in the dishwasher. All Jake had done was give her a ride home. They'd just had some dinner and some wine. She'd enjoyed the evening. She didn't feel manipulated. "He's leaving now, Phoebe. Don't worry about it."

In a rare demonstration of affection, Phoebe reached out and rubbed her sister's shoulder. "I'm worried about you. You know Dr. Larson said these first few months would be stressful. You've only been out of the hospital two weeks, hon."

Something about her sister's touch made Marcy uneasy, but she didn't push her away. She *was* stressed out. That didn't mean she didn't know what she was doing. "Drop it, Phoebe." She closed the dishwasher and, grabbing a towel to dry her hands, walked back into the family room. "Kisses around," she announced. "Dad's out of here."

Jake hugged and kissed the kids and promised to pick them up after work for their sleepover the following night. Marcy walked him to the front door as Ben and Katie filed upstairs for bed.

Marcy stepped out onto the front porch and closed the door behind her. Phoebe was supposedly out on the back porch having a smoke, but her sister wasn't always where she was supposed to be. She was a great one for eavesdropping. "Thanks for giving me that ride home," she said lightly.

"Thanks for dinner. It's lonely eating alone." Jake turned to face her. "I miss you," he said quietly.

She gave a half smile. It was on the tip of her tongue to say she missed him too, because standing here, she realized she did. But then she thought about what Phoebe had said about men and their manipulation. The truth was, she didn't always feel that she was thinking clearly. She would make that appointment to see Larson. Just to go over the blood tests. Maybe let him order another CT scan.

"You should call some friends," she said. "Go out with them."

"You are my friend." He brushed her bare arm with his fingertips, then let his hand fall.

She looked over his shoulder at the dogwood tree on

the front yard. They had planted that dogwood together when Katie was a toddler. "You sure this isn't about losing a good-looking wife?"

He met her gaze, his mouth drawn tight. "That's unfair, Marcy, and you know it. Do I think you're beautiful now? Of course I do! Do I find you desirable? What man in his right mind wouldn't? But you seem to forget who I fell love with. And that was you." He poked her in the chest above her breast. "Who you were . . . *are* inside."

He lowered his gaze, and a part of her felt ashamed. Jake had been so good to her all these years. And after the accident, he was the one who had insisted she have the plastic surgery; he was the one who had driven to Baltimore every night to be at her side.

She reached out to him in a feeble apology, grasping his arm, then letting go. "Jake, I can't do this right now." She rubbed her temples, realizing suddenly that she had a terrible headache. "I just can't."

"Fine," he said stiffly. She could tell he was angry with her. Angry and hurt. "We don't have to do it now. But we have to do it at some point." He turned away and walked down the sidewalk.

Marcy stepped in the front door, practically running into her sister. "Were you listening to our conversation?" she snapped.

"Of course not. I was going to bed." Phoebe started up the staircase. "'Night."

She was lying. Marcy knew she was lying.

"Good night," Marcy called after her. Watching her mount the stairs, hips swaying, she realized that she did need to see the doctor, just to be cautious. But right now, the best thing for her mental health was going to be getting Phoebe out of her house.

Chapter Six

Marcy sat on the cold examining table and clutched her skimpy paper gown to her naked body, her bare feet dangling over the edge. Now that she was here, she was beginning to feel foolish. She had a lot to accomplish today; she didn't have time for this. "I didn't mean for this to sound like an emergency this morning, Dr. Larson. I really didn't have to come in today. This fuss isn't necessary."

"There's no fuss." He was leaning over a small desk built into the exam room wall, studying lab reports in her medical record file that was thick enough to be a dictionary. "Apparently I had a cancellation this morning." He offered a quick smile she was certain was meant to be reassuring. "You're just lucky. If you'd called a minute later, you might have had to wait until September to see me. You know how I like my tennis in the summer."

She exhaled, unable to resist a grim smile. "But you said yourself, I'm fine. You said you found nothing wrong in the examination."

He removed his reading glasses, turning to give her his full attention. George Larson looked like a small-town doctor in a made-for-TV movie. Mid-sixties, graying hair, he had a friendly, weathered face. But Marcy had heard his grandfatherly looks were deceiving; he had a mean backswing for a man of retirement age.

"You look great. Blood pressure is good. Heart rate, pulse. Perfect. Your jogging seems to be making you younger by the day." He lifted his hand, pausing. He still wore his wedding band though his wife had passed away more than two years ago. Marcy admired his devotion.

"But," she urged.

"But you didn't call me for any physical ailment, did you?" He folded his arms over his chest. Waited.

She fiddled with the edge of the paper gown, focusing her attention on the spotless tile floor. "No, I guess I didn't."

"So what's up?"

She hesitated, then lifted her gaze to his kind brown eyes. "Is it possible, due to the brain trauma I suffered, that I could be experiencing episodes of . . . paranoia?"

"Paranoia?"

She gestured lamely. "You know. Thinking someone is watching you when there isn't anyone there."

"Who do you think is watching you?"

She shrugged.

"Well, I mean is it the KGB, or our guys?"

She looked up to see him smiling. He didn't seem to be terribly concerned. She chuckled and realized it felt good to laugh at herself. It had been a long time since she'd been able to do that. Maybe she never had.

"It's hard to explain. I just get this weird feeling that I'm being watched." She brushed her hair back, choosing her words carefully. "Dr. Larson, I'm not a woman easily spooked. I mean, I lock my doors at night and I check the backseat of the car before I get in, but I'm not one of those women who imagines the boogey man or a rapist around every dark corner."

"But you're feeling that way now?"

She shrugged, trying to find the right words to express the peculiar feeling she'd been experiencing. It had happened on the beach that night with Jake, on the porch, on the road running, and a couple of times in town. Now it was right out in public places, not even necessarily in the dark. It was just so unlike her—at least unlike the Marcy she had known before the accident. "It's not all the time. Just every once in a while I feel like someone is watching me. But no one is there."

"Trouble sleeping?" he asked.

She shook her head.

"Feeling the need to drink more heavily than your usual glass of wine or cold beer on occasion?"

She shook her head.

"And you're not taking any drugs, not even anything over the counter? No diet pills to keep your girlish figure?"

She smirked. "No drugs, Dr. Larson. So far, the jogging and pushing away from the table is working."

He studied her for a moment, his arms still crossed over his chest. "You know," he said after a moment. "In a way, you *are* being watched."

She frowned. "What do you mean?"

"Well, since your recovery, you've been a bit of a town celebrity. Especially with your plastic surgery and weight loss. People are naturally fascinated by stories like yours. They're watching you. Some maybe even wishing they were you."

She laughed at the absurdity of his comment.

"Marcy." He stepped closer, dropping one hand into his white lab coat pocket. "You can't be entirely immune to the attention. Some people are more sensitive than others. Maybe you're just sensing it."

"You mean like picking up vibes?" she asked, not completely buying it.

"Sort of."

She looked away, her gaze settling on the old-fashioned

black-and-white eye chart on the wall. "So you don't think I'm crazy?"

"Do you think you're crazy?"

She scowled. "Certainly not."

"Good then. Now, I don't mean to put my nose where it doesn't belong, but I'm going to do it anyway. What's going on with you and Jake?"

She considered telling the physician that nothing at all was going on, or just saying it was none of his damned business. Instead, she answered honestly. "I don't know. Things weren't going well between us before the accident. We seemed to have grown apart." She made herself look him in the eye. "Separation seemed a logical step."

"And this is what you really want?"

She sighed and slid down off the examination table. "You know, the truth is, Dr. Larson, I don't know what I want. I just know I want more than I had before the accident. I want to be happy."

"Because you're thin and beautiful now?" he questioned pointedly.

She hesitated. He was expressing the very thought that had been spinning around in her head for days. "No," she answered, firm in her resolve. "Because I deserve it."

He smiled. "That's what I was hoping to hear." He picked up her medical file and started for the door. "I want you to go ahead and have those couple of tests that we talked about done at the hospital. No hurry, just in the next week or two. And please, try to relax a little. You don't have to make up for the six months you lost in the next six weeks."

She nodded. "I'll do that."

"And you really should consider seeing Dr. Dubois or at least a counselor. Just to give you an outlet to talk through some of what you're going through."

"Thanks, Doc." Marcy padded barefoot to the changing cubicle. "Sorry I bothered you. I knew it was nothing."

"No bother at all. Take care."

He left the room and Marcy stepped behind the curtain, her confidence strong again. Seth had left a message on her answering machine last night asking if she'd like to get together for dinner tonight. He hadn't said if it was for business or pleasure.

She pulled off the paper gown and grabbed her clothes. She'd call Seth back when she got out to the car and accept his invitation. Why not? Ben and Katie would be with Jake tonight. And Dr. Larson had said she needed to relax. Maybe a date with a man who seemed to be genuinely interested in her was just what the doctor ordered.

That evening, Marcy found herself at a candlelit table at her favorite seafood restaurant in town, sitting across from Seth Watkins. It was the first date she had had since she was in college.

"More wine?" he asked, already filling her glass from the bottle he'd ordered.

"Whoa. That's enough." She took her glass from his hand, her fingertips brushing his. His touch brought a certain excitement to her. A little thrill of something akin to forbidden fruit.

He refilled his own glass, emptying the bottle. They'd had a nice evening. A great meal with a luscious dessert to share, and now, wine, a soft breeze off the bay, and the romantic lull of music in the background. Despite her hesitation, Marcy had found it easy to talk to Seth, or at least listen to him. He was only two years younger than she was and had attended a rival high school. He'd kept her entertained half the night telling her tales of his high school days as the starting quarterback of the varsity football team.

Seth took a sip of his wine and leaned forward on the table. "I've had a nice time tonight, Marcy."

"Me, too." She set down her glass, thinking she'd probably had enough. "It was so good of you to do all that extra leg work on the shopping mall property."

"I'd like to say it was all part of my job, but I have to admit, I did it partly because it was for you. I just couldn't wait to see you again."

She moistened her lips, not quite sure she was comfortable where this was going. Maybe it was the expensive gold chain around his neck, or the fact that his haircut probably cost more than hers. There was just something about him that made her feel she should take a step back.

But then she told herself she was being silly. It was only natural to feel this way after being with the same man for so many years. Having the same dull conversations, eating the same dull meals every night. Seth was just different from Jake, maybe not a he-man, but what was wrong with that?

"You know." He took her hand in his and turned it over, caressing her palm. "You're a very beautiful woman, Marcy." He gave her a boyish grin. "I just can't seem to stop looking at you. Marveling."

Seth was saying the things she thought she wanted him to say, things she'd dreamed her whole life of hearing, but somehow they didn't ring quite right in her head. "Seth," she said, "you understand, I'm just separated. I'm still married."

"Is that a problem for you?" His handsome blue eyes held her gaze. "Because it's not a problem for me," he murmured.

"Marcy."

Phoebe's voice jarred Marcy from the trancelike state Seth had held her in. She jerked her hand from his, but not fast enough for her sister to miss it. Marcy could tell by the sparkle in her eye.

"When you said you were going out, I didn't think you meant *out* out." She walked—no, *slinked*—up to the table in a white miniskirt and tank top, her blond hair brushing her tanned shoulders. "Phoebe Matthews," she said, offering Seth her hand.

He rose from his chair, gawking. "Seth Watkins," he managed.

Phoebe let him linger over her hand before withdrawing it. "So I take it my sister didn't tell you there were two of us."

"N . . . no." He managed a grin as he sat back down.

"Seth is a real estate agent," Marcy explained. "I . . . I really hadn't gotten to talk with you about it, but I'm . . . I'm looking at some property."

"Well." Phoebe turned her eyes on Seth again. "A nice-looking real estate guy like Seth, I might find myself looking into some property, too."

"Would you like to join us?" he asked, hovering over his seat. "I could grab a chair."

"No, no, thanks. My friends are all in the bar." She cupped her hand around her mouth and whispered to her sister, "Have you seen Ryan pass through here? He might have been with that new guy, Savage."

Marcy shook her head.

"Ass," she muttered as she dropped her hand. "Well, I was just headed for the little girls' room." She tapped a manicured hand on the table. "You two have fun. Nice to meet you, Seth. I won't wait up, Sis," she sang as she walked away. Her tone left nothing to the imagination. She was encouraging Marcy to sleep with Seth.

Marcy reached for her purse. "I think I should go." All she could think of was, thank goodness she'd insisted on meeting him here rather than letting him pick her up.

"Are you feeling bad?" Seth stood up, reaching for her arm.

"No." She shook her hands, not wanting him to touch her. "Yes, actually . . . a headache." Suddenly she felt over-heated, overwhelmed. She pressed her thumb and fore-finger to her temples, fearing that if she didn't get out of the restaurant, she was going to be sick. "Thank you so much for dinner." She walked away from the table. "I'll call you Monday."

He put out his hand to her, but she was already out of reach. "If you wait a sec for me to pay the bill, I'll walk you to your car."

She shook her head, hurrying through the dining room. "Talk to you tomorrow."

The Bloodsucker watched through the window as Marcy walked out of the restaurant, into the parking lot. The area wasn't particularly well lit, but he knew it was her. He knew the sway of her hips.

He felt his heart skip a beat. This was a public place. Riskier than the lonely street where he had picked up Patti. And so many people had seen him here. In the bar. In the restroom. Maybe sitting in the car.

But he wanted her.

He licked his lips, feeling the excitement build in-side him as he watched her glance up and down the row of parked cars before reaching for her car door.

The Bloodsucker knew he had to make his decision quickly or the opportunity would be lost.

Quick. Quick. A decision. A smart decision. Maybe being seen first *was* smart. Who would suspect a man who appeared openly in public at the site of the abduc-tion? Even paid with a credit card, leaving written, easily traced proof that he'd been there?

He pushed open the door, his gaze fixed on her.

She had gotten into the SUV, but she hadn't started the engine yet. The automatic locks wouldn't click until she started the engine and put it in reverse. The Blood-sucker was clever. He made it his business to know these things.

She was looking around. Looking for what? Who? Him?

The Bloodsucker's breath caught in his throat in a moment of fear, and he stepped back, into the shadows of the restaurant's lobby.

Marcy grasped the steering wheel. Reached down. The engine turned over.

The chance was lost.

The Bloodsucker closed his eyes, disappointed. Angry.

He heard Granny's accusing words in his head. *Stupid. Worthless.* The anger boiled up into his throat, and for a moment he was afraid he was going to throw up.

The green SUV pulled out of the parking lot, and then Marcy was gone. Gone from his grasp.

Behind him he heard voices. Laughter. People leaving the restaurant. He walked out into the parking lot, jingling his keys in his pocket as he headed to his car.

Someone waved as if they were his friend. "'Night."

The Bloodsucker smiled. Waved. "Good night. Have a nice weekend." He knew no one was really his friend. He had them all deceived.

Inside the safety of his car, he breathed a sigh of relief. He pulled out onto the street, checking his watch. It was close to eleven, and Max hadn't been fed. Poor doggie. He needed to get home, but he was feeling jittery. Marcy had left him a bundle of nerves and energy.

On a deserted street, he passed a young woman walking a little white dog. All alone.

A blond-haired woman.

The Bloodsucker glanced up at the one condo on the street. Almost no lights. Most of the balconies were still boarded up. It would be July before the summer season was in full swing.

He signaled, turned the corner, and pulled over. His

heart was pounding again. Granny told him not to do it. This was impulsive. He wasn't smart enough to pull it off. He'd leave evidence. He'd get caught. He was smart enough. He popped open the trunk, locating latex gloves and the chloroform-soaked gauze, sealed in a baggie. With one last brilliant thought, he grabbed Max's spare leash he kept in the car. "Max," he called as he slammed the trunk and slipped the baggie into his pocket. "Max! Come, boy!"

April gave the leather leash a tug. "Heel, Bootsy."

The poodle dropped back to walk beside her again, but the moment the dog heard the man's voice, she darted ahead.

"Max! Come on, boy," a man called as he walked up the sidewalk toward her.

April glanced around. She hadn't really been paying attention to where she was going when she'd left with the dog, using the excuse that she'd walk her. The little white mop wasn't even hers. She just needed to get out of the condo for a few minutes, away from her mother-in-law's whining. Away from her kiss-ass husband.

"Hi," the man said, approaching.

"Hi," April responded hesitantly. The guy looked normal enough, but who knew these days?

"I was out walking my dog, Max, and—" He held up the leash. "I guess the snap broke or something. Did you happen to see a dog run by? So big." He gestured. "Brown and scraggly."

She shook her head.

"I just can't believe he took off like this," the man went on, looking up the street one way, then down the other. He really sounded upset. "I'm scared to death he's going to get hit by a car before I find him. He doesn't have much in the way of street smarts."

Bootsy walked up to him and sniffed with interest.

April tugged on the leash. "Boots."

"Oh, it's okay. I love dogs." The man crouched down and petted the shitzu. She couldn't see his face very well. The street lamp was out overhead. It was still early in the season. She and her husband liked this time of year in Albany Beach before it got too busy, but everything wasn't quite up and running yet.

As the man stood up, freeing Bootsy, he turned his head suddenly. "Did that sound like a cry to you? Like a dog hurt?"

April listened. She hadn't heard anything. Just a car on the street behind them.

The man turned, hurrying around the corner. "There," he called over his shoulder. "Did you hear it? There it is again. "

April hurried after him, pulling Bootsy along. It was so dark in the shadows of the condo building that she could barely see the man as he ducked around the parking garage pillar.

"Oh, God, I hope he's not hurt," he said.

She took another step, barely around the cement structural pillar, and felt a hand clamp over her mouth and nose. Something rough. An unfamiliar smell. Medicinal, but sweet.

April opened her mouth to scream, but of course she couldn't. He wrapped his arm around her shoulders, pinning her hands down. She was dizzy, disoriented. Suddenly nauseated. She felt the leash pull from her hand. Her vision swam. The last thing she saw was her mother-in-law's white dog running through the dark parking garage, and then the blackness swallowed her.

"Jake?"

"Hey," he said sleepily on the other end of the line. "Marcy?"

"I'm sorry. It's late." She perched on the side of the

bed in her flimsy nightshirt she'd bought to replace the flowered tents she had once worn, and cradled the cordless phone on her shoulder. "I shouldn't have called so late."

"No, no it's okay." He sounded more awake now. "You all right?"

"Sure, I'm fine." She got up to pace. "I just called to . . . to see how the kids were."

"Fine. Great. Asleep, I think."

"So you went out and saw a movie?" She reached the bathroom door and turned around, going the other way.

"Yeah, an Arnie movie. It was the only thing we could all agree on."

She nodded. "And I guess you had dinner?"

"And ice cream." Jake paused. "Are you sure you're okay? You don't sound . . . like yourself."

She didn't tell him she didn't feel much like herself. Or, actually, that she didn't know for sure who she was anymore she didn't know how she was supposed to feel. "I'm fine, really." She plopped down on the bed again and brushed her hair out of her eyes. "I guess I just missed the kids."

"Phoebe there with you?"

She glanced at the digital clock on the nightstand. It was eleven-forty. "Are you kidding, before midnight on a Friday night?"

He laughed. "I'll see you tomorrow?"

"You'll bring them home, right?"

"By dinner," he agreed.

She pressed her lips together, knowing he wanted to get off the phone, but just not quite ready to let him go. "Jake."

"Yeah, Marcy?"

"I . . . um, I've got something I want to talk to you about. You think we can get together some time in the next couple of days?"

"You want to tell me what it's about now?"

"Nah." She leaned back, falling onto the bed. "Not a big deal. It can wait."

"I've got a Lions Club thing tomorrow night, and Sunday I promised my parents I'd come over. They've been bugging me for a week. The toilet in their powder room is stopped up again or something, so it will have to be Monday. Lunch?"

"Lunch, Monday," Marcy agreed and hung up.

Lying on her back in the bed in the dark, she held the phone to her breast. She stared up, watching the ceiling fan go around.

She thought about her quasi date. About Seth. She knew he was attracted to her. And she certainly liked the attention. So what had spooked her tonight?

"Please," April whispered, fighting back another sob. She made herself relax in the chair. There was no sense fighting it. She was trapped. Fighting the confines of the chair and all the tape only weakened her. Made her wrist start bleeding again. But what was she going to do? *What was she going to do?*

She tried not to think of her husband, Barry. About how frantic he must be, looking for her. And her mother-in-law—this was all her fault. If Darlene hadn't started in about them moving to Orlando again, none of this would have happened.

The man seated in front of her moved and she flinched, opening her eyes so wide that it hurt the muscles on her face. "Please don't do it again," she sobbed, fighting another round of sobbing hysterics that she knew would get her nowhere.

He didn't say anything. He just watched her from the bench at the table, dressed in that silly plastic suit, a weird look on his face. Sick creep.

And he seemed like such a nice man. Just a man looking for his dog. Another sob rose in her throat as she realized for the hundredth time what a terrible mistake she had made. What it would probably cost her. She hiccuped. She didn't even believe now that he had a dog. And where was Bootsy? That was what she wanted to shout at him—*Where the hell is little Bootsy?*

He just kept staring at her. It was making her crazy. What did he want? He hadn't raped her, at least not when she had been awake. And if he had kidnapped her to kill her, why hadn't he just done it and gotten it over with? Maybe he was having regrets . . . maybe that was it.

April took a breath, trying to calm her pounding heart. Maybe she could reason with him. Maybe he didn't really want to do this terrible thing he was doing. She made herself look right at him, try to make eye contact. "If you let me go," she whispered, "I wouldn't tell anyone. I don't know anything to tell, really." Her lower lip trembled. He was listening. Did that mean he was considering what she was saying? An inkling of hope fluttered in her chest.

"You . . . you could just put me back in the trunk. Drop me off somewhere," April continued. "I wouldn't tell. I swear it."

Now he didn't look like he was listening. He was just staring at her. At her feet.

"Do—do you think—"

"Please stop talking. This isn't right." He rose, throwing his arms in the air impatiently. "This just isn't right. None of it is right." He waved the blade. "You're not saying any of the things you should be saying."

Fresh tears filled her eyes. "I'm sorry," she said. "I'm sorry." He took a step toward her and she went on, faster, frantically. "T—tell me what you want me to say. Just tell me. I—I'll say it. Please."

He took another step closer, now between her and the lamp on the table. "You would, wouldn't you?"

She nodded rapidly. "Anything."

"But Marcy wouldn't," the Bloodsucker snapped.

"M . . . Marcy? Who . . . who's Marcy?" April shook her head pathetically. "I don't know Marcy."

"Marcy's my friend." He turned his head, looking at her petite, suntanned ankles. He was bored. This wasn't the way he had meant for this to go. And now he was disappointed . . . unsure of what to do next. How to make it right.

"I could be your friend," April whispered.

He studied her for a moment. She had the blond hair. The blue eyes. It was all there. Everything he needed. He stared at the blade in his hand . . . at the sweet stain of red streaked across the cold metal. "No," he said after a moment. "I don't think so."

"But I could. I swear I could," she moaned. "Please."

His gaze fell to her ankle again. He remembered something he had seen on TV the other night. Something that had stuck in his head.

The Bloodsucker squatted in front of the chair.

"What are you going to do?" she screamed.

He glanced up, impatiently. "Now, didn't I say not to raise your voice? Didn't I tell you that I didn't like that?"

"Yes, yes," she said so quietly, so apologetically.

She came across to him as weak. Pathetic. Just a little dull. Nothing like his vibrant, energetic Marcy.

He drew back the scalpel and cut across her ankle, rewarding him with a fresh spew of blood.

She screamed.

He didn't care.

"I don't understand why I can't go to Atlantic City with Chain," Ashley protested angrily, hands planted on her hips, black-painted mouth drawn back in a frown.

Claire looked up from her easy chair, closing the news

magazine on her lap. It was Sunday night, her evening to relax. She liked to read, watch a little TV. It had been a long weekend, and she really needed some down time.

A vacationer, April Provost, twenty-six, had disappeared from Albany Beach Friday night, and Claire was petrified what the implication might be. The husband had reported her missing around one in the morning. Claire hadn't gotten the call until six. She had interviewed the family to discover that April and her mother-in-law had had an argument prior to the young woman storming out of the condo on the pretext of taking the in-law's dog for a walk. The police had combed the area looking for the missing woman, who was a legal secretary in Pennsylvania and had only been married two years. There hadn't been a sign of April.

At noon on Saturday, the missing shitzu was found, leash still attached. The husband was still hoping his wife had just taken off, having had enough family vacation. April was coming up on forty-eight hours missing now, though, and as the minutes ticked by, Claire knew the chance of that kind of explanation was getting slimmer.

Claire blinked, focusing on Ashley again. "You can't go because you're fifteen years old. That's not even old enough to gamble in New Jersey!"

"I told you." Ashley rolled her eyes heavenward as if her mother were the most thick-headed person she had ever met. "It's not to go to a casino. It's to hear a band play."

"In New Jersey? You can't go hear a band play in this state?"

"Don't you listen to anything I say? Not the *Blood Thrill.*" The teenager threw up her hands in disgust.

Tonight she was wearing long black, baggy shorts that went to her knees and a black T-shirt sporting a bony hand grasping a skull in the fingers. Her inky black

hair was parted and pulled down in braids on either
side of her face. Not a terribly becoming hair style, in
Claire's opinion.

"Of course, not the *Blood Thrill!*" She threw up her
hands, imitating her daughter. "I've never even heard
of this band." She dropped her hands into her lap.

"Only because none of the band members are a hun-
dred years old like the old farts you like." She indicated
Claire's T-shirt sporting The Rolling Stones' "Forty
Licks" tour.

"Hey, Mick's not a day over ninety-five, I'll have you
know."

Ashley groaned in frustration. "Why do I even try to
talk to you?"

Claire glanced away. Obviously, joking around wasn't
going to work tonight. "What about your week of restriction? You broke curfew."

"I told you. Chain ran out of gas."

"And I told you, you call me when something like
that happens."

"Maybe I could, if I had a cell phone like I've been
asking you for, for like months." She crossed her arms
over her chest triumphantly.

Claire smiled. "Nice try. The fact is, you're still on restriction. No Chain. No concert in Jersey. No way. No
how."

"I'll trade you. You let me go to the concert, and I'll
redo the week's restriction." A sense of desperation
cracked in the teen's voice. "I'll give you a full week and
an extra day."

Claire got up, taking her empty glass to the sink. This
was obviously very important to Ashley, but at fifteen
she just wasn't sure her daughter was mature enough to
go so far for a night of entertainment, especially with a
guy and one called Chain at that. Claire hated being a
hard ass, but her gut instinct told her that her fifteen-

year-old daughter didn't belong in a sleazy nightclub with a bunch of kids dressed in psycho funeral attire.

She came back around the kitchen counter. Ashley was still planted between the family room and the hallway. "No, Ash. You can't go."

Her daughter looked away, tears clouding her eyes. "I'll go anyway."

"You pull a stunt like that and you'll be on restriction for a month. Two months." Claire pointed at her, something she had sworn as a teen that she would never do to her own child. Here she was, doing it anyway. "You know, your dad is making noise about you going to Utah to live with him. He thinks you'd get a better education."

"What? At that church school Rochelle teaches at?" she sneered.

Claire knew how angry Ashley was that her father had remarried and now had two more daughters. Daughters that, to Ashley, had to seem more important than she was to him.

"Ashley—" The phone rang, interrupting Claire.

Ashley dove for the cordless phone on the coffee table. "Drummond residence." She paused. She was obviously disappointed that it wasn't for her. She held the phone out. "For you," she said, not making eye contact. "Work."

"Chief Drummond," Claire answered, getting a little rush of adrenaline. Marsh had the shift. This was the call she'd been dreading.

"I'm sorry to ring you at home on your night off, Chief," he said grimly, "but I think you need to be here."

Their conversation lasted less than a minute. Claire hung up the phone, tossed it on the counter, and hurried down the hallway. She didn't want to take the time to get dressed in her uniform. She stepped out of her shorts, grabbing a pair of jeans out of the bottom drawer of her dresser. "Ashley!"

Claire hopped on one bare foot, then the other, pulling up her jeans. She grabbed the badge in a leather case, issued for these circumstances. "Ashley."

"I'm coming," her daughter shouted from down the hall. "Sheesh!" She stuck her head through the doorway.

Claire crouched in front of her closet to spin the lock on the safe where she kept her sidearm. It was a Cougar, a Beretta subcompact. A gift from her father the day she was sworn in as police chief of Albany Beach. "I have to go to a scene." The safe door clicked open. She glanced at her daughter as she grabbed the cool metal of the pistol grip, unsure of what to do about Ashley. Obviously she couldn't take her to the scene. She could drop her off with the grandparents, but that would take more time. And she was fifteen. Old enough to watch other people's children.

Ashley waited.

"I might be gone a while."

Still no response.

"When I go out the door, I want you to—"

"Lock it behind you, including the deadbolt, and set the security alarm," Ashley quoted from rote memory.

"Exactly." Slinging her gun belt over one shoulder, Claire grabbed her sneakers off the floor and hurried past Ashley. As she did, she reached up to stroke her cheek. Despite the dyed hair and black eyeliner, she still had the smoothest skin. Still smelled the same as she had when she'd been a baby.

Ashley followed her mother down the hall. "Hey, what's up?"

Claire shook her head. She didn't want to say until she was sure. Right now a thousand thoughts were flying through her head. None complete. "I'll call you when I'm on my way home, but if you want to go to sleep before I get back, that's fine. I've got my keys."

In the kitchen, Claire strapped on her holster, checked

her sidearm's safety, and wiggled one foot into a sneaker without taking the time to untie it. "You'll be okay?"

"I'll be fine," Ashley answered, sounding amazingly the way she had pre-Goth.

"Good." Claire stepped into the other sneaker, forcing a smile. "I'll be back as soon as I can."

Ashley let her out the front door into the dark yard. The security light clicked on as she crossed the driveway to her police cruiser and a lucent vapor glow illuminated the yard.

"Be careful, Mom," Ashley called.

Claire got into the car, smiling bittersweetly as she watched her daughter step back into the house and close the door safely behind her. It was nice to know Ashley still cared about her, even if it was just a little.

Chapter Seven

Claire pulled up to a familiar scene that she never got used to and hoped she never would. Eerie blue flashing lights radiating from police cars. The outline of an ambulance parked crookedly alongside the road, an ominous gray ghost in the darkness.

She parked the cruiser, cut the engine and, gripping the steering wheel, took a deep breath. Her heart was pounding in her chest, and her fingers were sticky with sweat. All the way here, she'd been praying this wasn't what it sounded like. But deep in the pit of her stomach, she already knew it was. On some level, she had known since the young woman disappeared almost two days ago.

A tap on the window startled Claire.

"Chief."

Glancing at Sergeant Marsh through the glass, she swallowed her fear. She was the chief of police in this town. Everyone looked up to her. They took her lead. She had to stay calm and do her job. If she needed to fall apart, she could do it later, privately.

The uniformed officer stepped back to allow her to climb out of the car.

"Marsh." She nodded.

"I hated to call you in, Chief," he apologized. He still looked like a Marine, with his buzzed gray hair, even in the tan and green Albany Beach police uniform.

"You made the right call." She did her best to remove every trace of emotion from her voice. "Who was first on the scene?" Her hand slid instinctively to her sidearm on her hip, and she then ducked under the yellow crime scene tape that blocked off the wide alley. She wondered absently where her boys had found it. It was rarely needed in a quiet resort town like this, and they had already used a roll with Patti's murder.

"Patrolman First Class McCormick."

She halted, looking back at Marsh. "Again? He was first on the scene with the Lorne girl."

He shrugged. "His bad luck. He was working overtime." He hesitated, then seemed to become concerned that he was in trouble. "McCormick said when he came on shift that you okayed the extra hours."

She started down the alley again, walking along the back of the cement block restaurant, trying to take in the crime scene as it unfolded in front of her. She was surrounded by confusion, which made it hard to focus. Lights flashing, cops, firemen, emergency medical technicians mulling around, talking quietly. She heard the station's only canine, Gus, barking wildly from the back of a unit. The stench of garbage assailed her nostrils. Seafood place. All summer, the garbage was picked up every morning; it still stank. But she had to look beyond the distractions and see the alley the way the killer had seen it. Recognize any evidence he might have left behind.

She walked up to McCormick, who had his back to her; she couldn't miss his buffed profile accentuated by the uniform. She placed her hand on his shoulder. "You okay, Ryan?" she asked quietly. She didn't want to embarrass him in front of the other officers, but he was her responsibility, too. Finding the bodies of two young women in two weeks couldn't be easy for anyone, not even a tough guy like McCormick.

He was stoic. "I'm fine."

"You were riding alone?"

He nodded.

Claire preferred that even her more experienced officers rode with a partner, but there was never quite enough money to go around and so that wasn't always possible. She glanced in the direction of the dumpster. One of her only two detectives on the force, Robinson, took a picture, and the flash illuminated, for just a second, a body lying on the black pavement. Claire caught a glimpse of a blue T-shirt and bare midriff where it had ridden up on the body. She focused on McCormick again, knowing she had to ask the question that had been burning in her mind since she got the call twenty minutes ago. "Give me your gut reaction. Same guy?"

"Same guy," he whispered. Now he sounded a little spooked.

She rubbed his arm, feeling hard the ripple of his biceps through his long-sleeved uniform shirt. It was no wonder he was popular with the ladies in town. "Who called it in?"

"Dishwashers." He pointed to two scruffy, long-haired, college-age boys standing in a lit doorway that obviously led to the restaurant's kitchen. Both were wearing dirty white aprons. Both looked scared shitless.

"They just walked out of here, and there she was?"

He nodded. "That's what they're saying."

"And when was the last time someone was in the alley?" She looked beyond the dumpster into the darkness, then in the direction she'd just come. She raised her hand to shield her eyes. Someone had pulled one of the police cars closer, flipping on the headlights. It gave them more light, but the high beams were almost blinding.

"Maybe an hour earlier. Another kid made a dumpster run. Said he tossed four Hefties in. She wasn't there, then. He swears it. And I checked—looks like four fresh bags of garbage in black bags on top."

"What time was that?"

"Between nine-thirty and ten. The call came into the station at eleven-ten. I arrived on the scene at eleven-fourteen and immediately called for backup."

She nodded. "Get the kids' names, phone numbers, addresses, and send them home."

"You don't want to talk to them?" he called after her.

She had already walked away. "I think they've been through enough tonight, don't you?"

Leaving McCormick behind, Claire approached the rectangular industrial-sized dumpster. One of her officers had found a battery-powered lamp like the kind she and her dad used to take camping when she was a kid. The officer clicked it on, and white light spilled across the pavement and the woman's body.

Claire swallowed the bitter bile that rose in her throat. Fought the wave of dizziness. "You bastard," she breathed.

She walked slowly around the body, taking in every detail, comparing it to Patti Lorne's crime scene in her head. Next to a trash receptacle. Body simply dumped with no care taken to "arrange" the victim. It was obvious what the killer thought of these two women. Nothing but trash. "Anyone touch anything?"

"Patrolman McCormick and then the EMTs checked for pulse, but nothing else," someone told her.

She snapped on a pair of latex gloves she fished out of her pocket and crouched beside the dumpster to get a better look at the girl's deathly pale face. She, too, had obviously been bled. She appeared painfully thin, her skin nearly translucent. Wrists were slashed again . . . no, just one. She leaned closer and caught a faint whiff of perfume that startled her. You just didn't expect a dead woman to smell good. The scent was subtle, flowery. Claire recognized it as a designer fragrance from a sample she'd picked up in one of her rare trips to a department store.

Claire felt her body tremble, and she laid her hand carefully on the pavement to steady herself. After a moment, she began her initial inspection again. One wrist slashed multiple times, with dried and congealed blood on the forearm; no puddle of blood beneath her.

"You catch the ankle?" a voice questioned from behind her. It was one of the county's emergency medical technicians, Kevin James. Early to mid-thirties. Nice looking. Friendly. Knew his stuff.

Claire's gaze shifted to a slender leg and saw a slash mark similar to the one on the victim's wrist. "Cut?" she asked.

"Looks like it." Kevin nodded in the direction of the body. "What do you think he's doing?" He looked away, then back at Claire. "Experimenting?"

Still crouching, she inched along the body to get a better look at the ankle. No blood puddle here, either.

She closed her eyes for a moment, thinking. So if the blood wasn't here, where was it? What was he doing with it?

Claire opened her eyes. "I need an evidence kit," she ordered to no one in particular. She didn't care who got it for her, so long as they did it now.

While she waited, she stepped out of the ring of light and pulled her cell phone from the waistband of her jeans. She punched in the familiar numbers.

"Mom?"

Claire hadn't realized she had been holding her breath until she released it. "Where are you?"

"In bed," Ashley answered incredulously. "Why?"

"I need you to get up," Claire whispered.

"What?"

Claire glanced at the police milling around April Provost's body. Someone had set the evidence kit that looked like a plastic tackle box near the feet of the dead woman.

Extra latex gloves, like the ones she wore now, lay on top, only they were blue.

"Ashley, honey, listen to me," Claire whispered harshly into the phone. "I need you to get up and check every window. Every door." She took another rattling breath, trying to calm her pounding heart. "Be sure they're locked."

"Mom—"

"Just do what I say for once and don't argue with me, damn it!"

"All right. All right. I'm going."

"Good. That's good," Claire said more calmly. "Check all the doors and windows and then recheck the security alarm. Be sure it's set, all zones."

"Mom, are you all right?"

"I'm fine."

"Chief Drummond," someone called. "A newspaper reporter is here. You want to handle it?"

"How do they find out so quickly?" she barked. "We haven't even identified the victim yet." Then into the phone. "Ashley, I have to go. I'll probably be gone all night. You stay put until I get there. I don't care if it takes me two days, *you do not leave the house.*"

"Okay, okay," Ashley breathed.

"'Night, baby. I love you." Claire hung up the phone and stepped into the bright light. "Tell the reporter to go home. We'll release a statement in the morning, once the body has been identified and next of kin have been notified," she ordered. "Now let's get this evidence collected and get this poor girl off the street."

"There you are." Jake slid onto the bench seat across from Marcy. It was Monday, noon. "I saw the car, so I knew you were here," he said. "I just didn't see you all the way back here when I came in."

She smiled, surprised that she was so genuinely pleased

to see him. "I ordered iced teas." She looked around at the diner filled with people, locals and tourists. Everyone seemed to be talking at once, the diner buzzing like a beehive. "The place is really hopping today. Loretta must be thrilled with all the business."

"Pulling her hair, more likely. I still don't think she's replaced Patti yet, so she's short a waitress." Jake folded his hands. "How are you?"

She nodded. "Pretty good. A little shaken like everyone else, I suppose. Who would have thought anything like this could happen here?"

He grimaced. "You saw it on the morning news?"

"I couldn't believe they were talking about our town. Another woman killed, this one thrown in an alley? I was just at that restaurant Friday night."

"You mean The Seahorse ?" he asked sharply.

The minute Marcy said it, she'd known she'd made a mistake. Now she was caught. She didn't know what to say.

"Marcy, I already know you were there with some guy."

She glanced up, unsure how to read his tone of voice.

"Now don't be angry," he went on, "but—"

"Phoebe told you." She scowled and reached for a pack of sweetener from a Styrofoam coffee cup at the end of the table. "Well, when she was informing on me, did she bother to tell you that it was a business dinner? He's a real estate agent?"

"Real estate? You're not selling our house without discussing it with me."

"I'm not selling the house. You think I'm nuts?" She glanced up. "Don't answer that until I tell you why I wanted to talk to you. Why I'm talking to the real estate agent. But first, I want to know what you think about the murder." She stirred her iced tea and licked the spoon. "You think what they were saying on the news is true? A serial killer here in little old Albany Beach?"

"I'll tell you what I think," Ralph cut in.

Marcy glanced up to see the dishwasher carrying an order pad, a pencil tucked behind his ear. He was wearing a white apron stained with the morning's dirty breakfast dishes, a big splotch of ketchup from someone's scrambled eggs across his belly. It made her think of blood.

"A probe," Ralph declared in a conspiratorial whisper. "That's what killed that lady walking her dog. A probe from another planet in another solar system sent here to do experiments on us. They been sendin' them for years. Government covers it all up, though, lickety split. Don't want us to know the truth."

Marcy looked at Jake across the table and knew he was hearing *The X Files* tune in his head, the same as she was.

"So what can I get you for?" Ralph asked, sliding his pencil from his ear.

Jake gave a little laugh. "You been promoted?"

"Nah. Dishes piled up to the ceiling in back. Just helpin' Loretta out. She thinks she hired a new girl, but she won't start 'til tomorrow."

"Small chef's salad," Marcy ordered. "And some crackers."

"A turkey club for me."

"You got it."

Marcy wrinkled her nose as Ralph walked away. "Did you ever notice that sometimes he smells like—"

"Cough syrup," Jake finished for her. "I guess he drinks it."

She sipped her tea, watching him shuffle away. "That or bathes in it."

Jake glanced in Ralph's direction and chuckled. "Oh, I don't think he's bathing all that often." He looked back at her. "So, you really want to know what I think about this dead woman?"

"What do you think?"

"That we need to wait until the police complete their

investigation to draw any conclusions. There's no need to panic."

"I'm not panicking. I just wondered what you thought. No murders in Albany beach in more than fifty years and now two in the same month? I mean, obviously you have an opinion. Everyone does."

"Again, I think we just sit tight and don't jump to conclusions." Jake tented his hands. "I have confidence that Chief Drummond will solve these crimes and the mystery surrounding them."

"But two women," she said softly. "Do you think . . . I should be afraid?"

"I think you should be careful. As I think you always should be," he amended, then glanced at his watch. "So what's up with the real estate agent?"

She drew a deep breath and raised her hand, palm toward him. "I want to tell you about my totally crazy idea, and it's okay if you tell me I'm nuts. I just want you to hear me out before you list all the reasons why it won't work."

By the time Marcy and Jake's salad and sandwich had arrived and they had eaten them and accepted a second round of iced teas, she had pretty much laid out her dream of opening a bistro, including how she was going to pay for it. Through the entire explanation, he had remained very quiet, asking only a few questions.

Marcy exhaled, watching Jake, waiting for a reaction. "So say something." She was so exited just talking about her restaurant that she felt like she was going to burst.

"Why?" he asked, his face impossible to read. "Why do you want to do this now?"

"Why?" She opened her purse and fished out her lipstick, taking her time in responding because she didn't want to hurt his feelings. "Because this isn't enough."

"What isn't?"

"My life."

He scowled. "The kids and me? We're not enough to make you happy?"

She carefully applied her lipstick. The old Marcy would have never dared this trick in public without a mirror. The old Marcy would have preferred one that was magnified to bring out all her imperfections.

"Me," she said carefully. "I'm not enough. This doesn't have anything to do with you or Katie and Ben."

"So, it's not enough to be thin and beautiful and have a family who loves you?" he demanded, raising his voice.

"Jake, I hated my job." She reached for his hand and squeezed. "You know I did."

He looked away. "No. I didn't know that. I just thought you hated me."

Tears welled in her eyes. She didn't know what to say because she honestly didn't understand yet what had been going on with her when she'd had the accident. But she felt like she was getting closer to the answer.

"I didn't hate you," she said softly, the realization washing over her like a cold shower. "But I think I hated myself."

Claire rose from her desk as the mayor walked into her office. It was eleven A.M.—it had taken him longer to show up unannounced than she'd anticipated. "Morris." She gestured emphatically as he opened his mouth to speak. "If you ask me if I've caught the killer yet, I swear to God, I'm going to pull this Beretta from my holster and shoot you. A jury of my peers, anyone who knows you, would never convict."

Morris took a step back, and for an instant, he looked scared. As if he feared she might just do it.

Claire dropped into her chair. "Twelve hours. We found her twelve hours ago. Her father-in-law just came in to identify her body, and while the ME made her initial report at the scene, we have to wait on the full report for details."

"So what am I supposed to tell the reporters?" the mayor huffed. This morning, he was dressed uncharacteristically in a suit and tie, to conduct TV and newspaper interviews, no doubt. The white leisure suit was not becoming, nor was the perspiration that beaded his sunburned, widescreen forehead.

"Don't tell them any more than you have to." She tucked rolls of film she had taken last night into an envelope.

"You know what they're saying, don't you?" he prodded. "That Albany Beach has a serial killer. A serial killer who is murdering young women."

"Looks like they might be right."

"What?" the mayor exploded.

She took a cleansing breath before she responded. Her head was pounding, she was hungry, and she needed to go home and check on Ashley. She'd be getting up soon. Claire wanted to get into uniform, too. She was still in the jeans she'd pulled on last night. Somehow, wearing the tan and green just made her feel more competent.

"You heard me, Morris. I don't want you giving any details to the press, but in my opinion, the guy who killed Patti Lorne probably killed April Provost."

"That's ridiculous! There's no connection between these two women. Patti was the town tramp. Some ex-boyfriend or drug dealer killed her."

"Maybe. But whoever did it killed April, too. It's the same MO. Slashed wrists, allowed to bleed to death, dumped beside a trash receptacle like an old mattress. It has to be the same guy." She came around her desk, not giving him a chance to speak again. "Now, I have to get to the drugstore and get these crime scene photos developed. Then I'm going home and getting a shower.

You need me, call me here and Jewel will patch you through."

The mayor looked at the envelope in her hand in repugnance. "You're going to take those pictures to the drugstore? I thought we sent things like that out to be developed."

She glowered, irritated that he was still holding her up. "We usually do, but I don't want to wait." She shook the envelope. "I'll run the machine myself so no employee has to see what's in here."

"You can do that?" He looked unconvinced.

"I'm trainable, Morris. Now, if you'll excuse me."

Her phone buzzed as she grabbed the door knob. She turned back. "Yeah, Jewel?"

"Captain Gallagher on line two, Chief."

Claire contemplated letting Jewel take a message. She could talk to Kurt later. But then she thought better of it. "If you'll excuse me, Morris, I need to take this call." She pointed to the door. "You wouldn't mind closing it on your way out, would you?"

Claire slipped back into her chair behind her desk and waited until the mayor was gone before she picked up the phone. "Kurt."

"Claire." It was his concerned tone. "I just called to see how you're holding up."

She ran her hand over her face. Truthfully, she didn't know how she was holding up, but she certainly wasn't going to hand that to him on a silver platter. "I'm just peachy, Kurt. I've got two dead women, dumped, and a sick bastard on a learning curve who appears to like blood."

"Come again?"

"I don't want this out, obviously, but this time I've got one slashed wrist and one slashed—hell, I don't know, looked like the ankle to me, but it was hard to tell with the dried blood."

"You think he's doing some kind of *research?*"

She stared at the envelope on her desk that contained the film to be processed. "I don't know what he's doing, Kurt."

"You're sure it's the same guy?"

"Pretty, young, blond. Died of blood loss. Dumped near a trash receptacle." She kicked back in her chair, throwing one heel up on her desk. "Gotta be the same guy."

"What about the husband? He a candidate? You know, reads the papers, gets a clever idea. He brings his wife for a little weekend getaway, offs her to make it look like Albany Beach has a serious slasher problem?" he thought aloud.

"I'm going to interview him this afternoon, but my gut says not."

"You want me to send someone down to give you a hand?"

"No." She didn't have to think twice. "I can handle this, Kurt. I just need some time to get my evidence together, compare the two vics. Of course, I can't tell you off the top of my head what they had in common, other than blond hair. Patti was a waitress, only one step up from a hooker, and our tourist was married and a legal secretary. She was here on vacation, for God's sake."

"I'm not saying you definitely have a repeat offender here, but if you do, sometimes the correlation isn't obvious," he said. "This kind of investigation takes your thinking cap."

"Listen, I have to run." She grabbed the envelope with the film again. "Thanks for calling."

"Claire, I really wish you'd—"

"Hanging up, Kurt." Claire dropped the receiver into its cradle and made a beeline for the door before the phone rang again.

* * *

"Your date's here," Phoebe called as she rose up on her knees on the floral couch in the living room and peered out the window from behind the drapes.

"He's not my date." Marcy glanced in the hallway mirror, tucked her hair behind her ear, and slipped on an earring. "And I have to say, I don't appreciate you running to Jake telling him where I'm going and with whom." She cut her eyes at her sister, who was still looking out the window.

"I didn't mean to tell him, Marcy. I really am sorry. It just slipped out." She came off the couch. "Of course, sooner or later he's going to find out you're dating. No harm in making it sooner rather than later. You don't want the poor guy to think he's got some chance of moving back in."

Marcy put on the other earring. She wanted to tell her sister that she was not dating Seth, but in order to make it fly, she'd have to tell her why she *was* seeing him. She knew she'd eventually have to inform her sister that she was seriously considering buying a restaurant, but she was hoping to get her out of the house first. Phoebe was going to be royally pissed when she found out.

"Do I look okay?" Marcy stepped back for Phoebe to see. She'd dressed in a just-above-the-knee-length khaki skirt, a black sleeveless shirt, and high-heeled sandals. She hoped the outfit was more professional-appropriate than date-appropriate, but her ego prevented her from wearing the dreary shapeless style she had once worn.

"I was going to say I'd like to borrow the skirt, but it is a little long, isn't it?" Phoebe reached around Marcy's waist, grabbed the waistband of her skirt and gave it a tug upward. "And it's snug. You putting on a little weight, sweetie?" Phoebe looked up with those big blue eyes of hers.

Marcy pulled the skirt down an inch, refusing to take the bait. "Actually it's a size six, so it probably wouldn't fit you anyway."

The doorbell rang.

"I'm leaving!" Marcy hollered into the family room. "See you guys! Be good for your Aunt Phoebe and don't stay up too late."

"Wait, Mom." Ben ran into the front hall, barefoot, shirtless in athletic shorts. "You think we could go back to the store? I know which carbon dioxide monitor we need, and I really think it should be installed right away. You just can't be too careful these days, you know." He drew himself up to his full four-foot-eleven. "What with all the environmental hazards these days."

"Phoebe, don't open the door." Marcy turned to Ben, catching his hand to lead him back toward the family room. She'd told the kids she was going out with a friend, but she hadn't elaborated. She *knew* she shouldn't have agreed to let Seth pick her up, but he'd insisted. "I think a trip to the Big-Mart tomorrow can be arranged."

Phoebe opened the front door. "Seth. How nice to see you again."

Marcy looked over her shoulder to see her sister all smiles. *So much for not letting Ben see Seth.* Marcy leaned over and whispered in Ben's ear. "I have a secret that I'll tell you later."

Ben glanced apprehensively one more time at the stranger in the doorway chatting with his aunt. "A good secret?" he asked suspiciously.

"Definitely." She led him into the family room, giving him a kiss on the top of his head before letting him go. "Your sister on the phone?"

He plopped on the couch and grabbed his video game controller. "Of course."

"Well, tell her I said good-bye. I probably won't be home until after you're in bed, but tomorrow I'll tell you my secret."

Ben held his controller tightly in his hands, staring straight ahead at the TV. "Dad know your secret?"

She smiled tenderly. She was just beginning to realize how hard this separation was on the kids, especially Ben. They really missed their dad. "He does. Of course he does. Now I have to run."

In the front hall, Marcy grabbed her purse off the bottom step. "Thanks for staying with Ben and Katie, Phebes." She smiled at Seth. "I'm ready."

"You kids have a good time," Phoebe called after them as they walked down the sidewalk. "Thanks for the pen, Seth. Stay out as late as you like, Marcy," she sang, her meaning obvious. *Sleep with him; I'll cover for you.* Marcy felt her cheeks color with embarrassment, but when she looked at Seth, he was grinning. He was apparently thinking along the same lines.

"You look great tonight," he said as he opened the car door for her.

It was a little silver BMW sports car. He'd mentioned several times the last time she saw him that he'd just bought the car. She knew she was supposed to be impressed. She wasn't, and she didn't even know why. "Thanks."

He strode around the front of the car and climbed behind the wheel. "In fact, I was just thinking what a good-looking couple we make."

She laughed aloud, thinking he sounded like he was in high school and was escorting her to the junior prom. "Seth, we *are* going to see those other two properties, right?"

"Yeah, right. Of course, of course. I just thought we might have a drink afterward." He glanced sideways at her, flashing his baby blues. "Did I mention to you that I was captain of the football team my senior year in high school? I—"

"You did." She laid her purse on her lap. "Now tell me about these properties, and give me the bottom line on what they have to offer. I'm looking for honesty, here, not the Taj Mahal."

Two hours later, Marcy had seen both new properties, one presently rented to a family-style Italian place which would be moving after the season, the other way out of her price range on the edge of the boardwalk in Rehoboth. When they had finished looking at the place in Rehoboth, Seth drove west, toward the bay, instead of south toward Albany Beach.

"I thought we were going out for a drink back in town," she said, glancing at the unfamiliar surroundings.

"We are." Grin. "My place, if that's okay with you. It's a great condo on the bay. I make a mean cosmopolitan."

Marcy wasn't sure what to say. After all, she had agreed to a drink. She'd just assumed he meant out somewhere in public. Now she wasn't sure how she felt about Seth. About being alone with him. She tried not to let her imagination run wild. She thought about the dead woman they'd found behind The Seahorse. Her pretty blond hair, her smile. Marcy had seen her picture on the news and on the front pages of all the papers. So far, her killer was unknown. The police didn't even know if it was someone she knew or not.

Marcy didn't know all the details, but the whole thing was making her uncomfortable. April Provost had just been in town for the weekend; it didn't make sense to Marcy that she could have known her murderer. Unless, of course, it was someone who had followed her there. Maybe her husband. But the papers hadn't mentioned that he was a suspect. Besides, how could he have known Patti? Anyway you looked at it—known killer, unknown, related murders or not—it still added up to two dead women. Something like that happening just naturally made a woman want to be more careful.

"Here we are, home sweet home." Seth zipped into a parking space in front of a three-story white stucco condo. There were three buildings just alike in a row, facing the bay.

Inside Seth's place, she set her purse on a table near

the door. He walked around, flipping on a couple of recessed lights. It was a nice place, decorated with lots of glass and white wood and paintings of the ocean and seashells. There was a couch and a loveseat in pale pastels and a big glossy coffee table book on seaside paintings displayed prominently. She doubted Seth had done the decor himself. Except for two dog bowls on the floor in the kitchen, the place looked like a furniture store.

"Check out the balcony," he told her as he switched on a stereo inside a media cabinet.

Jazz music seemed to slide from the seams of the high-ceilinged, open living area. She didn't know where he had the speakers hidden.

Seth stepped into the galley kitchen and produced a stainless steel cocktail shaker. He gave her the impression that he made a lot of mixed drinks, probably for a lot of women. She opened the sliding glass door and stepped onto the balcony.

The moon was just beginning to rise in the sky, casting white light in a beam across the water. She walked forward and leaned on the rail, breathing in the warm, humid night air. The living room and balcony were actually on the second story, jutting out over the bay so she could hear the water lapping on the shore below.

Marcy stared into the darkness and wondered what she was doing here. She had gone out with Seth on the pretense of looking at more property, but that wasn't the only reason she'd come. She knew it. Seth knew it. He had asked her out because he wanted to sleep with her. She'd come because . . . she was tempted.

"Here we are." Seth stepped onto the balcony carrying a martini glass in each hand.

"Thanks." Marcy accepted the drink and took a sip. It was strong.

"You're welcome." He slipped his hand casually around her waist. "You see, I told you what a great view I had."

She leaned on the rail again and tipped her glass. She was flattered that Seth found her attractive, that he obviously was interested in having sex with her, married or not. But she could see now that he didn't seem to be terribly interested in her personally. Though they had now been out five or six times to look at property or discuss their findings, he hadn't asked her any questions about herself. When they weren't talking about what he could sell her, he rattled on about his own accomplishments, the possessions he had accumulated, and where he was going on vacation.

Marcy didn't have a lot of experience with men; she'd begun dating Jake in college. But they had gone out for months before he'd even tried anything more than a kiss. By then, they not only knew each other well, but were already half in love.

In the last few years, Marcy had occasionally caught herself spotting a nice-looking man and fantasizing what it would be like to flirt with him, maybe even hop into the sack with him with the abandon Phoebe seemed to possess. But now, standing here beside Seth, opportunity obviously at hand for the taking, the idea of having sex with someone she didn't know was not terribly titillating.

"I bought this place at a steal. An old lady went into a retirement home and her kids wanted to unload it," he told her, moving closer. "How's your drink?"

As he spoke, his mouth glanced her ear. It didn't produce the effect she guessed he was hoping for.

"Good; it's good." She inched away, her forearms sliding across the black wrought-iron rail. She found herself thinking about Jake. About the promise she had made to him fifteen years ago in the same church where she'd been baptized and confirmed. She knew they were living in a modern age. Couples who were separated *dated* all the time—just the way Phoebe *dated*. That didn't mean it was right. "Listen," she told Seth, "I don't know what other properties you have to show me, but I'm thinking the old Mexican place would best suit my needs. Minus the sombreros." She gave a little nervous laugh and took another sip of the martini.

He inched closer and his hand appeared magically on her hip again. "I think it's a good choice, Marcy, but I wouldn't want you jumping to any rash conclusions. We should take our time. Study our options." His last words were a whisper in her ear.

He brushed his lips along the line of her jaw. "Damn, you're hot tonight, Marcy," he breathed. "I just can't take my eyes off you."

Marcy took a deep breath, turned to Seth, and pushed her drink into his hand. "I have to go."

"What?"

She strode off the balcony, through the living area to the door, where she grabbed her purse. She had hesitated because she didn't want to look stupid. Feel stupid. She'd spent a good portion of her adult life feeling inadequate, and she hated it. Funny thing was, standing here, she didn't feel stupid or inadequate, just thankful she'd had the nerve to put a stop to this before she did something she really didn't want to do.

"I'm sorry, Seth." She offered a quick smile. "I need to get home. It was really great of you to show me those other places. Give me a few days to think, and then I'll get back to you."

He stood in front of his pastel couch, his polo shirt matching the fabric, a martini glass in each hand. He appeared flabbergasted. Apparently the jazz from the invisible speakers and the cosmopolitans on the deck usually worked better for him than they were working tonight. "You're just leaving?"

He was obviously irritated with her. She didn't care.

"Yup. Afraid so."

He set the glasses down on a glass-topped table. "Women don't usually walk out on me like this."

Definitely irritation, bordering on anger now. She still didn't care.

"Don't worry about giving me a ride home." She grabbed the doorknob. "I have a friend around the corner. I'd been meaning to stop by and see her anyway."

Before Seth could say another word, she slipped out the door and closed it behind her. Not sure if she wanted to laugh or cry, she ran down the steps, fumbling in her purse for her cell phone.

There was no friend to visit. She was going to have to call someone to get her—the question was, who? Phoebe was the logical answer, but as she stepped into the parking lot, she found herself dialing Jake's number. She waited for a break in traffic to hurry across Route One.

"Please let him be home," she whispered reaching the median strip. "Please be home."

"'Lo."

"Jake?"

"Marcy?" He hesitated. "You okay? I just got off the phone with the kids. Ben said you'd gone out with a friend."

She glanced over her shoulder to be sure Seth hadn't followed her in his car, then hurried across the northbound lane of Route One. "I . . . yeah. Yeah, I'm fine, but I need a big favor. Could you come get me?"

"Get you?"

She grimaced as she stepped safely onto a sidewalk. "I kind of got myself into a jam. The car's at home."

"Tell me where you are."

She crossed the street, deciding to walk another block or so north, just to get out of Seth's vicinity. She told him where to find her in Rehoboth.

"Just pick you up on the corner?" he asked. "You sure you don't want to go inside somewhere? A restaurant? A mini-mart?"

"I'll be fine." She laughed with relief. "I'll be right here waiting for you, Jake." She hung up and tucked her cell phone into her purse as she crossed another street. She slowed her pace, her sandals click-clacking hollowly on the sidewalk.

On this street there were more shadows; the street lamps weren't as close. She glanced over her shoulder suddenly. There it was. That weird feeling . . . like someone was watching her.

Marcy saw no one.

She hurried to the designated corner and stood under the street lamp beside a mailbox. Jake would be here in fifteen minutes, even if there was traffic.

A car passed by, rock music blasting from its stereo. It was the third week in June, and the tourists were really beginning to pour in.

She noticed a man walking his dog across the street. She couldn't see his face. He passed two teen girls walking hand in hand on the sidewalk, laughing.

Marcy studied the buildings around her. It was an older section of town. A lot of turn-of-the-century houses that had been converted into summer apartments. There were lights on in the closest house. Shadows moved behind the drapes; someone obviously was home.

Still fighting that feeling she was being watched, Marcy looked behind her again. The man with the dog had stopped, but he wasn't paying any attention to her. His dog was squatting on a patch of grass between the street and the sidewalk. Harmless.

So why was the hair standing up on the back of her neck? Why did her stomach suddenly feel so weird? Empty. The drink? She *was* a little light-headed. She'd only had a yogurt and one of Ben's french fries for dinner. It probably hadn't been wise of her to pour vodka on top of it.

Marcy pushed a lock of blond hair behind her ear. As she did so, she caught a reflection of her image in the window of a parked car. The woman looking back at her truly *was* beautiful. But it didn't feel the way she always dreamed it would. All these years she had believed her unhappiness and discontent was due to the way she looked. A notion suddenly struck her. What if that hadn't been it at all?

The Bloodsucker nonchalantly opened the back door of his car and let Max jump in. "Good boy," he murmured, trying to appear, to the causal observer, to be just another vacationer taking his dog out for an evening stroll. Maybe taking a ride to the nearest mini-mart to pick up chips and drinks for the wife and kids. He smiled at the domestic thought.

When he was in his early twenties, he had fantasized marrying, having an adoring blond wife, two adoring children. One boy, one girl, of course. They'd be blond with blue eyes, too, and they would all live in a cute little Cape Cod in a nice neighborhood. When he cut his grass on his riding lawnmower, neighbors would wave. Maybe walk over, lean on the fence, and invite the family over for a backyard barbeque.

The Bloodsucker had never attended a backyard barbeque. Never even owned a gas grill. But if he had a family, a wife, two kids, he'd have to get one, wouldn't he?

He'd made the mistake of mentioning having a family to Granny once. She said no woman in her right mind would want him. An idiot like him. A worthless, whining excuse for a man. If his mother didn't want him, what made him think any other woman would want him?

Dry, bitter old bitch.

The Bloodsucker closed the back door of the car, licking his chapped lips. As he walked around the car, he dared a glance. There she was, standing under the street lamp, the glow of the light making her hair look like it was spun gold. He didn't know what spun gold was; he'd just read about it somewhere once. But he knew it had to look just like Marcy's hair.

Taking his time, he opened the driver's side door of the car. She was so beautiful that when he gazed at her face, his stomach grew tight. The thing down there in his pants grew tight. Hard. It made him uncomfortable. Then he thought about Granny and her tight-lipped sneer. Things loosened up a bit.

The Bloodsucker climbed in behind the wheel, debating. It was as if she was waiting for him. But tonight was not supposed to be the night; he had a busy day tomorrow. To take Marcy now, to put her in his trunk, would be impulsive. Nothing was ready. He wasn't ready for her. Impulsiveness was bad. It was dangerous. It also turned out to, sometimes, be disappointing.

He had picked up April on impulse, and it had been a mistake. Marcy was who he had wanted. He'd only taken April because he was so frustrated that night at the restaurant. Because Marcy had been so close, but unobtainable. He'd known the minute April had woken in the chair that she wasn't right. That her blood wasn't the blood he needed.

He'd even tried a little experimentation, hoping to create a little excitement. A little something he had seen on TV about a teen girl who committed suicide. He didn't care what any experts said, though, the ankle didn't bleed as well. The blood didn't seem as rich. As tantalizing.

Maybe it was just because April hadn't been Marcy. She just hadn't been able to stand up to her beauty. Her strength. With April, the sense of power hadn't lasted as long as he had expected it to, leaving him slightly disappointed. Kind of like when you wanted a vanilla chocolate swirl ice cream cone and you stopped to get it, only by the time you got there, they were all out of chocolate for the night. The vanilla was always good.

Sweet, creamy, cold. But there was still that sense of dissatisfaction at not getting what you had your heart set on.

His gaze strayed to Marcy again, and he contemplated taking her now. He imagined himself walking right up to her, smiling, drawing her into his confidence. He knew she'd talk to him, never suspect, because he already knew she liked him. By the time she realized something was wrong, it would be too late.

No, he told himself firmly. Not tonight.

He needed to stop at the grocery store and pick up dog food. Max was out. He had to be very careful with the chloroform not to give her so much that it poisoned her. And if he stopped for dog food with Marcy in the trunk, only lightly drugged, she might wake up. Even gagged, someone might hear her thumping around in there while he was in the store.

The Bloodsucker was disappointed, but not overly so. So what if tonight wasn't the right night? It would come soon.

He glanced Marcy's way. Smiled. Started the engine and pulled away. Part of the fun of the vanilla chocolate swirl cone was the anticipation.

Chapter Eight

Marcy and Jake rode back to Albany Beach in silence. It wasn't until they passed the carved sign in the median strip that read, *Albany Beach, If you lived here you'd be home now*, that she had the nerve to speak.

"Thanks for coming to get me."

He slumped in the driver's seat, one hand on the wheel, the other on the door. "You know, I'm a pretty patient man," he said quietly. "But my patience is wearing thin with this whole *finding yourself* quest you've got going here."

His remark hurt, but it wasn't unfounded. She studied her left hand without its wedding band and engagement ring. "It wasn't a date, Jake." She took a deep breath, daring a glance at him in the semi-darkness of the car. It had been hard to call him, but she was glad she had. He made her feel safe. As ridiculous as it seemed right now, considering the circumstances, even loved. "I thought it was a date, sort of, but I was wrong."

He glanced sideways at her. "If you think I'm going to believe for one second that any man would turn you down, looking the way you do these days, you—"

"Jake, I made a mistake. I thought it was what I wanted,

and I was wrong." She closed her eyes for a moment, then opened them. "The truth is, I don't know what I want."

"Tell me about it," he muttered.

His sarcasm stung, but she couldn't blame him for his reaction. She wasn't too pleased with her behavior right now, either. "The good news is, I feel as if I'm getting closer."

"And am I included in this new life plan of yours? I mean, I obviously wasn't included in the whole restaurant thing."

She studied his face for a moment and then hesitantly reached out to brush his cheek with the back of her fingertips. "Can we go to your place?"

He glanced at her, then back at the road.

"I thought maybe we could talk for a while," she said, refusing to let him rebuff her. "Without the kids. Without Phoebe. Phoebe makes everything so much more complicated."

"I don't know, Marcy. You're really screwing with my head. Dr. Larson warned me this was going to be hard, that there was going to be an adjustment period, but this isn't at all what I expected." As he spoke, he flipped on the directional signal and made the turn toward his rental, away from their home. "You can't keep doing this to me. Acting like you still care for me one minute, then going out on dates with other men the next."

"I'm sorry," she breathed. "I didn't mean to hurt you. It's just that I've been unhappy for so long . . ." She let her sentence trail into silence, and for several blocks they were both quiet again. He parked in the lot behind his condo, and side by side, they walked down the sidewalk and took the stairs.

He unlocked the door and opened it for her, stepping back.

She walked in, glancing around. She hadn't been inside before. She always dropped the kids off at the door, picked them up outside. "Nice."

It was a two-bedroom, right on the ocean. A comfy living area with a denim-covered couch and chair, a big TV, and scattered end tables. The colors were soft tans and whites with splashes of blue. There was a galley kitchen all in white and a short hall that led to the bedrooms and bath.

Marcy sat on the end of the couch and let her purse slide off her shoulder. Jake opened the double glass doors that opened onto the balcony and a rush of cool night air blew in. She leaned back and closed her eyes, smelling the salt of the ocean, hearing the waves crash on the beach.

"You want something to drink? I think I have some beer. Maybe some rum."

Marcy laughed. When she opened her eyes, he was standing there in front of her looking completely unamused.

"No, thanks. I already had part of a drink on an empty stomach." She winced. "Bad idea."

"Something to eat, then?" He hooked a thumb in the direction of the small, open kitchen.

Standing there in a pair of cargo shorts, a surfer's graphic tee, and flip-flops, Jake appeared ten years younger than his thirty-seven years. He looked like he needed a haircut. Looked like he needed a hug even worse.

She got up off the couch and stood in front of him. Her heart was hammering in her chest. "I'm sorry, Jake," she whispered.

"For what?"

"The accident. For nearly killing myself. For waking up looking like this and turning our whole lives upside down." Her voice grew stronger. "For not being the same person I was when I went off that bridge."

She hesitated, searching his gentle brown eyes for the man she had once known. The man she had fallen in love with. "I know I'm not the same woman who crashed her car six months ago. I'm not even the woman you married. But I just can't be that Marcy anymore. I'm tired of feeling miserable about myself. Tired of hearing myself complain."

To her surprise, he half smiled and rested his hand on her waist. "I'm glad you called. I mean, I'm pissed that you were with some guy, but—"

"Nothing happened. I swear it," she whispered. "He took one step toward me, and I was out of there." She snapped her fingers.

He looked away, then back at her again. "Good. I'm glad. I'm also glad I was the one you thought to call." He hesitated. "As far as the other stuff . . . I just want you to be happy, Marcy."

She pressed her lips together, afraid she might cry. It had been a long time since she had felt this kind of intimacy with Jake. Too long. And until this moment, she hadn't realized how much she missed it. She wrapped her arms around his neck and hugged him, reveling in the feel of his arms around her waist, the scent of his skin, and the sound of his breath in her ear.

She laughed. Sniffed. "So what have you got in that bachelor's fridge of yours?"

Jake prepared a gourmet meal for them of tuna pita sandwiches, carrot sticks, and lemonade. They sat on the balcony overlooking the ocean in the folding lawn chairs he'd bought at the dollar store, and ate and talked. They went for a walk on the beach, hand in hand, and then back to his place to talk some more.

It seemed as if suddenly there were so many things they wanted to tell each other. They talked about her dislike of her job as the bookkeeper with the construction company and her dream of the restaurant. The amazing thing was, he had a lot of good ideas on how she could make it work. They also talked about the accident. Jake told her things that had happened in the months that she was unconscious. Some big things, some just little that he said he'd wished she'd been there to share with him.

Somehow the night got away from them, and before they knew it, the sun was beginning to rise on the ocean's dark horizon. They sat on the balcony, wrapped in beach towels, and sipped coffee in silence as the sun went from an orange streak of light in the darkness, a bare hint of the day to come, to a glowing red-yellow ball in the sky, full of promise.

Jake drove Marcy home so she'd be there when the kids got up. They talked about him coming in for break-fast, but agreed it wouldn't be fair for the kids. Neither said anything about Jake moving back in, taking an-other stab at living together as husband and wife, but they both knew it was on the other's mind.

Jake walked her to the front door the way he had in the days when they'd been dating. "I really am glad you called me, Marcy. It means a lot to me to think you think I'm still a big part of your life."

Standing on the front porch step, she turned to face him and reached out tenderly to stroke his beard-stubbled cheek. He was going to have to hustle to get home, get a shower, and make it to work on time.

"Of course you're a part of my life. You always will be. You're the father of my children."

"Damn it, I don't just want to be the father of your children."

The strength of his conviction surprised her.

"I want to be your friend, your lover, your mate."

She closed her eyes, savoring the moment between them, truly thankful, maybe for the first time, that God had saved her the night she drove off that bridge. "I should go in," she whispered. "And you'd better get home. You'll be late for work."

"Call me later. If you want to go ahead with that Mexican restaurant property, we should have someone look over the sales contract." He caught her chin between his thumb and forefinger and pressed his mouth to hers.

Marcy slipped her arm over Jake's shoulder and parted her lips slightly. How long had it been since Jake had made her feel this way? All warm and tingly from head to toe. How long had it been since she let herself feel this way?

The kiss was over sooner than she wanted it to be, and Jake was headed for his car. "Talk to you later."

She waved and let herself into the quiet house. Without turning on any lights, she slipped upstairs. There was no sense in going back to bed. She wasn't even that tired. Her mind was already racing with all the things she needed to do if she was really going to buy that property. In her bedroom, she undressed and then stepped into the shower. She took her time under the warm water, washing and conditioning her hair, shaving her legs. She couldn't stop smiling. Last night was one of the best nights she could remember having in . . . forever.

She chuckled to herself. And who would have thought it could have been with her husband? The husband she was separated from? But somehow Jake seemed different to her now. More like he was in their college days, but still different. Witty, charming, thoughtful. Kind of like an aged wine?

She stepped out of the shower and grabbed for a bath towel.

"So how was it?"

Marcy jumped at the sound of Phoebe's voice and clutched the towel around her dripping, naked body. "Phebes! You scared me half to death." She slid the towel around to tuck in the end above her breasts so it would stay put and reached for a smaller towel to wrap up her hair.

Phoebe was stretched out on her bed, still made from the previous day. And Marcy had a feeling her sister had been listening for her to come in. There was no way she was going to get away with saying she hadn't been out all night, she was just up early.

"So?" Phoebe probed. She was wearing a pair of gym shorts and a skin-tight tank top.

"So, what?"

"Did you have a nice evening?" Phoebe's tone said everything. She wanted to know if Marcy had enjoyed having sex with Seth in his bachelor pad on the bay.

Marcy stood in front of the sink and, glancing in the mirror at the reflection of her sister, reached for her toothbrush. "I had a very nice evening, thank you." She didn't know why, but she didn't want to share her time with Jake with anyone else. She cared less about Phoebe thinking she was sleeping around than she cared about her and her husband's privacy.

Looking at her sister sprawled on her bed, Marcy knew that if she was even going to consider asking Jake to move back in, Phoebe was going to have to be out of here first. There just wasn't room in this house for two women, not two women who were so different.

"How'd that job interview go yesterday? At a crab house, right?"

Phoebe sat up on the bed, leaned against the headboard, and picked up the book Marcy had been reading. When she saw it had to do with parenting teenagers, she dropped it with disinterest. "It went well. They're probably going to offer me the job."

"That's great!" Marcy brushed her teeth, glancing in the mirror again. "You don't sound excited."

"It's a crab house, for Christ's sake, Marcy. I used to own a seafood restaurant, and now I'm going to manage an effin' crab shack?"

"You'll look cute in the short shorts and shirt tied under your bosom," Marcy teased.

Phoebe didn't laugh as she climbed off the bed. "Look, I'll find a job."

"I know you will because your unemployment has got to be running out soon." Marcy leaned over the sink, rinsed her mouth, and came into the bedroom. "Right?"

Phoebe walked out, sour-faced. "I'm going out to have a cigarette."

Marcy stuck her head out the door into the hallway. "Thanks for watching the kids last night. Katie has a softball game tonight, but I'll take her. We'll probably go out for dinner afterward, so if you have something to do, go ahead."

She wanted to shout after her that she should feel free to start looking for a place to live. It might take weeks to find something this time of year in her price range. But she bit her tongue. She had already riled her sister enough this morning. And if she went to the bank later in the week to apply for the loan, she was going to have to rile her even further.

With that unpleasant thought, Marcy padded bare-foot down the hall to Ben's room and opened his door. "Hey, sleepyhead."

"Mom?"

She could barely make out his form in his bed in the dark room. "I thought you might want to go have breakfast with me at the diner?"

He kicked off his sheet and scratched his bare belly between his boxer shorts and T-shirt. "So early?"

"I have to get some tests done at the hospital first, but I thought you might like to tag along. I think Katie is baby-sitting."

He sat up. "Could we go to the Big-Mart too?"

She smiled. "You bet." She closed his door and went down the hall to the next. "Katie?"

The teen groaned and rolled over, taking her pillow with her to cover her face. "Just a few more minutes."

"You said you wanted to be up by six-thirty so you could have a shower."

"I know," Katie moaned. "We're taking the kids to

some kiddy amusement park today. The Schmidts will be here at seven-thirty to get me."

"Just think of that big fat paycheck," Marcy teased her daughter. "But you'll be back in time for your softball game, right?"

"I'm taking my uniform. They said they'd drop me off so you can meet me there." Katie was still talking through her pillow, her voice muffled. "Then I think I'm going to Emily's to spend the night. That okay?"

Marcy frowned. She was really looking forward to the game and having dinner with the kids tonight. She thought she might ask Jake to join them. But she knew better than to try to put herself between Katie and her friends. It caused nothing but hate and discontent.

"That's fine. Let me know before you leave."

Marcy closed the door behind her and headed back to her bedroom, pulling her towel off her head as she went. Before the accident, a day this full had been daunting. Sometimes she used to feel as if she was dragging through mud, taking the kids here and there, running to the grocery store, attending their various athletic events. She had blamed it all on how fat she was, how unhappy she was with her life. Perhaps her weight had had something to do with being so tired all the time, but looking back, could she have been depressed and not even realized it? If so, exactly why had she been depressed? A good job, a loving husband who didn't spend more money than they made and who came home faithfully to her every night? Two healthy, happy children who did well in school and knew the difference between a smoke detector and a carbon monoxide detector? She shook her head. Had she been crazy?

Alex, one of Jake's co-workers, poked his head through Jake's office doorway. "Your wife's here. Coming up the hall." He glanced over his shoulder, then back at Jake.

"Damn, but she's hot. Wearing a skirt like that with legs like hers." He winked. "Ought to be illegal in this state."

Chuckling at his own joke, Alex disappeared down the hall.

Jake checked his watch. It was only nine-thirty. Marcy had had some medical tests to take this morning at the hospital. He hoped everything was all right.

She walked into his office.

"Mar—" The minute he saw the short white skirt and the swing of her hips, he realized it wasn't Marcy. Same eyes, same face . . . almost. The plastic surgeon's work truly had been incredible, but this wasn't his wife. "Phoebe."

He was surprised she was here, but not that Alex had gotten her and Marcy confused. People in town were mistaking the two sisters for each other all the time now. He was disappointed a little, though, that it wasn't Marcy. He hadn't expected to see her until Katie's ball game tonight, but he'd just been sitting there at his desk daydreaming about her.

"Hi, sweetie." Phoebe came around his desk, placing a paper cup of gourmet coffee and a bag from the local bakery in front of him. She leaned over and kissed his cheek.

She was wearing a strong perfume that was too earthy for him, too musky. He preferred Marcy's subtle floral scents. He glanced at the pastry bag, wondering what the hell she was doing here. "Uh, thanks."

"Hazelnut high-test, two creams, one sugar, and a cream-cheese bear claw. I got the last one because I know how you like them." She parked her shapely butt on the edge of his desk, stretching her long legs out in front of him.

He kept his gaze on her waist up, sure he'd catch a glimpse of more than he needed to see if he wasn't careful. Phoebe didn't always wear panties. And Alex was right. Her skirt was short this morning, even shorter than usual. "Is . . . is Marcy ok?"

"Everything doesn't always have to be about Marcy, Jake. I know she thinks so, but we only perpetuate that. I came to see how *you* were." She opened the pastry bag and pulled out the bear claw, arranging it on a napkin for him.

He had no idea what she was talking about. "How I am?"

"You've been really good about this whole break-up with Marcy, but I know you have to be hurting. You don't deserve what she's doing to you. I know she's my sister and I love her and I don't mean to speak badly of her, but . . ." She lowered her head.

Jake was still lost as to what Phoebe was talking about and he didn't have time for her dramatics this morning. He had a lot of work today, and he intended to walk out of this building at five o'clock, come hell or high water.

Talking to Marcy last night, he realized he had to take part of the blame for her unhappiness the last few years and his own apathy toward her and their relationship. He'd spent too much time behind this desk and not enough with his wife and kids. And when he had been at home, he'd been too busy putzing around the yard or watching a ball game on TV when he should have been playing ball with his family or taking his wife out on a date. He should have sensed Marcy's unhappiness a whole lot sooner and tried to help her figure out what was wrong. He wasn't willing to take all the blame; part of it certainly had to rest on her shoulders, but he felt like it was fair to share.

"Phoebe, what are you talking about?" Jake tried not to sound as irritated as he felt.

"I mean this thing with Marcy and that Seth guy. I know you knew they were dating, but . . ." She stopped and started again. "But now—"

"Now, *what?*" Had something happened last night that Marcy hadn't told him about? Was that why she had called him to come get her? Had this Seth character tried to—Jake felt his face grow warm and his hands clenched instinctively into fists. He wasn't a violent man, but if that guy—

"I shouldn't say." Phoebe shook her head. "I've already said too much. I should go."

She lifted her butt off its perch. This close to her, he could see fine lines starting to appear around her mouth and eyes. She was beginning to age, and it seemed as if it was happening quickly.

"I'm trying to find a job, you know. Trying to get out and a place of my own. Marcy says she wants me out." She gave him a sad smile. "And I understand, she wants her privacy to . . . well, for whatever reason."

"Phoebe—go back to last night. What happened to Marcy last night?"

She demurred.

It might have worked for some women, but he wasn't buying.

"I shouldn't," she simpered.

He narrowed his eyes. "Tell me."

"Well . . ." She sighed, as if ashamed and then shook her head. *More dramatics.* "She stayed out all night, Jake." She grabbed his arm, rubbing it. "I'm sorry to be the one to have to tell you she's sleeping around, but I'm caught between wanting to be loyal to my sister and not wanting to see you get hurt."

He almost grinned, but was able to control it. Phoebe must have caught Marcy sneaking into the house this morning and assumed she'd been out with the real estate guy. She obviously thought Marcy had spent the night with him, and Marcy hadn't told her any differently.

Jake didn't know why, but that tickled the hell out of him. Made him feel good; as if he and Marcy had a little secret together.

Jake reached for the coffee. "I need to get to work,"

he said gruffly, mostly because he was afraid he might laugh out loud. And it wasn't fair. Phoebe had been nothing but good to him. He didn't know what he would have done without her all those months, if she hadn't been there to help with the kids and the house.

She squeezed his shoulder. "If you want to talk or . . . I don't know, grab something to eat, you know you can call me, Jake. You've got my cell phone number." She moved toward the door. "I know it must get lonely there by yourself in that condo."

He pressed his lips together and nodded. Phoebe walked out, and Jake grinned the rest of the morning.

"Marcy Edmond," an older woman in a pale green smock announced.

Marcy patted Ben's knee. "I just have to get this blood test and one more test, then we can go have breakfast. You wait here."

He nodded and went on zapping some creature on his hand-held video game.

"Good morning," the woman said, waiting for Marcy at the door that led into the lab area of the hospital. She wore a name badge that said "Volunteer. Hi, my name is Madge."

"Good morning."

"This way, please."

Marcy followed her down the hall, and they halted at the third door on the left.

"Alan will take care of you." The receptionist dropped the lab request sheets on the corner of the counter and headed back up the hall to her desk.

Marcy ducked into the small room and took her seat on the chair that reminded her of one of those old-fashioned school desks. The phlebotomist turned around, and she realized she recognized him. He was the same person who had taken her blood in the hospital before she was released. He had a friendly face. "Good morning."

He smiled and reached for several glass tubes in a tray. "Good morning. It's nice to see a smiling face around here. You know, I'm not the most popular guy around town, especially first thing in the morning."

She laughed. He was an attractive man in his thirties, probably, with blondish brown hair and dark brown eyes. He was wearing a white lab coat open with tan trousers and a yellow oxford shirt.

"Oh, I don't know why you'd say that." She flipped down the arm ledge of the chair and offered her best vein.

"Because I use big needles on people." He turned to face her, snapping on latex gloves. "People are funny about that. They holler. They faint." He reached out and gently pressed two fingers in the crook of her elbow.

"I promise I won't do either."

He grinned and pulled the rubber strap from his lab coat pocket. "Can you make a fist for me? Good." He tied off her arm and grabbed the syringe from the counter behind him.

Marcy's gaze strayed to the many colorful posters on the wall of the small lab. One showed the types of blood and what percentage of the population had each.

"Little stick," he told her.

She didn't flinch.

He filled four glass tubes of blood, removed the syringe, and placed a cotton ball over the tiny drop of blood that oozed from her skin. "Hold that up there for just a sec while I get a Band-Aid." He lifted her arm in the air.

Marcy followed his directions, watching him as he placed each vial of blood in a compartment in a tray on the counter.

"Scooby Doo or boring brown?" he asked.

She laughed. "Definitely Scooby Doo."

He opened the Band-Aid, and as he placed it in the crook of her elbow, he met her gaze. "You don't remember me, do you?" He had a nice voice. Not feminine, but gentle. It reminded her of Jake's voice.

"Actually, I do. You took care of me when I was here in the hospital, right?"

He smiled. "I saw you almost every day for three months. I always do the morning rounds on the wards before coming down here to the lab." He smoothed the Band-Aid in the crook of her elbow and tossed the wrapper in a trash can. "I have to tell you, I've been working here for ten years, and you're the closest to a miracle I've ever seen. I was really pulling for you. We all were."

"That's nice of you to say." She got up. "Obviously, I'm happy it worked out."

He chuckled with her. "Well, have a good day, Marcy. Just follow the blue line. It will lead you to the waiting area to get that CT scan."

"Thanks." She followed the blue line, and a receptionist behind a glass window asked her to have a seat, saying it would only be a minute. As Marcy sat and picked up a gourmet food magazine from a table, she debated whether she needed to go back and get Ben.

"Mrs. Edmond?"

She glanced up to see a man dressed in a county EMT uniform; she didn't recognize him. "Yes?"

"Sorry, I'm sure you don't remember me. Kevin James. I was there the day of your accident. My partner and I . . . we were one of the first on the scene."

She chuckled. "No, sorry, I can't say I do remember."

He shook his head, grinning at her. "You know, I see medical miracles all the time." He brushed back his sandy blond hair. "I know that happens, but . . ."

"Yeah, I know." She smiled back. "Pretty amazing."

"Mrs. Edmond." A technician appeared in the doorway. "We're ready for you."

Marcy dropped the magazine on the table, rising. "Nice to meet you, Kevin."

He nodded, thrusting his hands into his pockets, and continued along the corridor. "You have a good day."

"You, too."

Marcy followed the technician back to the CT scan room and they had her in and out of there in twenty minutes.

The tests Dr. Larson had ordered completed, she returned to the waiting room. "You ready to hit the road?" she called to Ben.

He bounced out of his chair, grabbing her purse she had left with him for safekeeping. "Can we go to the Big-Mart first?" He hurried in front of her, headed for the glass doors leading out into the parking lot.

"I was thinking we would eat first. I'm starved."

"But, Mom—" He pushed through the door just as someone was trying to come in.

"Whoa there!" Chief Drummond stepped back, letting Ben push through.

"Ben, you need to watch where you're going." Marcy hurried through the door, behind him, grabbing her purse off his shoulder. "I'm sorry, Claire. You know a man. Always barreling ahead without looking to see where he's going."

"Sorry," Ben said sheepishly, studying Claire in her uniform. "That a real gun?"

Claire smiled down at him, resting her hand on the butt of the revolver in a holster on her hip. "Sure is, and I bet you're such a smart guy that you know never to touch a gun. You see one, you find an adult."

He nodded. "Did you know, Chief Drummond, that twenty-seven percent of all handguns are illegal?"

"You know each other?" Marcy asked with a laugh.

"Sure. Ben and I are old buddies. He interviewed me in January for a school report, right?"

He nodded. "Chief Drummond is really quite knowledgeable on crime statistics in rural and urban areas."

"Is she now?" Marcy couldn't stop smiling. Ben sounded so grown up so often that she felt like she had missed out on something. When had this happened? When had he developed such a vocabulary?

"You doing all right?" Claire asked Marcy. She gave a little nod toward the hospital waiting room.

"Oh, yeah. Yeah, I'm fine. I just had a CT scan and some blood tests. Dr. Larson says it's routine for patients with head trauma. He'll probably want me to do this once in a while for the rest of my life."

"Good." Claire smiled. "I'm glad to hear it."

Marcy reached out and touched Claire's arm. "How about you? This second murder . . ." She had never been particularly demonstrative with other women, but her heart went out to Claire. Two women dead and no real leads, apparently. She knew that had to be hard to handle.

"I'm doing okay." Claire nodded, lowering her gaze.

"Still no idea who could have done it, though?"

She shook her head, adding a half nod. "Well, we're still investigating. Lab results can take days, weeks . . ."

"I know you're doing your best." Marcy smiled, trying to sound reassuring. "Say, you want to get together for lunch this week? Or maybe coffee?" Never in her life had she asked an acquaintance to go somewhere or do something. She just had never been the kind of person to reach out to others. Maybe that was changing, too.

When Claire didn't answer right away, Marcy got a little nervous. "I mean, I know how busy you are, and if you don't have the time—"

"No." Claire looked up with those striking blue eyes of hers. "I'd like that. Can I call you? My schedule is pretty hectic, but I really could use a quiet lunch with a friend."

Marcy bubbled inside. Claire had called her a friend.

It had been a long time since she had been able to think of herself as someone's friend. "That would be great. I'm in the phone book." She reached for Ben's hand. "Let's let Chief Drummond get to work." She glanced at Claire once more as they went down the sidewalk toward the parking lot. "Have a good day."

"You, too."

"I didn't know you did a report in school about crime," Marcy said, letting go of Ben's hand to let him go around the front of the SUV to get inside. "I'd really like to read it." She waited for him to buckle his seat belt before she started the car. "I know I was only asleep six months, but in ways, Mommy feels like she'd been asleep a lot longer than that."

"Can I have pancakes and toast?" Ben asked.

"Little heavy on the carbs, there?" She cut her eyes at him as she pulled out onto the street. The diner was only a few blocks away.

"I used to get sausage, but I read what they put in that stuff." He wrinkled his nose. "Not just guts and brains and stuff, but did you know what percentage of rodent hair is legally permitted in packaged food in this country?"

A few minutes later, they were seated in the diner. They'd run into Patrolman McCormick on their way in, and he'd practically asked her on a date right in front of Ben. Apparently word of her and Jake's separation was getting around. She thanked him politely but turned him down. No matter what happened with her and Jake, there was no way she was dating anyone Phoebe had dated.

"Well, hello, little lady." Ralph sauntered up to the table. "Just can't stay away from old Ralph, can you?"

"I'll have coffee and a waffle with fresh strawberries." She glanced over her menu at Ben. "I was going to have sausage, but after the conversation I just had with my son, I've thought better of it."

Ben giggled. "Can I have a small orange juice, pancakes, and two pieces of whole-wheat toast, butter on the side?"

Ralph scribbled on the pad of paper in his hand. "I think old Ralph can see ya get that."

Marcy glanced up at the diner counter. Loretta was busy running the cash register, and there was a young woman she didn't recognize changing the filter on the coffee machine. She looked nervous. "That Loretta's new waitress?"

Ralph glanced over his shoulder. "Yup. That's Kristen Addison, college girl. Come to stay with her aunt and uncle for the summer. You know the Addisons off Oak? I think she's a nurse. He's some kind of big wig at one of the plants."

"Actually, I do know them." Marcy tucked the menus behind the napkin holder on the table. "Their son Ty used to baby-sit Ben. We know the family from church."

Ralph tucked his pencil behind his ear and winked at Marcy. "That coffee and juice be comin' right up."

She watched him walk away, glad to see him go. The man just gave her the creeps.

"So," she said, turning her attention back to Ben. She had made him leave his video game in the car. "Tell me about this carbon monoxide thing we're buying today. Why do we need this in our house and how on earth did we live without it this long?"

Chapter Nine

"Hey, Mom, can I ask you a question?"

Katie sat on a stool on the other side of the kitchen counter, slicing cucumbers for the salad for dinner. Marcy had picked up fresh tuna steaks to grill; it was one of her daughter's favorites. Phoebe had said she had a couple of errands to run and then she was going out with friends. It was the perfect opportunity for Marcy to spend some time alone with her children, especially Katie, who was hard to catch these days between her baby-sitting job, her girlfriends, softball, and the almighty telephone. It seemed that in the three weeks since Marcy had been home, she and Katie had really had very little time together alone.

"Sure." Marcy ducked so that she could see her daughter on the far side of the kitchen cabinets. "As long as it's not too personal."

Katie made a face. "Like I would want to know anything like that. *Please.*"

Marcy laughed and went back to squeezing juice from a fresh lemon into a small glass bowl. "What is it?"

"Why haven't you gone to see the van?"

"What van?" The minute it was out of her mouth,

Marcy realized what she meant. *The* van. The van she had driven off the bridge. The van that had nearly killed her. "Oh, you mean *our* van. Our new van that I totaled." She tried to make light of it.

Katie nodded, gathering up cucumber peels in her hands to carry around to dump in the sink. "Dad wouldn't let me see it. It's at the junk yard, you know. That place with all the fencing and the dog that always barks. Ben thinks it's as big as the one in the Harry Potter movie, but I told him that was stupid." She looked at Marcy as she stuffed the peels down the garbage disposal. "So why haven't you?"

Marcy leaned on the counter, the lemon in her hand. "To tell you the truth, I hadn't really thought about it."

"I don't know how you couldn't. I saw the picture in the paper after it happened. In the picture, they're using a crane to pull it out of the water. It wasn't a very good picture, pretty dark and smudged, but it looked really awful," she said tentatively.

Marcy shifted her gaze to Katie's face. "You think I *should* see it?"

She lifted a slender shoulder. Katie had gotten so pretty. She had her Dad's sandy brown hair and his dark eyes, yet she was utterly feminine. And she had apparently not inherited her mother's penchant for weight gain, either. She was the perfect size for a thirteen-year-old, neither too thin nor too heavy. She was going to be a beautiful woman by society's standards, but more importantly a beautiful person inside. She seemed to have none of the insecurities that Marcy had already accumulated by the time she was her age.

"It didn't look like a person would survive, coming out of it." Katie flipped on the garbage disposal switch and turned on the water. The sound was so loud that it prevented either of them from hearing each other.

Marcy took the moment to try and figure out where Katie was going with this conversation. She was pretty certain it wasn't so much about the car as about the fact that Marcy *had* survived. Had Katie been thinking about the van and the shape it had been in, all these months?

Marcy waited until Katie turned off the switch to the garbage disposal and the room was quiet again except for the distant sound of Ben's afternoon cartoons on the TV in the family room. "Do you want to see the van?" she asked her daughter.

Again, the only response was the slight rise and fall of Katie's shoulder.

"Because maybe we could go together," Marcy said carefully. "If you wanted to."

Katie turned away, presenting her back to her mother, and Marcy realized by the way she trembled that she was crying. "Katie?" Marcy dropped the lemon on the counter, swiped up a dishtowel to dry her hands, and walked up behind her daughter to put her arms around her.

"I'm sorry, Mom," Katie choked. "I saw the picture, and I knew there was no way you could live. I didn't care how many candles they lit or what people said about miracles."

Marcy wrapped her arms tightly around the teen, breathing in her little-girl scent that wasn't so little girl now. Once she had smelled of baby powder and peanut butter. Now it was shampoo and conditioner, deodorant and nail polish. "Ah, sweetie, it's okay."

"No, it's not." Katie sniffed. "Dad knew you were going to get better and wake up. Ben knew." Her voice trembled. "But Aunt Phoebe and I, we were just sure you were going to die. We talked about it when we were alone. You know, what was going to happen when you died." A sob escaped her lips. "I just *knew* you couldn't live through that car wreck," she repeated.

"Katie, honey, don't cry. It's all behind us now." Marcy turned her daughter around. She knew how teens could be about physical contact with their parents, but Katie wasn't resisting, for once. "There's no need to cry now.

I'm all right. I know I don't look the way I used to and that's weird for you, but I'm still your Mom. I'm still the same person inside."

"But you don't understand." Katie clung to Marcy, wetting her mother's linen shirt with her tears. "You've always been there for me. Always believed in me. Told me I could do anything, be anything. And I—" Another sob. "I didn't believe in you. I didn't think you would get better."

Marcy closed her eyes, pulling Katie tightly against her, wishing that she could take away her daughter's pain and the guilt she obviously felt. Marcy had learned the hard way that it didn't matter if the pain was justified or not, it was still just as real.

"Katie, it's all right that you realized I might die. You're just practical, that's all. The odds *were* against me. You were probably the only sensible one in this house, thinking I was never going to come to." She said nothing about Phoebe; no matter what she thought of her sister's handling of the situation, she didn't want Katie in the middle of it.

"I'm sorry, Mom."

Marcy tipped Katie's head back and pushed the damp hair away from her eyes. She wanted to say no apology was needed, but if Katie felt it was, she knew she needed to accept it. "Apology accepted," she said softly. "Now, no more tears over this. I'm alive, and I'm going to be fine." She wiped at her daughter's tears again, mainly because she wanted to savor the moment of closeness they were sharing. "And if you feel like you want to see the van, I'll take you to see it. We'll do it together."

Katie stepped back, her quota for mother's hugs probably filled and then some. "Even though Dad said no?" She wiped her eyes with the back of her hand.

"I'll talk to him. If you feel you need to see it, I think that's a reasonable request."

"That's okay, then. I don't need to go."

Marcy walked back to the counter and grabbed the lemon to finish squeezing the juice from it. "So you *don't* want to see the van?"

The teen shook her head. "Nah. No sense in flipping Dad out. You saying it's okay is enough." She walked out of the kitchen. "I'm going to call Miranda. Tell me when dinner's ready."

Marcy stood in the kitchen, lemon in hand, perplexed. She wasn't quite sure what had just happened there between her and Katie, but she had to think it was something good.

With a sigh, she walked to the refrigerator to retrieve the tuna steaks. As she dropped the brown wrapped package on the counter, she heard the front door open. "Marcy!"

It was Phoebe. And she was pissed. No one could miss the shriek of fury in her sister's voice.

"In the kitchen," Marcy called. She pulled the olive oil from the cabinet above the stove and calmly added a few splashes to the fresh lemon juice for the tuna.

"Just what do you think you're doing?" Phoebe demanded, marching into the kitchen on spiky high-heeled sandals. "Are you trying to make me the laughing stock of this town?"

Marcy put the cap back on the olive oil, taking her time in screwing it on. "What are you talking about, Phoebe?"

"I've been to the bank this afternoon." Phoebe halted in the center of the kitchen, both hands planted on her hips. Her hair was pulled back in a tight, high ponytail, and she was wearing too much makeup. In the bright fluorescent light of the kitchen, the pink lipstick and blue seventies-era eye shadow made her look harsh.

Marcy stirred the lemon and olive oil with a pastry brush and sprinkled in some fresh thyme. So Phoebe had found out. And just the way she had hoped she wouldn't.

Marcy should have known no one in this town could mind their own business. "No one at the bank should be discussing my personal business," she said, annoyed by the thought that an employee had mentioned her application for the business loan to anyone. She'd be calling the manager in the morning to complain.

"I went in to withdraw some cash, and that snotty Carla Perkins looks up at me and asks me if I intend to work for my sister in her new restaurant. Imagine my surprise."

"Phoebe, I—"

"*You're* buying a restaurant after what I've just been through!" She practically screamed the last words.

Marcy's first thought was to point out to her sister that the last seven months of her life hadn't been a picnic, either, but she kept that thought to herself. This conversation was about Phoebe. Of course. They always were.

Marcy calmly stirred her marinade for her tuna. "The loan may not even go through. I just didn't want to say anything to anyone until it was a sure thing."

"How are you getting the money to do this? Banks don't loan money to women on disability in the process of getting a divorce! Not that kind of money!"

"I resigned from my job. I haven't collected disability since I came home. As for the money, I'm using what Mom and Dad left me."

"You still have the money they left you?" She almost sneered the words.

"Yup. And then some. Jake and I never touched it. I invested it."

"Of course you did." Phoebe began to pace. "Little Goody Two-shoes invests her money," she mocked. "The evil twin blows it all on men and bad stock tips, and you, of course, come out ahead on the deal!"

Marcy turned around and leaned on the counter, crossing her arms over her chest. It used to be that when she

looked at her sister, her first thought was of how beautiful she was. How much she wanted to look like her.
What she would give to be her.

How could she have been so shallow? How could she
not have seen beyond the pretty face and size-eight jeans?
Marcy wouldn't want to be Phoebe now for anything.
She'd take her old body, her old face back, before she
would be this bitter, selfish, angry woman.

"I didn't mean to hurt you by keeping it from you,"
Marcy said quietly. "I just had to make some decisions
on my own without anyone else giving me advice."

"Hey, who am I to be giving advice?" Phoebe threw
up her hands. Reaching the wall, she turned on her high
heels and started back in the other direction. "God forbid I should say anything, be consulted, even though
I'm the one with experience running a restaurant. *I'm*
the one who owned one."

Marcy wanted to say *owned* was the operative word
there, as in past tense, but she bit her tongue. Phoebe
had owned a restaurant and it failed for several reasons,
the biggest one being that her sister had no head for
numbers, especially when it came to money. Marcy was
good with money, and she thought she had an eye for
what would make money; she didn't intend to make the
same mistakes her sister had.

"Does Jake know about this?" Phoebe demanded.

"Yes."

"And when were you going to tell me?" Phoebe's voice
quivered. "At the grand opening? Or were you going to
give me a ring ahead of time? Maybe offer me a position as your hostess?"

"Phoebe, I don't know what else to say, except that
I'm genuinely sorry you heard this way." She beseeched
with open hands. "I didn't do it to hurt you. It's just that
I need to get on with my life. I need to put the accident
behind me and start fresh."

Phoebe walked out of the kitchen without saying a word.

Marcy followed her. "Where are you going?"

"Out. I'll be back for my things."

Marcy ran her fingers through her hair in frustration. She wanted her sister out of her house, but not this way. With their parents deceased, they only had each other. On her deathbed, her mother had made Marcy promise she wouldn't let Phoebe separate herself from her sister, her only family ties left, no matter what. "Phoebe, please don't leave angry. You don't have to go now. Not tonight. Certainly not like this."

Phoebe jerked the front door open and walked out.

"Phebes, please—"

She swung the door hard, slamming it in her sister's face.

Marcy didn't go after her. Instead, she walked back into the kitchen and called Jake on the phone. "Hey."

"Hey," he said.

She could hear him smiling.

"I've got four tuna steaks and only three diners." She opened the package from the seafood market. "You want to join us for dinner?"

"Sure. When?" His tone was light, teasing.

"Now."

"Be right there."

Marcy hung up the phone and walked to the kitchen door that led to the family room to call the kids to get ready for dinner. She wasn't going to let this fight with Phoebe upset her or change her plans to open the restaurant if she could get the loan. She felt badly for Phoebe, but in time, her sister would get over her hurt feelings. Phoebe had lived her whole life ignoring how her actions would affect Marcy, always doing what she thought was best for herself. It was time Marcy tried doing the same.

*   *   *

The Bloodsucker sat in his car watching the sister tear off in her sports car. She'd stomped into the house mad, left even angrier. He wondered what the sisters had fought about. He'd never had a sister. A brother either. He suspected he had cousins, but Granny had never said and to ask . . . he just didn't.

The Bloodsucker's gaze settled on the house again, where he knew Marcy was inside. He knew he was taking a chance sitting here in her neighborhood before it was even dark and in his own car, at that. Anyone could see him. Recognize him.

But that was working to his advantage, wasn't it? Everyone *did* see him. He was right there under their noses and yet they didn't see him. Not for what he really was.

Granny said no one saw him because he was a no one. She said it was because he was an insignificant speck on the rear end of mankind. But the Bloodsucker knew that it wasn't true. They didn't see him because he was so clever. Because he was so smart.

He'd been smart with April, hadn't he? Lured her right in with the old lost-dog trick. He giggled. Even kids didn't fall for that one. Didn't April ever have a policeman talk to her class when she was little? Tell her how dangerous a ploy like that could be?

April had been fun for a while. She had cried like Patti. Sobbed. He had asked her if she found him attractive and she had said she did. But she could have been lying. Women did that. They lied. They cheated. They abandoned their children.

The Bloodsucker grabbed the hem of his T-shirt and twisted it.

Women thought they were so powerful. All this women's lib crap. They thought they held the power of the world in their hands because their thing was different than a man's thing. But they were wrong. That wasn't where the power was. It was all in the blood. And they could be depleted of their power. A smart man, a clever man, knew how to do that.

The Bloodsucker glanced at the nice Cape Cod house with its freshly cut lawn and pretty flower beds. If things had been different, if it hadn't been for that bitch, for the bitches in his life, this might have been his house. Marcy, ugly duckling turned swan, might have been his wife. Ben and Katie his children.

He forced himself to release his T-shirt. He smoothed out the wrinkles, taking a deep breath.

He was getting antsy. He knew he had to be careful. He couldn't be greedy. But he wanted Marcy. He *so* wanted her.

And no one suspected him. No one had even questioned him yet. How could they? Why would they? Claire Bear had no idea. She was running here and there, frantic. Holding meetings. Ordering reports. Looking beautiful and tough at the same time in that snappy uniform of hers. But she had no real evidence. He'd been too careful. He was too smart for the chief of police, and he was too smart for Marcy Edmond.

The Bloodsucker would prepare the place for her. The opportunity would present itself.

"Bad day?"

Phoebe glanced at the man sitting two barstools down, and then stared straight ahead again, sipping her rum and Coke. "You could say that."

He hesitated, then slid down to sit beside her. "Can I get you another drink?"

"It's a free country." She downed the last of the rum and Coke, tipping back the glass to let the cold liquid run down her throat. Numb her mind. It was her third and she was already drunk, but she'd have another anyway.

The man pointed to Phoebe's empty glass and his own beer bottle. "It's been a while," he said when the bartender brought them both fresh drinks.

She shrugged. She was chilly in the short skirt and bare top; the air conditioning was turned up too high. But she knew she looked good in it. Her suntan was just about at its peak. She did the tanning bed thing year round, but there was nothing like a real beach tan. "I've seen you around town."

"I mean us. It's been a long time since you and me . . ." He slid his hand across the polished bar to stroke her hand.

She glanced down at his hand touching hers. "Not working tonight?"

He shook his head. "Nah. Actually I was out today putting in some applications in some other places. Ocean City. Salisbury. Thinking about moving. My uncle's got a place in Ocean Pines he'll rent me cheap if I do the upkeep in the building for the other tenants."

"So you're getting out of Dodge, are you?" She took a sip of the fresh drink. Her head was really spinning. She wished she hadn't thrown up her lunch. She was hungry now. So hungry that her stomach felt as if something was gnawing inside her from the inside out. It was the same feeling she always got when she and Marcy argued. The ugly, fat bitch. She laughed aloud at herself, realizing she could no longer use those adjectives to describe her sister.

"Something funny?"

She turned to him, the gnawing inside her turning to a dull ache as she thought about what she wanted. What she needed. On the ride over to Calloway's tonight she had come up with a plan, and when she was sober again, she'd really think about it. She'd made a lot of mistakes in the past. A lot of the bad things that had happened to her were her own fault. She knew that. Bad choices in men. Her overspending. But she wasn't going to screw up this time. She was, at last, going to have what she wanted. What she had wanted since her college days— before she'd dropped out to go to Mexico with that guy whose name she couldn't remember right this minute.

"Just telling myself a joke." She smiled, giving him her full attention.

He leaned closer. "So you want to get out of here? Go to my place? I've got some prime California gold." He winked. "On the house."

She seriously considered his offer, for both the weed and the place to sleep for the night, for a moment. Billy wasn't bad in bed, especially if you were high and drunk, and his sheets were usually pretty clean. But the idea that his girlfriend Patti was dead gave her the willies. She thought about what she had read in the paper. They said she'd bled to death and though it looked like a suicide, it wasn't. What if he killed her? She'd certainly heard him threaten to do it on more than one occasion. Besides, it was early yet, surely something better off than Billy Trotter would come along.

"Nah," she said. "Thanks, but I think I'll just sit here for a while. I'll probably head home soon. I need to get my tail out on the pavement and find a job, too, before everyone gets the good ones for the summer."

He nodded, sliding off the bar stool. That was something she'd always liked about him. He was so easy-going. Whenever she blew him off, he didn't take it personally like some men did.

"So another time," he said, tipping his beer in her direction in a toast. "I'm a patient man."

She raised her glass and then took a long swallow. "Another time," she whispered.

When Marcy set out on her jog after dinner, she'd had no intention of heading this way. She had thought she would take her usual route into town, cut through the diner parking lot, and start for home. But she was feeling good this evening. She had passed that heavy feeling of fatigue in the first mile and now she was exhilarated. Taking the long way home would only add another mile, mile and a half to her run, and it would be a challenge.

She glanced up at the dark, ominous sky. If only the rain would hold off.

She hated running in the rain; the pavement was slippery and she didn't see well. Besides, she'd bought real running shoes and she didn't want to mess them up. The kid in the athletic store who had sold her the sneakers told her not to get them wet or they would never be the same. He told her that most real runners had a pair of shoes for dry days and another pair for wet. She didn't consider herself a real runner yet, but she'd keep that idea in the back of her head, just in case. Who knew what would happen over the next few months? Once, she had gotten out of breath walking to the end of the driveway too fast to meet the mailman. Now she was running five or six miles at a time.

Marcy took even, deep breaths, taking care how she placed one foot in front of the other on the dark pavement, her gaze fixed straight ahead. The sound of her pounding footsteps echoed in her head as she found the right rhythm.

Last night, dinner with Jake and the kids had been great. Like the old days. No, better. Marcy couldn't remember a time when she had felt so good about herself. Last night she and Jake and the kids had laughed, telling each other silly stories about things that had happened when they were little. They had talked about Katie's desire to go jet skiing, and they had decided they would go together as a family. Ben wanted to go camping, and they discussed planning a family trip in the fall. Marcy wasn't crazy about camping, but she loved the idea of doing anything as a family. Before the accident, they had all drifted apart, each going their own separate ways, caught up in their own troubles. At least, she knew she had been.

Marcy pressed her lips together, feeling a stab of pain in her chest that was almost physical. She had been so miserable last fall . . . and why? Was it the failure of the last diet? Jake working so much overtime and leaving her with the brunt of the housework and still holding down her full-time job? Or had it been Phoebe who had been in the throes of the restaurant foreclosure, her bankruptcy, and the divorce, and so needy?

When Marcy thought back, she remembered mostly looking at herself in the mirror. Wishing she were beautiful. Thin. Attractive to men other than her husband. What had been wrong with her? Had she really been that small-minded?

Tears stung her eyes because she knew she had been, and she wiped at them with the back of her hand.

What a terrible person she had been. Her sister's whole life had been falling apart—again. Her beautiful, thin sister's marriage was over after she caught the jerk cheating on her with a cocktail waitress. Her sister's beautiful condo on the beach had been foreclosed by the bank. She was childless and would remain so because of infertility, and Marcy had been standing in her bathroom crying because she had two healthy, bright children and a pooching baby belly.

Suddenly she was ashamed. Ashamed of herself and her insensitivity to Phoebe's plight. Sure, her sister had brought most of her troubles on herself, but that didn't mean they hurt any less, did it?

Phoebe hadn't come home last night, and Marcy hadn't heard from her all day. She hadn't even answered her cell phone. Marcy would try again when she got home. She'd apologize again for not telling her sister about her restaurant plans and then try to move on. She wasn't going to back down and allow Phoebe to stay, but she'd offer to help her any way she could.

Thunder rumbled overhead, and she glanced up at the sky. Dark clouds were moving in swiftly. There was a storm coming out of the west the way they usually did on the shore.

She glanced up ahead and spotted the fencing of the junkyard Katie had told her about. Well, she was already here, no need to turn back. Besides, at this point, it would be faster to run past the junk yard and take Webb's Road. It would lead her within a quarter of a mile of her neighborhood.

Reaching the gate, Marcy slowed to a fast walk. Panting, she approached the gate. There was some kind of plastic woven in and out of the links to prevent passersby from seeing inside. She pressed her hands to the warm metal and leaned forward to peer inside.

A dog's ferocious bark startled her, and she stumbled backward as it hurled itself into the other side of the gate.

"Oh!" Marcy cried, clutching her chest, her heart racing a mile a minute. Then she laughed at herself. Katie had warned her that the owners had a dog. It was just Ben's Fluffy, the three-headed mutt from the Harry Potter book. Nothing to scare her out of her panties.

She laughed again and began to walk down the country road, headed for the shortcut home. So maybe coming to see the van after closing, on foot, with an impending rainstorm, was a dumb idea. Tomorrow she'd call the junkyard and ask if she could come by and see the van. Didn't that make more sense?

Thunder rumbled overhead and Marcy caught a streak of lightning out of the corner of her eye. The humid, early evening air was changing rapidly as the impending summer storm grew closer. She could almost feel the electricity in the atmosphere as she pushed one foot in front of the other and fell into an easy jog.

The storm came faster than she had anticipated. It always did, didn't it? Especially if you were jogging too far from home in new running shoes or trying to get paper bags of groceries into the house. She felt the first drops of rain as she turned onto Webb Lane. Dense pine woods lined both sides of the narrow country road; she hadn't remembered it being so secluded. But it wasn't far to her road, not far at all.

Marcy felt strange all of a sudden. It was that now-familiar sense that someone was watching her. She glanced behind her. It wasn't yet sunset, but the storm had darkened the sky so that, in the woods, it was quite dark.

She thought of the silly slasher movies Katie and her friends liked to watch when they had slumber parties. Didn't Marcy always tell the girls that anyone stupid enough to walk into a dark kitchen, knowing there was a madman with a butcher knife in the house, deserved to die for sheer idiocy? Did that rule extend to thirty-something women jogging on country roads close to dark while their town was possibly being stalked by a serial killer?

Marcy spotted a stop sign ahead and heaved a sigh of relief, laughing at herself and her imagination. Her road was just ahead.

Then the rain began to fall in earnest, and she groaned. "Not my new sneakers."

At least it wasn't far to her house now. Maybe they could be saved. She ran harder, her feet making squishy, slapping sounds on the black pavement that was growing wetter by the moment.

A car approached from behind, and she glanced over her shoulder, hoping maybe it was someone from her neighborhood. The car didn't have its headlights on, though, so she couldn't see much. Maybe they could give her a ride. It whizzed past.

"Serves me right," she muttered. "Ben told me that the radar showed the storm coming in before sunset."

She heard another car behind her. Headlights appeared. Marcy glanced over her shoulder. The driver was slowing. It looked like it was Jerry from across the street. He had a blue car. The driver's-side window went down, and she slowed to a walk as he pulled up beside her.

"Need a ride?" Jerry called.

It wasn't Jerry.

The driver must have seen the surprised look on her face.

"It's Kevin," he said quickly. He pointed to his uniform shirt with his name embroidered on a patch. "Kevin James. I saw you in the hospital the other day. Didn't expect to get this lucky—you know, running into you again."

She couldn't resist a smile, despite the fact that the rain was now coming down even harder. He was flirting with her. She had to admit she was flattered, even if she wasn't interested. He was attractive. Clean cut. He had a nice smile.

"Come on. Don't you want a ride home?" he asked, looking ahead to watch for oncoming cars.

She glanced ahead. She thought she could make out the dark outlines of the houses in her neighborhood. It really wasn't much farther.

"I know, you don't know me very well. Taking rides from strangers and all that. Is there someone I can call for you, at least?" He held up his cell phone.

Thunder cracked overhead, and lightning streaked the sky, and Marcy involuntarily flinched. The storm was suddenly right overhead. The sky was opening up, the rain pouring in sheets.

"I just live up here in Seashore Acres." She ran in front of the car. If she got her sneakers off right away and put them over the central air vent in her bathroom, maybe they'd dry. She climbed into Kevin's car. "Thanks."

"You bet." He grinned, hooking his thumb in her direction. "Hey, buckle up. Sorry, but it's a rule in my car. I've seen too many auto accidents."

She laughed as he pulled away and reached for the seat belt. "You don't have to tell me." Her seat belt clicked. "The only time I think I've ever driven anywhere without it, I ended up in the drink." She tried to make light of it. "My son must have been furious with me. He's a bit of a safety nut. Seatbelts, regular fire drills at the house."

"That's Ben, right?"

She nodded, smiling hesitantly. How did he know Ben? "Yes."

"Met him at the elementary school. I went in to talk to his class—you know, career day or something like that." Kevin nodded. "Smart young man. He asked a lot of good questions."

"Thanks, he is bright." She chuckled. "That doesn't mean he can't be a handful sometimes. You have kids, Kevin?" Marcy had always found it hard to carry on casual conversations with people. She was beginning to realize now that it really wasn't hard at all. She just had to stop being so self-conscious, stop thinking about herself and what others thought of her, and instead think about the person she was talking to.

"Nah. Not lucky enough to find the right woman yet, I guess."

He flashed her a smile that was cute in a bashful kind of way. He was younger than she was, but not a lot younger.

She wondered if he'd be interested in going out with Phoebe. Maybe a nice guy like Kevin was just what her sister needed to make a fresh start. "Oh, I'm sure she's out there somewhere," she assured him. "You just have to keep looking."

"I don't know." He shook his head. "You can't imagine what it's like out there. Hard. You know what I mean?"

Marcy glanced up to see a car approaching. Then she realized he had passed the entrance to her development. "Oops. I'm sorry. I wasn't paying attention. The entrance is back there." She pointed.

"I'm sorry. I knew that." He touched the heel of his hand to his forehead. "I'll just turn around up in that driveway up ahead. I don't think I'd better back up in this rain."

The approaching car passed and Marcy realized it was one of the town police cars. As it went by, she saw Claire, who waved. Marcy lifted her hand to her ear, signaling for the police chief to call her. Claire nodded as she went by.

"Here we go." Kevin slowed, signaling, and turned into the driveway of a house just past the neighborhood. He backed out and pulled onto the road, going the way they had come.

Two minutes later, Marcy was pointing out her house. "Right there."

"The blue one?" He signaled to pull over.

"Nope, next one up. The beige Cape Cod."

"I see it. Nice house."

"Thanks." He pulled into the driveway, and she hopped out. "Thanks for the ride, Kevin."

"You bet. Any time."

He waved and she slammed the car door, making a run for the front porch. Maybe, just maybe, her new running shoes could still be saved.

Chapter Ten

After grabbing a quick shower and stuffing her running shoes with newspaper to keep their shape while they dried, Marcy settled on the couch in a T-shirt, no bra, and a pair of cotton gym shorts she'd borrowed from Katie's laundry basket. The lack of the bra made her feel liberated. It was amazing how little things could make you happy after you'd survived plummeting off a bridge into icy water and wrapping your face around a tree.

Marcy tried Phoebe's cell phone and when she got only her voice mail, she left a third message. "Phebes, it's Marcy. I'm worried about you. Would you call me, please?"

Then she called Jake. In a rare moment of sisterly love, Katie was playing a board game with Ben on her bedroom floor. Marcy knew it wouldn't last long, so if she wanted a moment of privacy, she'd have to grab it now.

"Hello."

She smiled at the sound of Jake's voice on the other end of the phone line and it delighted her that she could feel this way about him again, after all these years. "Hey," she said. "How was your day?"

"Good. Even better now that you've called. Just about makes my day perfect."

It was almost like they were dating again. Marcy knew it sounded silly, considering how long they had been married, but she was enjoying it. It was nice to be pursued, even if it was by the man she had been sleeping with for the last fifteen years.

"My day was good, too." She straightened the shade on the lamp beside the couch. "Except that I got caught in the rain on my run. I think I would have ruined my new shoes except that this EMT who actually worked on me at the scene of my accident gave me a lift home."

"This a male somebody?"

"As a matter of fact it was, Mr. Nosy." She tucked her bare feet beneath her and reached for her water bottle. "But you're safe. He was cute, but not my type. A little young for me."

"It's going to take me a while to get used to the idea of all these men hitting on my wife," he teased.

She laughed. "So did you get a chance to crunch those numbers for me? I know I should have done it myself, but my head is still flying in a million different directions. I was afraid I would make a mistake somewhere, and when you're talking this kind of money—"

"You don't want any mistakes," he finished for her. "Hang on a second. I brought the paperwork home with me. I've got your copy of the contract, too. Marv says it looks good."

For the next half an hour, Marcy and Jake talked about the restaurant. She wanted to borrow enough money to buy the property and get it off the ground, but no more than she absolutely had to. Jake had done a good job with the numbers, and she liked what she heard.

"This is do-able," she said, almost surprised by her conclusion.

"It is. I know you can make it work, Marcy."

She pressed her lips together, her chest suddenly tight with emotion. Jake didn't know what it meant to her to have his support. "You mean that, don't you?"

"Of course I do. I wouldn't say so if it wasn't what I really thought." He paused. "We're talking about my life, too, Marcy. At least I hope we are. And the kids'."

"I told you. I'm not touching their college money, no matter what." A sound coming from the direction of the back porch startled her, and she got up off the couch. "That's weird," she said.

"What?"

She had left the drapes open on the glass French doors, but standing in the light of the family room, she could barely see onto the screened porch. The storm was moving east to dissipate over the ocean and the sky was no longer illuminated with streaks of lightning. It was pitch black out.

"I just thought I heard something outside." She walked up to the French doors, seeing herself in the reflection. Nervously, she checked the lock. It was set.

"Probably just the wind, branches kicking up against the siding," Jake said, unconcerned. "I need to get out there and trim those azalea bushes before they take over the back yard."

"Yeah, probably just the azaleas." Marcy pressed her hand to the glass door, squinting. The security light hadn't come on. No one was there. She glanced at the fireplace along the same wall. It was gas now, but it had once been wood burning. Maybe a branch or something had fallen into the chimney. There was a cap on top, but it had blown loose before in a storm just like this one.

"You want to drop by tomorrow and pick up this packet with your proposal for the bank?" Jake asked. "You can get the contract, too."

She pulled the drapes closed across the doors. "You think I should do this if the bank gives the okay?"

"I think you should do it, Marcy. There aren't many people who get a second chance at life. You'd better use it."

Marcy returned to the couch. "It's just so scary. It's so much money that it doesn't seem real."

"Yeah, but done right, this kind of restaurant does great in this town. You invest in a little advertising, run some fun specials like you were talking about the other night, and people will be driving over from other towns. Summer traffic on Route One be damned."

"You really think so?"

A sound at the front door made Marcy bolt off the couch. "What the heck now?" she muttered as she turned around to look through the front foyer to the door.

"What is it?" Jake asked. Now he did sound concerned.

"Probably just something else brushing against the house." Marcy walked slowly around the couch, her gaze fixed on the white, paneled front door. She thought she had locked it, but she had been in such a hurry when she'd come in from running. She'd been wet and hadn't wanted to drip puddles on the floor.

"You want me to come over?" Jake asked.

"No. No, we're fine." She gave a little laugh as she stepped into the foyer, the tile cool on her bare feet. "I'm just rechecking the door. I seemed to get spooked so easily these days. You know me. I was never like that before."

She reached out to be sure the deadbolt was thrown, and just as she did, the doorknob turned. Marcy involuntarily made a sound as she jumped back.

"Marcy!" Jake called in her ear.

The door opened and Phoebe stepped in, soaking wet.

"Ah, hell, it's just Phoebe." Marcy pressed her hand to her pounding heart. "Phoebe's here, so I'll go. Talk to you tomorrow."

Marcy hung up the phone. "Look at you," she chastised, still trying to catch her breath from her scare. "You're soaked."

"I know. It's really raining hard out there. But I got us something to eat. Chinese and frozen yogurt." Phoebe held up two damp brown paper bags. The aroma of hot Szechwan chicken and steamed rice rose from one of the bags.

Marcy took them from Phoebe. "We ate earlier."

"So eat a little more." She smacked Marcy on her rump as she passed her, headed up the stairs. "Let me change and I'll meet you in the kitchen." She ran up the steps calling down. "Chopsticks are in the drawer next to the wooden spoons."

Marcy carried the bags of food into the kitchen. This was always the way it was with Phoebe. A big blowup, she'd take off, and then eventually she would show up again after a few hours, a few days, sometimes even a few weeks. When they were juniors in college, Phoebe had disappeared for three months. Marcy and their parents never heard a word from her until she called collect from Guadalajara saying she needed to have money and a plane ticket wired to her so she could get home.

Marcy flipped the overhead light on in the kitchen and dropped the bag of Chinese food on the counter. She pulled two pints of frozen yogurt from the other bag and stuck them in the freezer. By the time she had unloaded the clean dishes from the dishwasher and put them away, Phoebe had appeared in shorts and one of Marcy's new T-shirts, her hair wrapped up in a turban on her head. Marcy hadn't even taken the price tags off the shirt, but she didn't say anything. At least she knew Phoebe wasn't in Mexico.

"Beer?" Phoebe asked.

"Nah."

Phoebe opened the refrigerator and pulled out two bottles. "Come on, it will hit the spot on a hot, humid summer night. It's light beer, for cryin' out loud."

Marcy laughed. "Oh, all right. Just one." She grabbed the basket of paper plates off the counter and carried them to the kitchen table.

Phoebe took the chair across from her and began to dig out the little boxes from the brown paper bag. She pulled a plate from the basket. "You're having some, aren't you?"

Marcy twisted the cap off her beer and took a sip. Phoebe was right; it did hit the spot. "You go ahead. I think I'm saving myself for the Cherry Garcia frozen yogurt calling my name from the freezer."

Phoebe dumped half the box of rice onto her plate and then piled the chicken and Chinese vegetables on top. Marcy was still fascinated that her sister could eat so much and stay thin. Like their mother had always said, different metabolism.

Marcy watched Phoebe eat a couple mouthfuls and wash it down with the beer. "Listen, Phebes, about the other night—"

"Say no more." Phoebe held up her chopsticks. "I'm the one who should be apologizing. It was silly of me to get all upset about you wanting to open a restaurant. I should be happy for you." She stuck a piece of chicken in her mouth. "I *am* happy for you."

"Phoebe, it was insensitive of me. After all you've been going through—"

"I don't want to hear it—you just took me by surprise is all," she said with her mouth full, getting up out of her chair. "End of discussion. You want another beer?"

"No." Marcy took a sip from the brown bottle in her hand, still more than half full.

"So tell me about your place." Phoebe slipped back into her chair with another bottle of beer in her hand. "You're thinking a French Bistro? That's such a great idea. We don't have anything like that around here."

Marcy and Phoebe sat up until late talking about the restaurant. Ben and Katie said good night and went to bed, and the sisters talked for another hour. Finally, Marcy gave in.

"I have to go to bed, Phebes," she said, beginning to collect the beer bottles to place in Ben's recycling container in the broom closet. "I'm beat."

"I'm right behind you. Long day, but I got a job and a lead on a one-bedroom apartment."

"That's wonderful!" Marcy backed out of the closet, genuinely thrilled for her sister. "Where?"

"The job is an assistant manager's position at The Volcano. You know, that trendy place in Rehoboth."

Marcy nodded. "And the apartment?"

"Over some business." She gave a wave. "It's nothing great, but it will work until I get my feet back on the ground."

"Of course it will." Marcy was so excited by the idea of getting her house back, her life back, that she could barely keep from doing a dance across the kitchen floor.

"I'll be upstairs in a minute." Phoebe began to gather her paper plate and utensils and the littering of little white boxes across the kitchen table. "I'm just going to clean up and take the trash out to the dumpster. You know how Chinese can stink up the kitchen by morning."

"All right." Marcy paused in the doorway. "So I'll see you in the morning?"

"You bet." Phoebe grinned and leaned over to remove the lid from the trash can.

Upstairs, Marcy checked on Ben and Katie. They were both asleep. She went into her bathroom and brushed her teeth. Only then did she realize she'd forgotten her glass of ice water she liked to keep beside her bed at night to sip if she got thirsty.

Marcy went back downstairs. The lights were out in the kitchen, but the hall light was still on. She wasn't sure if Phoebe was still up or not, but as she passed the powder room, she heard a sound. She halted at the door.

It sounded like her sister was throwing up. She hesitated, then called out. "Phebes?" She rapped on the door lightly with her knuckles. "You okay?" She heard the toilet flush.

"I'm fine," Phoebe called cheerfully. The faucet in the sink came on.

Marcy stared at the closed door. She knew what she had heard. "You sure?"

"Yeah." Phoebe walked out of the bathroom, wiping her mouth with a hand towel. "You were smart not to have the Chinese. I think I must have accidentally ordered the hot Szechwan dog instead of the chicken." She headed for the stairs. "'Night."

"Good night," Marcy called after her.

In the kitchen, she filled a glass with ice and waited as the automatic dispenser poured cold water in a stream into the glass. Phoebe had acted strangely tonight. Even stranger than she usually did after they had had a fight. Manic almost.

Marcy flipped off the kitchen light and padded barefoot down the hall. Remembering the sounds she had heard on the back porch earlier, she decided to leave the hall light on. Climbing the stairs, she wondered if she was just being overly sensitive with Phoebe. After all, the two of them had been through hundreds of battles, and whenever her sister needed something from her, like now, she did come back with her arms full of gifts and just the right words. And honestly, did it matter? What was important was that Phoebe had landed a job and would be out of Marcy's house soon.

Maybe then she'd be ready to talk to Jake about moving back in.

The following Friday night, Marcy stood in the front foyer with Jake. He was waiting for Ben and Katie to grab sweatshirts. They were going out to a movie with their Dad, and Marcy had insisted they go back upstairs for something warm. The air-conditioning was always turned up too high in the theaters in the summer.

"You sure you don't want to come with us?" Jake asked, sliding his arm casually around her waist.

His touch made her feel good. Sexy, not just physically, but in her head. "Nah, you guys go have fun. Since it looks like this loan for the restaurant really is going to go through, I need to present the bank with our personal financial records. Tonight I plan to balance our checkbook and tally the money market and savings accounts." She gave him a playful push on his shoulder. "Have you looked at our checkbook lately? You ought to be ashamed of yourself, a CPA and your checking account hasn't been balanced since Thanksgiving?"

He grinned, almost boyishly. "I am ashamed. I guess while you were in the hospital, it just wasn't a priority." He rested his other hand on her waist and faced her. "You were my priority, Marcy. Fat, skinny, scarred, or stunningly beautiful."

He reached out to caress her cheek, and she laid her hand over his. "It's nice to hear you say that."

"I mean it," he whispered, his dark eyes searching hers.

She slid his hand to her lips and kissed it. "Phoebe is moving out in the next couple of days. Once she's gone, I . . ." She swallowed the lump in her throat, and with it, her fear. "I think we should talk about you moving back in."

"I can be packed in an hour." His tone was light, teasing, but he got his point across. He wanted to come back to her bed.

"Now I'm not talking about the way we were," she said. "I think we could probably both use some couples counseling, but—"

"But we're not ready to give up on our marriage yet," he finished for her.

Smiling, she shook her head, and he lowered his mouth to hers.

"Mom!" Ben shrieked as Jake brushed his lips against Marcy's. "Katie's teasing me. She says she's going to hide my telescoping fire escape ladder again!"

Ben bounded down the stairs, and Marcy pulled out of Jake's arms. She felt as if she and Jake needed to take this slowly, and the kids were already confused. She didn't want to make things worse.

"Tattletale!" Katie accused her brother, chasing after him.

Marcy couldn't resist a smile. At thirteen, her daughter was so mature in so many ways; the responsibility she was taking with her baby-sitting job, starting her period, her interest in boys beyond sticking her tongue out at them. But in some ways, Katie was still just a little girl, and Marcy intended to savor these last fragments of her daughter's childhood.

"Katie," Marcy called up the stairs as Ben hit the bottom step and hurled himself into his father's arms.

"Dad!"

"What have I said about tormenting your little brother?" Marcy asked patiently.

"You said 'don't'." Katie offered a nearly perfect teenage smirk. "But it's just so easy."

Ben stuck his tongue out at his sister as Jake lowered his feet to the ground. Katie stuck her tongue out at him.

"Enough already, you two," Jake said and pointed to the door. "Get your stuff and get in the car if we're going. The movie starts at seven-thirty, but we need to get into line to get our tickets early."

"Bye, Mom." Ben bounced out the door, dragging his gray sweatshirt behind him. "See you in the morning."

"Later, Mom."

Jake caught the front door with his hand as Katie disappeared out the door carrying her own and her brother's overnight bags. "You sure you want to stay home alone tonight?"

"Phoebe is supposed to be by. Apparently she really did get the job and the apartment. She called earlier and asked me if I had any boxes to pack her stuff."

"I can come by sometime this weekend and haul the boxes out of here, if she wants."

"That's nice of you." Marcy ran her palm over his chest. "But I'm afraid to make the offer. I don't want to do anything to delay this move." She brushed her hair back over the crown of her head. "I know she was really great to you and the kids while I was sick, but it's time she went back to leading her own life."

"I know. You're right." Jake leaned on the doorknob. "I don't know what's going on with her, anyway. She's been acting pretty strangely."

"You think so, too?"

He shrugged. "I don't know. Maybe it's my imagination or maybe she's just pissed that we took the bank card back and told her she needed to start supporting herself again."

"You're probably right. She—"

"Dad! You coming?" Ben hollered from outside. "We're not going to get the tickets if we don't hurry!"

Jake looked at Marcy again.

"It's all right," she said. "Go. We can talk later."

"We'll meet you at the ballpark in the morning. Ben plays at nine-thirty. Enjoy your evening." He leaned to offer a good-bye kiss, and she accepted.

His kiss made her warm to the tips of her bare toes. "See you later."

As Marcy walked into the family room, she heard Jake back out of the driveway and checked her watch. She had a good five hours to herself before bedtime; even with Phoebe stopping by, she could get a lot accomplished. Passing through the room, she picked up Ben's discarded handheld video game, an empty glass, and a women's fashion and health magazine Phoebe or Katie had left on the coffee table. She dropped the game in the basket at the edge of the couch and, balancing the glass, turned the pages of the magazine to close it so she could add it to the magazine rack. As she flipped the pages, a heading caught her eyes.

Vomiting To Be Thin: An Epidemic

The words struck something in Marcy, and she lowered the glass to the coffee table to glance at the article. There were photos of thin, beautiful women and colored boxes with their stories. The article was about bulimia and young women who wanted so badly to be thin that they were willing to make themselves vomit regularly in order to control their intake of calories.

Reading the words, Marcy thought of Phoebe. The women in the article sounded so much like her sister that it scared her. Marcy eased onto the edge of the couch, horrified by her sudden realization. She had always known what bulimia was, of course, but it had never occurred to her that her sister would do such a thing. Even considering how overweight Marcy had always been and how badly she had wanted to lose weight, she had never been able to fathom anyone actually controlling her weight this way.

Marcy slowly closed the magazine, staring without seeing as she went over in her mind how many clues she had seen of this condition with Phoebe. The fact that she was always thin, despite how much she ate, the fact that she had terrible teeth, unlike Marcy's healthy ones and had had to have them all veneered a few years back. And to actually catch Phoebe throwing up after a big meal . . .

Marcy got up off the couch, grabbed the dirty glass, and dropped the magazine into the rack as she passed it on her way to the kitchen. Obviously she needed to talk to Phoebe about this, but she knew she'd have to be careful how she handled it.

In the kitchen, she put the glass in the sink and then went back into the family room where the computer sat on a desk in a corner on the far side of the room. She already had all her bank statements and the checkbook register out. She slipped into the chair and clicked the mouse, leading her into the accounting program she used. When Phoebe came to pack, she decided, she'd feel her out. She doubted her sister would admit easily to such a disease, but if it was true, Marcy would do whatever she needed to do to help Phoebe get better. After all, no matter what, they were still sisters and they still loved each other, right?

In forty-five minutes, Marcy was on her feet, pacing the family room. She was hoping she was mistaken, but she knew she wasn't. Within minutes of beginning to balance her household checking account and review her money market and savings accounts, she realized money was missing. A chunk of it. The accounts were a mess. Money had been moved around, making it harder to do the math, but there was definitely money missing, to the tune of at least ten thousand dollars.

How could that have happened? Could Jake really have spent that much above and beyond their household expenses in the months she had been in the hospital?

She found it unlikely. If he had spent savings, he would have told her. Especially since it looked like some of the kids' college funds had been dipped into, as well. Only her own investment account with a stock brokerage company, where she kept her inheritance, appeared not to have been disturbed. It was the only account that didn't have Jake's name on it.

The first logical conclusion was that her husband had taken the money for some reason or another, but she didn't think that was true. Obviously she would have to talk to him, but she had a sick feeling in the pit of her stomach that he wasn't going to know what she was talking about. She just knew he hadn't removed it. The money had been transferred too haphazardly, in odd increments; it just wasn't like him to do anything that way, especially when dealing with finances.

She thought of the bank card she had confiscated from Phoebe not too long ago. With that card, the bank account numbers, and a couple of passwords, she would have had access to all the accounts Marcy and Jake shared.

Marcy felt like she was going to be sick. She always used easy, stupid passwords like her first pet's name, her mother's maiden name—all things Phoebe would have known.

Could her sister really have been stealing from her?

There was a sound at the front door, a key turning the lock, and Phoebe appeared in the doorway, as if on cue, with an armful of cardboard boxes. "Marcy!" she hollered. "You here? I could use a little help."

Marcy heard boxes hit the floor. She felt as if her stomach was in her throat. Her first impulse was to confront Phoebe and just ask her if she knew anything about the missing money.

But Marcy knew Phoebe. If she did know anything about it, she wouldn't say so. She certainly would never come out and admit to any wrongdoing. It just wasn't in her, never had been. Marcy remembered a time when she had been ten or eleven. It had been summer, and a neighbor had been keeping an eye on them while their parents were at work. Their mother had made a cake and left it on the counter, instructing her daughters not to eat any.

The sisters hadn't set out to eat the cake. First they just admired it. Then, the temptation too great, they had intended to just have a taste of the frosting. One lick off their fingertips. But it had been so good that they had kept returning for snitches of the cake. By the time their mother arrived home from work, the confection was half eaten. Their mother had made it to take to a sick friend, and she was furious. Marcy had crumbled almost immediately, confessing her sin and offering to make another cake and pay for the ingredients out of her own allowance. But Phoebe had made no such confession, not even when their mother asked her if she had eaten the cake, too. She had lied, saying no with the sweetest, most innocent, look on her face. Later, Marcy had asked Phoebe why she had let her take the fall alone for eating the cake. Phoebe's reply had been simple. Marcy was already being punished; there was no need for both of them to get into trouble. She had been completely without remorse. The memory was silly, insignificant, but for some reason it had stayed with Marcy all these years.

Marcy watched her sister in the foyer, trying to gather the boxes she'd dropped. She'd get no confession out of Phoebe. If Marcy wanted to confront her sister, she would have to have her facts straight first. She would have to talk to Jake and then to the bank. As she walked around the couch, toward the foyer, she decided she would say nothing yet, not even if Phoebe noticed she was balancing her accounts. She'd let Phoebe pack her stuff and move out; if she had stolen the money, it would be easier to do what had to be done with her sister out of the house anyway.

Marcy picked up a cardboard box that had slid across the tile floor and come to rest on the edge of the family room carpet. "You want me to take this upstairs to your bedroom?"

Phoebe dropped her purse from her shoulder on the small table in the foyer where she'd already set a bottle of wine. "Nah. Leave it. I'm going to leave a lot of my stuff in your basement for now, but I'll have to get a few things from down there. That looks sturdy enough to hold some kitchen stuff."

"You want me to take it downstairs? If you tell me what you need from the boxes in the basement, I might be able to get it for you."

"No!" Phoebe snapped. Then she gave a little laugh. "Everything's a mess down there, and I know that makes you crazy. I can do it. I know what I'm looking for. I don't really need any help, except maybe to get this stuff in my car."

Marcy lowered the box to the floor, studying her sister's face. She looked pale, despite her summer tan, and very thin. Thinner than she had been when Marcy was released from the hospital. Looking at her now, she could see that it was very possible Phoebe was bulimic, and she wondered how she could have missed it.

Bulimic and a thief? Marcy wanted to tell herself that Phoebe had been so clever to hide both from her, but the truth was, Marcy knew she was at least partially to blame. She'd spent so much of her life thinking about herself, stressing over her own life, that she might not have noticed if Phoebe had sprouted wings.

"You eat?" Marcy asked Phoebe. "I was just getting ready to pop a frozen dinner in the microwave."

"I'm stuffed from a late lunch." Phoebe pressed her hand to her flat belly. "But I brought wine." She lifted the bottle and set it on the table again. "I thought we could celebrate my getting the job."

Marcy didn't really feel like celebrating at this moment, but she didn't want her sister to suspect anything was wrong. "Okay, great," she managed, grabbing the bottle of Chardonnay. It was expensive. Far too expensive for a woman out of work living with her sister . . . unless maybe she was helping herself to her sister's bank accounts.

"Just let me fill up these first couple of boxes, and I'll join you." Phoebe grabbed two boxes and passed Marcy in the foyer. She opened the door under the staircase that led to the basement and stepped down, pulling the door behind her. "I won't be long."

In the kitchen, Marcy chose a light meal from the freezer and popped it in the microwave. She wasn't really hungry, but she would try to eat anyway because she knew she needed to.

Realizing that she had left all of her bank statements out on the desk in the family room, she went in and gathered the papers and stuffed them in a small plastic file box. She exited the money management program on the computer and pushed the file box under the desk. She could hear noises directly below as Phoebe banged around in the basement. What on earth was she doing in that end of the basement? She must have stuff everywhere, which was typical. It would never have occurred to Phoebe that her sister might want to use her own basement for storage.

Marcy returned to the kitchen, chastising herself for being so mean. What if she was wrong about Phoebe? What if she was just jumping to foolish conclusions?

She didn't know what to think. Phoebe seemed happy tonight. Excited about moving.

She opened the door of the microwave that she had heard beep from the other room and peeled the plastic back off her dinner. She stirred it with her fork and punched the buttons to start the microwave again. She leaned against the counter, arms crossed over her chest.

Was it silly to think that Phoebe could have believed she could get away with stealing that much money from her? Even if she thought Marcy was going to die, didn't she realize that eventually Jake would have seen there was money missing from the accounts? Even if she thought Jake wouldn't catch on, wouldn't she have moved out, maybe even tried to run, when Marcy miraculously awoke from the coma?

It just didn't make sense to steal that much money and then hang around. Maybe Phoebe hadn't really meant to steal it. Maybe she saw it as *borrowing* the money and had intended to pay it back just as soon as she got on her feet again.

The microwave beeped again.

Marcy walked into the foyer and opened the basement door. Cool, damp air hit her in the face. She heard noise, then nothing. "You sure you don't want any help?" she called down.

"Be right up," Phoebe hollered cheerfully.

Marcy closed the door again and returned to the kitchen to check her dinner.

The Bloodsucker stood in Marcy's backyard in the cover of some bushes, watching her through the kitchen window as she put her dinner in the microwave. He almost felt sorry for her, alone in the house, eating a frozen meal. He hated eating alone. Of course, he didn't hate it as much as he had hated eating with Granny.

He wondered what Marcy would do if he walked up to the house, rang the doorbell, and offered to join her so she wouldn't have to eat alone. They could sit at the table and eat and laugh. He could tell her how his day went at work, and she could tell him all about the new restaurant she was opening. Of course, she hadn't mentioned it to him directly, but he knew about it anyway. Small towns were like that. Everyone knew everyone's business. It was why Granny had insisted they always keep to themselves, why he had never had any friends growing up.

The Bloodsucker studied the back yard for a moment, trying to figure out how he could get closer. He wanted to see Marcy better. Wanted to watch her as she ate, lifting her fork to those lovely lips the plastic surgeon had created.

He had been closer to her earlier, when she'd been in the family room, so close that he could have reached out and touched her, felt her pulse, her blood rushing through her veins, had it not been for the glass doors. But then a neighbor had stepped out on his patio to start his grill, and the Bloodsucker had been forced to retreat to the bushes along the woods line. By the time he got situated, Marcy had closed the curtains on the French doors and he couldn't see her anymore.

He was disappointed, and yet he realized it was probably a good thing. Being so close to her again had made him want to reach through that glass and take her, and he knew that was stupid. And the Bloodsucker wasn't stupid, no matter what Granny said. Snatching a woman from her home or from her car would be too risky because it was too easy to accidentally leave evidence. He wasn't stupid; he watched *CSI* on TV like everyone else. Even wearing gloves and a hat, he knew that he could leave something behind in a house or in a car. Fibers from his clothes could be traced, even DNA tested if he left behind a hair with the follicle still attached. No, no matter how badly he wanted Marcy, he knew he shouldn't take her from her home.

Hiding in the bushes, the Bloodsucker had been just about ready to return to his car when he had gotten lucky. Marcy had appeared in the kitchen to make her lonely dinner.

He could see her now, leaning against the kitchen cabinet in her shorts and T-shirt, her blond hair tousled from her shower after she ran. He loved to watch her run. He loved to think about her blood coursing through her veins, pumped by her heart. Marcy was strong. She was powerful. How else would she have survived all that had happened to her?

He had to have that strength. He just knew it was meant for him.

The Bloodsucker stepped out of the lilac bushes. Despite the dangers, he couldn't help himself. He had to get closer.

Chapter Eleven

The microwave beeped, jolting Marcy out of her daze, and she slid the hot plastic tray onto a plate, grabbed a fork and a napkin, and carried them to the kitchen table. Behind her, she heard Phoebe coming through the basement door.

"It's amazing how much stuff a person accumulates, isn't it?" she called from the foyer.

Marcy set her dinner and the napkins on the table and went back for wine glasses, the bottle of wine, and a corkscrew. She could hear her sister lowering the boxes to the floor and stacking them.

"I want you to come over to my place for dinner just as soon as I get settled in," Phoebe continued. "I know it's going to get lonely for you here with Jake gone."

It was on the tip of Marcy's tongue to tell her sister that she was going to ask Jake to move back in, but she resisted. Considering her suspicions, she didn't exactly feel as if she wanted to confide in Phoebe right now.

"Wouldn't that be fun?" Phoebe appeared in the kitchen doorway.

"Um, yes. Sure, that would be great." Marcy set the

glasses down and handed her sister the bottle and cork-screw. "You do the honors. My dinner's getting cold."

Phoebe glanced over Marcy's shoulder as Marcy slid into the kitchen chair. "Doesn't look too appetizing. Want to go sit in the living room, enjoy our wine?"

"Here's fine. Actually, it's pretty good, and I feel like I need the portion control." Marcy took a bite of chicken. All these years she had thought herself weak because she had been unable to control what and how much she ate. Because she had seen herself as some kind of pig compared to Phoebe. Thinking now that her sister might have been making herself vomit all these years made her sad. Sad for Phoebe. Sad for herself and all the time she wasted worrying about such things.

The cork popped, and Phoebe poured the wine into the glasses.

"Easy there." Marcy watched her sister fill her glass to the rim. "What are you trying to do, get me drunk?"

Phoebe lifted her glass in toast. "Maybe not drunk, but a little silly wouldn't do you any harm." She tipped her glass to touch Marcy's. "Cheers."

"To your new job," Marcy said, trying to sound enthusiastic.

"To my new life."

As Marcy raised her glass to her lips, movement at the window caught her eye. Was it her imagination or had she just seen a man looking in her window? She froze. "Phebes?"

"Good, isn't it?"

"Phoebe, listen to me." Marcy tipped her glass to her lips, but didn't drink. "Don't make it obvious, but I want you to glance at the kitchen window. I think there's someone there."

"Well, what the hell are they doing at the window?" Phoebe strode right toward it. "Hell, they shouldn't be standing outside. Tell them to come in and join the party!"

"Phoebe, don't!" Marcy dropped her glass on the table, spilling wine, and darted across the kitchen. As Phoebe reached the window, Marcy grabbed the string on the blind and gave it a tug. She released it, and the miniblinds fell over the glass.

Phoebe planted her hand on her hip, annoyed. "I didn't see anyone."

Marcy could feel her heart pounding in her chest. Was she just being paranoid again? A man outside her window? The other night she had thought someone was on the porch. How ridiculous was that?

No. Marcy set her jaw. She didn't care how ridiculous it sounded, she knew what she saw, and it was a man outside her window. "Make sure the windows are all closed and locked," she said, running across the kitchen.

"Marcy! What are you doing?"

Marcy grabbed the phone off the counter as she raced for the front door. She turned the deadbolt as she punched in 911.

"911," a woman's voice announced. "What is your emergency, please?"

"This is Marcy Edmond at 223 Seahorse Drive in Albany Beach—"

"Marcy!" Phoebe cried, trying to grab the phone from her. "What are you doing?"

"I think there's a man outside my house, looking in my windows," Marcy said into the phone.

"All right, ma'am, we'll send out a patrol car. Are your doors locked?"

Marcy leaned against the front door, gripping the phone. She took a deep breath. "Yes, they are."

"And are you alone, ma'am?" the 911 operator asked.

"No, my sister is here with me." Marcy glanced at Phoebe, who was rolling her eyes. She was obviously angry, but Marcy didn't care. She saw what she saw.

"Just stay inside the house, Mrs. Edmond, and the

police will be there in a few minutes. A call has already gone in to the Albany Beach police department dispatch."

"Thank you." Marcy let out a deep breath as she walked into the dark living room.

"Do you feel comfortable enough to disconnect, ma'am, or would you like to remain on the line until the police arrive?"

"You can hang up." She knelt on the couch and closed the blinds behind it. "I'll be fine. Thank you." She hung up and climbed off the couch.

"What do you think you're doing?" Phoebe exploded. "Calling the damned police because you think you see something outside?"

"Not *something*. A man." She shook the phone at Phoebe. "I saw a man looking in the kitchen window at us."

"I cannot believe you're wasting the police's time with something like this." Disgusted, Phoebe walked back into the kitchen to retrieve her glass of wine. "You know, people are going to start to talk. First this restaurant escapade; now you're seeing men in windows—"

"Restaurant escapade?" Marcy demanded. Once upon a time, she would have dropped her tail between her legs and run from such criticism, but no longer. She took a step toward Phoebe. "This is not an *escapade*. I'm about to sink my life's savings into this business, and let me tell you—"

"All right, all right." Phoebe held up her hands in surrender. "I'm sorry."

Marcy glared.

"I said I'm sorry," Phoebe repeated more gently, making eye contact for just a second. "I *am*, sis. I'm just a little sensitive about the subject, that's all."

Marcy exhaled slowly. "Okay." She pressed her lips together. "I'm sorry, too. I didn't mean to jump on you." She pointed toward the kitchen window covered now by the shade. "But I'm telling you, I saw someone in that window. And not a neighbor's kid, either. Someone who didn't belong there."

"Well, the police will be here now." Phoebe took a drink of her wine. "They can walk around the yard and make sure whoever it is, is gone."

A couple of minutes later, the doorbell rang and Marcy hurried to the foyer. She peered through the small, round viewer to see Claire standing at the door in a pool of light given off by the lamps on either side of the door.

"Claire?" Marcy flipped the deadbolt and pulled the door open. Behind Claire's patrol car in the driveway, she saw a second pull in.

Claire glanced over her shoulder. "McCormick. He must have heard the call go out over the radio." She looked back to Marcy. "You okay?"

Marcy nodded. "But I saw a man looking in the kitchen window. Phoebe and I were having something to eat, and I looked up, and there he was."

Claire's gaze moved past Marcy to the moving boxes, to Phoebe in the family room doorway. Phoebe was still holding her glass of wine.

"Having a little celebration, ladies?"

Marcy glanced over her shoulder, caught Claire's meaning, and gave a little laugh. "No. Well, yes. Phoebe just got a new job, but I'd had only one sip of wine, I swear it, when I saw the guy."

Patrolman McCormick swaggered up the front walk, flashing a flashlight beam over the lawn. "Got us a Peeping Tom, have we?" He reached the porch and spotted the twin sisters. He nodded. "Ladies."

"I just arrived," Claire said. "Check the perimeter and the neighbors on both sides. See if they saw anything. You know how it is, a lot of times people don't call until after the guy has cased the place, and then robbed it while they're gone. Later the victims remember the guy standing in the flower bed staring in the window a few days back."

"Will do." McCormick went back down the steps, stepped over a bed of pansies, and headed around the front of the house.

"That what you think it was?" Marcy asked. "Someone looking to rob us?"

"Hard to say. You didn't recognize the guy?"

Marcy shook her head. "But I really didn't get a good look at him. He was there and then he wasn't."

"Well"—Claire clicked on the Maglight flashlight in her hand—"I'm going to check around back, too. Would you mind turning on any lights you have on the outside of the house?"

"There are motion detectors. They should come right on. Which is strange, because they didn't."

Claire nodded. "Which window?"

"The kitchen on the back of the house. I'll lift the blind so you can see which one it is."

"Stay inside." Claire adjusted her uniform hat. "Lock the door, and I'll come back and let you know if I found anything."

"Thanks." Marcy offered a quick smile and backed into the foyer, closing the door and turning the dead bolt as directed.

"Whoever it was, if it was anyone, is going to be long gone by now," Phoebe said with a bored sigh.

"You're probably right." Marcy walked into the kitchen and opened the kitchen shade. "But I'll feel better knowing there's no one out there. Remember, you're going to your new place and the kids are gone. I'll be here alone all night."

Phoebe lifted her shoulder. "Whatever. I guess I'll get the rest of my stuff together while the cops do their thing."

Phoebe left the room, and Marcy picked up her dinner to reheat it. Halfway across the kitchen, she realized she wasn't hungry anymore. She dropped it in the trash can, rinsed off her fork, and threw it in the dishwasher. By the time she had added a load of dirty whites to the washing machine in the laundry room off the kitchen, the doorbell was ringing.

"Nobody there, huh?" Marcy asked, opening the door to Claire again.

"No. And Patrolman First Class McCormick said he didn't see any footprints under the window, but that doesn't mean someone wasn't there." Claire slipped her flashlight through a loop on her belt.

"And my neighbors didn't see anything either?"

"No one home on the right."

"The Satchels. That's right." Marcy clicked her fingers. "They went to see her mother in North Carolina."

"I spoke to John Coffey on your other side." She gestured with her thumb. "Says he and his wife were watching a movie, but they hadn't noticed anything unusual. What we did find is that your motion detectors don't seem to be coming on. Obviously, I don't want you outside tonight changing light bulbs on a ladder in the dark, but you need to look into that tomorrow."

Marcy nodded, fighting the urge to feel foolish. "I didn't mean to waste your time, Claire. I know you've got a lot going on."

"Which is why I'm glad you called." Claire met Marcy's gaze. "You know," she said softly, "we've got two dead women in this town. I don't want to scare you, but we have very few clues other than that." She hesitated. "Right now, the only connection seems to be that they were both beautiful, blond-haired, and blue-eyed."

Marcy lifted her hand to her cheek in shock as she realized what Claire meant. Marcy vaguely knew that both women had been young and blond, but eye color had not been mentioned. She had seen photos of both victims in various papers, but she hadn't made the connection that they were both beautiful until Claire said it. "You think the same man killed both of them? Killed them because of what they looked like?"

"I honestly don't know, Marcy. We're still investigating. Waiting for some reports from various labs on trace evidence, which there's very little of. It's just something to keep in mind. I want you to be safe."

Marcy nodded. "I am. I'm always careful." She thought about her run to the junkyard the other night. "I'll be more careful," she amended.

"Well, everything looks okay here, but I'll send a patrol car around a couple of times tonight just to be sure. You call if you see anything. Don't feel like you're bothering us; it's what we're here for."

"Thanks." Marcy held the door open. "And when things slow down for you, we'll have lunch?"

"You bet." Claire started down the driveway. Patrolman McCormick had already pulled out. She turned back. "I will. I mean it."

Marcy waved and stepped into the foyer, closing the door behind her. Then, for a moment, she leaned against it, thinking about what Claire had said. The man who had killed Patti and the tourist might have targeted them for their appearance. Marcy's whole life, she had wished more than anything else that she could be beautiful. What Patti and the other woman's family wouldn't do now to have their loved ones back, overweight and plain.

"They gone?" Phoebe stepped into the foyer from the basement, a big box in her arms to add to several more that she had already stacked there.

"Yup. There's no one there."

Phoebe gave her sister an *I told you so* look and walked into the kitchen. "I'll get the wine," she called. "Meet you in the family room."

Marcy settled on the chair by the fireplace, her favorite reading chair, and glanced at the book she'd left on the table beside it. Maybe when Phoebe left, she would just curl up here and read and leave the checkbooks and accounting until tomorrow when she and Jake could go over them together.

"Here you go." Phoebe pushed the wineglass into Marcy's hand. She must have left her own in the kitchen. "You look beat."

Marcy half smiled, sipping her wine. She wasn't tired, but she was worn out. Worn out with Phoebe. But of course she couldn't say that. Not right now, at least. "I'm fine."

"I know you say you have a million things to do, but you ought to take the evening off, enjoy the peace and quiet." Phoebe set the wine bottle on the table beside Marcy's chair. "Just sit here and read. I know how much you enjoy reading and you say you never have the time."

Marcy glanced at the book—a cozy mystery by one of her favorite authors. "Actually, I was thinking the same thing."

"Well"—Phoebe looked at her watch—"I should go. I've got a lot to do if I'm going to sleep in a bed with sheets tonight." She looked up. "Unless you want me to stay."

"No, don't be silly." It was the last thing Marcy wanted right now. She'd sooner have a killer outside her window than spend the rest of the evening with her sister, trying to pretend nothing was wrong when the bank statements on the other side of the room were saying something different.

Phoebe hesitated. "You know, I've got more stuff here than I thought. I was wondering—"

"How you were going to get it all there?" Marcy asked. The same thought had crossed her mind. "Because there's no way those boxes will fit in your little sports car."

Phoebe grinned. "Exactly. You mind—"

"Take mine." Marcy just wanted her out of the house. Now. "The keys are on the counter next to the phone."

"You sure?"

Marcy closed her eyes, tilting her head back to rest it on the chair. She was beginning to develop a headache. "Take it, Phoebe. Bring it back tomorrow."

"Great." Phoebe was already on her way to the kitchen.

"But leave me your keys," she called after her. "Ben has a game in the morning and Jake and the kids are meeting me there."

"No problem."

In twenty minutes, Marcy had her sister and her boxes out of the house and gone and the front door locked again. She returned to the family room and sank into the chair.

What was she going to do if Phoebe had stolen from her? Just make her pay it back? Call the police? She just didn't know. Over the years, Phoebe had taken advantage of her in so many ways, but as far as she knew, this was the first time she'd ever committed a crime in the process. It just seemed too hard to believe it could be true, and yet . . .

Marcy set her wineglass down and closed her eyes. Her head hurt worse, and now her stomach was upset, too. Whose wouldn't be? It hadn't exactly been a great evening. She'd discovered that her sister might be bulimic *and* stealing from her, and some pervert had been staring in her window. She didn't think the guy could be the same one who had killed those two other women, but it sure set her nerves on edge.

Maybe it was time Jake came home. She'd certainly feel safer having him here if there was a serial killer on the loose targeting blond-haired, blue-eyed women.

Marcy felt herself drifting off to sleep. She knew she ought to get up and do something. It would be a shame to waste her entire evening on her sister and a prowler, but suddenly she was so tired. Maybe she'd sit here a few minutes longer . . . .

A beeping sound startled Marcy. She must have fallen asleep. She didn't know how much time had passed, but she thought only seconds . . . maybe minutes.

Opening her eyes, she blinked groggily. She could still hear the beeping sound, loud and obnoxious. What was it? She slid forward in the chair, planting her bare feet on the carpet.

It was coming from the hallway. The smoke alarm? She lifted her head to look around the room. She didn't see any smoke. Didn't smell any. And that wasn't the right sound.

She slid out of the chair, still not quite clear-headed, and stumbled into the hall. The sound was definitely coming from here. She stood for a moment, trying to figure out where it was coming from. As she lifted her gaze to the smoke detector, she saw another small white, dome-shaped contraption right next to it.

Ben's carbon monoxide detector? She hadn't even realized he'd installed it. He'd asked her if he could. She remembered now him asking where the big ladder was too, but she didn't know he'd done it.

She stared at the detector. It was definitely going off, its little red light blinking at her. Blink. Blink.

Marcy knew she should have let Ben buy the more expensive one. Obviously, this one was malfunctioning. But she had thought the idea was a little silly to begin with, so she'd just bought it to placate him.

She stared at the little blinking, bleeping monster. Now she was going to have to figure out how to shut it off. Pull its batteries?

Her head was still fuzzy from her catnap.

Or was it?

Somewhere in the back of her mind, she remembered what Ben had said about carbon monoxide poisoning. The stuff was colorless, odorless. It produced headaches, dizziness, and stomach ailments, but usually over a period of time. And most people who were poisoned in their homes were poisoned by faulty heating systems. It was summer. The heater wasn't running.

This didn't make any sense.

Of course the detector was malfunctioning. She slowly walked into the family room, thinking that if she could drag a chair down the hall, she could rip the guts out of the thing and shut it up. It was really getting on her nerves now. Bleeping. Blinking. Bleeping.

She was halfway across the family room when it occurred to her that she should get the ladder, not a chair. A chair didn't make sense.

But she was still so groggy . . .

A symptom of carbon monoxide poisoning.

She walked slowly into the kitchen and picked up the phone. For the second time that night, the second time in her life, she dialed 911.

"911. What is your emergency?" It had to be the same monotone voice as before.

"This is Marcy . . . Marcy Edmond at 223 Seahorse Drive in Albany Beach again."

There was a pause.

"Yes, Mrs. Edmond, what is your emergency?"

She leaned against the kitchen counter, suddenly feeling very nauseous. "My son . . . The carbon monoxide detector in my house is going off. I don't see how there can be any carbon monoxide, but . . ." She could hear herself speaking, but it didn't sound like her voice.

Dreaming?

The detector continued to bleep.

"Mrs. Edmond, listen closely." Marcy could hear other voices in the background, the click-click of a keyboard. "We'll send the fire department right over, but you need to get out of the house."

Marcy gave a little laugh, brushing the hair out of her eyes. "I called earlier. I thought someone was looking in my window."

"Yes," the operator said. "I see that now."

"But no one was out there," Marcy said unsteadily. "I guess it would be all right if I went outside . . . just for a minute."

"Mrs. Edmond, where are you now?" the operator said loudly.

"The kitchen."

"Go outside, Mrs. Edmond. Take the phone with you."

Marcy shuffled down the dark hallway, the phone in her hand. She was afraid she was going to throw up. She turned the deadlock and opened the door. Outside it was hot. Humid. But the air felt good on her face.

She heard a voice, and then remembered the phone. Stepping out onto the porch, she lifted it to her ear again.

"Mrs. Edmond?" the woman was saying, concern in her voice. "Are you still there?"

Marcy sat down on the top step. "I'm here." She took a deep breath. "I'm still here."

"Someone is coming to help you, Mrs. Edmond. The firemen will be there in just a couple of minutes."

Marcy could already hear sirens in the distance. They were sending fire trucks to shut Ben's detector off? Marcy hung her head. She still felt lousy, but her stomach was beginning to settle a little. She took a deep breath and then another.

The next thing she knew, the sirens seemed to be surrounding her. A small white panel truck pulled into her driveway. County emergency medical technicians. A fire truck on the street in front of the house. Two fire trucks. Two people in EMT uniforms hurried up the sidewalk, carrying bags in both hands.

"Mrs. Edmond?"

"Yes." She lifted her head. Someone took the phone from her.

"Mrs. Edmond, can you hear me?"

She took a deep breath. "Yes." She looked up to see a young man with a stethoscope around his neck stooped in front of her. She didn't recognize him. It wasn't Kevin James. "I can hear you. I'm feeling better." She felt as if a cloud was lifting from her head.

They were paramedics. Two of them, a man and a woman.

"We're going to take your blood pressure, Mrs. Edmond. You think you've been exposed to carbon monoxide, is that right?"

"My son's detector went off." She pointed behind her. She had left the front door open and light from inside spilled onto the porch. She could hear the stupid thing still bleeping. "I don't know if something is wrong with it or what."

"But you're feeling badly?"

She nodded. "I had a little wine. I was tired and dozed off."

Two firefighters with masks on their faces brushed past her on the steps and went into the house.

"I guess the thing woke me up," she said, allowing the man to take her pulse. "That was when I realized I felt bad."

"Let's try a little of this, Mrs. Edmond." The female paramedic drew a clear plastic mask down over Marcy's nose and mouth. "It's just oxygen," she explained.

"Ma'am?" A fireman loomed behind Marcy. "Do you have something in the house that runs on natural gas? Heating system, maybe?"

She shook her head, pulling back the mask so he could hear her. "An electric heat pump runs the air conditioner."

"Gas stove?"

She nodded. She was feeling better already. Much better. Her head was clearer, and it wasn't pounding the way it had been. She pulled the mask down again. "Gas stove and also the fireplace. It has a pilot, I think. I haven't been burning it, though. Not in the middle of the summer."

"We'll check it out, ma'am."

The paramedic closed his hand over Marcy's and eased the oxygen mask down again. "Just give this a couple of minutes and you'll be feeling better."

"We need to get her away from the house," the male paramedic said. "You feel as if you can walk? If not—"

"No. No, I'm much better," Marcy said, her voice muffled by the oxygen mask.

Carrying their equipment, the paramedics walked her to their truck. An ambulance crew had arrived, and two men ran up the driveway with a stretcher.

"I'm not going anywhere," Marcy said, pulling the oxygen mask off. She sat down on the bumper of her sister's car in the driveway.

Marcy heard another siren, and a police car came tearing into her neighborhood.

"You really should be transported to the hospital, Mrs. Edmond. A doctor should have a look at you. Carbon monoxide poisoning is serious, ma'am. The carbon monoxide combines with the hemoglobin, the oxygen-carrying protein of blood, and deprives the tissues of oxygen."

"I said, no," Marcy repeated. She handed the oxygen mask to one of the paramedics. "The last time I rode in one of those things, I slept six months." She didn't mean to sound superstitious, but there was no way she was getting in that ambulance.

"She's not going?" one of the men with the stretcher asked.

"Refusing medical care," the female paramedic said.

"Look, I'll go see my family doctor on Monday."

The police car had pulled in across the street, and Claire hurried up the driveway. There were fireman everywhere, walking across Marcy's lawn, going in and out of the house.

"Marcy?" Claire crouched in front of her. "Twice in one night," she teased. "What's up?"

Marcy closed her eyes for a second and then opened them. "I don't know. It's so weird. Ben installed this carbon monoxide detector, and it went off. I must have fallen asleep in the living room."

Claire glanced in the direction of the house. "Is Phoebe still here?"

"No. She left a while ago. She went to her new apartment." She lifted one hand, realizing she was still slightly muddled. "I don't even know where it is. She was a little vague."

"The kids?" Claire kept eye contact; her voice had a calming effect in the midst of all the confusion. "They're not home, right?"

"With Jake."

"You want to call him?" The police chief pulled a cell phone from her pocket.

"Thanks. That would be great." Marcy punched the numbers and waited. Jake didn't pick up, and she got a recorded message saying the number she had dialed wasn't in service. He must have had his phone off during the movie. "What time is it?" she asked.

Claire stood up. "Ten."

Marcy offered her back her phone.

"No, you keep it." Claire patted Marcy's hand. "Keep trying while I talk to the firemen and see what's going on."

While Claire was gone, the paramedics took Marcy's pulse and blood pressure again. They had her sign several forms, including one that said she was refusing the recommended medical treatment. By the time Claire came back down the driveway, Marcy had tried Jake two more times, unsuccessfully, and the paramedics were pulling out.

"How are you feeling?" Claire asked.

Marcy got up off the bumper of her sister's car. "Much better. Fine." She brushed the blond hair from her eyes. "Was there really carbon monoxide in the house?"

"Apparently so. Ben probably saved your life." Claire

glanced at the house and then at Marcy again. "Has Jake been doing some work in the basement?"

Marcy shook her head. "No. Not that I'm aware of. He's been gone, remember."

"What about the door from the basement outside? Do you normally keep it locked?"

"Of course." Marcy rested a hand on her hip, trying to think. "It wasn't locked? I haven't been down there in a few days, but the kids know it stays locked."

Claire shook her head. "I'm going to check with McCormick in the morning. He's already gone off shift, but I could have sworn he said he checked it when we were here earlier, and it was locked."

Marcy met Claire's gaze, wondering if the police chief was thinking what she was thinking. Did this have to do with her prowler?

"Listen, I need to ask you something personal," Claire said.

"Okay."

"You and Jake, how are you getting along these days?"

Marcy smiled, suddenly feeling almost shy. "Well."

"Yeah?"

Marcy crossed her arms over her chest. It was getting late, cooler out. "With Phoebe out of the house and in her own place, we were thinking about giving it another try. Jake says he's willing to go to marriage counseling."

"That's great."

"But why do you ask?" Marcy studied Claire's face, then glanced over her shoulder and back at her. "What did the firemen find?"

The police chief didn't answer.

"Claire?"

Claire frowned. "We don't know anything for sure yet, but there was definitely a level of carbon monoxide in the kitchen and the family room and—" She hesitated, then met Marcy's gaze. "It looks like the exhaust on the gas system has been tampered with."

Chapter Twelve

"Tampered with?" Marcy murmured, thinking maybe she hadn't heard Claire correctly.

"They think so, but as I said, we'll need to get someone else in there to be sure." Claire rubbed her temples. "This is beyond what our local volunteer fire guys usually do, but they suspect someone deliberately altered the exhaust system so that carbon monoxide was released into the house."

"You mean intentionally?" Marcy tried to consider the possibility, knowing it couldn't be true. This kind of stuff happened on TV. In novels, not in real life. Not in her life. "It couldn't have been done accidentally, like bumping into something or—"

Claire studied her with a penetrating gaze. "They think it was intentional. You're sure Jake hasn't done any—"

"Claire," Marcy said firmly. "Jake would never do anything to harm me or the kids. You have to know that."

The police chief nodded, obviously deep in thought.

Marcy turned to watch the house for a moment. The firefighters had gone through every room and opened the blinds and windows so that light spilled into the darkness from every room. She looked back at Claire suddenly. "You think someone came into the house through the basement? The man I saw in the window? Could he have come back?"

"It's possible."

Marcy sat on the bumper of Phoebe's yellow sports car again and dialed Jake. Still no answer. She tried his place too. Nothing. "I can't imagine the movie ran this long," she said, trying not to worry.

"You think they went out to eat afterward?"

Marcy frowned. "They were supposed to buy their tickets in advance, then have dinner, then go to the movie. What time is it now?"

Claire glanced at her wristwatch. "Ten-fifty."

"It's not like Jake to be out so late with the kids. Ben has a baseball game in the morning. He's cranky if he doesn't get enough sleep. Jake's cranky if he doesn't get enough sleep."

One of the neighbors walked up the driveway, barefooted in a white tank T-shirt and wrinkled work pants. Up to this point, the firefighters had blocked the way, keeping onlookers back. "You okay, Marcy?" His name was Al Nelson; he owned a small plumbing and heating company in town and lived across the street and down one house to the left.

"I'm fine. Just a little problem with the gas line or something." Marcy didn't want to go into any details.

"Kids okay?"

"With Jake." She smiled. "Thanks for checking on me, but you might as well go to bed." She looked beyond him to a couple of other neighbors gathered at the end of the driveway in various stages of dress and undress. Mrs. Murphy was wearing a zebra-striped housecoat; pretty racy for a Hungarian woman in her seventies. "Everyone might as well go to bed."

"Not staying here, are you?" Al thrust his hands into

the pockets of his olive work pants. "You know you're welcome to stay at our place."

Marcy glanced at Claire. She hadn't thought about where she was going to sleep tonight, but obviously it wasn't going to be here. She imagined the house would have to be inspected by someone from the gas company before they were allowed to go back in. "Jake's coming to get me."

"Glad you're okay." Al turned away. "Give a holler if you need anything. 'Night."

"Good night." Marcy returned her attention to Claire, who was looking at Phoebe's car.

"You said Phoebe left a while ago?" Claire asked.

"Less than hour after you and Patrolman McCormick left here." Marcy patted the bumper of the sports car. "She took my SUV. The dope realized, once she had all those boxes ready to go, that there was no way she was going to get them all in this tiny trunk. She's always doing things like that, always borrowing my car or my—"

"Where'd the boxes come from?"

"Where'd they come from? I guess she had most of them from the last time—" Marcy halted in mid-sentence. That wasn't what Claire meant. "Mostly from the basement," she said softly, rising off the bumper. She felt a sinking feeling in the pit of her stomach as she shifted her gaze to meet Claire's.

Sinking feeling? More like free-falling.

The implication was too awful to even consider. The idea of a prowler, or even a serial killer stalking her was far more bearable. And yet . . .

"I want you to think carefully," Claire said. "Did you go into the basement with Phoebe tonight?"

"No," Marcy heard herself say in a small voice. Suddenly she felt as if she were sleepwalking. This all had to be a dream. Maybe everything since she woke up in the hospital was a dream. Maybe she was still lying there in

a coma. It seemed just as feasible as what was happening now. "I offered to go down and help her out, but
she . . . she said she could do it herself."

Tears filled Marcy's eyes as she thought about her
discovery in her bank accounts earlier in the evening.
She had intended to say nothing to anyone, to make no
accusations until she talked to Jake. Until he looked at
the accounts. But now . . .

"Claire." Marcy took a deep breath. "Phoebe doesn't
know I suspect yet. I'm not even positive"—she went on
quicker than before—"but I think she may have been
stealing from us while I was in the coma."

Claire followed her with clear blue eyes. She was the
epitome of the calm civil servant in the midst of what
seemed like chaos. "You think so? What's led you to that
conclusion?"

"I've been meaning to do it for two weeks, but I just
sat down to work on our bank accounts tonight. Nothing
has been balanced since November. Jake said he hadn't
had the time all these months, and I believe him. Our
household finances were always my job and . . ." Marcy
let her voice fade.

"What did you find?" Claire prodded.

"Money missing from our accounts." She went on before she lost her nerve. "Accounts my sister either had
access to by means of the bank card Jake gave her months
ago, or accounts she could easily access because I was
stupid about my passwords." She pressed her lips together, afraid she was going to cry. But if she started
now, she feared she would never stop. The more she said,
the more she became convinced that her sister had
done this awful thing. "I used my first pet's name, for
heaven's sake."

"I hate to ask," Claire said, "but you're sure Jake didn't
take the money? Maybe he just moved it, and in the
confusion of the last month, he hasn't gotten a chance

to tell you? Or . . ." She left other possibilities unspoken.

Marcy hugged herself, knowing what Claire was suggesting—maybe Jake had a gambling problem, another woman on the side. There were many reasons why a husband might remove money from a joint account without telling his wife. Any husband but Jake. "I'm telling you, it wasn't Jake. He wouldn't do that. Besides, the money was transferred more than once online before it was removed from the household account. Jake wouldn't be able to access our accounts online without the passwords. He doesn't know I had a Persian cat named Butterscotch when I was five!"

A crackly voice came over a radio Claire wore at her shoulder, and she excused herself and walked onto the lawn to stand in the dark. She answered in some police jargon and then stepped back into the circle of light cast from the security lamp over the garage.

"You don't think Phoebe would do something like this, do you?" Marcy asked. "I mean, why would she?"

"Did your sister know you would be here alone tonight?"

"Yes." Miserable, Marcy looked away. She could already see the direction this conversation was going. Someone had taken money from the bank accounts assuming it wouldn't be missed if Marcy died or just never awoke from her coma. But then she did wake up, so that same someone tampered with the gas exhaust? She wasn't ready to even consider the possibility that it might have been her sister. "But what . . ."

Marcy raised her hand and let it fall to her side, searching for some other explanation. Any other explanation. "Could the man outside the window have anything to do with this? I mean, I know I saw a man, but Phoebe was really pissed when I called you. Maybe she knew him? Maybe he was making her do this for some reason?"

"Did your sister try to prevent you from calling us?"

Marcy tried to think back. "No, but . . . but she acted as if it would be a mistake. She said if I started doing wacky things like that, people would think I was nuts."

"What people?"

Marcy shrugged.

"All right." Claire reached out and patted Marcy's shoulder. "You try and call Jake again. I'm going to track down the fire chief and see what's up here, but Al's right. You can't stay here tonight."

Claire left Marcy in the driveway and disappeared into the house through the front door that remained open. Marcy watched her approach one of the firemen standing in the foyer with some kind of meter in his hand.

Her hand trembling slightly, Marcy dialed Jake's cell phone. It rang, and just as she thought the recorded message was about to come on, she heard Jake's voice. "Jake?" Tears welled in her eyes again.

"Marcy? Marcy, honey, what's wrong?" he said in her ear. "Are you okay?"

She bit back a sob. "I need you to come home."

"We're getting into the car now." His voice was filled with concern. "Ben, hop in. Come on, hurry up."

"I've been trying to get you for an hour." Marcy gripped the cell phone, refusing to let herself fall apart. "There was no answer at the condo, and your cell phone wasn't on. I knew the movie had to be over, so I couldn't understand—"

"We bumped into Phoebe at the mall. She took us out for ice cream to celebrate her new job. I just forgot to turn my phone back on until a few minutes ago."

A fresh well of emotion bubbled up inside Marcy. "Phoebe?" she said. Her sister had said nothing about stopping at the mall. She had said she was headed to her new apartment to settle in for the night. A new emotion gripped her. Fear. She was afraid for her family. What if

Phoebe did have something to do with all this? "Is . . . is she with you now?"

"No. She went to her new place." He sounded confused, now frustrated. "Why? Marcy, what the hell is going on?"

Over the phone, she heard a car door slam and Jake start his engine.

"Honey, are you sure you're all right?" he repeated.

"Just come home. There are fire trucks and police cars in the driveway, but I'll explain when you get here."

"Fire trucks?"

Marcy hung up and, with both hands, wiped at the tears that ran down her cheeks.

Marcy was still sitting in the driveway on the bumper of Phoebe's car, waiting for Claire to come back with her report from the fire chief when Jake pulled in to the neighborhood. He slammed on the brakes in front of the house, parking catty-corner across the driveway like he was a stunt driver in some movie. Through the open window, she heard him bark for the kids to stay in the car. She met him halfway down the driveway.

"What's going on?" Jake pulled her into his arms, and she dropped her head to his shoulder thinking she had never felt anything quite so good.

"A problem with exhaust on the natural gas. I fell asleep in the family room. Ben's carbon monoxide detector went off." She lifted her head to look into his brown eyes. "He probably saved my life, Jake."

He pulled her hard against his chest, his voice filled with emotion. "Talk about a cat with nine lives."

She let him hold her a second longer and then made herself take a step back. "But there's more to it, Jake."

He hooked his thumb in the pocket of his shorts. "More?"

"Let me go talk to the kids for a minute, and then

you and I need to speak with Chief Drummond. She's inside right now with the fire chief."

Jake just stood there in the driveway staring at their house with the windows and door thrown open and firemen wandering in and out as Marcy went down the driveway toward the car.

"Mom," Ben cried, thrusting his head out the open window of his father's car.

Katie threw open the door. "Mom, what's going on? Did the house catch on fire?"

Marcy draped one arm around her daughter and opened the front driver's-side door to let Ben out. "You guys can't come in the house. None of us can tonight. I just need a hug, and then you have to get back in the car and wait for us." She pulled them against her, their slender, bony bodies feeling so good.

"But why are the firemen here? Did the house catch on fire?" Ben demanded, craning his neck to see. "I don't smell any smoke. You can usually smell it. People sometimes smell smoke before they even see the fire."

Marcy reluctantly released her children. "There was no fire, but there was some kind of gas leak and a carbon monoxide buildup." She looked down at Ben in the light of the car's overhead dome. "Your detector went off."

"Cool!" he declared. Then he glanced at his mother, knitting his brows. He looked so much like his father when he did that. "Gas leaks don't cause carbon monoxide buildup, Mom. Only faulty burning of the fuel or a break in the exhaust system."

Katie hung on to the car door, staring at the house. She looked scared, bewildered, but she was doing a good job of hiding it. "Is our stuff all right? I've got important stuff in my bedroom. Those firemen aren't like poking around, are they?"

"They're just airing out the house," Marcy told Katie.

"And I don't know exactly what's wrong with our gas, I just know something wasn't working right and carbon monoxide was in the house. Now, I need both of you to get in the car and wait for me and Dad."

"You're coming to Dad's with us?" Ben climbed back into the front seat and slammed the door.

"Cool," Katie said, getting into the back of the car.

"We'll try to be quick." Marcy patted Ben's arm through the window and went back up the driveway. Jake was talking to Claire on the front porch. When she approached, they were both looking pretty grave.

"Chief Drummond filled me in," Jake said stiffly.

"Pretty far-fetched, huh?"

"I didn't touch any of our money," Jake said. "Not in all those months. Nothing but the household account I deposited paychecks into. Hell, I'm not sure I could tell you what accounts we have." He turned his attention to Claire. "I know we don't know each other well, Chief Drummond, but I'm telling you, I did not move or take any money from our joint accounts. I don't have a girlfriend, and I had no intention of skipping town with any money and abandoning my family. That's not the kind of guy I am."

Marcy's throat constricted with emotion again. Jake was right. He wasn't that kind of guy. It was one of the reasons she had fallen in love with him back in college, and again in the last couple of weeks. You just didn't run into many men these days with basic beliefs in loyalty and morality. And to think she had even considered a man like Seth Watkins. Maybe Phoebe was closer to the truth than she realized. Was she nuts?

"Do you know where your sister is right now?" Claire asked.

Marcy shook her head. "I guess Jake told you that he ran into her at the mall. Coincidence, I suppose." She wasn't sure she believed it, but right now she wasn't too sure of anything. "Then I would assume she went on to her new apartment. She didn't say where it was, though."

"She didn't tell me, either," Jake joined in.

"I asked, but I guess . . ." Marcy tried to recall the conversation. "I guess we must have gotten interrupted because she never did say."

"She have a cell phone?"

Marcy nodded.

"Well, I'm making no accusations, mind you." Claire gestured. "But I think she and I need to talk. Could you call her?"

Marcy felt numb. "Sure. I guess." She watched Claire reach for her cell phone. "But not on your phone. She might not answer. The number calling in comes up on the display." She bit her lip, looking inside the open front door. "You think I could go in and get my phone and maybe some shoes and my toothbrush?"

"According to the fire chief, the carbon monoxide has dissipated to an acceptable level, but you should probably stay out since you were already exposed. How about if I get your phone for you, and Jake goes in and gets anything you might need from the house for the night?"

Marcy nodded silently.

"I'll just get some overnight things for you." Jake reached out to massage her shoulder. She could tell he was in shock about Phoebe, too. "Anything else besides shoes and clothes and your toiletries?"

"Um, my makeup bag. It's right on the bathroom sink."

"I'll be right back." He brushed his mouth against her cheek and walked inside with Claire.

"Found it," Claire said, coming out of the house a minute later holding up her cordless phone. "Right where Jake said it would be in the kitchen."

Marcy took it. "What do I say?"

"Pretend nothing's wrong. You just called to see if she needed anything before you went to bed. Try to find out where the new apartment is. We'll go by and pick her up."

Marcy hesitated, biting down on her lower lip as she tried to think about what she would say. She dialed her sister's cell phone. It rang. And rang. She got Phoebe's cheery mailbox message. "It's Marcy. I just wanted to see how you were making out at your new place. Call me. I'll be up a while, still."

"No answer." Marcy lifted the phone.

Claire exhaled slowly. "Listen, I've been thinking. I don't mean to scare you, but I don't think you should go back to Jake's tonight either. Could you just take the kids to a hotel?"

Marcy stared at Claire in confusion. "Sure, but why?"

"Because I don't know what's going on here." Claire's building frustration was obvious. "I don't know if your sister has anything to do with any of this. I don't know if the man you saw tonight does. I don't know if they're connected. I don't know if this has to do with Patti and April's killer."

"You want me to go somewhere my sister won't know to look," Marcy said softly.

"I think it would be wise. Until I get a chance to speak to her. I'll send a car out to patrol all the apartment buildings in town. Maybe someone will spot your SUV. We've got a record of the tag number."

Marcy leaned against the front porch rail and looked down at lavender pansies that had been crushed beneath the boot of one of the firefighters. "I can't believe this is happening. I can't believe Phoebe would really try to hurt me."

Jake walked out of the house, onto the porch with a gym bag over his shoulder. "I just grabbed what I could find. The kids already have their stuff."

Marcy slipped her arm through Jake's. "Claire wants us to stay at a hotel tonight and not your place."

Jake looked at her, at Claire, and back at her again. "Oh . . . Okay."

"Tell me where you want to stay and I'll have one of my cars escort you." Claire seemed preoccupied now.

"No, that won't be necessary." Marcy took a deep breath, clearing her head. "The kids are scared enough as it is. I don't want them thinking they're in danger. If Phoebe did do this, it was about me. Remember, she knew the kids would be with Jake until morning."

"Just about you," Claire repeated thoughtfully, as much to herself as to Marcy.

Marcy tried to read the police chief's face. "What are you thinking?"

Claire shook her head. "Don't worry about it. I'm going to give Jake some phone numbers. The station house and my personal cell. You call the station house and leave a message for me as to where you'll be." She started down the steps to the sidewalk, and Marcy and Jake followed. "Then I want you to take your son and daughter, go to the hotel, and try to get some sleep. I'll talk to you in the morning."

Jake glanced at the house.

"Don't worry. I'll be sure everything is locked up," Claire assured him. "Right now, you just need to get Marcy to bed. By all rights, she should be in the hospital right now getting checked out."

Jake looked to Marcy.

"I'm fine," Marcy said. "I'm not going to the hospital. I'm going with you and Ben and Katie. I don't want the three of you out of my sight right now."

Jake turned to Claire. "You're sure—"

"Everything is going to be fine." Claire patted him on the shoulder. "Just take your wife and children and go. We'll talk in the morning, I promise. By then, maybe I'll have something to tell you as far as when you can go home."

"And what about Phoebe?" Marcy asked. "I wouldn't want to accuse her of—"

"Let me talk to her before we make any more allegations," Claire interrupted firmly. "Now, go on. Get some sleep. You've had a long evening."

Claire watched Marcy and Jake walk down their driveway hand in hand, her mind racing in a thousand directions. Was the man Marcy saw earlier in the evening connected to the carbon monoxide? To have a better idea, she'd have to get an expert in to tell her how long the poison had been leaking into the house. What if there was no man, or if the prowler was unrelated to the carbon monoxide? Weird coincidences happened all the time.

And where did Phoebe fit in?

Claire had a hunch. A sick hunch that didn't involve coincidences at all, but cold calculation. She had to get back to the station house to look into last year's records before she was going to be ready to voice her suspicion. She turned back to the house, spotting the fire chief. "Tobby, you got everything under control here?" she called from the sidewalk.

He gave her a thumbs-up.

"Go ahead and close the house when you think it's safe. I'll leave one of my officers here to be sure it's all secure and the front door is taped off before he leaves the premises. Talk to you tomorrow?"

He waved and, calling orders to the other volunteer firemen, he disappeared into the back of the house.

Claire gave her officer still on the scene instructions and then got into her cruiser and radioed the night dispatcher to let him know she was headed in. She was supposed to have been off hours ago. Luckily, Ashley had gone to spend the night with a friend so Claire could get away with pulling a double shift.

She eased the cruiser onto the main road, watching

the Edmonds' car taillights disappear around the curve ahead of her. Her heart went out to the family. They were such nice people, and they had been through so much. To think the situation might even be worse than they realized bothered her. It just wasn't right. It wasn't fair. But as her father had taught her as a child, life was rarely about fairness, and dwelling on life's injustices only prevented her from doing her job. So she would do her job as the chief of police of this town, and she would tuck her emotions away.

Claire didn't do the filing at the station so she wasn't even sure she could locate what she was looking for tonight, but she knew there was no way she was going to be able to sleep until she pored over the accident report from the near-fatal last December on March's Bridge. An accident that she wasn't sure now had been an accident at all.

The Bloodsucker sipped his coffee. Good old Loretta made the best damned coffee on the East Coast. At least that was what he had heard others in the diner say. Some locals expressed that opinion. Some tourists. He didn't really know because he hadn't much of an opportunity to sample the coffee up and down the East Coast.

What he *was* sure of was that Loretta had the best éclairs around. He thrust his tongue into the center of the pastry and sampled the sweet, yellow pudding-like center that he loved. It was his second one. A greedy piggy. That's what Granny had called him. A greedy piggy. If she had seen him eat two éclairs in one night, she probably would have pushed his nose in it, rubbed it all over his face. Or worse . . .

The Bloodsucker took another sip of the coffee that seemed even more delicious after the bite of chocolaty, pudding-filled éclair. He should have asked for decaf. He wouldn't sleep well tonight.

He wouldn't sleep well anyway. It was Marcy. She was keeping him awake. He couldn't stop thinking about her and her beautiful face. Her smile and the nice way she talked to him. He couldn't sleep because he couldn't stop thinking about her blood.

Going to her house tonight had been unwise. He'd been there too many times already. Even parking his car on the other road and cutting through the woods was dangerous. Someone was going to recognize him, realize he was out of place in that setting. That was part of the trick of deceiving people—always looking like you belonged, even when you didn't.

The Bloodsucker lifted the coffee cup to his mouth. He was seated in a booth in the diner near the back. Fit right in. Nobody thought it was in the least bit odd that he would be here this time of night.

As he sipped the coffee, he saw a car pass the diner and he took a second look. A grin broke out on his face. He couldn't believe his good fortune! Never in a million years had he expected to see Marcy again tonight.

What was she doing out so late?

It had to be a sign. A sign that the time was just about right.

It was time for him and Marcy to be together. He could taste his anticipation, sharp and tangy on his tongue. He was so clever. So smart. He already had the place prepared for her. Already knew where she would go when he was done with her.

Chapter Thirteen

Marcy sat on the edge of the double bed in the hotel room and leaned over to kiss Ben's cheek. Katie had protested at having to share a bed with her little brother, but she'd been appeased by the promise of breakfast out in the morning and, after Ben's ball game, a trip to the outlets to buy the tankini she wanted.

Both children were asleep now—Katie sprawled out in shorts and a tee, her hair spilling over the white pillow case; Ben curled in a little ball, knees to his chest, his thumb near his mouth. It seemed like only a very short time ago that he had sucked his thumb. Now he appeared so old to her at nine, nearly grown up.

Her nine-year-old who had probably saved her life with his safety obsession. She'd never tease him again about it.

"You okay?" Jake asked, coming out of the bathroom in boxers and a gray T-shirt.

She nodded. She really *was* ok.

"Then let's see if we can get some sleep." He left the bathroom light on and closed the door all but a crack so the kids could find their way in the dark if they needed to. "Tomorrow is probably going to be a long day."

He took her by her hand and led her to the bed they would share tonight. She sat down obediently and let him remove her sneakers and then lay back on top of the sheet, her head on the pillow. Jake had already pulled the bedspreads off at Ben's request; riddled with germs, he had explained.

Jake went around the other side of the bed and climbed in. For a moment they lay side by side, only inches apart, unmoving. The only light in the room was the streak that fell from the crack in the bathroom door and a faint patch that leaked from behind the generic curtains over the windows.

"Do you really think Phoebe would try to harm me?" Marcy asked. She turned to look at Jake and then crawled closer, dropping her head on his shoulder. He made her feel safe. And as she ran her fingers over his chest, she felt a stirring of excitement inside her. There would be no hot sex between them tonight, not with their children asleep beside them, not with everything that had happened tonight. But lying close like this, she could feel the promise of future nights crackling in the air.

Jake wrapped his arm around her and slipped his hand beneath her shirt to brush her skin with his fingertips. "I don't know, honey. It sounds crazy, but—"

"But she's done crazy things before," Marcy whispered. "The trip to Mexico, marrying that guy in Las Vegas she'd met at the slot machine."

"Vic," Jake offered.

"Vic," she repeated. "And then there was the time she put all that money into the buffalo farm." She chuckled, but felt sad rather than humored by her sister's antics. "Ah, Jake," she groaned. "What are we going to do about the money?"

"One thing at a time. Let's find out what happened at the house first. If she tried to poison you, she's got bigger problems than theft charges."

"Maybe there's something wrong with her. Maybe she's

sick." She glanced at him, biting down on her lower lip in indecision. "I think she might be bulimic, Jake."

He scowled. "Of course she is. She's been barfing up all the good meals we've fed her for years. Where've you been, hon?"

She stared at him. "You knew?"

He shrugged. "I guess I didn't know for sure until she moved in after your accident. I heard her in the bathroom a couple of times."

"Did you say something to her?"

"Sure. I even offered to get her some help. She said it wasn't true. She just had a flu bug."

"And that was it?"

"Marcy, you can't help people who don't want to be helped."

She was quiet for a minute. How had she missed the signs and Jake hadn't? Men were notorious for being unperceptive. Had she been that caught up in her own misery? Apparently so.

So she hadn't realized Phoebe was ill. That was no excuse for her sister to steal from her. "But we worked so hard to save that money," she mused aloud. "Part of that is supposed to be for our retirement."

He kissed her shoulder, and she could feel the warmth of his mouth through the fabric of her shirt. "I should have been more careful, less trusting. I was just so damned worried about you."

She smoothed his bare arm beneath her fingertips.

"But money can be replaced," he said. "I can make more. Your French Bistro, with its magnificent homemade soups and breads, is going to be such a success that in a few years, ten thousand dollars will mean nothing to us." He rubbed her bare stomach beneath her shirt. "I'm just glad nothing happened to you, that you're safe. I almost lost you once. I can't bear the thought that it could have happened again."

She smiled in the darkness. The sincerity in his voice

touched her in a place he hadn't touched in a long time. Her experience tonight made her realize how precious moments of happiness were. How easily they could be shattered. A person could lose their brakes and drive off a bridge at any moment, breathe in noxious fumes anytime.

"When we can go home, I want you to come too. I don't want a divorce, Jake. I want you." She rolled onto her side to face him. "That is, if you still want me." She gazed into his dark eyes. "If you'll give me another chance."

He threaded his fingers through her hair and drew her head closer until her lips touched his. "Another chance? I'd give you a hundred. And not because you look like a million dollars, though that *is* a decent perk." He grinned the way he had back in the old days. "I'd give you another chance because I love you, Marcy. Always have. Always will."

"I love you, too," she whispered, tearing up.

He kissed her again, this time quick. An end to the conversation. "Let's get some sleep."

She rested her head on Jake's shoulder, and within ten minutes she heard him breathing rhythmically. However, sleep did not come so easily to her. Taking care not to wake him, she scooted over onto her side of the bed. She glanced at the sleeping forms of her children and thought about what Jake had said about nine lives. She really was fortunate. Tonight could have turned out so differently. She needed to keep that in mind in the days and weeks to come. No matter what happened with Phoebe, she had to prevent herself from wasting time, wasting energy, wasting her God-given gifts and talents again.

Her thoughts strayed to her sister again. How could Phoebe have stolen from her? Had she been that desperate for money? For what? And if so, why hadn't she just asked Jake if she could borrow from them? And what about the carbon monoxide in the house? Why would Phoebe have tried to kill her? Surely not to cover the theft? That didn't make sense.

Marcy squeezed her eyes shut, trying to stop thinking about it because the more she thought, the more confused she became. She tried to relax, to think about the restaurant, to think about the waves crashing on the beach only a few blocks away. Sleep still eluded her.

Claire carried the file down the dim hallway to her office and flipped on the bright fluorescent overheads. She cringed as they flashed on and filled the room with artificial light. It had taken less than an hour to find the file; pretty amazing considering the way records were kept around here. She was pushing to switch to computer files and do away with paper, but with the budget she had to work with and the old bat who was in charge of record-keeping, it was a miracle she wasn't hauling stone tablets to her office.

Claire checked her watch as she slid into her chair behind her desk. Twelve-thirty A.M. Jake Edmond had called her from his cell phone to say that they were staying at the Seascape Hotel on Driftwood, and that as an extra precaution, he had dropped off his family, parked his car in the apartment building garage down the street and was walking to the hotel.

Claire knew Marcy didn't want to think the worst of her sister, but she could tell that Jake already did. Either he knew Phoebe better than Marcy, or he was just more realistic. Either way, he had been clear on the phone. He wanted Phoebe picked up, and he intended to press charges on the theft once the situation at the house was investigated. He wanted her locked up until they had a better idea what was going on. He didn't want to take any more chances with his wife's life, and Claire couldn't blame him.

She flipped open the manila file on her desk and glanced at Marcy's original accident report. It contained the usual information: the time it was called in, the exact location. Single car accident, single passenger ejected from the car. Routine, in a way. It was scary how life and death could be trivialized to such generic words on paper.

She flipped to another page. The first officer on the scene's initial observations, written in McCormick's stiff, masculine print. The details were pretty grim. Marcy had been pulled from the water by a guy in a tow truck only a minute or two behind her. She hadn't been breathing when he fished her out. He had started CPR. The emergency medical technicians had resuscitated her at the scene. It was unknown exactly how long her brain had gone without oxygen. *Severe facial trauma* was noted.

But these details weren't what she was looking for. Claire went through several more pages, looking for the specific report she knew had to be here. She grabbed the can of Diet Pepsi on her desk and took a swig. It was sweet and flat and disgusting. She forced it down and went on with her search.

She found the copy of the report from Alan's Auto at the very bottom of the file. Of course, she didn't know how much help it was going to do her; she knew nothing about cars or brakes. She read the report in Alan Junior's scrawled handwriting. *Brake failure. Brake fluid leak due to partially severed brake line*, it read. The "report" was actually a bill for his services. $42. Then there was an arrow with a word written in the margin. She turned the piece of paper around to get a better look. It was an old-fashioned carbon copy. Hard to read. What did it say?

Intensive?

Claire looked away, rubbed her eyes. That didn't make any sense. What was intensive? She stared at the word again.

Not *intensive*. It said *"intentional"*, followed by a question mark. Alan Junior had noted that he was concerned the brake lines might have been cut intentionally. Apparently the report from Alan's Auto had been filed properly, but never read. She knew *she'd* never seen it.

"Son of a bitch," Claire muttered.

No, *you little bitch* is what she should have said.

Claire got up from her chair. This was all circumstantial at this point, of course, but she had enough to bring Phoebe Matthews in for questioning. She was putting out an APB for her and Marcy's vehicle.

She jerked open the door to her office and headed for the fishbowl. She was going to order the all-points bulletin, and then she was going out and looking for Marcy's SUV herself. It was the least she could do, considering the evidence lying on her desk.

The cell phone beside the bed jingled, startling Marcy. She must have been half asleep. She grabbed it and punched the receiver button to keep it from ringing again and waking Jake or the children. She glanced at the bedside clock. *One thirty-two* the red numbers glowed.

"H . . . hello?" Marcy whispered.

Jake rolled over on his side away from her.

"Marcy."

It was so like her own voice that it could only be one person. Marcy felt a shiver trickle up her spine. "Phebes?"

"You just won't die, will you?" her sister said. Her voice was a mixture of sarcasm and indignation.

Marcy sat up on the bed, swinging her legs over the side onto the floor. Her sister's words chilled her. She really was sick, wasn't she? "Phoebe, where are you?"

"Don't worry," Phoebe sighed. "I'm not coming back to get you."

"I . . . I didn't say that."

"I give up. You win."

Marcy glanced at the kids in bed only two feet from her. Ben stirred. She got up and stood in the middle of the room in the dark in indecision for a moment. She had to go somewhere to talk. The bathroom? No. She was suddenly sick to her stomach. That little room was too confining; besides, it was tile. If she talked to Phoebe on the phone, her voice would echo. She might wake the kids.

"I don't know what you're talking about. What do you mean, I win?" Marcy unlatched the metal bar that prevented someone outside the hotel room from coming in, even with a key, and turned the doorknob. Outside, the air seemed cool, refreshing, despite the high June temperature. She flipped the mechanism so she wouldn't lock herself out and then walked over to lean on a railing along the walkway that ran the length of the hotel between the rooms that opened to the outside and the parking lot.

"I mean you win. You get it all. The man, the cute, smart little brats, one boy, one girl, of course. One big fucking happy family. *And* the successful restaurant," Phoebe finished caustically.

Marcy brushed her hair from her face. "You're not making any sense."

"Don't you get it?" Phoebe shouted.

"No. No, I don't get it." Marcy gripped the cell phone. "Tell me where you are and I'll come. We'll talk about it."

Phoebe laughed, but she didn't sound like herself. "What? So you can send the cops after me?" She sounded . . . *hollow*. Gone was her vibrancy. Her confidence. She sounded scared. Alone.

"I wouldn't do that."

"Why the hell not? I would, if I were you." Phoebe laughed that lifeless laugh again. "Of course, that's the crux of the whole matter to begin with, isn't it?"

Marcy didn't understand what Phoebe was talking about. She was scaring her.

"It's about being *you*, you twit," Phoebe said when Marcy didn't respond. "Don't you get it? I always wanted to be you. You always had everything going for you. You were always so smart and I was so stupid. You always made all the right choices. I made the wrong one every time."

"Don't say that," Marcy whispered. "It's not true. I was fat. Ugly—"

"You think I wouldn't have traded my face for yours to have what you had?" Phoebe cried.

Marcy squeezed her eyes shut. She had never had any idea her sister felt this way. It made no sense, of course, but that really didn't matter at this point, did it?

"And you always got all the nice guys, didn't you?" Phoebe continued. "And I ended up with the ones who just wanted to get in my panties."

"Phoebe—"

"You don't know what it was like," she said, lowering her voice. She sounded so desperate. "I wanted him *so badly* for so many years."

"You wanted who?" Marcy demanded, suddenly angry. She was tired of her sister's dramatics. Tired of letting her control her feelings.

"Jake. Jake, of course."

"Marcy," the Bloodsucker crooned, slowing down his car as he turned onto the dark street. "Marcy, I see you. I'm coming for you."

He could feel his blood pumping in his heart. Pulsing. Throbbing in his head and in his groin.

He still could not believe his good luck. Marcy in the darkness. No one around. No witnesses to see her disappear.

Because he was clever. Smarter than them all. There would be no witnesses until he was done and then the whole world would be witness to his cunning. His brilliance.

The Bloodsucker felt stickiness on his fingertips. Pudding from the chocolate éclair. He couldn't be leaving evidence anywhere, now could he? He licked his fingers greedily and gazed up to look at her again, so lost in her phone conversation that she didn't see him coming.

"Jake?" Marcy whispered, shocked by her sister's confession. "*You wanted my husband?*"

"I wanted him long before he was your husband," Phoebe ground out. "Don't you remember? He was my boyfriend first. I introduced you two. We were out—"

"No. No, we met at the bar. It was a whole group," Marcy said, wracking her brain. It had been so long ago. "He wasn't your boyfriend. He was just some guy you had met in Econ class."

"But I *wanted* Jake to be my boyfriend," Phoebe whispered, and then her voice caught in her throat. "He was so sweet. Such a damned nice guy. I wanted him to love me, to look at me the way he looked at you."

Marcy heard the sound of gravel crunch on the road, and she looked up to see a car pass the hotel. Nothing else was stirring. She turned around, leaned against the railing. "Phoebe, I never knew."

"Of course you didn't know!" She took a shuddering breath. "When you went into the hospital to have the kids, I prayed. I prayed you would die in childbirth, and I would be there to comfort Jake. To console him."

"No, Phoebe," Marcy whispered, horrified she would say such a thing. Marcy loved Phoebe. She had always loved her. Didn't sisters love each other?

"But you didn't die. Because you were strong. Stronger than I could ever be. So I decided to help you along."

Marcy felt her throat constrict with emotion. Emotion so powerful that she couldn't quite identify it. Regret, pity. She felt so damned guilty. And then there was the anger, the anger that was bubbling up inside her. "You tried to kill me in the house tonight?" she demanded. "How could you!"

Phoebe gave a little laugh. "Oh, sweetie, that wasn't the first time. You see, I'm not only lousy with men and investments and business ventures, but I'm also lousy at attempting to kill people."

Marcy heard Phoebe pause and the click of a disposable lighter. Her sister was lighting a cigarette.

"You know," Phoebe said. "I tore my favorite denim skirt climbing under your minivan in the parking lot where you worked to cut the brake lines. It's not really a cut, of course. You're supposed to slit them so the brake fluid drains out slowly. That way the driver is already on the road by the time the brakes fail. You know, you'd be surprised the information you can find on the Internet."

Marcy shuddered. "You caused the accident that did this to me?"

"Did what?" Phoebe snapped viciously. "Made you thin and beautiful?" She chuckled without humor. "Joke was on me, huh? I try to kill you, or at least turn you into a vegetable so your husband will divorce you and marry me, and you walk out of the hospital looking like some fucking movie star."

"Phoebe, you have to tell me where you are. You have to turn yourself in. You're sick. You need help. I can get you help if you'll just—"

"I didn't call for your help, Sis," Phoebe said acidly. "I've been calling you for years to help me and look where it's gotten me." She inhaled deeply on her cigarette, and Marcy heard her exhale. "I just called to tell you that I left your SUV near the diner. My stuff's inside, but you can sell it, give it to the Salvation Army, whatever."

Near the diner? That was only two blocks from the hotel. Was Phoebe out on the street? Marcy ran barefoot down the walkway, stepping out into the parking lot. She looked up the street in the direction of the diner. "You're not at your new apartment?" she stalled, hoping she might see her sister on the street.

"There's no new apartment," Phoebe mocked. "No new job. I made that all up." She spoke now as if Marcy were a foolish child who had to be handed an explanation. "When Jake found out tomorrow morning that you were dead, poor thing, he was going to call me. Just like he did when you were in the accident. He was going to *call me,* and I was going to be there to comfort him. What was I going to need my own apartment for?"

"Phoebe, listen to yourself," Marcy begged, wiping at her tears. "You know you don't mean what you're saying."

Phoebe made a sobbing sound. "I thought it would be just like before. He was going to call me, and I would come back to live with him and the kids. Come back to take care of them. With you gone, it would have only been a matter of time before Jake fell in love with me. Don't you see that, Marcy?"

"No, what I see is my sister, who I love, who needs help. I should have seen it sooner. I don't care about the money, I only—"

"You know about the money?" Phoebe's voice quivered.

"I know," Marcy admitted softly. "But the money doesn't matter to me. You do."

A flash of light caught Marcy's eye and she glanced up. Headlights. A car. The same one she had seen moments ago? She wondered if she should go back into the hotel room. But what if her sister was only a block or two away?

"Phoebe, please tell me where you are."

"I told you. Your car is right on the street near the diner."

"I don't care about my car," Marcy cried. "I just—"

"Hey sugar," Phoebe said. But she wasn't talking to Marcy; her voice had changed. There was someone else there with her.

Marcy stepped off the sidewalk, into the street. If she walked to the stop sign, she'd be able to see the diner. She ran down the middle of the street, her bare feet slapping on the cool black pavement. If she could just get to Phoebe, she knew she could talk some sense into her. Get her to realize she needed psychiatric help.

The car she had seen went to the end of the street that ran perpendicular to the hotel, then backed into a driveway to turn around. Marcy's heart fluttered. Who was out at this time of night? Why were they turning back? Had they seen her? Was it the man she had seen in the window?

Was there even a man? If so, who? Was he someone Phoebe had hired to help her with the gas ventilation system in the basement?

"Phoebe, who's there with you?" Marcy darted for the sidewalk, still running in the direction of the diner. "Please tell me where you are. Let me come to you!"

"How are you tonight?" Phoebe said, still talking to someone else.

A pause, then, "Yeah, yeah, I guess it is a little late to be out walking." Then Phoebe laughed, her voice low. Sexy.

"Phoebe!" Marcy kept her eye on the car approaching her as she ran for the stop sign. She was afraid, but not for herself. For Phoebe. It sounded like her sister was catching a ride. The newspaper said it was believed Patti had caught a ride with someone the night she was kidnapped. "Damn it, who are you talking to?" Marcy demanded.

"A ride?" Phoebe said. "Well, that depends on which way you're going." It was that sexy, playful tone Marcy knew so well. She'd heard her sister use it a hundred times with men. A thousand times.

"Phoebe, listen to me," Marcy shouted into the phone. "Tell me where you are this minute. Tell me who you're talking to. I'm coming for you."

"I gotta go," Phoebe said, this time directly into the phone. "Talk to you later, Sis. Or not . . ."

"Phoebe—!" Marcy shouted. "Don't—"

She heard a click too distinct to misinterpret. Phoebe had hung up.

"Phoebe!" Marcy cried. Under the light of a street lamp, she punched her sister's cell phone number in.

The car was crossing the street, pulling up to the sidewalk. Marcy stepped back into the shadows of a condo building as she listened to her sister's cell phone ring, unanswered.

The dark-colored sedan rolled to a stop. Still listening to the phone ring in her ear, Marcy looked back in the direction of the hotel, ready to run.

The window glided down. "Marcy!"

"Oh!" Marcy cried, changing directions, running to the open window when she recognized the female voice. "Claire! You scared me half to death."

"Me? What about you? What the hell are you doing on this corner"—she looked her up and down—"half dressed in the middle of the night?"

Marcy heard the locks on the doors click open.

"Get inside, Marcy."

Still breathing hard, Marcy opened the door. She saw now that the car was an unmarked police car. That was why she hadn't recognized it the first time it went by. "Claire, I'm so glad you're here." She dialed her sister's number again. "I was talking to Phoebe. You have to drive me to the diner. She says she left my car on the street there. She knows we know she tried to kill me."

"I've already put an APB out for her," Claire said grimly. "It's worse than we suspected, Marcy. I hate to tell you this, but—"

Marcy lifted her cell phone to her ear again. "Phoebe tried to kill me in December. She cut my brake lines. She told me." The phone rang again. Rang and rang. "She was talking to me on the phone. She was leaving town, I guess, but then she was talking to someone," she gushed. "Claire, please . . ."

The chief of police turned the car around in the intersection and headed back toward the hotel. "I'll go look for her, but you're going back to the hotel, and you're going to stay there if I have to handcuff you to the bed."

Marcy hung up again and pressed the phone to her chest. Still no answer, and her phone battery was beginning to die. "I don't know who she was with, Claire." She looked at her friend anxiously. "What if—"

"Calm down," Claire said firmly. "I'll find her. You just spoke to her. How far could she have gotten?"

Marcy stared at the phone in her lap. She was trembling from head to foot. "You're right," she whispered. "How far could she have gotten? You'll find her and then we'll get her the help she needs." She looked to Claire. "Because she's sick. She really is."

Claire patted Marcy's hand. "I know. She has to be. We'll get her the help she needs." She pulled into the hotel parking lot.

"I can get out here," Marcy said. "Please, find her."

"I want you to go inside," Claire said as Marcy climbed out of the car. "I want you to go to that hotel room and lock the door. I want you to stay there until I come back. Do you understand me?"

Marcy swallowed hard, fighting to gain control of her emotions. Sweat trickled down her temple, and she brushed it away. "I'll wait inside. I'll try to keep calling her cell."

"Good." Claire leaned over to see Marcy from the driver's side. "Now I'm not going until I see you go inside."

Marcy ran barefoot across the parking lot, down the walkway, and pulled open the hotel room door, bumping right into Jake.

"There you are," he muttered, pulling her into his

arms. "Where the hell have you been? I was just getting ready to call Chief Drummond."

Marcy closed the door behind her and threw herself into his arms. "Jake, you're not going to believe this."

Claire drove up and down the empty streets directly around the diner, looking for Phoebe Mathews, and then fanned out. She called both her available patrol cars to join in the search and verified with the dispatcher that the APB had gone out so state and local police in the area would be looking for her. Of course, she had located Marcy's SUV right where Phoebe had said it would be, so they no longer had a vehicle to look for. That was going to make it more difficult to find her.

Claire drove around for an hour before she returned to the hotel where the Edmonds were staying. The door opened the moment she tapped lightly on it.

"Please tell me you found her." Marcy gripped the door, white-knuckled, her beautiful face pale in the poor light.

Claire's heart went out to her. After all that had happened to Marcy, and now to have her sister disappear like this. Surely she had to be as worried as Claire was, considering the murder of the two women. But she didn't voice her concerns aloud; it didn't seem necessary when she met Marcy's gaze. "We didn't find her, but we will." Claire tried to sound confident. "She'll turn up."

"That's right." Marcy gave a little laugh, now holding tightly to her husband's hand in the doorway. "Phoebe is always doing crazy things like this. She'll turn up."

Chapter Fourteen

Phoebe woke up slowly, like after a hard night of drinking. She was confused. Dreamy. She thought she was lying on her side in what felt like a small, enclosed space. The air stank of exhaust. Plastic. Whatever she was in was in motion. A car?

She opened her eyes, but could see nothing. Her head swam and her stomach lurched and she closed her eyes again. Where the hell was she?

Flashes of what had happened that night flitted through her head. Disjointed thoughts.

All the shit with Marcy. The ice cream with Jake after he and the kids had gone to the movie. He'd been such a sweetheart. He was so good with Katie and Ben. So nice to her. They would have been so happy together. She would have made him a happy man. She would have made him love her.

Then everything had fallen apart. The botched carbon monoxide leak. She'd researched it on the Internet. It should have worked.

She should have just hired someone to stage a robbery and shoot Marcy. Right in that beautiful face of hers. People did it all the time.

Now the police were looking for her. They knew.

She opened her eyes again, trying hard to remember what had happened. How she'd gotten here.

She remembered talking to Marcy on the phone. Marcy, who had been babbling about how they would get her help. How the money she had taken from the bank accounts didn't matter. Money she'd blown on manicures, drinks for guys she didn't know . . . coke. God knew what else.

And her sister was going to get her help? Right.

But after the phone call, what had—

Suddenly, in her mind's eye, Phoebe saw a car pull up. Someone she knew. She'd remembered smiling, leaning on the door. Flirting. She'd hung up on Marcy. There was nothing to say.

He'd offered Phoebe a ride. She was going to ask him to run her out to Route One. She'd be able to hitch a ride from there.

He'd slipped his arm around her and then—

That son of a bitch! He'd put something over her mouth and nose. Something that had . . .

Phoebe opened her eyes again. The motion beneath her, around her, had changed. She was in the damned trunk of his car!

Why the hell would he—

Suddenly, she was afraid. More afraid than she had ever been in her life. He seemed like a nice enough guy. But he wasn't. He wasn't because he was the guy who had killed Patti and April.

Suddenly, Phoebe's heart was pounding so hard in her chest that she grew light-headed. What was she going to do? *What the hell was she going to do?*

The car had slowed when the motion changed. An old road, maybe.

Then the car stopped, and she held her breath. She heard a dog bark. She didn't know what she should do. Did she pretend to still be knocked out?

A car door opened. She heard his voice. He was talk-ing to the damned dog.

Her mind raced. She was shaking all over. Maybe if she pretended to still be asleep, she might be able to get away when his back was turned. But maybe she should just come out of this damned trunk swinging. The ele-ment of surprise.

She went to move her arms and legs in the confined area and realized they were tied together.

Tears filled her eyes. She was usually one tough broad, but this . . .

The trunk popped open and she squeezed her eyes shut, lying motionless.

"Out of the way, buddy. Good boy. Don't want to step on you."

Phoebe felt his hand touch her shoulder, and it was all she could do not to scream. He was wrapping her up in something. Something crackly. She felt it brush her bare leg, and she realized it was some kind of plastic.

Shit! Was he going to suffocate her in it?

But he just wrapped her up and then lifted her into his arms. She opened her eyes just a little.

"Waking up, are you? You feeling all right? I know, stomach's a little upset, but that passes."

He was speaking so gently to her. So kindly. People never talked to her that way.

She looked up at him, half scared out of her mind, half pissed. She didn't try to fight her way out of his arms because what would be the point? She couldn't run, couldn't even crawl, trussed up like a turkey the way she was. "What are you doing with me?" Against her will, her voice trembled.

"Now, don't get upset. I just want to talk to you."

She studied his face. He looked like such an ordinary guy. Not a killer. And yet she knew . . . she *knew* he was.

"Please," she whispered, fighting tears.

"Now, don't get yourself all upset," the Bloodsucker

said, carrying her through the dark barn. He didn't need the lantern because he knew his way in the dark. He walked to the picnic table, then around it to the chair that was now enclosed by a little wall he'd built on three sides of it. The wall was hung with plastic for spatter and could easily be removed and burned. Then he could just replace the plastic again.

The Bloodsucker knew this wasn't Marcy he held in his arms, and he fought the disappointment. He'd known it the minute she'd leaned into the car, opened her mouth, and spoke. He'd had a moment of indecision then; take her, or leave her. But he needed someone so desperately. Ached so for her that he told himself he could pretend Phoebe was Marcy. He could make it work because he was clever. It worked in the movies. Spencer Tracy had just pretended Katharine Hepburn was all those heroines and look at what had happened with them. In real life, theirs had been a true, lasting relationship. A relationship built on mutual love and respect.

The Bloodsucker lowered Phoebe into the chair that he had already covered with plastic. "Now, sit right there," he ordered. It wasn't like she could go anywhere—not with her arms and legs taped.

Keeping an eye on her, he went to the table, picked up the lighter, and lit the lantern, casting light on the table and a circle around it, including the chair. He looked at Phoebe. She was staring round-eyed at him. He picked up a roll of tape and she flinched.

"Don't be afraid," he said, coming to her, reaching out and stroking her hair. "Don't be afraid, Marcy, dear."

Marcy? Phoebe thought wildly. *He thinks I'm Marcy?* "No," she whispered, shaking her head. She tried to stand up, but he pushed her back in the chair. "I'm not Marcy."

"Hush," he said, picking at the roll of duct tape, trying to find the end.

She attempted to stand up again, but he shoved her back, harder this time.

"I'm not her," Phoebe said frantically. "You . . . you've made a mistake."

"I said shut up. Shut up or you'll ruin everything," he snapped. The tape made a horrendous tearing sound as he pulled it off the roll, wrapping it around her waist, around the chair. Then he grabbed her left arm, twisted it so the pale side of her arm faced upward. He slapped it onto the chair arm, yanking the right arm with it and began to tape her arms down with more duct tape.

Phoebe bucked wildly, rocking the chair. "Let me go! I'm not Marcy! You've got the wrong woman!"

He grabbed the back of the chair and steadied it. "I know that," he sneered. "But you could just play along, couldn't you! Just once, you could think of someone else instead of yourself!" He shouted in her face, spittle flying.

She pulled back against the chair, panting hard. Scared half to death. "You wanted Marcy," she whispered, suddenly realizing what he was saying.

He gave a little laugh. "You don't think I wanted you, did you? Little slut. Thief." He walked to the table and began to step into some kind of plastic jump suit.

Her gaze moved from him to the tray on the table. A tray covered by a white towel. Phoebe knew what he had done to the other two women. She knew what was under that towel.

"Please," she said frantically. "If . . . if you want Marcy, I . . . I can help you. I can help you have her. I . . . I swear I can."

He was pulling something that looked like a shower cap over his head. He glanced at her with interest.

"I can. I can. I'll do it," she said. "I swear I will. You know I will."

"And why would you do that?" he asked, seeming truly perplexed.

"Because . . . because you want her. And . . . and because you deserve to have what you want. My . . . my hair's not really even blond anymore. Hasn't been since

I was thirteen. I bleach it. Look." She lowered her head. "Look at the roots."

"You would give me Marcy because I want her?"

She watched him step into a plastic shoe cover, her chest suddenly swelling with hope. "I would. For you. For you, I'd do anything."

"Liar!" He snapped on the other shoe cover, jerked the towel off the tray, and grabbed something shiny off it.

Phoebe recoiled in horror as he came toward her with the scalpel. "Well . . . for me, too," she said quickly. She stared at the scalpel, shaking all over. "Because I hate her. I've always hated her."

"Why?" he asked, actually fascinated that one sibling could do such a thing to another.

"B-because I always wanted to be her. Never could be. She—she was always so smart. Such a good person. P-people always liked Marcy. Loved her."

He lifted the blade to let it catch the light, thinking of the warm blood. Of its scent. It wouldn't be Marcy's blood, just like April's hadn't been, but there was no reason why he couldn't enjoy it anyway. Drink the power. "But not you?" he questioned. "You never loved her?"

She shook her head.

"And you would give up your sister's life in exchange for yours?" He stood in front of her now.

She nodded, tears running down her cheeks. "Please. Just let me go. I'll take you to her. I . . . I'll help you get her in the damned trunk, if you want."

The Bloodsucker lifted the blade. "You know," he said. "I actually considered letting you go. Letting you go because you're not who I wanted. I know how black your blood will be."

She stared up at him, blue eyes wide with terror.

"But you deserve to die," the Bloodsucker snarled.

The blade bit into Phoebe's wrist, searing her flesh, and blood bubbled up. She threw her head back and screamed. Not just in pain, in fear, but in bitter frustration. All these years she had wanted to be Marcy, and now at last, she was in her chair.

Phoebe Mathews's body turned up two days later in a dumpster at a condo construction site on the edge of town. Claire hadn't gotten her first cup of coffee down when she received the call from the station.

After hanging up, she dressed slowly in her police uniform, watching herself in the mirror. No need to hurry now. Phoebe was dead, her body dumped like the last two women's. A tear ran down Claire's cheek as she sat on the edge of the bed to slip on her shiny black shoes, and she wiped at it angrily. There was absolutely no doubt in her mind now; what glimmer of hope she had clung to was gone. She knew she had a serial killer on the loose in her town.

Claire rose slowly from the bed and reached for her Beretta to strap it around her hips, dreading having to leave her bedroom. She had a serial killer stalking women in her town, and she was going to have to go to Marcy Edmond's house this morning and tell her that her sister was dead. Murdered. Bled to death by some sicko son of a bitch and dumped in a trash heap.

Her gun fastened properly, Claire strode down the dark hallway to kiss her sleeping daughter good-bye. Her whole life, Claire had dreamed of being the police chief of Albany Beach and now . . .

The job sucked.

The following morning Marcy sat at the kitchen table with her coffee and stared at the newspaper headlines. There was a high school graduation photo of Phoebe smiling at her, as beautiful and vivacious as she had ever been.

Somehow, Marcy managed a bittersweet smile. It seemed as if it was only a few days ago that this graduation photo had been taken, and she and Phoebe had had their whole lives ahead of them. And now . . .

Jake walked into the kitchen. "You don't have to read that," he said quietly, leaning over to brush his lips against hers. "We ought to just stop the paper."

"No," Marcy said, surprised she wasn't crying. No tears left, she supposed. "It's all right." She pointed to the counter. "Coffee's made. Hazelnut. Your favorite."

"Another cup?" Jake asked.

"Please." She handed him her mug. "The headlines say the police are almost certain the same man killed all three women," she said, staring at Phoebe, who stared back at her.

"They'll catch the bastard, now. I have every confidence in Claire."

Marcy nodded. "Me, too."

Jake brought her the mug, filled to the brim with aromatic coffee, and sat across the table from her with his own. "You know, I was thinking. What would you think about taking a vacation? Getting the hell out of Albany Beach for a few weeks?"

"Until Claire catches him, you mean?"

"No, of course not," he protested. "Well, maybe, but not just because of this." He gestured to the newspaper.

Marcy cupped the warm mug in her hands and stared into the pool of black coffee, not wanting to sound like a nut job, but needing to tell Jake the truth. "You know, this is going to sound crazy, but for weeks I've felt like someone was watching me, and now . . ." She looked up. "It's the strangest thing, but the feeling is gone. I'm not afraid anymore."

"You think he was watching you? Maybe both of you?" Jake didn't act like he thought she was crazy.

"I don't know," she whispered.

"Well, think about the vacation idea. We could take a month, six weeks even. We could go west like we always talked about. Maybe rent one of those motor homes you drive."

"It's tempting," she thought aloud. "But I've got all that work to be done if I'm going to open the restaurant by Columbus Day."

"We'll leave the real estate agents and the bankers to deal with it and shoot for a later date." He dismissed her argument with a wave. "I just feel like we need some time to be alone. Just you and me and Ben and Katie. Besides, it would be so unlike us to take off like this that I feel like we ought to do it." He grinned. "Mesa Verde? Rafting down the Colorado? It would be such an adventure."

Marcy lowered her gaze to the newspaper in front of her again. Her sister stared back at her with those big blue eyes of hers, full of wonder . . . and a sense of adventure.

Leave all her worries behind and take a trip to the Grand Canyon, Marcy thought. It was certainly the kind of thing Phoebe would do. Would have done . . .

Marcy looked up. "Okay."

"Okay?"

She smiled across the table at Jake, her faithful, beloved Jake. He had never even known Phoebe had been in love with him. "Okay, let's do it. We leave the day after the funeral, so you better get cracking." She got up from the table and carried the newspaper to the trashcan. Without bothering to read the article on her sister's murder, she tossed it. She and Phoebe had shared enough unhappiness in their lives. This wasn't the way she would remember her.

The Bloodsucker stared at the face of Phoebe Mathews on the front page of the newspaper. Smiling.

She wasn't smiling anymore.

Of course, when he picked her up, he had thought

she was her sister, Marcy. He had wanted her sister. All those months Marcy had lain in that hospital bed like Sleeping Beauty, he had wanted her.

And now Marcy was gone. Gone with her family on an extended trip. That's what Loretta had told him. She had slipped right out of his hands.

In a way, he had to concede, she had outsmarted him, and if there was one thing the Bloodsucker admired, it was intelligence. So Phoebe had been his consolation prize.

But he wouldn't dwell on that. And really, he had done Marcy a favor in getting rid of Phoebe. He didn't know if Marcy had ever realized what a real twisted bitch her sister had been, but she was better off without her.

And Phoebe had turned out not to be such a bad choice, anyway. She had begged for her life, pleaded. Offered him everything from money to illicit sex. Then he had killed her, slowly, the way he liked it. The way it had to be.

The Bloodsucker decided, in a moment of supreme generosity, that he would not pursue Marcy Edmond, his ugly duckling turned swan, his Sleeping Beauty. Not even when she returned to Albany Beach. She had outsmarted him fair and square. Besides, there were other beautiful women out there, just waiting for him. Other pretty blondes.

"That all I can get you before you get to work?" The new waitress at the diner smiled as she tore off the Bloodsucker's check and handed it across the table to him.

"That's it." He folded the newspaper and slid out of the booth. Her name was Kristen. She was a college student staying with her aunt and uncle and cousin for summer. The Addisons. He knew them. Nice family. "Thanks," the Bloodsucker said, leaving a generous tip.

"You're welcome." She flashed a smile, her blue eyes sparkling with youth.

The Bloodsucker knew she was strong. He had seen her carry piles of dirty dishes to the back. And not just strong physically, but mentally; she was studying nursing in college. A man found that kind of strength exciting. Invigorating.

And fortunately, he knew just how to tap into it.

MEMORIES FADE, BUT FEAR NEVER DIES

A victim of amnesia, Jillian Deere only knows that she was left by an unidentified man at a Virginia hospital with a gunshot wound to her neck. But she has the strangest feeling she belongs elsewhere. *Something* is drawing her to the small Delaware town of Albany Beach—a town caught in the grip of a seemingly un-stoppable serial killer . . .

The victims have all been blond and blue-eyed, just like Jillian. One by one, they've disappeared from the beach town's quiet cottages and wind-swept streets, only to be found horribly murdered. Jillian can't imagine why she remembers Albany Beach or what it means. The only person she can turn to for help is lifeguard Ty Addison. Despite the almost ten-year difference in their ages, Jillian finds herself falling for his beach-bum good looks. And then the first memory flashes to horrifying life . . .

Haunted by her tragic past, unsure of whom to trust, Jillian is desperate to uncover the truth about her identity before it's too late. For someone is watching Jillian from out there in the dark. Someone who knows exactly who she is . . . *his next victim* . . .

**Please turn the page for an exciting sneak peek of
Hunter Morgan's
SHE'LL NEVER KNOW
coming next month from Zebra Books!**

Chapter One

There were times when a woman realized she was at a defining moment in her life, and Jillian sensed that when she walked into the old-fashioned diner in Albany Beach, Delaware, that hot July 1 afternoon. She didn't know a soul in the diner. Didn't know a soul in the town . . . or on the earth for that matter, except for the doctors and nurses who treated her in the hospital in Portsmouth, Virginia, and Mrs. Angelina Jefferson of the Amnesia Society. Still, even being a stranger in an unfamiliar town, Jillian felt an overwhelming sense of exhilaration when she stepped through the door. Something was going to happen to her in this town, something wonderful. She could feel it in her bones.

As Jillian made her way to one of the stools at the lunch counter, she took in her surroundings. The diner was right out of the fifties, like a scene from *Mayberry RFD* with its shiny chrome trim, Formica counters, and out-of-date, plastic-upholstered booths. Close to five in the afternoon, the place was busy with what looked to be tourists and locals alike. Among others, she spotted a woman in a beach cover-up sharing a milkshake with her daughter, a nice looking blond man in his mid-thirties drinking a cup of coffee while he read the paper, and a young scruffy guy, mid-twenties, in sunglasses, eating scrambled eggs and bacon, who appeared to have a serious hangover.

No one seemed to give her any mind as she settled on the stool; it was almost as if she belonged there. As if she had been there before.

" 'Lo there, little lady." A man in his mid-fifties, with thinning salt-and-pepper hair leaned on the counter opposite Jillian. "What can I get you for?"

She hesitated, glancing at the large, poofy-haired waitress in a floral apron at the cash register, then back at the man in the dirty, wet, white apron. "I was wondering if I could get a soda?"

"You bet. See, I'm a jack-of-all-trades 'round here. Loretta"—he indicated the obese woman at the cash register laughing with a young, good-looking uniformed cop—"she owns this place, but she can't run it without me. Can you, Loretta?" he called to her.

Loretta flapped a pudgy hand, dismissing him without a glance, and went on ringing up the cop's bill.

"See, I can get your drink, bus your table when you get through, and then wash that glass, clean as a whistle." The jack-of-all-trades, who looked more like a dishwasher to her, pursed his lips and gave a low whistle.

Jillian half smiled, forcing herself not to pull back from the stranger, who frightened her a little. She was still on shaky ground here. She felt uncomfortable everywhere, with everyone, but yesterday, when Angelina Jefferson had come to the hotel to see Jillian off, she'd been straightforward with her advice. Angel, her advisor with the Amnesia Society, who had turned out to be a true angel sent from heaven, said the only way for an amnesia victim to become part of society again was to immerse herself in it. Jillian had to go to public places like restaurants and museums, and she had to talk to people in libraries, in line at the grocery store, even if she had to make herself do it. Angel said that some form of paranoia was common with most amnesia victims and that Jillian would just have to work through it. It was the only way to become a part of the world again, one of the living.

"I was hoping to get that soda to go, if it's not too much trouble," Jillian said, making eye contact with the dishwasher.

"No problem, sweet thing. I got Styrofoam cups here with lids." He grinned as he picked one off the top of a stack. "What would you like old Ralph to get you?"

"Cola, high test," she answered, proud of herself for knowing the answer. Six weeks ago when she woke in the hospital, she couldn't have responded to his question. She hadn't known who she was or how she got there, no less what cold beverage she preferred. Now, at least, she knew a few things about herself. She knew she loved the color blue, and the Beatles, and despised diet soda. It was a little thing, but it was one more "baby step" as Angel called it.

"Coming right up." Ralph filled the cup with ice, leaned on the rear counter, and hit the button to dispense the soda. "Staying the week on vacation? Longer, maybe?"

"Actually, I don't know. I didn't have any specific plans," she said, trying to be vague without sounding like a fruitcake. "I have a few weeks off, and I'm just driving up the coast, stopping here and there." It was only a half lie. She *was* driving up the coast, stopping here and there. Only right now, she had the rest of her life off because she didn't know what job she was supposed to be returning to in what state.

"Albany Beach is a great little town." Ralph popped a plastic lid onto her cup and grabbed a straw from a box. "We still got a few vacancies, but you better grab one up quick, if you mean to stay. Fourth of July is a big holiday here. We have a parade with fire trucks, a band, the whole enchilada. And some say we got the best view of the Atlantic Ocean of anyone." He winked.

Jillian took the cup from Ralph's hand. When his fingertips brushed her skin, she didn't recoil the way she had whenever someone touched her the first few days in the hospital after she woke from her surgery. Angel said it was normal for an amnesia victim to get spooked by human touch and that it would fade with time and regular contact with others. "Thanks for the soda." She slid off the bar stool.

"You bet." Ralph followed her to the cash register where Loretta was just handing the cop his change.

"Have a good day, Patrolman McCormick." Loretta punched the drawer of the ancient cash register closed.

"You bet." The officer picked up his paper to-go bag and turned to Jillian. He nodded, acknowledging her, as he slid his wallet into the rear pocket of his pressed tan uniform pants.

Jillian smiled and nodded shyly as she turned to the woman behind the cash register. "Just the drink."

"Large Coke," Ralph offered, looking over the proprietor's shoulder at the cash register.

"You've got a stack of dirty dishes calling your name, Ralph." Loretta hooked a thumb in the direction of the kitchen behind the lunch counter. "Hop to it."

Ralph looked at Jillian. "You have a fine day—sorry, I didn't catch your name."

Jillian hesitated, a little uncomfortable with giving the stranger her name. But then she thought, what the heck, it wasn't her real name. What did she care? She'd probably be gone by morning, anyway. "Jillian," she said. "Jillian Deere."

"Nice to meet you, Jillian Deere." Loretta handed her the change from her dollar bill and a big smile. "You come back and have breakfast with us, you get the chance. I make the best blueberry hotcakes on the East Coast. Ask anyone."

Jillian picked up her drink. "I just might do that. Thanks. Have a good day." On her way out, a blond man in his mid-thirties coming in the door held it open for her.

"Good afternoon," he said, smiling wider than she liked. He was wearing a navy blazer with a name tag with a realty company name on it. She only caught his first name. *Seth.* He didn't look like a Seth to her. He was a little too polished, his teeth a little too white.

She offered a quick, perfunctory smile, walking through the doorway to the stair landing. She didn't make eye contact purposely. "Thanks."

He turned to watch her go the way she had observed that construction workers and highway employees often did when a pretty woman passed. "You bet."

He was still ogling her when she took a quick look over her shoulder halfway across the parking lot. Jillian picked up her pace, hurrying to her car. A loaner from the Amnesia Society. The private organization did what it could to help "unidentified" amnesia victims rebuild a normal life. They provided places to live, cash, even used Hondas with a hundred and twenty thousand miles on them. The only stipulation the organization had was that if recipients ever got back on their feet again, they were to make a donation to help others in the same predicament they had experienced. *If they ever got on their feet again.* Angel's ominous words still terrified Jillian.

In the car, she dropped her drink into the cup holder on the console, rolled down the window, and slipped the key in the ignition. The Honda's engine turned over and purred. She backed out of the parking space and pulled out of the parking lot. As she turned onto the street, she noticed the police officer from the diner sitting in his marked green and tan car, still in the parking lot. Again, he nodded solemnly, but this time he flashed a cocky smile.

Jillian gripped the wheel and buzzed down the street.

The cop was flirting with her. Sort of. And she didn't know how she felt about it. In the last few weeks, she'd run into men in the hospital, in stores, who flirted with her, but she still wasn't certain how to respond. She could look in the mirror and see that she was beautiful, by present standards, with her long blond hair, slightly upturned nose, and bright blue eyes, but it really didn't mean anything to her. Right now, she'd have exchanged this face and her Coke for a few memories in a heartbeat. How could she flirt with a man not knowing who she was or who she had relationships with? What if she was married?

Of course she had entered the emergency room wearing no wedding ring, and as Angel had pointed out, she didn't even have an indentation of a wedding band on her left ring finger. Women who were recently divorced, or even robbed, had at least the imprint of a ring. Jillian had no proof she was married or had a significant other, just a weird feeling that there had been someone in her life. A man she loved.

That, of course, led to the next question. Where the hell was he? She signaled and turned off the main road onto a tree-lined street. She had no idea where she was going, only that she was getting closer to the ocean. She could smell it on the hot, humid, late afternoon breeze.

If Jillian did have a husband, why hadn't he been looking for her? No one had called or come to the hospital in search of a blond, blue-eyed woman in her mid-thirties in the days after she turned up at the hospital. No one had contacted the Portsmouth police, or any police in the state, not even weeks later when she had recovered and had nowhere to go.

In the days following her mysterious arrival at the door of the Portsmouth ER bay, Jillian had talked with a psychiatrist, several psychologists, and had even been hypnotized, but no one had been able to help her draw any conclusions. She didn't know who she was or where she had come from, and she didn't know who had shot her and why. She had continued to be listed as a Jane Doe until the hospital put her in contact with the Amnesia Society and Angel had come to her rescue. Literally.

And now, here she was, on her quest to find herself. Angel had suggested taking a few days to drive around the area and see if anything looked familiar, or perhaps jolted her memory. She said that many amnesia victims who did not have a friend or relative identify them, often found their identity on their own just this way. Either they spotted a familiar house that turned out to be theirs, or they bumped into an old friend in a grocery store who asked them if they'd been on vacation. Angel said the world was full of surprises; it was just a matter of going out and looking for them.

Full of surprises? The elderly woman with her flame-red hair and ever-present cigarette dangling from the corner of her lipsticked mouth had that one right. Jillian was surprised every day, nearly every hour as she slowly uncovered aspects of the personality that was somehow locked inside her head.

Jillian spotted a small green street sign that read *Juniper*. She turned onto it without signaling, a sense of excitement coursing through her blood. There was something about the street name . . . or maybe the street. The way the maple trees hung over. Checking to be sure no one was behind her, she slowed down to less than twenty miles an hour, gazing from one side of the street to the other. She was obviously in an older section of town. The multiple-story condos had given way to small, square, cedar-sided and whitewashed cottages. Some were freshly painted, others a little worse for wear. On other streets, she had seen tourists walking with children in bathing suits in tow, carrying armfuls of chairs and wet beach towels. On this little side street, she spotted an elderly woman in her side yard taking down laundry from a clothesline. A middle-aged couple sat on a porch snapping fresh beans. They both waved as she drove by as if they had known her her whole life.

Jillian's heart skipped a beat. Did they? That was silly, of course, to think that in two days' time she could get in a car and drive home. But it was fun to fantasize about, if only for a moment.

Ahead, she spotted beach dunes covered in sea grass to prevent erosion and signs warning that cars would be towed for parking in unmarked spaces. It was a dead end. She pulled into the last parking spot on the end of the street, parallel to the sidewalk, just in front of an old restored motorcycle—vintage fifties. She got out of the car, leaving her purse and locking the door. Jillian had no idea where she was going or why. Her new sneakers seemed to have a life of their own.

Gazing up at the brilliant blue sky, she heard the crash of ocean waves and smelled the tangy salt air. The wind whipped at her hair as she stepped off the cement sidewalk onto a wooden one that led around the cottage directly ahead of her. She followed the creaky path around to the front of the house that faced the ocean. It was small, with a white-painted front porch, flowerless window boxes, and pale green shutters that looked like they still worked. An orange *Vacancy* sign hung in the window, framed by pale yellow gingham curtains.

Jillian gazed up at the house, at the single small window on the second story that faced the ocean. She hesitated, glanced over her shoulder to see if anyone was watching her, and then mounted the steps to the porch. Obviously no one was staying here if there was a vacancy sign in the window. What harm would it be to have a look?

The painted gray floorboards beneath her feet creaked and gave way slightly as she walked to the window, cupped her hands over her eyes and looked in. There was a bright, cheery kitchen with a round wooden table and dish cupboards with glass fronts. She crossed in front of the front door to look in the other window. It was a living room or maybe a parlor. Furniture was covered in pale sheets, but instead of seeming ghostly, the room beckoned her.

"Have I been here before?" she whispered, pressing her fingertips to the cool glass windowpane.

The house gave no reply.

After a moment, Jillian turned around and hooked her arm around one of the wooden posts that fortified the porch. A path led directly from the steps, through a break in the sand dunes, onto the beach. It was a breathtaking sight, the mounds of fine white sand, the waving dune grass, the wide beach that fanned out in either direction as far as the eye could see, all leading directly to the Atlantic Ocean's edge.

She smiled and slid down to perch on the top step. The wind tangled her hair, but it was a hot, humid wind. On impulse, she slipped her feet out of her sneakers and peeled off her new white athletic socks. She wiggled her toes, enjoying the freedom. This was a nice place. Maybe a nice place to stay a few days? Ralph's description of the upcoming Independence Day parade sounded charming.

She thought of the vacancy sign in the window behind her and wondered how much the cottage would cost to rent for a few days, maybe a week. Probably too much. She had money, but her resources, for now, were dependent on Angel and the Amnesia Society. She didn't want anyone to think she was trying to take advantage of the generosity of her benefactors, staying in an oceanfront house when she could very well take a room a few streets back at a budget motel.

But there was something about this cottage . . .

A long shadow fell over the sand in front of Jillian, and she glanced up to see a young man with sun-bleached blond hair, wrap-around sunglasses, and a great tan walking over the crest of the dunes. He was shirtless, wearing fluorescent orange swim trunks and carrying a gym bag that had the Red Cross symbol on the side. A lifeguard.

She found it fascinating that she could recognize the symbol for the Red Cross, or a vintage motorcycle, but she couldn't remember her own name. Funny how the mind worked.

The lifeguard stepped onto the wooden walk that ran directly in front of the cottage. As he approached the house, he gave a nod and offered a lopsided, boyish grin. He had a nice smile that made her want to smile back.

"Hey," he greeted.

She nodded.

He walked past the front steps, barefooted, swinging the bag. He looked like he was headed home. It had to be five-thirty by now. Quitting time?

She watched him pass, admiring his muscular, tanned shoulders. It was one of the interesting quirks she had learned quickly about herself. She obviously liked men. Found many sexually attractive. She couldn't remember having sex, yet she knew, innately, that she had enjoyed it a great deal.

The lifeguard got to the end of the walkway, about to disappear around the side of the house, when he turned around. "Can I help you with something?"

Before she could reply, he lifted a tanned shoulder in an easygoing half shrug. "You look kind of lost."

Jillian threw her head back and laughed, surprising not only the man, but herself as well. He walked back toward her. He was still smiling, but obviously puzzled.

"I'm sorry," Jillian said, pressing her hand to her mouth, still chuckling. "I didn't mean to be rude. No, I'm fine. Thanks for asking."

But the lifeguard didn't go. He stood there, all six foot something of him, looking down on her sitting on the step, still smiling. "I gotta ask. What's so funny?"

She looked up, squinting in the bright sunlight, still

amused. "What you said, it was just so . . . apropos."
Apropos? What kind of person had she been that she
used words like *apropos?*

"Why's that?" He slid the bag off his shoulder and
parked one bare foot on the bottom step beside hers.

"I just—" She shook her head, burying her face in
her hands for a minute. How pathetic was it for a woman
her age to be spilling her guts to a kid who looked to be
young enough to be her son.

"Got lost on I-95? Thought you were in Maine, and you
wound up in little old Delaware?" he prodded teasingly.

She lifted her head. "Actually, even more bizarre than
that." She hesitated, but there was something about the
lifeguard's warm hazel eyes that just made her want to
tell him her whole wretched story. "Before I go on with
the crazy story, you mind if I ask you a crazy question?"

"Shoot."

"Have you ever seen me before? I mean, I realize that
obviously you don't know me, but I don't suppose, by
any chance, you've seen me around town?" She sounded
so pathetically hopeful.

He shook his head. "Nope. I'd remember your eyes if
I had." He seemed to sense her disappointment. "But I
only live here in the summer," he went on quickly. "I
grew up here, but I've been gone a while. I just graduated from Penn State."

Jillian did the quick calculations in her head. That only
made him twenty-two or twenty-three. He was young, all
right . . . but not young enough to be her son.

"So tell me your crazy story," he said. "I'm dying to
hear it now."

She took a deep breath. "Well, I am sort of lost because . . . because I'm not exactly sure who I am." She
said it without giving herself time to think, to get the
words out of her mouth before she lost her nerve. She
hadn't told many people about her predicament yet. So
far, most people she encountered already knew.

"Interesting." He nodded his head, not sounding as if he quite believed her, but intrigued.

"Amnesia," she explained. She threw up her hands and let them fall to her pale, bare knees. "I know. Sounds like something out of a soap opera, but I was injured and left at a hospital without any identification on me. When I woke, I didn't know who I was. I still don't," she finished, thinking it sounded pretty far-fetched to her, too.

"Wow." He thrust out his hand. "I'm Ty."

She clasped his hand, warm and firm. He smelled faintly of coconut suntan lotion. "Jillian Deere."

He looked at her as if to say *Are you for real?* "As in Jane Doe?" he asked.

She laughed. "You know, you're the first person that's gotten it." She made a face. "I just couldn't see myself spending the rest of my life as *Jane Doe*. It would be like toting a red flag around that said, *'I'm an idiot. I don't know who I am or how I got here.'*"

"Nah, I don't think anyone would say that. But I like it." He waggled the finger he pointed at her. "Pretty cool, actually." He dropped his bag in the sand and crossed his arms over his chest. "Out of curiosity, how did you find your way to Albany Beach, *Jillian Deere?*"

She liked the way he said her name. "I just got in the car and drove here. I've been in Virginia recuperating in a hospital; I was in a coma for a few days. Then I woke up with the amnesia. When I was released, some nice people helped me out. They loaned me a car and some money."

"Sounds pretty scary." He leaned on the porch rail, closer to her than he had been before. "I don't know if I would have had the guts to do it."

"It didn't seem like I had much of a choice."

"And no one came to the hospital looking for you? No one contacted the police or some missing persons bureau or anything?"

She shook her head. "The police said it could be that I was there in Portsmouth on vacation or business. But who knows? I just could have gotten off the interstate in the wrong place, or had a change in flight plans and wandered from a nearby airport into some kind of trouble. Someone could be looking for me, but in another part of the country. They say it happens."

"Wow, spooky," Ty said thoughtfully. He glanced at her. "So like you could, like, have a husband, kids and not know it?"

"Well, the doctors say I've never given birth, so I suppose that's good." She lifted her left hand. "And no wedding ring, either." She stared at her finger. "Somehow that seems a little sad to me."

Jillian met his hazel-eyed gaze for a moment, then looked away, surprised by the emotion that stuck in her throat. Most of the time she could remain pretty removed from all this. Often, it was as if it was someone else it was happening to. Like she was watching a movie.

"Well, I just got off work." Ty broke the silence. "Lifeguard. And I'm starved so I'm going to get something to eat." He paused, then pointed in the direction of the street. "You wanna come?"

"Oh, no, I couldn't." She raised her hand. "Thanks, but—"

"But what? You've got someone holding dinner for you? Got somewhere else better to go? Or are you just trying to get me the hell off your porch?"

She laughed. "Well, obviously it's not my porch."

He tilted his head in the direction of the street. "Then come have something to eat with me."

Jillian hesitated. What kind of thirty-something woman went to dinner with a twenty-two-year-old?

"Come on, it'll be fun," he dared her.

He was cute. And nice. And she didn't like eating alone; it reminded her of just how alone she was. "Okay." She hopped up, grabbing her sneakers, stuffed with her socks. "Sure. Why not? It's not like I have anywhere to be, is it?"

On the street, Ty walked up to the motorcycle she had parked in front and strapped down his bag with a couple of bungee cords.

"So that's yours. I was admiring it earlier."

He rubbed the gas tank with the heel of his hand. "An old Chief made by the Indian Company."

"A 1958," she said. "The last year they really made them until the company was bought in '99."

"How'd you know that?" he asked, obviously surprised.

Not as surprised as she was. She stood there staring at the red and black painted motorcycle. "I have no idea," she murmured.

He studied her, blond brows furrowed as he slipped into a pair of ratty sneakers from his bag. "You recognize a bike from the fifties, know its obscure history, but you don't know your name?"

She opened her arms; his easy-going nature seemed to be contagious. "I told you it was a crazy story."

He laughed as he mounted the bike. "You just want to follow me?"

"Sure." Jillian jumped into the Honda and made a U turn in the street. Ty pulled out, and she followed him back toward the center of town. They ended up in the parking lot of the diner she'd been at less than an hour ago.

"What's so funny?" Ty asked, waiting for her when she climbed out of the car. He'd pulled on a wrinkled Radio Head concert T-shirt.

"I was just here." She pointed at the silver building that looked as if it had been constructed from an old railway car, with an addition tacked to the back. "When I came into town, I stopped for a drink."

"Two-for-one burger night. Loretta makes a mean quarter-pounder with cheddar cheese. None of that American crap."

They walked side by side across the gravel parking lot.

"Hey, Ty!" A blond women about his age stuck her head out the window of a car in the parking lot.

Ty took a second look and broke into a smile. "Anne. I didn't know you were home." He hooked his thumb in Jillian's direction. "This is Jillian. That's Anne." He pointed. "We went to high school together. She's at Virginia Tech now."

The blonde lifted her hand in greeting. "Nice to meet you." She started the engine of her car. "I have to run, Ty. Take-out for my mom and dad, but I'll catch up with you. You'll be home a while, right?"

" 'Til August tenth." He thrust his hands into his pockets, and he and Jillian headed across the parking lot for the diner again.

"So what degree did you graduate with?" she asked.

"American literature." He glanced at her, a wicked grin. "I know. What the hell am I going to do with that? My dad says the same thing about twice a week."

"You know, I wasn't going to ask you that."

"What's that?"

"I wasn't going to ask you what the hell you were going to do with the degree."

He grinned. "I like you already, Jillian Deere."

She thought for a minute. "Although I guess that *should* be my response."

He lifted one shoulder in what she now recognized as one of his favorite gestures. "As much as I hate to admit it, I can see my dad's point. He paid sixty-some thou for four years of partying, and now I'm qualified to lifeguard on a beach—the same thing I've been doing since I was seventeen. My older sister is an engineer making boo-coo bucks in Texas for some oil rig company." They walked up the steps and he held open the diner's door for her. "But I'm going back and getting a master's—I've been accepted into a program that will pick up most of the tab. I think I'd like to teach high school. Maybe on an Indian reservation, or one of those schools for problem kids. You know, the kind where you make them climb mountains, live in the desert. I want to do something cool like that before I really have to become an adult."

She laughed.

"You know what I mean."

She nodded. "I don't know how I do, but I do."

Inside, they passed the cash register with Loretta at the helm and took a booth toward the rear. There was a new assortment of customers from the ones she had seen before, but somehow they all seemed like friendly faces. In addition to the diners in tees and flip-flops, with bathing suits showing beneath their clothes, and a security guard of some sort, she noted a table of teens dressed in black, their hair dyed black. One girl had a ring through her nose and was sporting black lipstick. Goths. She'd seen a couple in Portsmouth. Apparently every town had them.

Ty slid into a booth, and she took the crackly fake leather bench seat across from him.

"Want a menu?" He offered her a laminated single page he plucked from behind the chrome napkin holder.

She dropped her purse beside her. "You don't need it?"

"Nope. I always get the same thing on burger night. Two quarter pounders with cheddar, pickles, ketchup, and mustard. No rabbit food. Side of boardwalk fries."

As she took the menu, her fingertips brushed his, and she felt a rush of warmth. She glanced up at him, her response surprising her. Not only had his touch not scared her, but it had felt good. He didn't seem to notice.

She pulled the menu from him, feeling silly. She didn't know exactly how old she was, but she knew she was too old for this kind of nonsense. She needed to get her hormones in check. "What are boardwalk fires?" she asked, reading the menu.

"I can tell you one thing, you're not from around here." He leaned back on the Naugahyde bench and stretched out a lean, tanned arm. "Just take my word for it. Order the boardwalk fries." He winked.

She tossed the menu on the table. "Okay, but I think one burger will be sufficient."

A college-age waitress in a pair of denim shorts and a white, tight-fitting knit shirt approached the table. The only giveaway that she was a waitress was her sensible white sneakers, the straws sticking out of her pocket, and the notepad in her hand. "Hey," she said, grinning at Ty.

"Hey. You off soon?" Ty remained relaxed against the bench seat.

The cute, blond-haired, blue-eyed woman grimaced. "Not until ten. I have to work an extra hour to get Loretta through the after-movie crowd,"

Ty motioned to the waitress. "This is Kristen Addison. My cousin. She's staying with us for the summer."

"I just couldn't go back to PA and suffer the summer with my parents again," she confessed.

"Kristen will be a senior at the U of D this fall. She's going to be a nurse."

Jillian smiled. She liked Kristen immediately. She had that all-American freshly scrubbed look. She was beautiful without makeup. "Hi, I'm Jillian."

"I picked her up on the beach," Ty said.

Jillian laughed, feeling her cheeks grow warm.

Kristen just shook her head, seemingly used to Ty's humor. "Nice to meet you, Jillian. You visiting Albany Beach for the week?"

"I'm thinking about it."

"So what can I get you?" Kristen poised her pencil. "I already know what goof-ball over here wants."

"I'll have a burger with cheddar, mustard, and relish. With the bunny food." She eyed Ty teasingly. "Boardwalk fries and a Coke."

"I'll get your order right in."

Kristen headed for the kitchen to place their order, and Ty began to systematically fold the paper placemat in front of him, advertising a local business, into a paper airplane. "You serious about maybe sticking around a few days?" he asked.

"It seems nice here."

"You want me to see what I can find out about that cottage? I think it's for rent. It's owned by this old lady in town. It's been there forever."

"I don't know. It might be beyond my price range. I have to be careful with my money."

He halted the plane construction to meet her gaze across the table. "I could check. It might be nice to chill out in the same place for a few days. Get your bearings."

"It would be."

He slid off the bench. "Hang on. Let me go grab my cell; I guess I left it in my bag. I'll make a few phone calls. My dad knows this Realtor. He's kind of a jerk, but he knows everybody in town." He dragged his fingertips along the table as he walked away. "Be right back."

A minute later, Kristen set two plastic cups of soda and straws on the table. "Burgers will be up in a couple of minutes."

"Thanks." Jillian picked up one of the straws and tore off the paper. As she dropped it into one of the sodas, the diner's door opened, and a very tall, slender woman in what she now recognized as a local police uniform walked in. Despite the uniform, blond hair tied back in a no-nonsense ponytail at the nape of her neck, and lack of makeup, the policewoman was what Jillian would have described as a gorgeous, willowy blonde. The officer stood in the doorway for a second, surveying the diners and then made a beeline toward the table of Goth teens.

"Get up, Ashley," she said to the girl with the black lipstick.

Jillian knew it was rude to eavesdrop, but she couldn't help herself. With no life of her own right now, other people's fascinated her.

One of the girl's companions snickered.

"Mom," the teen groaned, rolling her blue eyes lined thickly in black.

"Either you get up and you walk out of here, or I take you out," the policewoman threatened in a low voice that even Jillian could interpret as meaning business.

Ashley, obviously the policewoman's daughter, pushed her soda aside and reached for her purse, managing to make each movement dramatic.

"You're still on restriction. You were supposed to go straight to your grandparents after work so they could drive you home."

"I was on my way," the teen answered sourly. "I just stopped for a drink. Can't a person get something to drink if they're thirsty?"

"Yeah, can't a person stop for a drink if they're thirsty, *Chief Drummond?*"

The young man who spoke was tall and angular with the same shoe-polish black hair as his companions'. He wore a ragged black T-shirt and a chain around his neck that appeared to come from a gate or a fence. The necklace was so ridiculous in appearance that it was laughable, but obviously from the young man's tone of voice, it made him think he was tough.

"A person certainly can," Chief Drummond answered, imitating the boy's tone of voice, "*Chain,* unless, of course, she's a minor and her parent has deemed that she may not stop for a drink, not even if she is dying of thirst."

The female companion again sniggered, but when the policewoman eyed her, she shut right up.

Jillian couldn't resist a smile as she sipped her Coke. Obviously, the blond cop was a woman to be reckoned with, and Jillian immediately admired her.

The police chief stepped aside to allow her daughter to exit the booth. "Be sure to say good-bye to your friends, Ashley. You won't be seeing them, or speaking with them on the phone or the Internet, for another three days."

"Three days?"

The cop/mom crossed her arms over her chest. "The length of the extension of your restriction for this violation."

Again the eye roll, but young Ashley climbed out of the booth, dragging her purse behind her. Her mother let her pass and then followed her out the door where the two disappeared down the steps into the parking lot.

"Good news."

Jillian looked up to see Ty sliding into the seat across from her, setting down his cell phone.

"What's that?" she slid his straw to him.

"That house is for rent." He leaned forward as if he possessed a secret. "Cheap. Someone backed out of the lease for the month of July after paying half up front as security. I guess this whole mess with the serial killer spooked them. The owner just wants someone in the house, so she's willing to rent it for the balance of the rent. I warn you, it's basic. Small, no cable, no phone, and no air conditioning."

He named the price, and Jillian found herself smiling back at him. That was do-able. Very do-able. "Two questions," she said as she leaned back to allow Kristen to slide her plate in front of her. "One, when can I move in?"

He reached for the bottle of ketchup and began to

squirt all over his fries and on the hamburger. "Tonight if you like. Key is hidden on the property, and I know the secret place. You can sign the contract in the morning. And question number two?" He put down the ketchup bottle and squashed the bun on top of the first burger.

"I guess I'm asking these questions out of order," Jillian said, grabbing a fry that appeared to have been freshly cut with its skin still on. "But what serial killer?"

And don't miss Hunter Morgan's
SHE'LL NEVER LIVE
Coming in September 2004!

Her days are numbered . . .
. . . by a sadistic madman who calls himself the
Bloodsucker. All summer, he's been preying on blond-
haired, blue-eyed women in the small resort town of
Albany Beach—abducting them, then draining them
of their blood.

Women are dying—drop by drop . . .
Business is down. Suspicion is up. And fear runs ram-
pant. With people's livelihoods—and lives—at stake,
police chief Claire Drummond has her work cut out
for her. A single mom with a rebellious teen daughter,
she finds herself leaning on councilman Graham
Simpson for support. But it's hard to trust her own
heart when everyone is a suspect.

Meanwhile, the Bloodsucker spins a web to reel in his
next victim. He has set his sights high—on Claire. And
he knows the perfect way to get to her . . .
through her daughter . . .